HEARTS OF SAWYERS BEND #3

IVY LAYNE

GINGER QUILL PRESS. LLC

Contents

Also by Ivy Layne

Don't Miss Out on New Releases, Exclusive Giveaways, and More!!

Join Ivy's Readers Group @ ivylayne.com/readers

THE HEARTS OF SAWYERS BEND

Stolen Heart

Sweet Heart

Scheming Heart

Rebel Heart

THE UNTANGLED SERIES

Unraveled

Undone

Uncovered

THE WINTERS SAGA

The Billionaire's Secret Heart (Novella)

The Billionaire's Secret Love (Novella)

The Billionaire's Pet

The Billionaire's Promise

The Rebel Billionaire

The Billionaire's Secret Kiss (Novella)

The Billionaire's Angel

Engaging the Billionaire

Compromising the Billionaire

The Counterfeit Billionaire

THE BILLIONAIRE CLUB

The Wedding Rescue

The Courtship Maneuver

The Temptation Trap

Chapter One

TENN

" T ennessee Sawyer! Don't you dare walk away from me!"

Fuck. I knew that voice. I'd been dodging her for weeks. Couldn't a man enjoy an early morning run in peace? Apparently not.

I came to a stop on the neatly graveled path that ran from the back of my family's inn into the trails beyond. I didn't usually get up this early. My brother Royal was the early riser, which worked out great for me. He covered mornings and I rolled into the office at a reasonable hour, staying later to cover part of the evening shift. Better for the Inn and better for my sanity.

I didn't want to wake up this early every day. I was only up now because Royal had a romantic evening planned with his girl and I'd offered to cover. But there was something to be said for the cool of early morning, the light mist slowly burning off in the newly risen sun. The Inn gardens were dreamy and green, flowers laden with dew, most of the guests still in bed. Peaceful and quiet.

At least, it had been before Vanessa tracked me down.

I came to a stop in front of my brother Ford's ex-wife. No one should be this put together so close to sunrise. Her ink-black hair was swept back from her exquisite face with a narrow leather headband that perfectly matched her red lips and equally narrow red belt. The little black dress was too formal for a summer morning, but it showed her long, sleek legs to perfection.

Vanessa knew exactly how gorgeous she was. I wondered if she knew the strain of the last month showed through her polish. Jail could do that to a person. New lines fanned from beneath her eyes, matching the grooves that cut between her arched brows and beside her full lips.

Until recently, Vanessa had been a thorn in my side. Irritating, at times mildly painful, but otherwise, no more than an inconvenience.

My older brother Ford had divorced her years ago, getting out of the ill-fated marriage unscathed except for the hefty alimony check he wrote every month. Vanessa had been happy to leave it at that, more interested in Ford's name and money than the man himself.

That is, she'd been happy enough until Ford was arrested for my father's murder. No income meant no alimony.

Since the day those hefty checks had dried up, Vanessa had been on the warpath.

I scanned the garden, hoping to see an early rising guest or a member of the staff. Anyone. I had a few inches and at least eighty pounds on Vanessa, but that didn't mean she wasn't dangerous.

The last time we'd underestimated her, she'd nearly killed someone.

"Vanessa." I kept a safe distance between us. "What the hell are you doing here?"

"We need to talk, Tenn." She sidled closer. I backed away. I didn't see a weapon in her hands, but I wasn't taking any chances.

"We really don't need to talk," I countered. "And right now, I'm wondering why we don't have a restraining order against you. Probably because we never thought you'd make bail, and if you did, you'd never be stupid enough to come back here."

"Tenn, please, you're the only one reasonable enough to talk to me."

"I'm not all that reasonable. Not anymore." I knew why she was here. Everyone thought I was a soft touch. They weren't wrong. I had a habit of falling for the whole damsel-in-distress thing. Most of the time, the woman in question deserved my help. I'd paid for legal fees when an employee tried to leave her abusive husband, had covered rent for another when a sudden illness drained her bank account.

Maybe I'd been taken for a ride here or there, but my judgment was mostly sound. Then, Vanessa had started targeting me with her sob story and vague threats. I didn't mind stepping in when someone needed help, but I was done being seen as the family sucker.

My father had been murdered.

My brother Ford was in jail for killing him, though no one really thought he'd done it.

Since then, someone had tried to kill my oldest brother, Griffen, twice, and Vanessa herself had attempted to stab my brother Royal. It was irrelevant that she'd mistaken someone else for Royal in the dark. Royal was fine, but J.T. was still recovering from his near-miss at Vanessa's hands.

It was not a good time to be seen as a soft touch. I had no intention of being Vanessa's next victim.

"Vanessa, the Inn is private property. We made it clear you aren't welcome here. Do I need to call West?"

Vanessa's face blanched at the mention of the police chief. She sidled closer again, one arm held out, beseeching. Her beautiful features transformed into a seductive half-smile. It was a little scary how well she manufactured innocent desire. I wasn't falling for it.

"Tenn—" Before I knew it, she was in my arms, her body pressed to mine, mouth way too close to my neck. I shuddered in revulsion. Vanessa was one of the most beautiful women I knew. She was also a viper.

Closing my hands around her wrists, I pulled her closer as she hummed in her throat.

"I could be so good to you, Tenn. If you let me, I could —" She shrieked as I yanked her arms over her head, transferring her wrists to one hand and patting her down with the other. "What the hell are you doing? Let me go!"

"I'm looking for a weapon. Do you think I'm an idiot?" Not lingering on her curves, I checked for anything hidden on her person that could do damage. In Vanessa's hands, even a nail file could be a potential murder weapon.

"I'm not—"

"Save it, Vanessa." Finished with my search, I released her hands and shoved her back, putting a few feet between us. "First, I wouldn't fuck you with someone else's dick. Touch me again and I'll knock you the fuck out. I don't give a shit that you're a woman. Got it?"

"Tenn, I don't know what you—"

"Got it?" I repeated.

Vanessa ground her teeth together, glaring at me, her dark eyes narrowed. I was unmoved.

If I had the slightest inclination to feel sorry for her, it dissolved at the memory of Royal's girlfriend covered in blood, the hours in the hospital as we waited to find out if her best friend would survive Vanessa's attack. She'd come close to killing J.T. Could have killed Daisy. And in the end, her target had been my brother.

Yeah, this woman was poison. I slid my phone from the armband I used for running. "You know what? I think I'm going to call West anyway. Pretty sure trespassing is a violation of your parole."

"No!"

Great, more shrieking. I was done with this.

"I'll tell you who killed Prentice!"

I paused, finger hovering over West's number on the screen. "Keep talking."

Vanessa hesitated. She'd tried this game with Royal. He didn't think she knew anything. I wasn't so sure. She chewed at her red lipstick. "Give me enough cash to get away from here, and I'll tell you everything."

"How much cash?" She'd asked Royal for a cool million. Had she gotten smarter since then?

"Two hundred and fifty thousand."

She *had* gotten smarter. A million in cash took time. Two hundred and fifty thousand was doable. Not that I had any intention of handing that kind of money to Vanessa. Especially if she was going to use the money to jump bail. She'd almost killed a man. I wasn't rewarding attempted murder with a quarter of a million dollars.

Vanessa thought I was the same soft-touch I'd always been. The irony was, before she'd come after my family, before she'd hit Royal up for a million and then tried to kill him, I'd been considering helping her. Not because she deserved it. Mostly just to get her out of Sawyers Bend. Griffen was newly married and Royal had been falling hard for Daisy. Neither of them needed Vanessa around causing trouble.

I'd been planning to talk Griffen into giving her just enough to get rid of her. Then, she'd tried to kill my brother and I'd grown a nice, thick callus over my soft spot. If she hadn't gone over the edge, she might have gotten her cash. Instead, she'd lost her chance. Not that I was going to tell her that. Not yet. I had some questions first.

"What proof do you have?"

"Proof?" Vanessa echoed, glancing back over her shoulder at the empty gardens.

"Yeah, proof. Your word on who killed Prentice isn't going to get Ford out of jail."

"I don't have proof. I'll tell you who and why. With that, you can find your own proof."

I crossed my arms over my chest and shook my head. "No way. For a quarter of a million in cash, I want more than gossip and speculation. If you want the cash, bring me proof. Otherwise, I'll give you ten grand for the who and why. That's all it's worth to me, and that's generous."

I wasn't going to give her a goddamned penny no matter what she told me, but she didn't know that.

Vanessa wrapped her arms around herself, rocking from one foot to the other, chewing again at her lipstick.

"I don't have all day, Vanessa," I pushed.

"Ten grand won't get me anywhere, Tenn. I need to get away from here, start over. When he finds out I told you, my life won't be worth anything." Another furtive glance over her shoulder.

He. She'd said *he.* It was debatable whether Vanessa's information was worth anything, but the word had slipped out.

He.

Maybe she did know something.

"Ten grand is all I can get you on short notice." A lie, but she didn't need to know that. "Give me a name."

Another furtive glance over her shoulder. I remembered what she'd said when she'd stabbed J.T. Daisy had heard her mumbling, '*Kill Royal and I'm free,*' as if someone had sent her after Royal. She'd denied it later. But if it was true, if someone had sent her after Royal, maybe that same person had sent her to kill me. Maybe he was waiting in the woods or peering out from one of the Inn windows.

Since my father's death, it had been open season on the Sawyers. Someone was after us. I needed to know who. We all did. I tried one more time to get through to Vanessa.

"Who are you looking for, Vanessa?" I asked gently.

She started, eyes flashing up, wide and panicked. "No one. No one. I just... I need to get out of here, Tenn. I don't have a lot of time."

"Then give me a name and I'll help you." I was mostly lying. There was no way I was going to help this woman evade justice, not even for the name of my father's killer. She'd almost murdered J.T. But if she gave me a name that panned out, I'd help pay her lawyer's fees. Considering her lawyer was Cole Haywood, Ford's defense attorney, I knew exactly how expensive those bills had to be.

"Tenn," she sidled closer again, wheedling. "Surely we can work something out." She angled herself so I caught a healthy flash of cleavage and long leg. I rolled my eyes to the sky.

How desperate did she think I was?

It had been a while for me—I didn't partake of hot tourists like Royal had before Daisy—and my last semi-serious relationship had ended almost a year ago. I wasn't a

7

teenager, swayed by a flash of her tits into forgetting who she was.

"Like I said, I wouldn't fuck you with someone else's dick, Vanessa. And if you come one step closer, I'm going to deck you and then call West."

She stepped back, crossing her arms over her chest again, this time in petulance tinged with fear.

"I'm asking you for help, Tenn. We're family. You don't have to be such an asshole about it."

Was she serious? "Vanessa, get real. You broke Griffen's heart when we were kids, then made Ford miserable when he was stupid enough to marry you. That alone would be enough for me. But then you tried to kill Royal, and in the process, almost murdered JT. I have no idea what voodoo Cole worked to get bail granted, much less how you managed to cover it when you claim to be broke. Believe me, If I could pay to get you thrown back in jail, I'd do it in a heartbeat. There's nothing we can work out."

"I thought—"

"I know what you thought. I'm turning over a new leaf. No more damsels in distress for me. Someone else can field the sob stories. I'm out. Either give me that name of Prentice's killer or get the fuck off my property."

Vanessa stared at me, quivering with fury, before turning on her heel and storming down the path. I stayed where I was until she was out of sight, wondering if I'd made a mistake.

Chapter Two

SCARLETT

The beautiful woman stormed past my hiding place in the trees, her shining black hair streaming behind her, her perfect face caught between temper and something that looked a lot like fear. I watched her go, trying to tamp down my curiosity. What was she doing in the gardens of The Inn at Sawyers Bend just after dawn, dressed for a cocktail party?

Not your business, I reminded myself.

I had enough problems of my own without wondering about someone else's. I was here for a reason. Not *my* reason, but that didn't matter. If it were up to me, I'd be at home right now, just getting up, waiting for that first steaming cup of coffee before I shattered my peace and woke up my boys.

Instead, I was in a small town in North Carolina on a wild goose chase, caught up in a mess I didn't truly understand. I palmed the phone in the back pocket of my jeans and again considered calling Thatcher, demanding he come home. Like that would work. If it was that easy, I wouldn't be in Sawyers Bend in the first place.

I didn't care how all of this worked out, I just wanted Thatcher back. He'd assured me it wasn't that simple. If I wanted this to be over, he needed my help. So, I'd help. And once this was done, I was kicking Thatcher's ass.

A tall figure moved into my line of sight and my gut clenched. My first reaction was sheer female awareness. He was a fine specimen of a man: tall, with broad shoulders, a chiseled jaw, and thick dark hair. Definitely hot, his looks not in the least diminished by the irritation all over that handsome face. Was he the reason the black-haired woman had stormed off?

All at once, his face came into focus in my memory. Crap. This wasn't just any hot guy. This was a Sawyer. Royal? Tenn? I knew they both worked at the Inn, so odds were it was one of them.

The idea of approaching this hot, cranky man had my knees shaking. I wasn't afraid of men in general. Usually, I could hold my own just fine, even with oversized, annoyed men.

This one was more than I wanted to handle, especially in my ancient shorts and rumpled shirt, running on zero coffee and way too little sleep. I was far from my best, but I was going to have to woman-up anyway. I was in Sawyers Bend for a reason, and it was likely my best lead was about two seconds from marching right past me.

It was Go-Time.

Thinking only of Thatcher, I stood up from my crouch and stepped into the gravel path, bumping right into cranky-hot-guy. Instinctively, he stopped, hands coming up to steady me.

"Hey, you okay?" he asked in a deep voice.

"I think so," I said, my voice weak and fluttery in a way it rarely was in real life. I swayed, bracing myself by pressing my hand to his chest. I tried to ignore the sudden flash of heat at the feel of that firm, muscled chest.

No way, Scarlett. You have a job to do, remember?

I did remember. Didn't stop the need. This close, cranky-hot-guy smelled as good as he looked. So good, the swoon was on the verge of becoming real. Woodsy, salty, and undeniably male. How could he smell sweaty and clean at the same time?

Focus, Scarlett. Fortunately, I didn't need to think of what to say.

"Can I help you with something?" he asked politely. "Are you a guest at the Inn?" His eyes narrowed as if trying to place me in his memory.

"Just out for an early walk," I dodged. "I love to walk in the mornings." Lie, but he wouldn't know that. I cast around for something else to say.

"Are you here with your family? I don't remember you checking in." With a genial smile that smoothed away the cranky, he said, "I'm Tenn Sawyer. I run the Inn along with my brother."

I fumbled, not sure how to answer. I hadn't planned this out ahead of time. I'd only gotten to town a few hours before and was still getting my bearings. I knew I'd need to establish contact with one of the Sawyers, but I hadn't come up with a good cover story yet.

"I'm not here with my family. And my name is Scarlett." I stuck my hand out for a shake, cursing myself for giving my real name. Subterfuge was not my forte.

"Scarlett." He repeated my name, rolling the sound of it on his tongue, sending another thrill through my rebellious body. "How long have you been a guest at the Inn?"

"Um, not long. Still getting settled in," I babbled, wanting to escape and knowing I needed to stay. "I, uh, did you just get back from a run? Is there a trail you recommend?"

"There are a few," he said with another genial smile. Taking my elbow, he turned me back toward the rear of the Inn. "But it's a little early for a walk. Let me buy you breakfast instead."

It sounded like he was flirting, but the way he scanned the gardens—focused in the direction the black-haired woman had taken—made me think otherwise. Or maybe he was doing double-duty and flirting while he tried to get me out of the gardens. His fingers were steel on my elbow. If I tried to resist and head out for my fictional walk, I had no doubt he'd stop me.

"Uh, okay. Thanks." I could have breakfast with hot, not-so-cranky-guy. But not dressed like this. And not without checking on the package I'd left in my hastily claimed cottage. "I have to change first." I stopped and tried to pull my arm free. Tenn released me, pivoting to block my exit.

"That's fine. I'll walk you to your room," Tenn said, his expression all cool calculation. Not good. Did I mention I suck at subterfuge? He could probably see the lies all over my face.

"I'm staying in one of the cottages. If you wait here, I'll run back and change. Won't take a minute," I promised with a bright smile.

Tenn's deep blue eyes narrowed. *Shit.* "No," he said slowly, "you're not staying in one of the cottages. It happens that cottage access is limited this summer because of construction. I personally welcomed every guest to reassure them that the noise wouldn't detract from their stay. Like I said, I would have remembered you."

This was exactly the time for a quick comeback.

I was a late arrival.

I was someone's aunt, come to sleep on the couch for a day or two.

Anything.

Say something, Scarlett!

"I, uh, I'm really a guest. Maybe you just missed me at check-in?"

Another narrowed look. "Maybe I did. Why don't you show me your room key?"

Tenn Sawyer was hot, definitely back to cranky, and absolutely no idiot.

I didn't have a room key and he knew it. Now what? I didn't get a chance to figure that out. Those fingers of steel closed over my arm again, pushing me ahead of him on the path with a gentle shove. He muttered to himself, "This must be my day for trespassers."

"I'm not a trespasser," I insisted, trying to think of how to get myself out of this one.

"Well, you're not a local, and you're not a guest of the Inn. So where are you staying, Scarlett? And why are you in my gardens just after dawn?"

I couldn't answer either question. Not yet. I should have figured out a good cover story on the long drive to North Carolina. Instead, I'd split my time between distracting my travel partner and quietly panicking. When I got my hands on Thatcher, I was going to kill him.

"Look, I can explain—" I tugged against his hold, casting around for something to say. I couldn't tell him why I was there. I didn't fully understand it myself. If I tried to explain, he'd think I was either crazy or a criminal. Probably both. Neither of which would help me get Thatcher back.

Tenn Sawyer wasn't letting go of my arm. His teeth set, jaw in a hard line, he dragged me down the neat gravel path, the Inn looming before us. It was a gorgeous building, the stone and timber construction at home in the mountains, imposing and still welcoming. If I were here on vacation, I'd be in heaven.

"Hey, stop!" I gave another hard tug on my arm, trying to get free. I didn't have anywhere to run considering what I'd left in the cottage I'd commandeered, but being dragged to the Inn had panic spiking up my spine. What if I got arrested? I couldn't let that happen. Too much depended on me. Everything that mattered.

Almost too late, I remembered a move Thatcher had taught me from one of his martial arts classes. How to get away from someone who outsized you. Leverage. Leaning into Tenn, I bent over and turned at the same time, wrenching my arm from his grip.

Damn, that hurt. I had just enough time to register the pain before my feet went out from under me. Stumbling back with an embarrassing shriek, I hit the bushes on the edge of the path, branches breaking, stabbing through my shirt. Swearing, I fell in an awkward tumble of limbs.

I landed wedged between two bushes, firmly stuck, my long hair falling in my face. Above me, Tenn muttered something about annoying women. I ignored him, twisting to get my hair out of my eyes.

Immediately, I wished I hadn't. A familiar face stared up at me, inches away. The black-haired woman. Only now, her eyes were glazed, and she had a neat, red circle in her forehead.

Oh, my God. She looked shocked as if she couldn't believe she was dead. Neither could I.

I'd love to say I kept my cool and ordered Tenn Sawyer to call the police while extracting myself from the bush without disturbing the evidence around the body.

I did not.

I screamed my ass off, thrashing to get free, hysterical in my desperate need to get away from the first dead body I'd ever seen up close. She was still warm. Just minutes ago, she'd been so alive. So angry. Now she was dead, her little black dress dirty with mulch, the circle in her forehead matching the red of her lips.

At that thought, my stomach heaved. *Get a hold of yourself, Scarlett,* a small voice ordered from the back of my head. It was drowned out by the much louder voice screeching, *Oh My God Oh My God,* over and over. I barely registered being lifted, branches dragging at my hair, ripping strands from my scalp, tearing my old t-shirt.

Landing on my feet, I stared up into Tenn's hot-yet-cranky face, registering just how pissed off he was before I lurched forward and threw up on his shoes.

Chapter Three

TENN

"What was that for?" I stared down at my running shoes in disgust, aware puke was slowly seeping through the lightweight mesh. Ugh.

It was definitely my day for gorgeous, trouble-making women. Though this one was light years from Vanessa. Tall, slender, stunning. That, they had in common. But while Vanessa was always made-up perfectly, dressed to the nines no matter the hour, Scarlett wore clothes so old most women I knew would have tossed them in the trash.

I doubted she had a speck of makeup on her clear skin. She definitely hadn't used anything to cover those freckles. I was a sucker for freckles. Ditto for long, thick red hair, pink lips, and green eyes so clear they made me think of newly cut grass. Not to mention the full swell of breasts I'd felt when she'd tried to get her arm free. Or the flare of interest in her eyes when she'd bumped into me on the path.

For a second, I'd warmed to the idea of buying her breakfast, thinking maybe it was time to break my rule about hooking up with guests. Then, she'd lied about reserving a cottage and my interest morphed into irritation. Since I had to call West anyway, might as well turn in two trespassers for the price of one.

Scarlett—if that really was her name—heaved again. I stepped back to get out of the way, my irritation sidelined by worry. She was a trespasser and a disappointment, but something was wrong with her. She needed help.

Crouching down to her level, avoiding the waft of puke-scented air, I rubbed her back. "Hey, you okay? Do you need a doctor?"

"Body," she moaned. "Body in the bushes. Dead. She's dead." Her voice ended in a wail, her body dry heaving again.

Had she said body? There was a dead body in the bushes? What the fuck?

Hardly believing her words, I crouched further, looking past Scarlett's hunched form into the dense bushes beside the path where she'd fallen. A familiar pair of red leather sandals caught my eyes.

No. Fuck, no. How?

Pushing the bushes apart, I looked down into Vanessa's sightless eyes. The red circle in the center of her forehead stared back. Vanessa was dead. Shot, just like my father.

I would have heard the gunshot, wouldn't I? I knew guns, was a decent shot myself. There was no way I would have missed the sound of a gunshot. Unless... I thought back. While I'd been arguing with Scarlett, I'd heard something. A hiss-thump I'd taken for a car backfiring in the nearby employee parking lot. I'd looked down the path after Vanessa and hadn't seen anything, but taking in the neat red circle in her forehead, the sound fit into place. A silencer. What I'd heard could have been a silenced gunshot.

I straightened, mind racing. Vanessa and I had fought. I

was one of the last people to see her alive. But no one knew that. No one knew... Before relief could set in, I straightened and looked up at the Inn, took in all those floors of windows, all the guests who could have been staring outside just in time to see me get into a fight with Vanessa.

West's deputies would canvass the Inn. It wasn't that no one knew we'd fought, it was more how many witnesses were there? Odds were at least one. How many times had I stood at the windows in my office, taking in the view of the gardens? Too many. Looking away from the windows, I stared at Scarlett.

She'd started as an opportunity, then she'd been an annoyance. Now, she was my lifeline. I'd run into her less than a minute after Vanessa had stormed off. Scarlett was the only person on the planet who knew that Vanessa had been alive when we'd parted ways. The only person who knew exactly where I'd been every second between Vanessa's departure and her death.

She was a trespasser, and she was definitely up to something, but it didn't matter. I wasn't letting her out of my sight.

I pulled out my phone and dialed West. I'd been friends with our police chief for most of my life. Between my father's murder, the attempts on Griffen and Royal, and J.T.'s stabbing, we'd seen more of him than usual lately. He wasn't going to be happy about this latest development. None of us liked Vanessa, but no one wanted her dead.

Mentally, I corrected myself as I listened to the phone ring. One person had wanted her dead. And that person had gotten what he wanted.

"I take it this isn't a social call. What's up?" West answered.

"Vanessa's dead. In the gardens at the Inn."

West was all business. "Are you with the body now? Did you find her?"

"Yes and no. A guest found her."

"Stay with the body. Don't let anyone close enough to disturb the scene. I'll be there in ten."

West hung up before I could tell him Scarlett had literally fallen on top of his scene, then I'd made it worse by hauling her out of the bush. Remorse hit me as I took her in, arms scratched from the bush, t-shirt ripped, her hair tangled. She wiped her mouth on the back of her hand and straightened, her breath ragged.

"What happened?" she breathed, her voice shaky and thin. "She's dead. How?"

"I'm assuming someone shot her," I said dryly, instantly regretting it as Scarlett's face paled. She swallowed hard. I took her arm, gently this time, and pulled her a few feet away from the bushes.

"The police chief is on his way. After we talk to him, I'll take you somewhere you can get cleaned up. Just hang on a few minutes."

She tugged on her arm. "I don't need to be here for that. Just let me go and—"

"Save it. You found the body. West is going to need to talk to you."

"I'm sorry about your shoes." Scarlett's voice was weak. So weak I didn't have the heart to give her crap about my shoes. They were pretty gross for now, but a run through the wash would fix them up. Nothing was going to fix Vanessa. A wave of nausea hit me at the flash of Vanessa's face, that neat red circle in her forehead. For a second, I could relate to Scarlett's unsettled stomach.

I hadn't seen my father's body but I'd imagined it plenty of times, imagined that red circle in his forehead. Now, I knew exactly what it had looked like. The hole was cleaner than I'd pictured. Precise. I knew from West that the wall behind my father's desk had been covered in blood. Wherever Vanessa had been shot, there was probably a similar spray of blood. Evidence.

Swallowing the bile rising in my throat, I tapped my phone screen with my free hand, pulling up the number to the front desk. When the manager answered, I said, "Close the gardens to guests until further notice. Same for the terrace. I'll explain later."

"Yes, sir, I'll take care of it immediately."

The last thing I needed was a guest stumbling across blood spatter or a dead body. Not the kind of review that brought in the high-dollar bookings. Glancing back down the path to the cottages, I scanned for signs of any guests in search of breakfast. No one so far.

I hadn't lied to Scarlett. The cottages were a special case this summer. As always, they were booked solid until winter. Royal and I had been trying to build more of them for years. Guests loved the stone and timber cottages overlooking the river, the combination of privacy and lush indulgence.

Our father had turned down our proposal repeatedly, but once Griffen took charge, we were a go. Finally, the new cottages were taking shape, the noise of construction distanced from our guests by the cottage we'd kept empty as a buffer. Even with that, I'd made sure to touch base with every group when they checked in to make sure they knew their comfort was of utmost importance. Scarlett had not been among them. Of that, I was sure. At the moment, it might be the only thing I was sure of.

I swept the garden and the path one more time, my eyes avoiding the place where Vanessa's body lay, and pulled

Scarlett back onto the lawn beside the gravel path. "Scarlett, we need to have a conversation before West gets here."

She looked up at me, her green eyes unfocused. I closed a hand over her shoulder and gave her a shake. "Scarlett, look at me." She did as ordered, her eyes slowly clearing, the dazed expression draining away, replaced by horror.

"She's dead. The woman I saw earlier. Someone killed her right here."

"She is. And I think they did."

Scarlett tensed, her muscles ready for flight. I grabbed her wrist and tugged again, drawing her attention back to me.

"Take a deep breath. I need you to focus. Why are you here?"

Her face went flat. "I didn't kill her."

"I know you didn't. I ran into you only a few seconds after Vanessa took off."

Scarlett was no dummy. Her eyes focused to laser sharpness, locking to mine. "You couldn't have killed her either. I saw her go past me and then you came up the path behind her."

"Vanessa is dead and you and I are the only two people we know didn't kill her." Scarlett took a hesitant step closer to me. She was shaky, smelled like puke, and she was still gorgeous. All of that left me feeling like an ass when I pushed my advantage. "I was about to call the police chief to report you for trespassing. You and Vanessa."

I waited for her to work through that part. "I was trespassing," she admitted, "but you know I didn't kill her. You know I didn't."

"I do. So, I guess that makes us partners."

Scarlett's white teeth sank into her lush bottom lip. I forced myself to look away, catching her reluctant nod of agreement from the corner of my eye. I did not need to make this any more complicated than it already was.

West was the police chief. He was also one of my oldest friends. That wouldn't stop him from throwing my ass in jail if I was the best suspect for Vanessa's murder. My brother Ford was serving a ten-year sentence in prison right now for our father's murder. No one believed he'd killed Prentice, not even West, but Ford was the best and only suspect. He'd argued with Prentice just before Prentice had been found with a hole in his head.

Ford had been set up. We just hadn't been able to prove it. And now, here was Vanessa, shot in the head right after she'd argued with me in full view of most of the guest rooms in the Inn. I didn't want to be paranoid, but if it hadn't been for Scarlett's inconveniently convenient presence... I didn't even want to consider what that would mean.

Could Scarlett be in on it? I studied her from the corner of my eye. She'd been trespassing, had lied about staying in the Inn. Wouldn't be the first time someone grabbed cheaper accommodations and tried to use the Inn's amenities. It happened all the time.

She'd been awkward, embarrassed, and charmingly clumsy as she'd tried to lie her way out of my accusations. Then, she'd seen Vanessa's body and puked all over me. I flexed my toes in my soiled shoes, my stomach turning at the faint squish. The second we were done with West I was finding a hose.

Scarlett was still pale, still shaky. It was possible she was the best actress I'd ever met, but I doubted it. My bet was that she was in the wrong place at the exact right time to keep me out of jail.

Pretty, lying Scarlett wasn't going anywhere. Not any time soon.

Chapter Four

TENN

"What the hell, Tenn?" West strode down the gravel path, his eyes hard. "Who's this?" he stopped in front of us, looking over his shoulder at his lead deputy. "Get the scene secured. Coroner is on the way." His deputy nodded and turned, barking orders at the rest of her team.

West didn't wait for me to respond, scanning the gravel path as he approached. "She over there?" I pointed. West leaned into the bush and swore. "Should have stayed in jail," he said under his breath. Raising his head, he zeroed in on Scarlett. "Name?"

"Scarlett," I answered. "We ran into each other on the path."

West didn't acknowledge my comment. Eyes on Scarlett, he brought out his pad and pen, then clicked open his phone and hit the red 'record' button. "I'm recording this for accuracy. This is police chief Weston Garfield—" He went on to list the date, location, my name, and Scarlett's first.

At his raised eyebrow she said, "Hall. Scarlett Hall."

"Scarlett Hall," West repeated. "Are you a guest at the Inn, Scarlett?"

"No, sir," she said, her voice soft and scared in a way it hadn't been when I'd interrogated her. Then again, I hadn't had a gun on my hip or the ability to throw her ass in jail.

"Then why don't you tell me what you were doing on the garden path this morning," he prompted, holding up his phone so it could catch her answer.

I already knew whatever she said was going to be a lie. She surprised me just a little. I don't think she lied so much as left out most of the truth. "I was thinking about getting a room at the Inn, but it's kinda pricey, you know?"

West nodded. Rooms at the Inn started at $350 a night and went up sharply from there. Cheap, it was not.

"I wanted to check out the place, see if it was worth springing for a few nights, so I decided to go for a walk. I was on the path, back that way." She pointed toward the cottages, near where I'd first run into her. "I was off to the side, looking at the roses, when I saw her—Vanessa?— go by. She looked angry. A few seconds later, I bumped into Tenn."

"And where did Tenn come from?" West asked easily as if my freedom didn't rely on her answer.

"He was behind me, I guess." Scarlett knew exactly what West was asking. She pointed ahead of us at the Inn. "Vanessa walked off that way." Turning back to the cottages, she pointed again. "Tenn came from behind me, the opposite direction as..." A slight hesitation before she said the name. "Vanessa." Scarlett glanced at the bushes where deputies swarmed the area around Vanessa's body. She swallowed hard.

"And then what happened?" West prompted.

Eyeing the recorder, Scarlett went on, "I bumped into

Tenn. Wasn't watching where I was going. It's so beautiful here," she said weakly. She was good, believable and way less sketchy than she had been when I'd questioned her. "I was nervous once he told me who he was since I was, you know, not really a guest. I, uh, I lied about staying here, and he knew I was lying. He got, um, angry, and I'm pretty sure he was going to call you and report me for trespassing. He was dragging me back to the Inn..." A baleful glance in my direction from both West and Scarlett.

"He dragged you?" West asked.

"Yes. He had his hand on my elbow and was pulling me down the path. I tried to get away because he was freaking me out, and I tripped, fell in the bushes." Abruptly, Scarlett stopped talking. She swallowed hard again after another quick glance at where she'd fallen on Vanessa's body.

Taking pity on her, I finished, "She fell on top of Vanessa's body. I helped her up, and then she puked all over my shoes."

West gave my feet a sympathetic look. "And you?"

I filled in my part, starting with Vanessa accosting me on the path, back by the cottages. I didn't leave anything out, knowing that keeping things from West was the best way to find myself in jail, even with Scarlett as my alibi.

West made notes on his pad. Finishing, he attached the pen to the binding of the pad and shoved it into his pocket. Looking at Scarlett, he said, "You're not a guest at the Inn."

"No." Scarlett's eyes flicked to me then away, a faint flush on her cheeks. Good, she should be embarrassed.

"Where *are* you staying?" West asked.

She shifted from one foot to another, and I had the distinct impression she was trying not to look back at the path to the cottages. "I just got into town. I haven't—"

I wasn't taking any chances that this situation was going

to spin further out of my control. "West, can I borrow those?" I inclined my head at the shiny metal handcuffs clipped to his belt. Scarlett missed the gesture, her eyes drifting between the path to the cottages and the officers surrounding Vanessa's body.

West gave me a long look before tilting his head to one side and looking at the sky as if seeking counsel from someone far above us. He appeared to come to a decision. Unclipping his cuffs from his duty belt, he tossed them to me. My fingers closed around them in mid-air.

Scarlett didn't have time to register what was coming. Flipping the cuffs over, my hand shot out to grab her arm. I slapped one side of the cuffs over her wrist and the other over my own. Holding out my free hand, I said to West, "Key?"

With a rueful smile, he dropped the key in my hand. Scarlett looked between the two of us, her green eyes wide with shock and the beginnings of what I suspected would be an impressive display of temper.

"Are you kidding me?" She yanked at her arm. "You can't let him do this!"

West gave her a level look. "Would you prefer I book you for trespassing?"

Scarlett's face drained of color. This time, she couldn't stop her eyes from flicking back to the cottages. Why? What was back there? Shaking her head, sending her hair flying, she said, "No. No, you can't."

West let out a sigh. "I'll be straight with you, Miss Hall. I can't have you wandering off until we have a better idea of what's going on here. And I don't have enough people to assign one to guarantee your safety."

"My safety? I'm not the one who was shot." She gave another yank to her wrist and shot me a glare.

"No," West agreed, "but you were only feet away, and you two were the last to see her alive. Maybe you already told me everything you know—"

"I did!"

"And maybe the killer thinks you saw something. Something you might remember later. Do you really want to be on your own out there?" We watched Scarlett absorb his words, her face growing paler than I thought possible. I started to think she might faint.

West narrowed his eyes on me. "Are you going to take her back to the Manor?"

"I'm not letting her out of my sight until we know what the fuck is going on here."

Nodding down at our cuffed hands, West said, "I'm letting you get away with this because I'm short-staffed and it's easier all around if she's somewhere safe. Not many places around here safer than the Manor. I'll be checking in with both of you. I'm assuming she won't have any complaints."

I didn't bother to answer. West had known me all my life. He knew I wasn't going to hurt Scarlett. I just wasn't going to let her go. I didn't believe the bullshit story she'd given West. The Inn was expensive, but scoping out the place to protect her budget wasn't the reason she'd been lurking in the gardens.

Scarlett Hall was up to something. Something that involved my inn. I wasn't going to let her go anywhere until I knew what.

West glanced back at the Inn. "The coroner is here. I need to focus on the scene and the body. You closed the gardens?" I nodded. "Good. Get her out of here and stick close to the Manor. See if Royal can cover the Inn for a day or two. I want you two out of sight for now."

He glanced up at the windows to all those guest rooms, each with a perfect view of the gardens, then back to Vanessa's body in the bushes. "I don't like the way this lines up." A pointed look at Scarlett. "If she hadn't been here—"

"I know." I wasn't surprised West had come to the same conclusion I had. If Scarlett hadn't been in the gardens to see Vanessa storm off, those handcuffs would be on my wrists, and I'd be headed to a cell.

"I'm sending a deputy to escort you to your car and follow you home. I want you to text me when you're behind the gates of the Manor."

"Got it." I pulled my phone from my pocket and dialed the front desk again. When the manager answered, I said, "I need you to go to my office, grab my laptop in the backpack beside the desk, and bring it to the terrace. Keep the gardens closed. We've had an incident. West will fill you in when you get here."

"I'll check in later," West said, nodding to Scarlett and striding over to one of his officers.

Scarlett eyed me with suspicion. I could practically see her mind racing, see her concocting her newest bullshit story. I wasn't having it. I plucked her phone from her back pocket and shoved it in my own, pretending I hadn't seen her covert glances at the cottages.

"Ready to go?"

"Where are we going?" she stalled.

"My family's house. Heartstone Manor."

"You expect me to just go with you? What's your family going to say when you show up with a strange woman handcuffed to your wrist?"

I raised my eyebrows and shot her a grin. "That I'm a lucky man?"

Scarlett let out a huff and glared down at our joined wrists. This would be a lot easier if I didn't have to fight her.

"Look, I'm not going to hurt you. And if whoever killed Vanessa comes back to tie up loose ends, the Manor is the safest place you could be. My oldest brother used to work in security, and he has the whole place wired up. Guards, cameras—you name it, we have it. If a bunny rabbit hops too close to the house, they know."

Scarlett worried her lower lip with her teeth and looked at the sky, just like West had. I glanced up. Nothing to be seen, just puffy white clouds and summer blue sky. Whatever I was missing, Scarlett seemed to find her answer. Lowering her clear green gaze to mine, she gave in.

"Fine. I'll come with you. Doesn't seem like I have a choice." She pulled at the cuffs, the metal jangling.

"You don't." I turned as if to head back toward the Inn.

"Wait!" Scarlett turned the other way, our joined wrists dragging me along with her. "I told the truth when I said I was staying in one of the cottages. I just didn't exactly check in. I need to go back there before we leave."

That was all I needed to hear. Now I knew exactly where Scarlett had been squatting.

Chapter Five

TENN

S carlett kept pace with me as I strode down the path to the cottages. There was only one cottage empty right now, but it should have been locked up tight. "How did you get in?" I asked conversationally. Yelling at her wasn't going to get me anywhere. Might as well play nice considering we were stuck together.

"Get in to where?" Scarlett gave me an innocent smile.

"The cottage," I said through clenched teeth.

I was trying for nice, but this woman could test the patience of a saint. I am not a saint. If Royal were here, he'd make a joke or flirt. He'd find some way to diffuse the tension and win her over.

I wasn't a saint, and I wasn't my brother. I could be a soft touch when it came to a person in need, but I wasn't particularly charming. Royal was finesse, and I was the blunt hammer.

Scarlett gave me another smile, genuine laughter in her eyes. I tried not to notice the way amusement sparkled in all that clear green. I'd bet she was heart-stopping when she laughed.

Not that I cared.

Her mouth quirking to the side, she said, "Hypothetically, if I had broken into a cottage—not that I'm saying I did, because I didn't—"

"But if you had?" I prompted as we passed the first of the occupied cottages.

"But if I had," she mused, "I might have picked the lock."

I raised an eyebrow at her. "You can pick locks?"

A shrug of one shoulder. "Or I found a bathroom window that had been left open."

"Impossible. The staff wouldn't have left a window open."

"You never know. Do you have an eye on every single thing that happens here?"

"Yes," I answered, knowing it was a lie. There were too many moving parts to the Inn at Sawyers Bend. I had an eye on ninety-five percent of what went on in my inn, but even I had to admit things slipped my attention.

Her steps picked up their pace as we neared the last cottage, the one that was supposed to be empty. From the outside, there was no sign anyone had broken in. Scarlett came to a stop at the bottom of the porch steps and raised one eyebrow.

"What?" I asked.

"Aren't you going to open the door?" She shoved her free hand in her pocket, apparently prepared to wait me out.

We stared at each other, at an impasse. She wasn't going to show me how she'd gotten in. Stating the obvious, I said, "You won't show me because if you do, I'll have evidence to turn that trespassing charge into breaking and entering."

That faint flush hit her cheeks again. She muttered something under her breath, but I couldn't catch more than a hard 'ch' sound. "Look, I entered, but I didn't break anything. No property damage, I swear. I wouldn't do that. I'm also not going to admit to anything else considering you're close enough to the chief of police that he gave you his cuffs."

"Fair enough." I pulled out my master key and unlocked the door. Scarlett pushed past me, almost rushing to get into the room. Right behind her, I couldn't spot the reason for her hurry.

The main room of the cottage appeared ready for a guest, missing only the flowers and gift basket that would have been on the counter. Beyond the main room, the bed in the bedroom was bare of linens. Everything seemed to be untouched. I couldn't see any sign Scarlett had ever been in here.

A glance at her face told me she was as surprised as I was by the pristine cottage. Heedless of the cuffs connecting our wrists, she started around the couches in the living room, her eyes darting from side to side, tension gripping every inch of her body.

The cottage wasn't that big, and it was quickly clear that the main room and tiny kitchenette were empty. I barely kept my hand from being torn off as I followed her to the bedroom, also empty, the white walls and bare mattress bright in the sunlight pouring through the windows.

Into the empty cottage, Scarlett shouted, "August! August Hall, you'd better be in here!"

I wasn't expecting the tiny voice that drifted into the room. I wasn't sure from where. Under the bed? The closet?

"Mom? Is it safe to come out?"

Scarlett strode to the closet and threw the door open. Curled on the floor, headphones on his ears connected to a dark tablet, a small boy blinked up at us. Scarlett dropped to her knees, wrapping her free arm around the boy who looked at me in unabashed curiosity.

"When I couldn't find you—" Scarlett broke off, pressing her face to the boy's golden blond hair.

"You said to hide if I heard anyone coming. I wanted to listen to my game, so I went ahead and hid anyway, just in case."

"Okay, okay," she murmured, resting her cheek on his hair, eyes bright with tears that didn't fall. "You did the right thing. I was just scared when I didn't see you. I didn't want to leave you alone, and then— But you're okay. Everything's okay. Let's get you up, we need to get moving."

The boy tucked his tablet under his arm and stood along with his mother but made no move to leave the closet. "Who's he?"

I stuck out my hand. "Tennessee Sawyer. Who are you?"

The boy took my hand gravely and shook. "Tennessee like the state?"

"No, Tennessee like my Great-Great-Great-Uncle Tennessee Reginald Sawyer. But everyone calls me Tenn."

"I'm August Hall." August dropped my hand. "Can I call you Tenn?"

"Fine with me," I said at the same moment Scarlett said, "No. You can call him Mr. Sawyer."

August shrugged. "Where are we going?"

"You and your mom are coming to stay at my house for a while. You'll like it. It's practically a castle, and our housekeeper has a kid about your age." I pictured Nicky in my head. "Maybe he's a few years younger than you. How old are you?"

August tilted his head to the side and quirked the side

of his mouth the same way his mother had. "How old do you think I am?"

"Eight," I guessed.

His eyes shot wide, then darted to his mom. "He's smart." She shook her head, and August's eyes finally caught on the handcuffs joining our wrists. "Why are you wearing those?" That fast, the light left the kid's eyes and his lower lip trembled. "Are you under arrest?"

"It's a game," I said, thinking fast. "Your mom isn't in trouble, we're just playing a game."

"Yeah, about that," Scarlett cut in, "August, where's my backpack?"

"I hid it under the bed." He pointed at the dust ruffle concealing his hiding place.

Scarlett ruffled his hair. "Good thinking." Straightening, she caught my eye. "Why don't we take a break from the game for a few minutes? Long enough for you to clean off your shoes in the tub while I change into something a little less ratty."

"Sure, as long as August helps me." Just in case she was planning on taking off while I was barefoot and she was free of the cuffs.

"Fine," she said shortly. Getting away from me wasn't going to be that easy. Once I got her behind the gates of Heartstone Manor, escape would be nearly impossible.

I unlocked her end of the cuffs and reached down, holding my hand out to August. "Want to come with me? Your mom puked all over my sneakers, and I need to clean them off."

His hand sliding easily into mine, August wrinkled his nose. "Ewwww, gross. Benji did that in preschool once after we had birthday cupcakes and it soaked into my toes before my mom could bring me new sneakers. It was squishy gross."

One last look at Scarlett before we left her to change. "Five minutes." She nodded and dropped to scrounge under the bed for her bag. She wasn't going anywhere. Not while I had her son. The mystery of Scarlett deepened.

I mulled it over as I listened to August chatter about puke and Benji and cupcakes. Taking off my sneakers, I rinsed them in the tub until they were mostly clean. I could wear wet shoes until we got to the Manor as long as I wasn't walking in puddles of puke. *Squishy gross* about summed it up. Done with them, I grabbed a bar of soap and took care of my feet.

Of all the scenarios I'd been building in my mind, Scarlett having a son tagging along hadn't made the list. She'd seemed genuinely distraught when we'd entered the cottage and she hadn't seen him. So distraught it was hard to imagine she'd endanger him without a good reason.

Leaving him on his own in a cottage she'd broken into while she snuck around the Inn? What would drive her to do that?

I wasn't a parent. Nicky was the only kid I knew on a first-name basis, but I was pretty sure you didn't leave an eight-year-old on his own in a strange place.

Sticking my feet back into my wet but mostly puke-free sneakers, I looked up at the knock on the door frame.

My mouth went dry. Scarlett had been gorgeous in a torn t-shirt and threadbare, baggy shorts. In a light yellow sundress and matching flip-flops, her hair pulled back on one side with a flower-shaped clip, she was absolutely stunning.

Fuck.

I looked down at the kid in reflex as if to remind myself

that Scarlett was far more than a very pretty face. She was complicated. Likely up to no good. And my alibi. Definitely not hook-up material. But still. Damn.

She held up a hand, fingers gripping a blue toothbrush, a sheepish smile curving her pink lips. "Is the bathroom free? I won't make a mess, but I'd love to brush my teeth."

Nudging August ahead of me, I gestured back to the sink. "All yours. We'll just wait out here."

Scarlett nodded and squeezed August's shoulder. "You good?"

"Hungry. You said we'd get pancakes." His eyes were blue to her green, but I had a feeling that determined squint came directly from his mother.

Dropping a kiss to the top of his head, she smiled into his hair. "Why don't you talk to Mr. Sawyer about those pancakes? He's in charge now."

With a wicked grin and a wink that made my knees go weak, she disappeared into the bathroom and shut the door.

August rounded on me, his mind stuck on one track, and that track was called 'Pancakes.' I checked my watch. It was almost breakfast time at the Manor, and our current cook made pretty good silver dollar pancakes. "I bet there are pancakes at my house," I said. "And if not, we can make some."

It didn't look like I was going to work today. Or tomorrow. Might as well make some pancakes.

Chapter Six

SCARLETT

Tenn slapped the cuffs on my wrist just before he shut the passenger door to his SUV. The other end of the cuffs he closed over the door handle. So much for hoping he'd forget about them.

Did he think I was going to make a run for it with my son strapped in behind us? Not likely. Then again, he didn't know that. He thought I was a woman who'd left her eight-year-old alone in a stolen cottage while she planned a more nefarious crime.

Who was I kidding? I *was* that woman. Kind of. I hadn't been planning any kind of crime. If I was being honest with myself, I had no idea what I'd been doing. All I knew was that if I wanted to get Thatcher back, I had to come to Sawyers Bend and connect with the Sawyers. If I'd had any idea I was going to bump into one of them just after dawn, I would have figured out a cover story. And dressed better.

I'm not usually so slow. I'm a college professor, damn it. Generally, I'm considered fairly intelligent. Since the moment Thatcher had taken off, leaving me only increasingly cryptic messages, I'd been acting on instinct. When it came to intrigue, my instincts sucked.

I could teach the hell out of art history, create some pretty nice glass art, and sometimes did appraisals and verifications. Usually, I was a good mom. Usually. Not so much the last few days. Also, a halfway decent cook. Those were my main skills. Note that clandestine operations were not on that list. I might have been better at it if I'd had any idea what the hell was going on.

We turned out of the Inn at Sawyers Bend, a staff member following in my car, and passed through the far end of the town of Sawyers Bend. I'd arrived well after midnight and only got a few glimpses of the town. What I'd seen had appeared quaint and charming, like a small town in a movie. In the bright light of a summer morning, the town was even prettier than I'd thought, the main street already crowded with tourists.

Within a few minutes, we'd passed through town, heading up a winding road into the mountains. I should have been scared to leave civilization with a stranger. I was. Kind of. I didn't know any of these people. Definitely couldn't trust them.

Tipping my head back against the soft leather headrest of Tenn's luxury SUV, I let out a sigh. I was sorry that woman had died, but her death had solved a lot of problems for me. After I'd gotten Thatcher's garbled message, I'd withdrawn as much cash as I could, raided my emergency fund stashed in the freezer, loaded up August, and taken off for North Carolina. I hadn't slept since.

Considering the demands of an eight-year-old bladder, it had taken us almost twenty hours to get from our small college town outside of Boston all the way to Sawyers Bend, North Carolina.

Go to Sawyers Bend. That was all Thatcher had been able to tell me. That they were headed to Sawyers Bend, but he didn't know when they'd get here, and that the Sawyers had what they were looking for. If I wanted this to end, I needed to see if I could find it.

An impossible task. I was a stranger and a terrible liar. Two things that would not get me entry to any of the Sawyers' private spaces like the Inn or their historic Manor. Except here I was, Tenn Sawyer's new best friend, being taken to his home where I'd be forced to stay until they let me go.

Good luck or bad? Hard to say. For now, I was cautiously going with good. Given what Tenn had said about the security at Heartstone Manor, I never would have been able to sneak in on my own.

I could have gone after Tenn or one of his brothers, tried seduction to get in the house, but that would have caused more trouble in the end. For one thing, I had August. Leaving him alone in that cottage for twenty minutes had left me sick with worry. Leaving him while I went off with a strange man? No freaking way.

And second, there was Tenn.

I glanced away from the passing trees and snuck a look at Tennessee Sawyer. My life was cursed by handsome men. No, really. Cursed. My ex-husband was the most beautiful man I'd ever seen, and he'd been a major disappointment in almost every way a man could be. He'd been good in bed, but that was the best thing I could say about him.

I was currently having issues at work due to the new head of my department, another too-handsome man. This one had decided I should be his newest extracurricular activity if I wanted a full professorship. Forget that. Not only was he married, I was done sleeping with men just because they were hot. Been there, had the wasted years to show for it.

Which brought me to Tenn Sawyer. In another world, for another woman, seducing him would have been heaven. He was just as good-looking as my ex though in a totally different way. Taller and broader for one. I hadn't missed those strong thighs in his running shorts or the way the sleeves of his t-shirt stretched around his biceps. Add deep blue eyes, thick, wavy, espresso-dark hair, and that serious demeanor—it was hard not to be tempted.

You don't do temptation, remember?

That was right, I didn't. I'd dated a few times since I'd ditched my ex, but none of the guys had been worth a second date. Lately, I'd been too focused on the important things in life to focus on dating. Being a mom, teaching my classes, and my side hustle, selling my lampwork glass art and jewelry for extra cash—those things were my future, my real life. I didn't have time for anything else. I definitely didn't have enough patience for the meat market of dating.

Maybe Tenn Sawyer wasn't that tempting. I was seriously sleep-deprived, and I hadn't been this close to a man, outside of work, in a long time. I was sex-deprived and it was making me a little crazy. *He's probably not even that hot,* I told myself. *It's just your hormones.*

Yeah, right. Tenn Sawyer was exactly that hot, but he was not for me. Even forgetting that I'd sworn off men for the rest of forever, I was here under false pretenses. Another complication was the last thing I needed. Luck had landed me entry to Heartstone Manor, but that wasn't enough. If I couldn't find what Thatcher was looking for, my life was going to get extremely messy. I didn't think there was enough luck floating around the universe to get me out of this disaster unscathed.

The SUV turned and August sat up in the back seat. "Wow, are those gates? Where are we going?"

Tall, black iron gates framed by granite pillars blocked the road. Tenn pressed a remote clipped to his sun visor and the gates swung open. Turning back to grin at August, Tenn said, "I told you our house was practically a castle."

Tapping the screen on his dashboard, Tenn pulled up a phone number labeled '*Griffen*' and connected a call. A distracted, sleepy voice answered.

"Tenn?"

"You at breakfast?"

A muffled laugh. "Not exactly."

"Sorry to break up your morning, but we have a problem. I just drove through the gates, need you to meet me downstairs."

"Be down by the time you get here." The call disconnected and Tenn didn't explain. I didn't ask. We'd be at the house soon enough.

I'd only seen aerial pictures of Heartstone Manor, and those hadn't done the place justice. In the little research I'd managed before we left, I'd learned that Heartstone Manor had been built in the late 1800s by one of Tenn's ancestors to ease the homesickness of his English bride. The family had never opened it to tourists, never allowed it to be photographed.

One of the few Gilded Age mansions still used as a private home, it was completely inaccessible to the public. The art historian in me was salivating at the chance to see the inside. I was prepared to be wowed.

Wowed didn't cover it. The narrow, paved drive wound through the forest, the asphalt crumbling in places, weeds threatening to take over the road. In some spots, it looked like some effort had been made to trim back the growth, but in others, green shoots pushed right through the hard, black surface.

The house itself appeared out of the trees between one blink and the next, so large it was hard to imagine we hadn't seen it from the road. Three stories of granite, wings jutting out on each end, Heartstone Manor was majestic and looked oddly abandoned. Some of the windows were lit, proving it wasn't empty, and the grass between the granite blocks paving the courtyard was neatly trimmed, but where there should have been landscaping or flowers around the house there was only bare dirt. It gave the house an unfinished feeling out of place on a home so old.

Tenn noticed my look. "My father let the place go after the rest of us moved out. My oldest brother Griffen inherited the house. He's working on getting it back into shape."

"Oh," was my brilliant response, my brain too busy processing to talk. "How many of you live here? If you all moved out..."

"All of us. It's a long story." He pulled the SUV to a stop in front of steps leading to tall, iron-strapped wood doors. Jumping out, he had a word with the guy who'd driven my car from the Inn. The driver jumped out, handed Tenn the keys, and disappeared around the side of the house, my bags from the trunk in hand.

I watched my belongings disappear with him, feeling things sliding even more out of my control. I might have gotten myself inside the Manor gates, but I was completely cut off, at their mercy, and I had August to protect. When I got my hands on Thatcher...

August let Tenn help him out of the SUV, climbing the steps alone and waiting for us at the top. Tenn came around and opened my door, smoothly unlocking the cuff from the handle and securing it back on his wrist. Crap.

I knew how to pick a lock, handcuffs included, but without my set of picks I was screwed. I had a feeling Tenn wasn't going to just hand over my things. Added to that complication, I could pick a lock with two hands. Picking a lock with only my left hand? That, I'd never practiced. Why would I?

I'd taught myself to pick locks partly for fun and partly to liberate the household funds my ex liked to siphon off for his poker games. Someone had to make sure there was food on the table and the power stayed on. It sure as hell wasn't going to be him. None of that made me a career criminal or a master locksmith. I'd managed to open the back door to the cottage, driven by desperation, but that was the apex of my skills.

Even if I got the cuffs off, where was I going to go? I was miles from town. Tenn had my car keys, and there was no way August could walk out of here even if I got us away from Tenn. We were trapped. I looked up at the imposing facade of Heartstone Manor and at Tenn, a bemused smile on his face as he led me to where August stood at the top of the steps. Remembering the police chief promising to check in on me, I let out a breath.

I wasn't going to get away from Tenn, and I needed to be here even if I wasn't sure exactly what to do about it. Might as well go with the flow. For now.

Keeping pace beside Tenn, I took August's hand in my free one and tucked him behind me as Tenn reached to open the front door of Heartstone Manor.

Chapter Seven

SCARLETT

The door swung open before Tenn could turn the handle. A man who could only be another Sawyer stood in the open doorway, his blond hair rumpled from sleep. This must be Griffen, the oldest brother, the one Tenn had called from the gates. Beside him was a tall, slender woman in a bulky robe, her face pale, eyes wide as she took in the three of us.

Griffen stepped back to let us in. "What the hell is going on?" he demanded, his voice filling the two-story front hall.

"Are you okay?" the woman asked, her warm brown eyes on me then moving to Tenn. It felt like she was checking on me as much as Tenn, but I didn't answer. Until I had a better feel for the room, I was keeping my mouth shut.

A door closed on the other side of the hall and a couple strode in, hand in hand. The man was almost a carbon copy of Tenn, his hair a little more auburn than Tenn's espresso, but otherwise, they could have been twins. The woman was shorter than me, her face a little moony when she gazed up at the Tenn look-alike, the hot pink coils of her hair bright against her honeyed brown skin.

"Hey guys," the Tenn look-alike said. "Since when are you all up this early?"

Tenn raised an eyebrow at him. "Since I found Vanessa's body this morning when I came back from my run."

They all stared at us, faces blank.

"Vanessa's body?" the look-alike asked. "She's dead?"

"Shot in the forehead, just like Dad," Tenn confirmed.

"And who's she?" he asked, looking at me. I rolled my eyes to the ceiling, impatience warring with my nerves. Tenn had said his whole family lived here, but I hadn't expected to walk into a crowd.

"Her?" Tenn asked, shooting me a hard look. He raised his arm and mine followed with a metallic jingle, the handcuff connecting us shining silver under the crystal chandelier. "She's my alibi."

A cacophony of sound exploded, questions shooting from all angles. August hadn't heard about the dead body earlier, and I'd prefer he didn't get an earful now. I tugged at Tenn's hand with the cuff. He ignored his family's demands to look down at us.

"Ix-nay on the ody-bay," I said with a pointed look at August, peeking out from behind me.

"I know pig-Latin," his little voice piped up. God save me from smart-ass kids. Then again, if I didn't want little smart-asses running around, I probably shouldn't have procreated. Dragging Tenn's hand along with mine, I pressed my palms over August's ears.

Silence fell as the crowd registered August's presence. If it were just me, I would have stuck with keeping my mouth shut, but I had August to look out for. Trying for a friendly smile, I faced Tenn's family.

"Hi, I'm Scarlett. This is my son August. I know things need to be said, but August doesn't need to hear anything that might keep him up at night." I raised an eyebrow, hoping they got me. I'd learned the hard way that hands over the ears were not foolproof.

The woman beside Griffen rubbed a hand over her abdomen for a second before she took charge. "Of course. You can—" She inclined her head at my hands over August's ears. I dropped them.

He glared up at me. "I'm not a baby, Mom."

"I'm sure you're not," the woman said. "You're August? I love that name." August beamed up at her. "I'm Hope. This is Griffen, Royal, and Daisy." Hope pointed to each of them as she said their names. "Have you had breakfast, August?"

After a pointed look at both me and Tenn, August smiled at Hope, sensing an ally. "No, and Mom and Mr. Tenn promised me pancakes."

"Okay, we can make that happen." With a glance at the cuffs connecting me to Tenn, Hope turned to Griffen. "I need to go upstairs and get dressed. Could you introduce Scarlett and August to Savannah and Nicky, see if Savannah can feed August downstairs, and arrange breakfast for the adults in our office?"

Griffen pressed a kiss to Hope's forehead. "I'm on it."

Hope smiled at us. "Sorry to run off on you," she gestured to her robe, "but I'll be right back." Leaning down so she was even with August's face, she said, "Savannah's son is a little younger than you and I bet he'd love to have another kid to play with. Usually, he's stuck with the grownups around here. Do you think you could hang out with him for a while?"

"Sure! I know how to play with little kids. We have little kids at my school. But not in my class."

Hope gave him a bemused look, her hand drifting back to her abdomen in a gesture I thought was unconscious.

Based on the rock on her finger, I assumed she was married to Griffen. For our sake, it would be nice if she was as kind as she seemed.

Royal stepped in. "Daisy and I will hit the buffet in the dining room and make up plates, bring them to the office, and save Savannah the extra work." To me, he said, "Anything you don't eat?"

"Nope, whatever you have would be great." I'd eat anything, especially if it wasn't another drive-through meal shoved in my face on the road.

That quickly, the crowd dispersed, Royal and Daisy headed for the open double doors on the left side of the hall and Hope up the wide staircase to the second floor. Griffen, eyeing the cuffs again, led us to the right, through double doors that mirrored those Royal and Daisy had gone through. I tried to take in every detail of the house as we followed Griffen down a wide hallway.

The hallway opened on either side to rooms that should have been sitting rooms or galleries. Something formal, based on their placement in the house. Both were completely empty, dark squares showing on the wallpaper where paintings had hung. Weird.

We left the hallway to spill into a two-story library, every wall covered in leather-bound books except for the space taken up by a fireplace so big I could have stood comfortably inside and not had to bend even a little. My entire house would have fit easily in the library with plenty of room for my postage stamp of a yard.

I didn't get the chance to see more than that. A door on the far side of the library led to another hallway and a set of stairs that descended to the depths of the great house. Here, the feel shifted from elegant to medieval, the walls changing from plaster to stone as we turned on the landing and took the final steps to the lower level.

Once we were away from the main floor, Griffen turned to Tenn. "I'm assuming West is on the case?"

"I called him as soon as we found her."

A nod from Griffen. "Good." A glance at me. "Sorry for the long way around. The other entrance to the lower level is through the dining room and half the family is in there right now. I didn't think you'd want to explain the handcuffs."

"It's okay, Mr. Griffen, they're just playing a game," August assured him.

"Mr. Sawyer," I corrected automatically.

"But Mom, they're all Mr. Sawyer. How will they know who I'm talking to?"

I let out a sigh. I needed a good meal and either a vat of coffee or twelve hours of sleep to keep up with my kid. Usually, I was proud of his quick thinking. Hell, I was still proud of it even if it was momentarily annoying.

"Mr. Griffen works for me," Griffen said, a laugh in his voice.

I sighed. "Okay, August, but don't forget the Mr. part."

"I won't!" His pride offended, August sent me an affronted look. I ran my hand over his golden hair, not sure I wanted to leave him with this Savannah even if she did have a son of her own. I changed my mind seconds later.

A tall woman nearly ran into us, her strawberry-blond hair in a neat bun. She wore a long-sleeve gray dress in a tight herringbone pattern covered by a starched white apron. "Griffen, is everything okay upstairs?" Her eyes landed on the rest of us, processing Tenn, me, the handcuffs, and August in a heartbeat. Turning questioning gray eyes on Griffen, she waited for an explanation.

With a quick look at August, he did his best to talk around the situation. "Savannah, this is Scarlett and August. Scarlett and Tenn here are, um, playing a game, and they need to fill in the rest of us on the rules so we can help. We'll eat in my office. Royal and Daisy are making up plates in the dining room. Can August hang out with Nicky for a while?"

Savannah smiled down at August. "Of course, Nicky would love that. He doesn't have preschool today, and Mom came by to keep him company. She can look after August while you're all upstairs."

I wasn't so sure about that. Savannah seemed nice, but this was my son we were talking about. My free hand closed over August's shoulder as I searched for words. I wanted reassurance, but this woman—all of these people—were strangers. I had no clue what their reassurance was worth. Again, I was reminded how very far in over my head I was.

Savannah must have sensed my hesitation. With a sympathetic smile, she met my eyes. "I know you don't know me, but I promise we'll take good care of August. Whatever's going on, he'll be safe with us."

The metal around my wrist reminded me I had no choice but to trust her.

Leaning down, I pressed my forehead to August's. "I'll come to check on you soon. Have fun and mind your manners."

August tapped his forehead against mine, the gesture so familiar and comforting it brought tears to my eyes. "It's okay, Mom, I'll be good."

"I know you will," I whispered, pressing a kiss to his cheek.

My August could be a little smart-ass, but he was also sweet-natured, cuddly, and smart as a whip. Not for the first time, I wished I'd had any other option than to bring him along on this wild goose chase. If my parents had been in town... But they hadn't.

They were currently somewhere in Canada, enjoying their spiffy new RV and my dad's recent retirement. My mom could work from anywhere so they'd sold their house and headed out to explore the world. At least, those parts accessible by RV. They would have come home if I'd called. I knew they would. But they were at least three days' drive away and I hadn't had that kind of time. August and I were on our own.

Straightening, I ruffled August's hair and gave him a final reminder. "Use your fork."

August stared at the ceiling for patience. "I will!"

With a snort, I pushed him towards Savannah. "Thank you."

"Anytime," she said with a smile, taking August's hand in hers. "Nicky is working on using his fork, but he doesn't quite have it down yet. Maybe you can show him how it's done."

"I can. I'm really good. Sometimes—" August's voice faded as they turned the corner and disappeared.

I looked back to find Tenn and Griffen staring at me. Griffen's eyes dropped to the cuffs securing me to Tenn and his gaze hardened. "My office. I want to know what the fuck is going on. Now."

Chapter Eight

SCARLETT

Hope, Royal, and Daisy were waiting for us in Griffen's office along with three untouched plates piled high with eggs, bacon, biscuits, and pancakes. Small crocks of butter and jam sat on the coffee table in the middle of the office.

Royal and Daisy shared one couch. Tenn led me to the other, opposite them. Griffen pulled up an armchair beside Hope's and took his plate from the table.

Tenn leaned forward for his. I used the cuff to jerk him back.

"What?" he asked, eyeing his plate.

I lifted our joined wrists. "Seriously? You have my son. Do you really think I'm going to try to run?"

Cool blue eyes assessed me. He raised one eyebrow in a look so superior I wasn't sure if I wanted to smack him or kiss him. Ugh. No. I definitely wanted to smack him. In a slow, almost taunting drawl, he said, "I'm not sure *what* you're going to do, Scarlett Hall."

I deserved that. Dropping my arm to the couch, I let out a sigh. "Look, we got off on the wrong foot, and I understand why you don't trust me, but may I please have both my hands to eat? I haven't had anything decent to eat since yesterday at lunch and I'm starving."

Without another word, Tenn unlocked the cuff from his wrist. I would have preferred he removed the cuff on *my* wrist, but I'd take what I could get. I snagged my plate, trying to follow my own advice and remember my manners instead of diving headfirst into the fluffy eggs and pancakes.

Tenn filled in his family on the events of the morning so far. I had my mouth stuffed with a biscuit and jam when Griffen turned to me and asked, "Does all that line up for you?"

I swallowed, washing down the biscuit with a sip of coffee and wiping my mouth with a napkin before I tried to speak. I was feeling a little more human with some food in my stomach. "I didn't see Tenn talking to Vanessa, but I heard raised voices. Otherwise, yes."

"And there's no way Tenn could have gotten to Vanessa between the last time you saw her and when you found her body?"

"Hey!" Tenn's look of affront was so like August's earlier that I had to bite my lip to hide a smile. "I didn't think I specifically needed to say I didn't shoot her."

Griffen sent Tenn an impatient glare before turning his heavy gaze back to me. When we'd met at the door, Griffen had seemed friendly. Now, the weight of his eyes on me, I remembered that Tenn had said he used to be in security. I could believe it. Beneath the friendly welcome, he was as hard as the granite walls of Heartstone Manor.

"No," I answered, knowing a smart-ass response would not help me here. "Whoever killed her had to have worked fast. She went storming past me, and I watched her until she was out of sight. She caught my attention because she was dressed all wrong for dawn in a garden." I glanced at Daisy and Hope, guessing they would get it. "Little black dress, lots of makeup."

"Sounds like Vanessa," Hope murmured.

"And when did Tenn come along?" Griffen prompted.

"At most two minutes later, from the opposite direction. I guess if he sprinted he could have shot Vanessa, but he wasn't breathing hard, and I didn't hear anyone coming back past me. Based on what I saw, it's nearly impossible that Tenn shot her."

"What did you tell West?" Griffen asked carefully.

"Exactly what I just told you." I almost slouched in relief when Griffen's hard eyes swung back to Tenn.

"She was killed just like Dad," Griffen said, mostly to himself.

"And if Scarlett hadn't been on the path, Tenn would be the prime suspect, just like Ford was," Royal finished. His eyes, a deep blue that matched Tenn's, landed back on me. He studied me but addressed Tenn. "Why the handcuffs?"

Tenn joined him in examining me. When he spoke, Tenn's voice was as cold and hard as Griffen's eyes had been. "Scarlett was skulking around the Inn gardens after breaking into the empty cottage and stashing August inside."

Griffen, Royal, and Daisy all stared at me. I felt like a bug under a microscope. Of the three, Griffen looked the least surprised. He let out a sigh and shook his head. "You couldn't have been a normal guest, could you?"

"I wish I were." It was the truth. If I could go back, I would have checked in as a real guest, but... No. I couldn't use my credit cards. Not until I knew exactly what kind of trouble Thatcher had been dragged into. Places like the Inn at Sawyers Bend didn't take cash.

Griffen leaned back in his big leather armchair and propped his ankle on his knee, a steaming cup of coffee in his hand. Everything about him had shifted back to friendly welcome, including the easy smile on his face. I wasn't fooled.

"How did you get into the cottage?" he asked as if idly curious.

I took a sip of my own coffee and stayed silent. Griffen tried again.

"What were you doing at the Inn this morning, Scarlett?"

Everyone waited for my answer. I weighed my options. The truth was out of the question. Mostly because I wasn't sure exactly what the truth was. I wouldn't know that until I got my hands on Thatcher, and the only clue I had to his eventual location was Sawyers Bend and the Sawyer family. My conscience twinged—hard. The Sawyers seemed like good people. Normally, I'm not a liar. And I didn't have to lie now.

Stuck between the truth and a lie, I chose door number three.

Complete and utter silence.

The Sawyers waited. I took another sip of coffee, trying to hide my racing heart. Griffen ended the stalemate with a decisive nod. Transferring his attention from me to Tenn, he asked, "Does West have proof of the breaking and entering?"

Tenn shook his head. "Trespassing so far, but when I see him later, I'll let him know I found August in the closet of the cottage. That should be enough to add to the charges."

They discussed my crimes as if I wasn't sitting right there, my gut turning to ice as the full ramifications of what I'd done sank in. I was sitting in a mansion surrounded by the trappings of extreme wealth. There was no way I could fight these people.

Griffen's eyes on mine were cold green flame, the pretense of friendly welcome gone as quickly as it had reappeared. "Do you understand your situation, Scarlett?"

I took another sip of coffee, the hot liquid bitter in my mouth. Or maybe that was the taste of the angry words I held back. Trapped. I was trapped by Thatcher's idiocy, my own shortsightedness, and the dead body I'd fallen on top of.

I thought I understood my situation. I answered with a question of my own. "Who was Vanessa?"

Tenn answered as Griffen continued to stare me down. "Vanessa was our brother Ford's wife. They're divorced, and she hasn't been smart with her alimony. Now that Ford's in prison for killing our father, Vanessa has been hounding us for money. There were public arguments. She was a real pain in the ass."

"Lots of motive there," I commented, my mind racing. "Did your brother kill your father?"

"No," both Griffen and Tenn said.

Griffen set down his coffee mug and leaned forward, bracing his elbows on his knees. "I have one brother rotting in prison for a crime he didn't commit. I couldn't stop that." He glanced at Tenn. "Those are West's handcuffs?"

Tenn gave me a sly smile before looking back at his brother. "Yep."

Griffen nodded again and turned his attention back to me. "Looks like you'll be a guest of Heartstone Manor for the foreseeable future."

"You can't—"

Griffen cut me off. "I already am. I'm done with people who think they can fuck with my family. I lost one brother. I'll fill the woods with bodies before I lose another. No one is going to hurt you or August. I can promise you that. But as long as you're all that stands between Tenn and joining Ford in prison, you're not going anywhere."

Tenn shifted beside me, a stunned look in his eyes as he watched his older brother. He shifted his gaze to me and it was gone, replaced with a teasing expression I didn't know how to process. Another blink and he'd fastened the other end of the cuffs back on his wrist.

I ignored him and met Griffen's eyes, steeling myself to negotiate. "And if I cooperate, you won't press charges for the trespassing and the rest?" A nod of agreement from Griffen. I might have been a peasant petitioning the king. "Fine. But you don't keep my son from me."

"He'll have fun with Nicky, and Savannah and her mom are good with kids," Hope put in.

"That's great as long as I can see him whenever I want." I lifted my cuffed wrist. "And I am really done with these. Where am I going to go? Tenn said you have top-notch security."

"Don't forget that as much as I need you, whoever killed Vanessa will want you gone as soon as they find out I'm not under arrest." Tenn's eyes on me weren't cold or teasing. He almost looked like he cared.

"I gave the police chief my statement," I protested. "Why wouldn't that be enough?"

I could see the danger Tenn was in. Beneath the crap sandwich of Thatcher's mess, I was deeply glad I'd been there to save Tenn from a murder charge. Another few minutes either way and he'd be in serious trouble. I didn't even know him, and what I did know I wasn't sure I liked.

Liar, a voice whispered in my head. It didn't matter if I

liked Tenn or not. No one should go to prison for someone else's crime.

Tenn's problem, I understood. In all the worry over Thatcher, I hadn't really absorbed my own. As bad as those charges would be for my career, that wasn't as dangerous as being in the crosshairs of a murderer.

Tenn's next words drove the point home. "West has your statement, but what's that going to be worth if you disappear? The DA isn't the biggest fan of the Sawyers right now. I can guarantee that West is going to turn up at least one guest who witnessed my argument with Vanessa. Even if they couldn't hear me, things got a little physical—"

"What happened?" Royal cut in.

Tenn shook his head and let out an exasperated sigh. "Typical Vanessa. When I wouldn't hand over the pile of cash she wanted, she tried to screw it out of me. Right in the middle of the garden path. I had to shove her away. It probably looked worse than it was from a distance."

"Unless the police find evidence of another killer," I finished, "everything will point to you."

"Exactly. And you fell on the scene. Literally. Who knows what evidence you destroyed?"

"Maybe if you hadn't been manhandling me, I wouldn't have destroyed the scene," I shot back.

"Maybe if you hadn't been trespassing, I wouldn't have had to manhandle you."

We glared at each other, faces so close I could feel his warm breath on my skin. I leaned in, once more not sure if I wanted to slap him or kiss him.

Nope, still firmly on the side of a good, hard slap.

Daisy let out a low whistle, shattering the mood. Biting my lip so I wouldn't be tempted to say anything, I scooched as far away from Tenn as I could get.

"Maybe Hawk should take charge of the prisoner," Daisy said, laughter in her voice. "Otherwise, they're going to kill each other. Or, you know—"

"No," Tenn interrupted before Daisy could finish. "Scarlett's fine with me. West wants me to stay here for a few days. He thinks it's better if we're not visible. Might as well keep an eye on Scarlett while I don't have anything better to do." He shot me a grin. I shook my head as I fought the desire to grin back. What was it about this guy?

"Handcuffs?" I pressed.

Tenn leaned in, his mouth only inches from my ear. "We'll talk."

Pretending that was good enough, I lifted my coffee cup and sipped. The memory of that neat red hole in Vanessa's forehead kept flashing into my mind. Whatever else was going on, I couldn't let that happen to me. August and I were safer here, handcuffs or not.

Chapter Nine

SCARLETT

Royal and Daisy headed out, saying they'd taken the early morning off but Daisy had to help her grandmother at their bakery and Royal needed to get to the Inn. Apparently, the Inn's CFO, someone called Forrest, could have held down the fort, but he'd left Wednesday for a quick trip out of town.

Fortunately for Royal, Forrest was scheduled to be back by tomorrow. And it didn't look like Tenn was going into the office for a while.

I followed Tenn out of Griffen and Hope's office, surprised by the crew of maids who bustled in and cleared all evidence of breakfast. "Can we go check on August?"

"You know he's okay, right?" Tenn asked, leading me by the handcuff back toward the stairs we'd taken earlier.

"I'd rather see for myself." I tugged again at the cuffs. "Can't we take these off?"

Tenn shot me an amused smile. "Not yet. Soon."

What was he waiting for? I turned into the room where Savannah had taken August earlier to find a huge kitchen complete with long tables, more than one stove, and a staff of three busy making something that seemed to require a ton of vegetables.

Tenn gave them all a wave and pulled me through the kitchen to a narrow hall off the back. Here, I heard the familiar strains of August's voice. The tight ball in my chest eased. He sounded normal—cheerful and a little too loud.

We opened the door into a small set of rooms, the first with a low table occupied by August and a smaller boy with dark hair and Savannah's gray eyes. They each had a coloring book and crayons, their voices raised in conversation. I recognized the names they were throwing back and forth as belonging to August's favorite trading card game.

An older woman who had to be Savannah's mother sat in a nearby armchair, a magazine in her lap, her eyes on the boys.

"Mom!" August shouted when he saw me. "Nicky has Pokémon too!! Did you bring my cards? He said we could play, and he wants me to teach him some stuff, but I need my cards."

Crossing the room, dragging Tenn behind me by the cuffs, I gave my little guy a one-armed hug. "I left your binder at home, love-bug. I was worried we'd lose it. I'm sorry."

August's lip pooched out, but he said, "S'okay, Mom. We left fast."

Yes, we had. If August were a little older, I'd give him a lecture about privacy and family business. Since he was eight, I'd pretend he hadn't said anything. Looking at Savannah's mother, I held out my free hand.

"Hi, I'm Scarlett, August's mom. Thanks so much for including him. I can take him off your hands if—"

"Mom!"

"No, Gramma!!"

Two little boys turned beseeching faces to me. Savannah's mother took my outstretched hand in a firm shake. "You can call me Miss Martha. Everyone does. And, if you don't mind, I'd love to keep August with us. They've been getting along just fine. Nicky is dying to show him his toys, and later, we're going to take the soccer ball outside. August said he'd show Nicky his moves and help him practice his kick."

I couldn't bring myself to dim the hopeful light in August's eyes. As much as I wanted my baby boy right by my side, we'd come here in part because it was safe. The last thing August wanted was to hang with me when there was a new friend to play with.

"If you're sure. I don't want to impose."

A warm smile spread across Miss Martha's weathered face, a glint lighting her eyes as they noted the handcuffs tying me to Tenn. "I'm sure you know, sometimes two are easier than one."

I couldn't help my laugh. "I absolutely do know. I don't have my phone, but it looks like I'll be with Tenn today. If you need a break, just let him know, and I'll come rescue you."

The glint in Miss Martha's eye turned into a full-blown laugh. "Looks like you're the one who needs rescue."

"How do you know it's not me who needs rescue?" Tenn asked, grinning at Miss Martha.

She harrumphed and shook her head. "I know you, Tennessee Sawyer. Just because you let Royal pretend he's more charming doesn't mean you're not just as much trouble." A pointed look at me. "Give this one an inch, and he'll take a mile."

"Not fair," Tenn protested. "You don't know her. She's way more trouble than I am."

"I know she raised a smart and sweet boy who got Nicky to use a fork for every bite of pancakes and also remembered to say please and thank you."

"That's a relief," I said with a genuine smile, "but did he keep the syrup out of his hair?"

Another harrumph, this one followed by a smile matching mine. "We got cleaned up well enough."

"I see that," I said. "And thanks for the warning on this one." I tilted my head toward Tenn. "I'll get the better of him eventually."

"I have no doubt," Miss Martha agreed.

Tenn let out an exaggerated sigh, closing his hand over mine, interlacing our fingers. The affectionate contact was so unexpected, my mouth snapped shut. I followed him to the door, my lips silently curving as he loudly complained, "That's what I get for arguing with a woman who changed my diapers."

"And don't you forget it," Miss Martha called after us.

"Did she really change your diapers?" I asked, finding my voice again.

"A lot of them. We had a stepmom, but she had her hands full, and I have a twin sister. Avery. You'll meet her at dinner tonight. Miss Martha pinch-hit whenever Darcy needed her, which was a lot."

"Where was your mom?" None of my business, but I was curious.

"She took off when Avery and I were a year and a half old." His lips quirked in a bitter smile. "She liked the big house and the money but popping out kid after kid for Prentice wasn't her life goal. He gave her a big settlement, and a month after the divorce was final, he married our nanny."

"Oh." I wasn't sure what to say about that. For all the

discussion about his murder, no one had sounded particularly sad about their father's death.

"It wasn't as bad as it sounds. At least, not for us kids. I'll never know what Darcy saw in Prentice, but she was the best. Darcy was pure love."

I knew without asking that Darcy was dead. Tenn fell silent, his words weighted with old grief. I had more questions, but I kept my mouth shut. I knew what it was to lose someone I loved. I wasn't going to poke at him over a loss that still hurt.

"So," I said instead, "what now?"

Tenn stopped at the base of the stairs. "What do you want to do?"

I only had one answer. "Tour of the house? Please?"

Tenn appeared to think over my request. "We'll start with the library."

That sounded good to me. It would take days to explore all of Heartstone Manor. Not an issue since it seemed I wasn't going anywhere.

Thatcher had told me very little of what he needed. My guess was that he didn't know much himself.

I was working off of two pieces of information. One, that Thatcher was eventually going to end up in Sawyers Bend. And two, that he was after a work of art, one I'd seen myself, and if he didn't find it, heads were going to roll. Including, possibly, his own.

Roughly six inches tall, the bust of Roman Emperor Vitellius was fashioned of rock crystal on a marble and bronze base. Dating from the nineteenth century, the piece lacked historical or artistic significance and wasn't particularly valuable.

On top of that—no offense to Emperor Vitellius—but the bust was ugly. The base was okay, white marble accented with bronze, but the bust itself was... Let's just say that Emperor Vitellius wasn't going to win any beauty contests. When I'd originally seen it at the auction house, I'd estimated it would go for around $7,500.

I couldn't fathom why such an insignificant work would be the subject of so much drama. I'd guessed it had been stolen from whoever won it at the auction I'd appraised the piece for, but why? There had been far more valuable and desirable works in the same auction, all just as accessible once whoever stole it had broken in. What would have drawn the thief to this particular work? It made no sense. Yet here I was, looking for a needle in a haystack.

The library at Heartstone Manor was massive and, unlike the empty rooms we'd passed earlier, every shelf was full. Most were packed with leather-bound books, some of which I'd bet were quite valuable themselves. Here and there, small objets d'art were interspersed among the books, breaking up the monotony and creating an appealing sense of flow.

The artist in me appreciated the balance of color and space someone had created here. The art historian wanted to examine everything, from the carvings on the woodwork to the antique books and furniture, the oil paintings, and other objets d'art. The rest of me just wanted to find the damn bust, then Thatcher, and go home.

On one hand, I knew exactly what I was looking for. On the other, considering the scale of Heartstone Manor, the bust was a speck. How many places could someone hide something six inches tall in a house that had to be forty thousand square feet? An infinite number of places. If the piece wasn't on display, I could spend a year looking and never find it. Still, I had to start somewhere.

Dragging Tenn to the closest shelf, I scanned the books,

stepping back to look up—and up. How was I going to get to the upper shelves? I put that problem aside and lost myself in the search. Despite the high stakes, I found myself drawn more by history and beauty than an interest in the bust of Vitellius. The Sawyers had collected a fascinating selection of books, the subjects covering everything from history to art and architecture to science and philosophy. So far, no fiction.

Unable to help myself, I reached for a gilt and leather book, the title indicating it was a French Almanac, I guessed from the eighteen hundreds. Just in time, I snatched my hand back.

"You can look at it." Tenn's amused voice had my spine going stiff. Somehow, I'd forgotten he was there.

A flush of embarrassment heating my cheeks, I made no effort to touch the book again. "Not without gloves," I explained. "I don't know how delicate it is. Something this valuable shouldn't just be sitting on a shelf, but I've learned not to trust collectors to take care of their things."

Tenn's laugh was harsh. "My father wasn't into art or history unless it could give him more money or power. He could have bought something priceless and then shoved it here and forgotten about it."

I shook my head and stepped back, eyes drifting over the columns of shelves. "I don't know, whoever arranged this room had an eye for design. For art. It's hard to imagine that same person being careless with antiques. But I'd still rather have gloves on before I touch any of the books."

Now that the spell had been broken, I was aware of Tenn once more. He followed me as I drifted down the side of the vast room, my eyes greedily absorbing one treasure after another. Tenn said nothing, his eyes on me rather than the books and art. When I came to a sudden halt, he bumped into me, the hard heat of him a jolt, cutting through my art-induced haze.

Clearing my throat, I mumbled, "Sorry," my hand reaching to touch once more. The oil on my skin wouldn't damage this piece, but it was so rare, so delicate, the stroke of my fingertip was feather-light.

"Please, tell me you don't let Nicky run around in here." The thought of the child bumping into the ancient Roman flask was terrifying.

Tenn started to shrug, then stopped. "I doubt it. Why? Is it valuable?"

"May I?" I asked instead of answering, my fingers itching to touch.

Chapter Ten

TENN

I was transfixed by the reverent expression on Scarlett's face. I walked through this room all the time and couldn't remember the last time I'd really paid attention to the place. I liked to read, though I found myself digging into a good book on audio most often these days, but the Heartstone Library had never felt like my place. As children, we'd been forbidden to enter, and by the time I was old enough, I'd lost interest.

Watching Scarlett, the mix of awe and curiosity suffusing her entire body, I realized I might have missed something. She studied the short, squat piece of glass as if it were a hundred-carat diamond, her fingers hovering in the air, clearly longing to touch.

"Go ahead." I didn't bother to tell her to be careful. I already knew there was no one in this house who'd take more care than she would.

Shooting me an impatient look, Scarlett wiggled her cuffed wrist. "Undo me, just for a minute. If you jerk your arm, I might drop it."

I pulled the key from my pocket and released her. I had

no doubt I could chase her down if it came to that, but my gut said Scarlett wasn't going anywhere. Even if we didn't have her son, this room would hold her here for now.

Her touch delicate, she removed the bottle from the stand, turning it carefully, eyes narrowed, cataloging every detail.

"What is it?" I asked, needing to know what about the thing had her so transfixed.

Her voice was hushed when she finally spoke. "It's an aryballos. First-century Roman. A perfect and very rare example of the splashed glass technique."

"How rare?"

Absently, tracing a finger over the texture of the gray splotches obscuring the blue glass beneath, she said, "The last one that went to auction was six or seven years ago and it sold for around forty-thousand pounds."

I let out a low whistle. In a million years I wouldn't have guessed the small blue and gray bottle was worth so much. "Did you say first century? As in A.D.? And what's an aryballos?"

So very carefully, Scarlett placed the little bottle back on its stand. "Yes, first century A.D. Roman. An aryballos is a flask. This was probably used to hold perfume or oil." Her voice was distant as if she answered by rote, her mind caught by the piece itself.

"Why is it worth so much? The age?"

Scarlett shook her head, reaching out again to trace her finger over one of the gray splotches. "No, not the age. Or not just the age. See this? The technique is called 'splashed glass' and it was only used for a few decades in the first century, and then rarely on aryballos. It was done by attaching these gray chips to the already-blown glass and then reheating and reinflating the aryballos to create an effect that mimicked a mosaic."

She drew her hand away, tucking it behind her back as if restraining herself from touching again. Sounding as if she was a million miles away, she murmured, "I've never seen one in real life. What I do is lampwork, so not the same—I don't blow glass—but melting and shaping the chips of glass is one of the earliest uses of similar techniques. It's fascinating."

Something here was fascinating, but it wasn't the little Roman flask. Scarlett had been a lot of things to me in the short time I'd known her. A trespasser. A woman. A mother. Someone I'd like to get naked, though I'd barely admitted that to myself, much less to her. Since the moment she'd careened into me that morning, she'd been all of those things. She was a challenge, and ultimately, a lifeline.

Now, watching her absorb every detail of the ancient glass bottle, I wasn't quite sure what she was. So much knowledge and skill was tucked away in that head of hers.

Fascinating was exactly the right word. Not for the aryballos. For Scarlett. This woman was dangerously fascinating.

Reluctant to break the spell, I kept my voice low. "Are you an artist?"

Scarlett blinked once, twice. Her chin came up, a shield snapping down over her eyes. With a half-shrug of one shoulder, she went back to scanning the shelves of books. "Not really. I have a side gig making lampwork jewelry and some small sculptures and figurines."

"Then what's your main gig?" I had to know more.

"I'm an art history professor at Winsfield College." At my blank look, she added, "It's small. About an hour outside

Boston. I also do appraisals here and there. My specialty is glass art, though I have some expertise in related areas."

"You're an art history professor?" Of all the things I might have imagined for Scarlett, *college professor* was not on the list. "How old are you?" Dumb question, but I'd never had a professor who looked like Scarlett.

"Thirty-three, and I'm still an Assistant Professor. Not as impressive as it sounds." Her eyes swiveled from the books to focus on me. "How old are you?"

I let my mouth curve into a smug smile, sensing my answer would annoy her. I was beginning to love the way her cheeks flushed when she was annoyed. "Thirty."

"Humph. I should have guessed."

I let that one go, too curious about Scarlett to mind her implication that I was immature. I wasn't, but something about Scarlett brought out the desire to tease and poke, to have her attention centered on me.

Okay, maybe I was a little immature. Or maybe I was just interested. No. No maybe about it. Taking in her long waves of red hair, the swell of her breasts beneath the yellow sundress, the freckles scattered everywhere—no *maybe* about it. I was very interested.

Hey, she was stuck here anyway. Why not have some fun?

So many reasons that was a bad idea.

I was starting not to care.

"Did you always want to be a professor?" I wanted to know more, wanted to know who she was.

Her lips curved, and she glanced at me sideways, weighing her answer. Another half-shrug as if she'd decided the information wasn't classified. "No, not really. I wanted to study glassblowing in Italy, actually, but life got in the way. It wasn't practical to study abroad, so I switched my major to art history and, eventually, took up lampwork as a hobby."

"Do you still want to learn glassblowing?"

A half-grin in my direction. "I did get around to learning, but I don't have my own studio. Lampwork is small-scale. Think a blowtorch versus a furnace. My pieces sell pretty well. I've actually been thinking about leaving the college and working on that full time, but..." Her voice faded away.

"But?" I prompted.

She straightened, turning to face me. "But it's not just me, you know? I have a mortgage and a family to provide for. The college has health insurance, and the department is small, so I have a good shot at a full professorship and maybe tenure."

"You don't like it," I guessed, watching boredom film her eyes as she explained her future prospects.

She let out a short sigh. "Not really. I like teaching classes. Most of the students are great. But the politics make me crazy, and my department head is a total ass. A creepy ass. I go back and forth. Maybe when I get my nest egg built up a little more, I can think about leaving."

Wait, she'd said she had a family. "Are you married?"

Scarlett snorted with laughter. "No. I am most definitely not married. Been there, have the divorce to show for it. Not going there again."

"Never?" I pressed.

Another snort, this one less amused. "No way in hell. If I want another person to take care of, I'll get a dog."

"Not all of us need to be taken care of."

One russet eyebrow arched. "How do you know I was talking about marrying a man? Maybe I was with a woman."

Now she was fucking with me. Not that she couldn't be

a lesbian, but I'd felt that spark of interest, and it hadn't been in my personality. Looping my fingers around her wrist, I pulled her closer.

No resistance. Scarlett let me reel her in, her pink lips pressed together as she looked up at me, her wide green eyes flicking over my face. Dipping my head, I nuzzled the soft skin under her ear, breathing in the scent of peaches and warm female skin.

Lips pressing to the spot where her pulse beat a frantic rhythm, I tasted her rising tension. She wanted me. She might not choose to act on it, she might not like it, but she wanted me.

"This is a bad idea," she breathed. I waited for her to move away. When she didn't, I licked at the skin under my lips, sucking just enough for her to jolt against me but not hard enough to leave a bruise.

"It doesn't have to be a bad idea," I countered, wrapping my arms around her waist, pulling her flush against me.

My lips brushed hers, feather-light, giving her time to draw away. She didn't, tipping her face to mine, those pink lips parting a fraction. I took immediate advantage, kissing her again, tasting her, molding her soft curves to my body, claiming what I wanted.

Another few minutes and I would have missed the rap of knuckles on wood, the amused clearing of a throat. Fuck. Scarlett leapt back, might have tripped if I hadn't had a grip on her arm. I looked over to see Hawk watching us with an unexpected twinkle in his hard, dark eyes. Was that a smile on his face? Before I could be sure, the slight curve of his mouth was gone, and he was back to the very serious business of security.

"Am I interrupting? I'd come back later, but I have things to do. Griffen said you'd want a tracker."

Hawk approached, holding out a black band of fabric with a small box attached. It looked like a house arrest anklet. Turns out I wasn't far off. He reached us and I made introductions.

"Scarlett Hall, this is Hawk Bristol, the guy keeping us from being murdered in our sleep."

Scarlett stepped away from me smoothly as she held out her hand. "Hi, nice to meet the man keeping us alive."

Hawk gave a brief shake of her hand and held up the tracker. "This should be better than those cuffs. It's waterproof. Once it's on, I'll know if you try to take it off."

Scarlett's expression hardened. "Do I get a shock if I go over the boundary?" she asked, words dripping sarcasm. "I think I'd rather be cuffed than chipped like a dog."

"If I wanted you chipped, you'd never know." Hawk's flat tone made his words that much more terrifying. I had no doubt he could do as he said. I was glad he was on our side, but times like this, I was reminded that Hawk Bristol was a scary guy.

Dropping to his knees, he had the device clipped around Scarlett's ankle before either of us could stop him. Standing again, impervious to the shock and anger on Scarlett's face, he said, "Took me a while to engineer what I wanted, but this will sound the alarm if you attempt to leave the property. Once you're over the boundary, I'll be able to track you."

"What if I take it off?" Scarlett challenged, her jaw set. She looked ready to throw a punch.

Hawk cocked a dark eyebrow, amusement ghosting over his face before it sank into his normally dour expression. "You can try. You're more likely to hurt yourself than the tracker."

He raised two fingers to his forehead in a salute before turning on one foot and striding out of the library.

Scarlett glared down at her ankle in disgust. I unlocked the other side of the cuffs from my wrist and shoved them in my pocket, missing the excuse to keep her at my side.

"It's weird, but better than the cuffs, right?"

"I guess." She eyed her ankle, then my pocket, looking like she almost missed the cuffs, too.

Wishful thinking on my part.

Now that Scarlett had the freedom to move, I'd have to see what she did with it.

Chapter Eleven

SCARLETT

The rest of the day was a bust. I managed to talk Tenn into expanding our tour of the house, but so far, no ugly little bust of Emperor Vitellius. Worse, Tenn still had my phone. I didn't even know where he'd stashed it.

What if Thatcher called and I missed him? What if he needed me?

What if? What if? I was making myself crazy.

We checked in on August twice more to find him happy as a clam with Nicky, not yet bored with entertaining a younger child. When I'd asked if he was having fun, he'd whispered in my ear, "Mom, I get to be the big kid. I'm really good at it."

I believed him. He'd had a good example, after all. Reluctantly, both times I left him with Miss Martha and Nicky. Sometime in the late afternoon, Miss Martha went home and we discovered Savannah juggling the boys and dinner preparations.

In an unexpected move, Tenn came to the rescue. Taking in the lines of strain around Savannah's mouth and the increasing volume of the boys, he said, "I'll make a deal with you. We'll take the kids off your hands if you feed us all in my suite instead of the dining room."

"Done," Savannah immediately agreed. She sent me an apologetic look. "Griffen told me to set you up in Tenn's suite. There's plenty of room for you and August. I had your bags brought up from your car. I'd give you the keys, but I don't have them." We both shot Tenn an accusing look that he ignored. Savannah added, "He gives you any trouble, let me know."

Tenn shoved his shoulder into hers like she was an annoying little sister. "You know I'm not going to give her any trouble."

An enviably starchy harrumph and she shook her head. "Normally, I'd agree, but you've never handcuffed a woman to you before, so all bets are off."

He let it go, but as we let Nicky lead us to the elevator so he could show August how it worked, Tenn leaned in to ask, "Are you scared of me, Scarlett? Seriously?"

I didn't know how to answer. My gut gave a resounding, '*No.*'

I wasn't scared of him. Not the way he meant. Maybe I should have been, but Tenn had had plenty of opportunities to take advantage, and he hadn't pushed any further than I'd let him.

I wasn't afraid he was going to force me into anything.

I was afraid he wouldn't have to.

All I had to do was think of the heat of his lips on my neck earlier, the way I'd swayed into him, ready to do anything for one more touch... Yeah, I was in trouble. And Griffen had decreed I was staying in Tenn's room? Not good. Not only for my search—not good for me.

I took so long to answer, Tenn's face fell. Crossing his

arms over his chest, he followed us into the elevator. "Wait a second, Nicky. I have to lock the door before you can press the button."

Nicky was chattering a mile a minute about the folding metal door, the phone to call for help, how the elevator wasn't very fast, his voice filling the heavy silence between me and Tenn. My need to reassure Tenn had its own gravity, pushing, pulling, demanding I speak and erase the cloud shadowing his blue eyes.

I opened my mouth, then snapped it shut. Better if he thought I *was* afraid of him. Distance was good. Flirting, teasing, and neck-kissing were very bad ideas. Tenn was all kinds of trouble. Way too handsome. Good-looking men were off my list. Forever.

All of that was enough, but he'd basically kidnapped me. Did Stockholm Syndrome happen that fast? I'd be an idiot to trust him.

Don't forget that you broke into his cottage with the intent of talking your way into his house to search for stolen property.

My conscience was not helping. Okay, I wasn't an innocent here either.

Tenn didn't look at me, his shoulders stiff as I followed him and the kids down a wide hallway. I wasn't ready for how uncomfortable his reserve made me. In less than a day, I'd gotten used to his smile even when he was cuffing my wrist to his and dragging me to Heartstone Manor.

I tried to remind myself of the tracker on my ankle, the fact that I was a prisoner. Reserve was much better than charm. Of course, it was. Tenn was bossy, even manipulative, and was controlling me for his own ends.

It shouldn't matter that he'd given me exactly what I needed by bringing me to Heartstone. And it definitely shouldn't matter that I was the one holding back my real reasons for being there. As far as I could tell, Tenn had been completely upfront about his situation. He wasn't the liar here.

Ugh. Trying to convince myself Tenn was the bad guy wasn't working. I followed him into a spacious sitting room off another wide hallway. His suite? It was bigger than the first floor of our house. I spotted my duffel bag slumped in the corner. Yep, this was Tenn's suite.

Our suite, for the time being. I'd have to deal with the low hum that thought sent through my body. Later.

For now, I was going to concentrate on getting my phone back, searching the house, and keeping my distance from Tenn.

Tenn's suite looked like it was composed of a generous sitting room and bedroom. Nicky dragged August to the couch opposite the flat-screen TV and plopped down. "Can we watch cartoons? Please?"

We had rules about screens at home, but the day had been endless, and I didn't have it in me to fight over television. One day of extra screens wasn't going to rot August's brain. Shoulders sagging with fatigue, I leaned against the wall, unable to resist Nicky and August's pleading expressions. "It's fine with me if Mr. Tenn doesn't mind."

Without comment, Tenn picked up the remote and navigated to a channel showing all kids' shows. August bounced on the couch when one of his favorites was on. He and Nicky sank back in the cushions and zoned out, only rousing to murmur about the characters on the screen.

I took advantage of their distraction to get Tenn's attention. "I'd like my phone back."

"No." A wall had come down over Tenn's eyes. No humor lurked there. No flirtation.

I wanted to tease him out of his mood. I resisted. I was not here to flirt with Tenn Sawyer. And I needed my phone back. Thatcher was my priority, not worrying about a grown man who had his panties in a twist because I didn't trust him after he'd kidnapped me.

"At least let me see it."

His mouth pressed in a thin line, Tenn dug the phone out of his back pocket and woke up the screen, holding it up to show me. No missed calls. Damn. That was worse than Thatcher calling and not getting me. Why hadn't he called?

"Who are you working for, Scarlett?" Tenn's words were almost silent, far too low for the boys to hear over the TV.

Just as quietly, I murmured, "No one. I'm not working for anyone."

"I don't believe you," he said, that cloud of disappointment still heavy in his eyes, flattening his voice.

Meeting those eyes, ignoring the twinge in my gut at his expression, I shrugged a shoulder. "I'm not lying, Tenn. Not about this. I'm not working for anyone."

"Then why are you here?"

"Because you kidnapped me?"

"It's more than that." Tenn set his jaw in a mulish line.

"Yes," I admitted, tired of sparring with him. Just then, I was tired of everything, the stress of the past twenty-four hours suddenly too much. "It's more than that, but I can't tell you. You aren't the only one with problems."

Tenn's eyes stayed on my face until I had to fight the urge to squirm. Abruptly, he shoved my phone into his pocket and closed one hand around my wrist, tugging me closer. My sluggish brain had just enough time to remind me of all the reasons I should run from Tenn Sawyer before I found myself tucked into his side, his mouth at my ear, the warmth of his body easing the tension in mine.

Even as I relaxed into him, my better judgment told me to run in the other direction. Taking a deep breath, I ignored that little voice of warning in the back of my head. That always-suspicious part of me didn't trust Tenn as far as I could throw him. But then, it didn't trust anyone. The rest of me—most of me—was sure I was exactly where I wanted to be.

"Are you here to hurt my family, Scarlett?"

"No," I breathed without thinking. I didn't need to think. That was the truth. "This isn't about you. I don't really know what it's about."

Tenn drew his head back and I felt his eyes on me again, studying my face. "Are you running from someone? Are you and August in danger?"

I wasn't tall enough to reach his ear, so I settled for turning my face into his neck, telling myself it was for privacy from the kids and not because the woodsy scent of him was comforting. I murmured into his warm skin, "You mean other than Vanessa's murderer? I don't think so."

"You don't think so? But you don't know for sure?"

Tenn was getting a lot further like this than Griffen had over breakfast. I was too tired and felt too safe in his arms to guard my words.

Worry about Thatcher, frustration at not knowing what was going on, fear that I wouldn't find what Thatcher needed—it all pressed in on me, squeezing until I said, "I don't know anything. I'm not even sure exactly why I'm here, okay?"

My voice cracked on the last word, tears prickling my eyes. Pressing my face harder into Tenn's neck, I bit down on my lower lip, trying to force the tears away.

I could handle this. *I could.* Just like I'd handled everything else before this. I'd figure it out. Everything was going to be okay. I had to believe that was true. I didn't need Tennessee Sawyer or anyone else to solve my problems for me. I just needed dinner and a good night of sleep. That was all.

Tenn rubbed his hand over my back, soothing. If I hadn't been so exhausted, I would have pushed him away. His chin resting on the top of my head, he let out a long sigh. "My family has been through enough, Scarlett. If I find out you're lying about hurting them, I can promise you'll regret it."

"I'm not lying about that. I swear."

I wasn't. I didn't want to hurt anyone. I just wanted to find Thatcher.

And what happens if you have to choose between the Sawyers and Thatcher?

I had to hope that wasn't going to happen because if I had to choose, it wouldn't matter how much I liked Tenn Sawyer. Thatcher was going to come first every time.

Chapter Twelve

TENN

Scarlett melted into me, her lips grazing my neck, her breath soft and warm on my skin. I'd heard tears in her voice. Tears. She could be playing me, but I didn't think so.

I should shut her out. I should stash her and the kid in one of the empty guest rooms, put a guard on the door, and forget about both of them.

Not going to happen. However stupid it might be, I liked her exactly where she was—in my arms, the weight of her full breasts against my chest, the scent of peaches and woman teasing my senses. Whatever was going on that had driven the dauntless Scarlett to tears, it had to be big. She was in over her head, and she needed help.

Hadn't I decided no more damsels in distress? I hadn't had any trouble brushing off Vanessa. And now Vanessa was dead.

It hit me all of a sudden.

Vanessa was dead.

I hadn't liked her. She'd broken Griffen's heart and

made Ford miserable, but I'd known her half of my life, and now she was dead.

Scarlett's arm slid around my waist and tightened. Leaning back to tilt her face to mine, she murmured, "What? What's wrong?"

I shook my head, avoiding her eyes. "Nothing. Just thinking about Vanessa." I let out a long breath. "I didn't like her, but—"

"It's not your fault," Scarlett said before I could finish my thought.

How had she known? I found myself saying, "If I'd given her the money—"

"Then you'd be a few hundred grand poorer, and she'd still be dead."

"You don't know that," I couldn't help arguing.

Scarlett reached up to take my face in her hands, forcing my eyes to hers. "Look, I know we just met, and you kidnapped me, so I could be completely wrong about you, but I know for a fact that unless you're secretly The Flash, you didn't shoot Vanessa." I said nothing. The corner of her mouth quirking up, Scarlett tilted her head to the side. "Are you secretly The Flash?"

The kindness in her eyes undid me. I matched her half-smile. "Sadly, I am not secretly The Flash."

Her smile spread to fill her face. "Too bad, August would have gotten a kick out of meeting The Flash. But if you aren't him, then you couldn't have shot Vanessa. And if her killer was at the Inn waiting for her, then I doubt handing her a check would have saved her."

"If they were after the money—"

Scarlett cut me off again. "If they were after the money, they would have let her live to try again. More likely, based on what your police chief said, she was a tool to set you up for murder."

"Still makes me the reason she's dead." That thought landed like a lead balloon in my gut. Before it had a chance to settle, Scarlett lightly smacked my chest to get my attention.

"Don't be an idiot. She's dead because of the person who shot her. Who is not you. And you probably hate this idea, but you're not the bad guy, you're a victim. The only difference between you and Vanessa is that you aren't dead." Her eyes scanned my face slowly, pensive. "Really, when I think about it, you're lucky the killer wanted you in prison, because if he wanted you dead... It happened so fast, I bet Vanessa never saw it coming. You wouldn't have either." She stepped back and cast her gaze around the room. "Makes me glad you have all of this—the house, the security—between you and whoever killed her. If they can't have you in jail, they might just decide to try a bullet again."

I shook my head. "I don't think it's about me specifically. I think it's about my family."

"Then I hope the rest of your family is being careful."

So did I.

A knock fell on the door. I opened it to find Savannah pushing a rolling cart piled high with covered dishes. "Just like a hotel," Scarlett murmured beside me before moving to help Savannah. We got the kids set up at the coffee table while Savannah folded out hidden leaves at the sides of the food cart, turning it into an intimate table for two, complete with a linen tablecloth. Savannah set out a tall, white candle in a sterling silver holder and lit it with a flourish.

I grabbed the chair at my desk and another from the hall as Savannah produced an ice bucket already stocked with a bottle of white wine and lifted the covers off of our dinners. Steak, asparagus, and twice-baked potatoes. Scarlett let out a moan that instantly distracted me from my empty stomach.

Savannah gently rolled the table to the corner of the sitting room opposite where the boys sat at the coffee table, effectively giving us a romantic table for two complete with a view of the formal gardens behind Heartstone Manor. Or what used to be the formal gardens. The outline of the beds was still there, but they were barren, waiting for Hawk and his skeleton crew of grounds people to find the time to deal with them.

The grounds were Hawk's side gig, the lure Griffen had used to draw him from Sinclair Security in Atlanta to our small town in the mountains of North Carolina. The idea had been for Hawk to split his time between security and getting the gardens back in shape, but since he'd arrived, security had been a full-time job. The neglected flower beds had been cut back and cleaned up, but nothing grew there and probably wouldn't for another year.

Farther from the house, the swimming pool sparkled in the early evening light. The pool house behind it wasn't in great shape, but Griffen had fixed up the pool as soon as Hope mentioned she liked to swim. His devotion to his new bride paid off for the rest of us. It wasn't hot yet, never got truly hot at this elevation, but we'd be grateful for the pool in July and August.

Scarlett joined me at the window, following my gaze. Her eyes hit the sparkling water. "How did I miss that?"

"We haven't explored outside yet," I said. "Does August swim?"

"He loves it, but he doesn't have a suit."

"We can take care of that," I said absently, stepping back

and pulling out one of the chairs at our small table. "For now, dinner is served."

I barely noticed the meal, though I'm sure it was delicious. I was too focused on Scarlett. I asked her about teaching and spent the rest of the meal just enjoying her. Her enthusiasm for art history and for her students. The wrinkle in her nose when she talked about her sleazy department head and his plan to 'mentor' her. Clothing optional. I might have worried, but Scarlett's amusement, the tart way she'd brushed him off, told me she wasn't that concerned. I couldn't see anyone, even her boss, pushing this woman into doing something she didn't want to do.

Just as we were finishing our meal, August ran over, pushing into Scarlett's side until her arm came up around him in a hug. I watched them in fascination, unused to what a normal mother/son relationship looked like. Savannah was casually affectionate with Nicky, but they'd only been living with us for a few months, and I didn't run into Nicky that often. The separation between staff and family wasn't as strict as it had been in my father's day, but the lower level of the Manor, where Savannah and Nicky lived, wasn't a place I frequented.

August leaned into his mother with the confidence of a child who knows he's loved, knows he's always welcome, knows he'd never get the back of a hand for interrupting or being too loud.

"Mom," he said in what I think was supposed to be a whisper but wasn't in any way quiet. "Dessert?"

Scarlett craned her neck to check his plate. I lifted the silver lid to the remaining plate, revealing four perfect brownies.

August's eyes widened, his lips parting in awe. "Mom, please?"

Nuzzling his ear with her nose, she said, "One more chicken finger and two more carrots for each of you and you can have your dessert."

"Okay!" he shouted and bolted back to the coffee table to tell Nicky about the brownies.

Scarlett leaned toward me, lowering her voice to a much quieter whisper than August's. "Keep an eye on them, will you? Make sure those carrots don't end up shoved between the couch cushions."

"I'm on it," I promised, watching August stuff the required chicken finger into his mouth. When he got to the carrot, he rolled it around on the plate and glanced up casually. Spotting me watching, one shoulder shrugged, so much like his mother's shrug I grinned, and he picked up the carrot in resignation.

Soon enough, dinner was finished, the boys were munching on brownies, and Scarlett was chewing hers thoughtfully, eyes on the gardens outside the window. Despite her fixed stare, I had a feeling she was lost in her head and not the view of our derelict grounds. I was about to ask what she was thinking when my phone chimed with a text. Royal, wanting to touch base about the schedule at the Inn.

"I need to talk to Royal," I said, breaking into Scarlett's distraction. I wasn't sure she'd heard me when she dragged her gaze from the window to fix on my face. "I have to head to Royal's room to go over some things for work tomorrow since he's short-handed with Forrest still gone and me staying home."

"Oh, uh, okay." Scarlett looked over at August and Nicky, faces smeared with chocolate, eyes drooping. "I'd better get August a bath and then put him to bed." She glanced around the room, brows raised in question. I knew exactly what she was asking. We hadn't discussed sleeping arrangements. She wasn't going to like my answer.

"That couch doesn't fold out, but it should be wide enough for August. Savannah can get you a set of sheets and a blanket."

"And where am I sleeping?" A sardonic arch of one dark red eyebrow, challenge in her green eyes.

"You're sleeping with me." I'd thought that would be obvious. I wasn't expecting the flash of alarm in her eyes, the way she leaned back just slightly.

"You're not... I'm not..." Stalling, she regrouped. "You're not cuffing me again. And I'm not sleeping with you."

Partly to calm her down and partly to needle her, I said, "If you're talking about sex, I'm afraid I don't know you well enough for that. If you're still interested in a few days, we can consider it then." The alarm disappeared from Scarlett's face, replaced by a scowl. She balled up her napkin and lobbed it at my face.

"Smart-ass."

Glad she'd relaxed, I dropped the joke and leaned forward. "Scarlett, I won't cuff you again if I don't have to. And I'm not going to push you for anything you don't want to give, in bed or out of it. But you're staying with me until we have the shooter in custody. That's non-negotiable."

"Then give me my phone," she countered.

"Also non-negotiable." She wasn't getting that phone until I knew what she was up to.

Leaning back in her chair, she leveled a suspicious, assessing look at me for a long, silent moment. "If you try anything, I'll make you pay for it."

I grinned. "I know you would. And I promise I'll sleep on top of the covers. It's a big bed. Plenty of room."

Scarlett let out a harrumph that reminded me of

Savannah and Miss Martha. At least she wasn't arguing. Holding on to my advantage, I left before she could come up with more reasons she wasn't sharing a bed with me.

I could have put her in her own room with a guard on the door. We could spare the staff.

I'll admit it had burned earlier when she'd hadn't immediately told me she trusted me. I was over it. It hadn't taken much to understand Scarlett's reservations. I was a strange man who'd basically kidnapped her, West's approval aside. Now, I was demanding she share a bed with me. Sure, I'd said I wasn't going to touch her without permission. That was a line I'd never cross. I knew it wouldn't happen, but Scarlett didn't. Once she was asleep, she'd be defenseless. Of course, she was nervous.

My better nature urged me to let her off the hook. She wasn't going to get past one of Hawk's people if she tried to sneak off in the middle of the night. As I walked down the hall to Royal's room, I thought about it. Almost pulled out my phone to call Hawk to see if he could spare a guard for her.

My better nature was on Scarlett's side, but my gut won the battle. Scarlett was mine. I'd found her, and she'd rescued me when I could have been sitting in a jail cell.

Scarlett wasn't leaving my side. Not yet. Not until I was done with her.

Chapter Thirteen

SCARLETT

By the time he opened the door from the hall, I was tucked into the far side of Tenn's king-size bed, reading a paperback I'd shoved in my duffel and pretending I wasn't stressed out by the fact that I was half-naked in a strange man's bed.

Okay, I was wearing a loose tank top and sleep shorts, and Tenn wasn't exactly a stranger anymore.

Details.

I still wasn't sure I wanted to be there. And wasn't that the problem? *I wasn't sure.* I should have been running in the other direction. I should have demanded Griffen, the police chief, someone, anyone, give me my own room. This place was practically a freaking castle. It's not like they didn't have the space.

Yet here I was, tucked into Tenn's bed, waiting for him to come back. What the hell was I doing?

Savannah had shown up only a few minutes after Tenn left while I was still working on the boys' chocolate-covered faces with a wet washcloth. She delivered bedding for August and collected Nicky and the food cart. After thanking me for entertaining Nicky, she said her mom would be there tomorrow to watch the boys again.

Just before she headed out the door, she stopped, closing her hand around my arm with a gentle touch. I met her grey eyes, heavy with concern. "Are you okay with this?" she asked. "Hawk is a hard-ass, but he's protective. If I tell him you need space from Tenn, he'll step in."

I liked Savannah even more for bothering to ask. Tenn was her boss, in a way. At least, I assumed he was. I was a stranger, yet she was willing to go out on a limb for me. Glancing back into the room where I'd gotten far too comfortable way too fast, I asked what I really wanted to know. "Do you think I need space from Tenn? Am I safe with him?"

"Yes," Savannah answered, without a second of hesitation. "Tenn's a good guy. They all are, really." She stopped herself and drew in a short breath. "Except Bryce. You haven't met everyone yet since you ate dinner up here, but Bryce is their cousin and a total asshole."

"How will I know which one is Bryce?" So far, most of the Sawyers looked alike. Tall, dark-haired, and gorgeous.

"If you meet a guy who looks like the villain in an eighties movie, that's Bryce. Very blond, blue eyes, preppy, and a major jerk. Everyone else is good." She rolled her eyes. "Well, Finn can be an asshole, too, but he's mainly just full of himself. He'd never hurt a woman. And Tenn absolutely wouldn't."

"Thanks," I said, comforted by her reassurance.

"If you need anything, just dial 1 on any house phone and it'll ring through to me. There's tea and coffee and a mini-fridge with water and snacks in the cabinet by Tenn's desk in case he forgot to tell you." She tipped her head at the desk before corralling Nicky one more time and disappearing down the hall.

I grabbed a bottle of water from the cleverly hidden fridge and corralled my own little guy, herding him to the bathroom. After a day of travel and playing for hours with Nicky, August needed a bath. Not a problem here. Tenn's tub was practically a small swimming pool. I started the water and unpacked our toiletries, pouring a slug of bubble bath under the running water. August didn't need much supervision in the bath these days, so I was free to explore.

The bathroom was acres of white marble. Double counters with deep, square sinks. A side room just for the toilet, and another filled with linens and extra toiletries. A third door led to Tenn's expansive walk-in closet. He'd said the house had been neglected. Both the grounds and some of the rooms I'd seen downstairs supported that claim, but Tenn's bedroom and bathroom had to have been recently renovated. I watched enough home improvement shows to know that the fixtures in here were almost brand new. Another mystery. One I could ask about later. For now, I needed to get through tonight.

I'd worried for nothing. Tenn let himself back in quietly, careful not to wake August as he passed through the sitting room into the bedroom. Without a word to me, he disappeared into the bathroom and shut the door. I heard water run, a toilet flush, then nothing. He reappeared a few minutes later in a white t-shirt and boxers.

Opening a leather-strapped trunk at the foot of the bed, he pulled out a soft-looking knit blanket and got into bed on the other side, staying on top of the covers as promised. He fluffed his pillow, tossed the blanket out so it covered him from chest to toes, and rolled over on his side, facing me.

"I usually stay up later," he said, his jaw cracking with a

yawn, "but I got up early so I could cover for Royal and I'm dead on my feet after today. Wake me up if you need anything."

And that was it. All that worry and he was three feet away, on the other side of this huge bed, apparently fast asleep. Not only had he not made a move, he hadn't even looked at me. Not really. The female heart of me was miffed that Tenn hadn't spared a tiny glance at my legs, which looked pretty good in my sleep shorts.

Not that I care, I reminded myself. Men that good-looking are nothing but trouble.

Ugh, even I wasn't buying that line anymore. I snuck a peek at Tenn, his face relaxed in sleep, his bare forearm the only part of him I could see. Tanned skin, the hint of muscle. I dragged my eyes back to my book and started the page over. I hadn't read a word since Tenn had opened the door to the room.

After the tenth pass through the same page, I gave up. I thought about the small bottle of melatonin in my toiletries case, convinced there was no way I'd fall asleep with Tenn so close. But no. That stuff always knocked me out, and the last thing I needed was to be out of it in a strange place with August to look out for. Rolling over, my back to Tenn, I closed my eyes and tried to sleep. I must have been more tired than I realized. One second, I was wound so tight I thought I'd snap, and the next, I was out cold.

Normally, I wake here and there through the night. Just long enough to get up to pee or to listen to my quiet house and reassure myself that everything was as it should be. Not that night. Once my eyes were closed, I was dead to the world. My brain was silent, my sleep free of dreams.

My body had other ideas.

I'd fallen asleep on the edge of the bed, as far from Tenn

as I could get. When I eventually surfaced, faint morning light prodding my eyelids to open, I was on my side, every inch of me toasty warm, my torso draped over a hard, male body, my face buried against skin prickly with stubble.

Fuck.

How did Tenn always smell so good? And why was that the first question to pop into my mind? I should be asking myself how the hell I'd ended up splayed on top of him, one arm wrapped around his waist, one leg hitched over his hips, the pressure of a significant erection against my thigh.

Fuck.

Find another swear word, Scarlett, I ordered my sleepy brain. Fucking was the last thing I needed to think about while I was on top of Tennessee Sawyer.

At that thought, I became aware of the heat in my core. The soft weight of my breasts pillowed against his chest. The corded muscle of his arm around my back holding me close. Damn it. This was 100% on me. Tenn was laying almost exactly where he'd gone to sleep, and somehow, I'd maneuvered myself all the way across this massive bed until I was cuddled up to him. No, not cuddled up, I was practically on top of him.

All I'd have to do was shift the tiniest bit and that erection pressing into my thigh would be right between my legs... The heat bubbling under my skin jumped another few degrees. It would feel so good...

Wake up, Scarlett!! Get your head together.

No sex with Tennessee Sawyer.

Absolutely not.

For so many reasons. One, he's holding me captive. Two, I have to stay sharp for August, not get distracted by sex with a hot guy. Three, I already decided no more beautiful men. My hormones had led me astray before. Too much was at stake to make that kind of mistake now. And four—

I drew in a deep breath, smelling the woodsy scent of Tenn, and I forgot what the hell number four was supposed to be.

Why couldn't I have sex with him?

Realizing how close I'd slid to the edge, something else hit me. While I was lying there, trying to figure out how I'd ended up mostly on top of Tenn, he was already awake. Something about the way he held his body, the slight tension in the arm around me, gave him away. The bastard was awake!

The flash of outrage was gone as soon as it hit. *I'd* climbed on top of *him*. I wasn't exactly in the position to get pissed off that he was touching me. If I wanted him to stop, all I had to do was move.

Any second now. Really. Now that I was awake, I had no excuse for staying exactly where I was, my lips grazing his neck, my thigh pinning his hard cock.

Fuck.

Just one more second and I'd do it. I'd roll off him, get out of bed, and take a very cold shower. Soon.

Definitely soon.

A fingertip grazed the back of my neck, drawing a feather-light line from the base of my skull down between my shoulder blades to the edge of my tank top and back up, leaving flames everywhere he touched. Down, then up, not moving my clothing, not baring any more skin, just sliding back and forth.

Heat spread from that line around my rib cage to my breasts, down my spine to arrow between my legs. He was barely touching me, and all I could think about was how long it had been since any man had touched me like this.

Never. I'd never been touched like this, never felt a gentle stroke spark into white-hot desire. If those fingers felt so good between my shoulders, on my neck, what would they feel like between my legs? At that thought, I let out a low groan.

Fuck.

Now I couldn't pretend to be asleep. There was the slightest hitch in the path of those fingers before they kept going. Down the line of my neck, along my spine to stop between my shoulder blades and switch direction back up to my neck.

Why wasn't he pushing for more? I could feel his cock against my inner thigh, my leg still hitched up over his hips. Why hadn't I moved?

Why the hell would I when being draped over Tenn felt so good?

Because this is a terrible idea, you moron.

My brain and my body were not on the same page. I realized Tenn was just going to wait me out. He wasn't going to stop. He wasn't going to say anything. He was just going to stay like this, letting me dig my own grave.

Still not moving, my lips almost touching his neck, I said, "Well, this is awkward."

A low chuckle rumbled against my cheek. "Is it? I feel just fine."

The devil in me couldn't help it. I rocked my hips, sending my inner thigh sliding over his hard cock, only his thin cotton boxers between us.

Tenn sucked in a breath. His voice low, rough in my ear, he murmured, "Even better if you do that again."

Ready to argue, I lifted my head, propping myself up on one elbow, putting us almost eye to eye. *Way too close, Scarlett!! Back off. Get up!*

I wasn't listening to my brain. Not now. I parted my lips to say something. Anything.

Instead, I kissed him.

It was all me. Tenn didn't move. I brushed my parted lips over his, testing. Tasting. Firm, but that lower lip had a soft curve I couldn't resist. I nipped his plump lip, and he raised his chin the tiniest bit. Yep, this was all me. I could stop, I could get up, be smart—

Chapter Fourteen

SCARLETT

I kissed him again, tilting my head to the side, sliding my tongue over his lower lip to coax his mouth open. Following the instincts of my body over my brain, I surged up closer, sliding to straddle him as I took his face in my hands and kissed him like I'd die if I didn't.

I don't know what came over me. I knew better. I'd spent the last half-decade being smart and I blew it all at one taste of Tenn Sawyer. But damn, what a taste. His mouth matched mine, his lips soft and firm, his tongue right there with me, tasting, seducing, all of it so good my head spun.

It was spinning so hard, I almost didn't register his strong fingers closing over my ass in a tight grip. With a low growl of demand, Tenn flipped us, landing between my thighs, his cock pressed right against my heat, my legs wrapping around his waist as if we'd done this a million times. Tenn never stopped kissing me, his mouth hungry on mine, hips nudging that beautifully hard cock against my clit through his thin boxers and my sleep shorts.

He hit just the right spot and it was too much. Tearing

my mouth from his, my neck arched, the sweet, sharp tease of pleasure almost enough to send me over the edge. I couldn't remember the last time a man had made me come. Tenn was going to do it just from a kiss. Holy fuck.

I couldn't... I wasn't... My hands came up to capture his face, pulling him back for another kiss. More. I wanted more, wanted to come, wanted—

The sounds of a cartoon theme song hit me like a bucket of ice water. *August.* I was the worst mother on the planet. My eight-year-old son was in the other room, and I was messing around with a man I didn't really know with the goddamned door open. Tenn and I flew apart. My feet hit the floor, my cheeks flushed with shame instead of lust.

Tenn watched me, eyes heavy-lidded with desire, lips swollen from kissing me. Just the sight of him—the worn t-shirt stretched across his shoulders, the length of his leg, that muscled thigh. Those eyes. Those lips. Fuck. I wanted...

Leveling a pointed finger at him, I narrowed my eyes. "You're dangerous, Tennessee Sawyer. Keep your hands off me." I slammed the bathroom door on the sound of his laugh. We both knew who'd started that, and it wasn't Tenn.

I strode to the shower and turned it on the coldest setting, teeth gritted. A freezing shower would suck, but it was what I deserved. And maybe, just maybe, it would cool the lust that still had me aflame.

I'd been right. The cold shower had sucked. And wrong —because it didn't do much about the lust. What was it about Tenn? He wasn't the only hot guy in this house.

No, he wasn't, but he was the only one who could set me on fire with just a look.

I was spared the torture of being around him for most of

the day. By the time we all got dressed, the rest of the family was done with breakfast. We ate alone in the huge formal dining room, plates piled high with pancakes and eggs like the day before. Miss Martha and Nicky showed up to claim August, and then Tenn and I were alone.

Awkward.

Not because of Tenn. Because of me. Tenn acted like nothing had happened, as if I hadn't been seconds away from orgasm because of him. *Stop thinking about it*, I ordered, feeling my cheeks heat again. His eyes flicked to my face and back to his phone, the slightest curve at the side of his mouth giving away his amusement.

I did not throw a biscuit at him. I thought about it but managed to rein in my temper. It wasn't his fault I couldn't control myself.

Bullshit. It was totally his fault. I'd done just fine controlling myself for years. Years! Then Tenn barrels into my life and suddenly I couldn't keep my lips to myself? Totally his fault. I shoved another fork full of eggs into my mouth and scowled down at my plate.

"I have a proposal for you," he said easily. Of course, my mind immediately assumed he meant *that* kind of proposal. Not the ring kind, the naked kind. Mouth curving as he read my thoughts, he said, "Get your mind out of the gutter, Scarlett."

This time, I did throw the biscuit at his head. He caught it easily, setting it on the side of his plate. "Savannah doesn't allow food fights in the dining room. You throw it, you clean it up."

That statement intrigued me. "Do I want to know how you know that? Aren't all of you too old for food fights?"

He eyed the biscuit I'd lobbed at his head. "Apparently not. Anyway, do you want to hear my proposal?"

I gave him a single, regal nod, trying to claw back my composure. I was a college professor, for God's sake. I didn't throw food at the table. I also didn't kiss men I barely knew. Everything about the last twenty-four hours was wildly out of character. Thatcher had a lot to answer for.

Get real, my inner voice chided. *You can blame the trip here on Thatcher. Even the breaking and entering. That kiss, though... That's entirely on you.*

"I ran this by Griffen last night," Tenn began, "and you can say no, but you don't have much to do until West finds the shooter, so..."

"What is it?"

Tenn pushed aside his plate and picked up his coffee. "My family used to have a significant collection of artwork. You saw some of it yesterday in the library and scattered through the house."

I nodded, not sure where he was going with this. Prepared to wait, I slathered butter and honey over a biscuit.

"Some of it is missing."

My eyes bugged out of my head. Mouth full of biscuit, I chewed furiously.

"We don't know exactly what's missing and what's just been moved. Griffen and Hope found receipts that indicate some pieces were sold, but others are straight up gone. You've seen the gallery and music room."

I sipped coffee to wash down the biscuit, thinking about the tour the day before. The gallery and music room were in the front of the house on the first floor and normally would have been filled with art meant to show off to guests. Instead, both rooms had been stripped bare.

"I thought you were redecorating."

"Not exactly. My father started renovating a few years

ago, hinting that he was bringing home a new Mrs. Sawyer. Then, one day, the renovations stopped. He got as far as re-doing the master suite and the bathrooms in the family wing before he quit. He never said what happened, and the one time Ford asked, Prentice lost it so he let it go. At the time, we thought he was moving the art while there were contrac-tors in the house, but none of it ever reappeared."

"What do you want me to do?" I thought I knew, and if I was right, Tenn was about to make my life a whole lot easier.

"We need someone to catalog what's in the house so we can compare it to the list our attorney has and see what's missing and what's just been moved."

"Why me? Aren't you worried I'll steal something?"

Tenn raised one eyebrow. "You met Hawk, right? You really think you're going to get out of this house with a duffel bag filled with priceless artwork?"

"Good point." Not that it mattered. I wasn't a thief, though the Sawyers didn't know that. And, well, I *was* kind of a thief. If I found that little bust of Emperor Vitellius... But no. Not even then. I might use the statue to get to Thatcher, but after that, I'd return it to the rightful owner. As soon as I figured out who that was.

Getting back to business, I pointed out, "You know I'm not a professional appraiser? I do appraisals in my area of expertise, but I'm not qualified to do general appraisals."

"We know. We don't need anything appraised. We're more interested in a catalog. Take pictures, note where the piece was and what you think it is. At the least, it would be a start. We don't usually have an art history professor just hanging around the Manor with nothing better to do."

I shrugged one shoulder and sipped my coffee. "I guess I can help." I didn't want Tenn to know he was handing me exactly what I wanted. As an added bonus, something to do would keep me away from Tenn. A little distance might get my head on straight before I jumped him again.

Searching the Manor was the reason I was in Sawyers Bend. Somehow, through good luck disguised as bad, I'd ended up exactly where I needed to be. This whole thing was too good to be true. I'd arrived in town despairing over how to get close to the Sawyer family. Now, I had carte blanche to search their historic Manor.

Never mind that I was due for some good luck. I knew it didn't work that way. Not for me. Which meant I was missing something, some angle they had for offering me the run of the house and access to their art collection. Why? What could they have to gain?

Stalling, I said, "If you want pictures, I'll need my phone."

Tenn shot me that grin I wanted to hate. I didn't. It lit his deep, blue eyes from within, sending my belly tumbling over itself every single time he aimed it my way. "Griffen has an extra tablet with an app you can use to take pictures and notes. He set it up thinking he and Hope could work on the project, but they never seem to have enough time."

"And Griffen is good with me taking over? He didn't seem like he was my biggest fan yesterday."

Tenn smiled again, his expression softer this time. "Griffen is protective of his family these days. He doesn't trust you, but he trusts me. I promised him you wouldn't damage anything."

"I won't," I agreed immediately.

I took possession of the tablet after breakfast and headed upstairs with a bounce in my step, thinking it was only a matter of time before I found what I was searching for.

Hours later, I was bored, frustrated, and wondering what the hell had been wrong with Prentice Sawyer. He owned Heartstone Manor, a treasure in itself, as well as what had been rumored to be a renowned art collection. Instead of taking care of everything he'd been given, he'd let the house decay and lost half of the art.

Griffen had the house back on the right track, but the art collection was a fraction of what it should be. Granted, Heartstone was massive and it was always possible things had been packed away in a room in the attic or lower level, just waiting for me to stumble across them. Maybe.

I thought of the bust of Emperor Vitellius. It had been listed for auction by Prentice Sawyer, probably only weeks before he'd died. How many other pieces had been disposed of the same way? Where was the money? And why was Thatcher so sure the statue would end up back here?

Too many questions and I couldn't ask for the answers without giving away my part in the whole mess. Not a good idea considering I didn't exactly know what my part was. I was getting ready to bang my head against one of these beautifully papered walls. What if the bust of Vitellius wasn't here? What if Thatcher was wrong? Why hadn't he called? Was he hurt? Was he—

Stop, Scarlett. You can't do anything about Thatcher right now. Just keep your head down and look for the bust.

I was lecturing myself an awful lot lately, and it wasn't doing any good.

I needed a break, needed to clear my head instead of banging it against a wall. One more room, and I'd go outside, get some fresh air. Maybe see if the boys wanted to kick around the soccer ball for a few minutes. A sound in the hall caught my ear.

"I heard Tenn brought us a tasty little snack."

I looked up to see a man, early twenties at my guess, with platinum hair and bright blue eyes, his white polo shirt tucked into a pair of pants I was sure he'd call salmon. From where I was standing, they just looked pink. I narrowed my eyes, wondering if that belt had whales on it. I wouldn't be surprised. Yep, just as Savannah had described.

"You must be Bryce," I said, flicking a glance over my shoulder. "Savannah told me to look out for you."

I instinctively knew she was right to warn me. This man was dangerous. Not in the way Hawk or even Tenn could be dangerous. They were tough, but this man was mean.

And I was no one's snack.

Chapter Fifteen

TENN

At the sight of Bryce entering the room, I came to a halt outside the bedroom door. Savannah had told me she thought Scarlett was going through the rooms up here. I hadn't seen Bryce on my way up. How long had he been lurking around before sneaking into the room to take Scarlett by surprise?

I was ready to crush his face with my fist, and he'd only gotten out a few words. Typical. He'd always been a spoiled little snot. My Aunt Ophelia couldn't bear to tell her little prince, 'No.' Ever. My siblings and I were rarely all in agreement, but we were united in our hatred of Bryce.

I wanted to storm in and tell Bryce to get the hell away from Scarlett.

I stayed where I was, out of sight in the hallway.

The whole point of giving Scarlett the catalog project was to see what she did with it. We weren't going to learn anything about her intentions if she stayed glued to my side. This way, she could move through the house thinking she was unobserved, and we could see what she was up to.

So far, the plan had been a waste of time. She'd accessed

her email on the tablet Griffen gave her, but there was nothing of interest there. She'd checked her online shop, setting it on vacation mode, and replied to a few prospective clients. Not quite the criminal activity we were looking for.

After that, she'd pulled up her voicemail through her mobile provider's account, but there was nothing there, either. That done, she got to work cataloging the art she found as she worked her way through the house, room by room.

She'd made a few choice comments about the state of the house and the artwork she came across. Impolite but nothing my siblings and I hadn't said ourselves. Watching her on the tablet's hacked camera, my gut kept telling me that she was up to exactly what it looked like: searching for and evaluating the art in the house.

Except it was more than that. She entered every room with a spring in her step as if buoyed by fresh expectation. Every room left her deflated. Almost like she wasn't just searching for art to catalog. Like she was searching for a specific work of art. And not finding it. I'd have to have Griffen and Hawk check the footage and see if they had the same impression. If she was searching for something, what was it? And why?

She could have been simply looking for something worth stealing, but I doubted it. I didn't think this was about money. Not for Scarlett. She knew she wasn't sneaking some bauble past Hawk. Hours of watching her catalog art, and I was no closer to figuring out what she was up to. As much as I didn't want to leave her alone with Bryce, there was a chance he'd shake something loose.

The mostly empty guest room they were in was bright with the midday sun, leaving the hallway shadowed. I leaned against the wall opposite the open door, giving me a good view of Scarlett and Bryce. If they stared right at me they might see me, but between my dark shirt and jeans and the sunny room, I doubted it.

I was curious about Scarlett's reaction to Bryce. He was younger than me, and women seemed to think he was attractive. Okay, let's be real. I'm a guy, but I have eyes. Bryce looked like a young Greek god. What if Scarlett fell for his act? No way. She was too smart for that.

I scowled as I heard him call her a *tasty little snack*. Was he a moron? What made him think a woman like Scarlett was going to tolerate that kind of bullshit? I grinned to myself when she dismissed him, ignoring his taunt.

The grin faded when Bryce closed the distance between them. He lifted a finger, trailing it down her arm. Scarlett sidestepped, moving out of reach. My gut tightened at the unease she tried to hide. I was a dick for leaving her alone with a man who was making her uncomfortable. I did it anyway, waiting to see what happened next.

"Not interested," Scarlett said in an icy voice. "I'm here as a guest of Tenn's, helping catalog the family's art collection. Unless you can help with that, you're in my way."

"And where did Cousin Tenn find you? You don't look like any appraiser I've ever met."

"I doubt you've met enough art appraisers to make that kind of judgment. We come in all shapes and sizes."

"You know what I mean, honey." Bryce flipped his shaggy bangs off his forehead. They fell into a perfect swoop over his Sawyer blue eyes. Annoying fucker.

Scarlett's only response was to roll her own eyes. She barely spared him a glance before turning to study a painting on the wall. It badly needed cleaning but looked like an oil of some pastoral scene. The house was full of that kind of thing. It could be from a yard sale or a priceless work that belonged in a museum. Based on Scarlett's lack of excitement, I was betting it fell more on the yard sale end of the spectrum.

The room fell silent, the only sound the tap-tap-tap of Scarlett typing on the tablet screen as she made notes on the oil painting. She lifted the tablet and photographed the painting. Crossing the room until she was almost out of view, she stopped in front of a porcelain vase on a side table someone had shoved in the corner. Picking up the vase, she checked the bottom, snapped a photo, then moved back to take a second picture from the front.

Bryce propped his hands on his hips, glaring at the back of her head. "So, where are you from? Sounds like some-where up north."

"Boston," was all she said in response.

"And you came all the way down here to sift through our closets in search of art? What are you looking for?"

At that, Scarlett turned, one eyebrow raised. "Looking for? Griffen asked me to catalog what's here, not to search for anything specific." She tucked the tablet under her arm and studied Bryce like a bug under a microscope. "Is there something I should be looking for? Something you'd like me to find?"

Bryce paused, taken aback at her direct question. I couldn't tell what he was up to. This exercise had begun as a way to learn more about Scarlett. Now, I was more inter-ested in Bryce. I was almost positive Scarlett was searching for something. It hadn't occurred to me that Bryce might be doing the same thing.

Scarlett stared back at him with a bland expression, but the tight grip she had on the tablet told me she wasn't as relaxed as she seemed. Was it the conversation or Bryce himself that was making her nervous?

The stiffness in Bryce's face dissolved back into his smarmy smile, and he sidled closer to Scarlett. "Nah, I've searched the house already," he easily admitted. And wouldn't Griffen be thrilled to hear that?

Tapping on the tablet screen, Scarlett looked completely disinterested. "Find anything good?" she asked absently.

Bryce was right beside her when she looked up, a smug expression on his annoying face. I'd always hated Bryce, but it was a little alarming how much I wanted to shove him away from Scarlett. He wasn't touching her, was only looking at her, and still, I wanted him a mile away. Preferably with a bloody nose.

Bryce reached out to tuck a loose curl behind her ear. "Not until I saw you."

At the touch to her hair, she stiffened, her gaze flicking to the doorway, past Bryce's body blocking her exit.

That was it. I was done.

I could play the game with Scarlett. I knew she was hiding things from me, and I'd find out what they were eventually, but none of that was worth putting her through dealing with Bryce.

I could feel her unease all the way out in the hall. I could be an asshole, but I wasn't this much of one. I was the reason she was here. I was the one forcing her to stay at Heartstone Manor. I owed her my protection. More than that, I wanted to give it to her. No one was going to touch her without permission. Not me, and definitely not Bryce.

Fuck, it had almost killed me that morning, not moving while her luscious body pressed to mine. She had no clue how close I'd been to coming all over her soft skin, how hard it had been to let her take the lead. She'd made her way across the bed in the middle of the night, snuggling into me as if we'd slept together every night for years.

Scarlett had been the best armful I'd ever woken up to. Soft, warm, smelling of peaches and woman, her silky hair tickling my nose and falling over my arm, the heavy weight of her breasts pressed to my chest, the velvet skin of her inner thigh pinning my cock to my belly. And that kiss. Fuck. It had been a good thing August turned on the TV before things went any further.

This woman was mine.

We were going to have each other.

Thoroughly.

Eventually.

First, I had to rescue her from Bryce.

Chapter Sixteen

TENN

"Can I help you?" I asked from the doorway, striding in to take Scarlett's arm and turning her away from Bryce.

Bryce sneered at me. "Did I get too close to your toy? I was only making conversation."

Shifting position to put myself between Scarlett and Bryce, I took her free hand in mine, lacing my fingers through hers. "You okay?"

She nodded. "It was hard to focus with him interrupting, but I'm good." She wasn't. Her shoulders were stiff and her eyes were on the door.

"You ready for lunch?" Another nod. "Would you go downstairs and let Savannah know? Maybe we'll take the boys out in the yard for a picnic, give Miss Martha a break."

She was out the door a second later without sparing Bryce a glance. If I'd had any doubt how uncomfortable she'd been, that settled it. I'd had enough of Bryce and his childish bullshit. He opened his mouth, no doubt to say something asinine and offensive. I didn't give him the chance. Closing one hand over his throat, I shoved him back until he hit the wall, his mouth gaping like a fish.

Switching my grip, I fisted his polo shirt, holding him in place. He twisted and kicked out with one foot, but I wasn't budging. I'd grown up in a houseful of kids, including older brothers. I knew how to fight. Bryce had been raised an only child of a doting mother. All it took was a single punch to his gut and he was doubled over with tears in his eyes.

"I'd call you a pussy," I said, looking down at his hunched shoulders, "but I'd hate to insult one of my favorite body parts. If I ever catch you touching a woman in this house without permission, I'll beat the shit out of you. We have to let you stay here for the next five years. We don't have to put up with this bullshit."

"She's just working here," Bryce whined, straightening and wiping his eyes with the back of his hand. "It's not like she's someone important."

Sudden rage hit me, hot and fierce. I shouldn't have punched him.

Shouldn't have but did. It was worth it to see the shock in his eyes at the slam of my knuckles into my jaw.

Of course, he fell on his ass, whining about telling his mother. I leaned down, getting right in his face. "Remember when we were all kids and you'd pick on the little ones? Remember what would happen? Didn't Griffen break your nose after you teased Sterling when her mom died? Your mommy's plastic surgeon fixed it so I can't even tell. What do you think would happen if it got broken again?" Bryce just moaned. I was done with him. "I hear one word about you giving anyone in this house trouble, and I'll fuck you up so badly Aunt Ophelia won't even recognize you. I don't care if it's staff, family, a visitor—keep your fucking hands to yourself. Do you understand me?"

Bryce turned his face to mine, hatred shining in his eyes. I didn't give a fuck. We'd always hated each other. That would never change.

I nudged his side with my foot when he didn't respond. Not a kick, but a reminder that I could break a few ribs if he pissed me off.

"I understand," he ground out between his teeth.

"Good."

Done with Bryce, I strode from the room, going in search of Griffen. I found him in his office, conveniently with Hawk and without Hope. "Got a sec?"

Griffen set down his phone, and they both looked at me. "What happened?"

Guess my mood showed on my face. I flexed my fist, my knuckles tight from that punch. "I went up to get Scarlett for lunch and found Bryce with her. He was hitting on her and trying to get info about any art that she found. Wasn't taking no for an answer."

"And?" Griffen prompted, his sharp gaze taking in my clenched fist.

"And I punched him. Twice. After Scarlett left. Told him we'd beat the shit out of him if he tried anything like that again."

"What did he say?" Griffen asked carefully, leaning back in his chair.

"That he was going to tell his mommy, and that it didn't matter because Scarlett wasn't important anyway."

That last part still burned a hole in my gut. Not important? Who the fuck was Bryce to decide another human being wasn't important?

It was more than that, more than him being an asshole to a woman in my home. I'd known Scarlett less than 48 hours. She shouldn't be important to me either. But she was, and I burned to hit him again.

Griffen sat forward, bracing his elbows on his desk. "That little shit. Is she okay?"

"I sent her down to see Savannah about lunch. She looked a little shaken but otherwise fine."

Griffen and Hawk shared a look. Hawk spoke first. "I'll get her a panic button in case he bothers her again. I don't trust your cousin to be smart. He might go after her just to get back at you. And I'll talk to Savannah, see if she or any of the other staff are having problems with him."

"We have to let him live here," Griffen said, "but there's nothing that says we can't press assault charges if he goes too far."

"That's our only recourse?" At that moment I had a new reason to hate my father. He hadn't liked Bryce any more than the rest of us. Bryce was here as a threat.

"To get rid of him, yes," Griffen answered. "But we won't let it get that far. He isn't going to harass anyone under my roof."

Picking up his phone, Griffen opened a familiar video. Scarlett, seen through the tablet's camera, cataloging one of the upstairs bedrooms.

"She's looking for something," Hawk said, his eyes on the screen.

"That's what I see," Griffen agreed.

"I was wondering if you'd catch that," I said.

"She's too smart to try to steal something," Hawk commented, still watching the screen.

"Agreed." The methodical way she cataloged every piece she found, the clarity and detail in her notes all made it clear she might be a liar, but she was far from stupid.

"Tenn." I expected a warning. Griffen's concern took me by surprise. "We don't know why she's here. Be careful."

"I won't endanger the family," I promised.

Griffen held my gaze, his own open and full of emotion. My throat went tight. Griffen had left home when I was fifteen, thrown out by our father for getting in the way of a business deal. For so many reasons, most of them bullshit, we'd all let him go. I hadn't laid eyes on him, hadn't spoken to him for years. Not until he turned up at our father's funeral three months ago.

I'd been ready to hate him when our family lawyer announced that Griffen was inheriting everything.

Our father had been a complete asshole. That was a fact pretty much everyone agreed on. He'd loved to fuck with us, pitting us against each other until we were little more than strangers. He'd left each of us a trust fund—with a catch. If we wanted our money, we had to move into Heartstone Manor and live there for the next five years.

If we refused, we gave up any claim to our trusts. And if we contested the will, everything went to Bryce. Just in case we forgot that part, Prentice had offered room and board to Bryce and Aunt Ophelia for the five-year waiting period. I'm sure he was laughing his ass off in hell. He'd hated Bryce as much as the rest of us.

We'd all moved back into the Manor after the funeral as ordered. For the next five years, Griffen had control of everything, including our trusts. If he wanted to spend it all to the last dime, none of us could stop him. In fact, in his will, Prentice had encouraged Griffen to do just that.

Griffen had done the opposite. He'd hired Savannah to manage the house and gotten to work re-learning the ins and outs of Sawyer Enterprises. He'd married Hope, which had seemed weird considering she'd been the catalyst who'd gotten him thrown out in the first place.

Now that I was used to seeing them together, it didn't seem weird at all. They were in love and expecting a baby, their affection and domesticity settling down the household until it seemed like we might actually make it the five years without killing each other.

And more than that, Griffen had listened to us. Royal and I had been trying to get the extra cottages at the Inn approved for years. Griffen had reviewed our business plan and told us to go for it. He'd dragged Sterling out of the bottom of a bottle and given her a job. Piece by piece, he was putting our family back together. The last thing I wanted to do was fuck all of that up.

Griffen shook his head at my promise. "I'm not worried about the family, Tenn. I'm worried about you. Scarlett's an intelligent and beautiful woman. I can't fault you for being attracted. I'm not telling you to keep your distance, I'm just saying that she's up to something, and until we know what, be careful. I don't want to see you get hurt."

"I'll be careful," I said, pushing the words through my tight throat. Straightening, I added, "Bryce told Scarlett he'd searched the house for valuables. He could be full of shit, but you might want to have someone go through his room."

"I'm on it," Hawk said, a grim look in his eyes.

I left them plotting and went in search of Scarlett. I found her in Savannah's apartment behind the kitchens, talking to Miss Martha. When I walked through the door, she turned to me with a bland smile as if the scene with Bryce had never happened.

I wasn't fooled. I'd had a good reason for leaving her at Bryce's mercy. Still didn't sit right. I couldn't get the memory of her stiff shoulders out of my head. I kept seeing her eyes flick past him to gauge how far the door was. I'd fucked that up. Scarlett thought I'd rescued her. The truth was, I'd let her swing far longer than I should have.

"You up for a picnic?" I asked, ignoring the weight of guilt heavy in my gut. I'd make it up to her. Absolutely.

"Savannah is having lunch packed up now," Miss Martha said, her considering eyes moving between me and Scarlett. "The boys are helping her find a blanket for the grass."

Scarlett kept that bland smile on her face until we were out in the summer sunshine, the heat already building. Sawyers Bend never got Atlanta-hot, but that didn't mean a June day couldn't make us break a sweat.

One eye on the two boys chasing each other around the picnic blanket, Scarlett started to unload the basket, setting out sandwiches and cookies wrapped in wax paper. Every time she looked away from the boys or the food, her eyes landed on the sparkle of the pool across the gardens.

"I had one of the Inn staff bring over bathing suits for you and August. We can go for a swim later if you want."

Her wide grin was as bright as the sun, eclipsing the flat smile she'd worn since the encounter with Bryce. This was the real Scarlett. I loved getting under her skin, peeling back the layers of self-protection until I found the real her.

"I haven't been swimming since I took August—" She swallowed. "Since we went to Disney two years ago."

"No pool at home?"

Scarlett let out a belly laugh. "The pool on campus isn't kid-friendly. It worked for swim lessons, but we don't have a lot of opportunities to get in the water and have fun."

I was glad I got the bathing suits, then. I wanted to give Scarlett something, to make up for the scene with Bryce.

Taking advantage of the boys' momentary distraction, I said, "Watch out for Bryce—"

"Savannah already warned me," Scarlett cut in. "She said to look out for the asshole straight out of an eighties movie."

Her description surprised a laugh out of me. "As usual, Savannah is right. My aunt Ophelia, Bryce's mother, is sweet but kind of vague. Unless you're an unmarried man around her age with a fat bank account. Then, she's a shark. But she's always spoiled Bryce. I used to be jealous when I was a kid. My mom took off when I was a baby—she said the money wasn't worth putting up with Prentice and a pile of kids—and then, Darcy, our stepmom, died when I was twelve. Prentice had pretty much given up on being a father by then, and whenever Bryce and Ophelia would visit, Bryce would get away with murder, Ophelia jumping in to defend him no matter what."

Scarlett wrinkled her nose and shook her head, handing me a soda she'd pulled from the basket. It was still cold, dripping from the ice Savannah had packed it in. "I bet Bryce just loved that," she said. "Did he set you up to get in trouble and then call for mommy?"

I took a swig of my drink. Scarlett got it in one. "Pretty much exactly that."

"And you have to live with him? You can't kick him out?"

"I can't do anything. Not my house. Griffen is in charge, but inheriting the house came with a few conditions. He can't open it to the public, and he has to allow Bryce and Ophelia to live here for the next five years."

Not realizing I'd been eavesdropping, Scarlett said, "He admitted he'd searched the house for valuables. He was kind of clumsy about it, but I won't be surprised if he makes another approach, tries to get me to point him in the direction of easy-to-fence pieces."

"I didn't like his attitude when I came in," I said. "Hawk is going to give you a panic button. If Bryce makes you nervous, use it. But if you feel okay and think he's going to say something like that, can you turn on the recording app on the tablet and get it on video?"

The side of her mouth curled up before she took a sip of her own drink. "Good thinking. I can definitely do that. And thanks for the panic button. I don't think I'll need it, but you never know with guys like him."

She called the boys over to eat, pushing the conversation in other directions. I ate, watching the boys scarf down their sandwiches, distracted by thoughts of Scarlett in the bathing suit the Inn had delivered. It was pretty conservative, but that wouldn't matter. I'd had her body splayed out on top of mine, my hands all over her. I knew exactly how luscious she was.

With August sleeping on the couch and Scarlett's own caution between us, I wasn't going to see her naked any time soon. If the bathing suit was the best I could do, I'd take it and enjoy every second.

Chapter Seventeen

SCARLETT

I was in love with Heartstone's pool. I hadn't been swimming in ages, and never in a huge, private pool smack in the middle of paradise. It didn't matter that the gardens of Heartstone Manor were a mess. The view from the pool was spectacular. With the house on one side and the mountains everywhere else, the pool felt like a secret oasis.

An oasis occupied by two screaming kids. But I had an imagination. I could erase the kids and leave just Tenn and me, alone, mostly naked in the water...

No, not going to imagine that. It was bad enough watching him in his board shorts, tossing the boys high in the air so they could splash into the water over and over, without complaint. These days, patience is at the top of my list of sexy traits in a man. Combined with that body, that grin, his kindness... Ugh. I had to stop. I was not here for Tenn.

And I was not mostly naked. I just felt like it. In reality, the swimsuit Tenn's assistant brought over from the Inn gift shop wasn't the least bit sexy. No cleavage, and it actually managed to cover my ass, something I couldn't say for most of the suits I'd tried on lately. Still, when those deep blue eyes cut my way, I had the distinct impression he could see straight through the opaque navy fabric to absorb every detail of my bare breasts. And no, that thought did not get me hot. At all. Really.

Not even when we corralled the boys in the shallow end of the pool and he swam over to join me on the steps. Bracing his arms on the step behind him, he tipped his face back to catch the sun. Did he know what he looked like?

Chiseled muscle covered his chest, drops of water in his chest hair catching the light like diamonds against his tanned skin. And his face, those cut cheekbones, thick hair dark with water slicked back off his forehead. I could almost see him in the glossy pages of a magazine, advertising something expensive. His watch. The pool. It didn't really matter. You could balance a can of sardines on those abs and people would line up to buy them.

And yet, that image of Tenn didn't fit because Tenn was real. He was vital and present and way too potent to be contained by a photograph in a magazine. At that thought, at the heat deep inside as the word *potent* filled my head, I slid down the steps and sank under the water. I hadn't planned to get my hair wet, but I needed to cool off. His hard cock against my leg that morning had been *potent* as hell. I'd wanted it. Far too much. Kicking my feet, I crossed the shallow end of the pool, drifting closer to the boys. I needed to get out of touching range.

Kissing Tenn that morning had been a huge mistake. Massive.

Tenn Sawyer had been temping enough before I knew what he tasted like. How his hands felt on my hips, sliding over my skin. Now that I'd had a taste, all I wanted was more. I wanted to blame my libido, long-repressed and eager for control. I could, but it would be a lie and I really tried not to lie to myself. This wasn't just about his gorgeous face and that perfect body. This was about Tenn.

His external beauty was a distraction from the man inside. I was starting to believe he might be that most mythical of beasts—a good man. He was funny and kind and patient. Strong but not overbearing. I thought of the handcuffs and a shiver of lust hit me. I should be disgusted that he'd restrained me. With any other man, I would be. With Tenn, I couldn't help thinking about what I'd do if I had those cuffs. I could pin him down, straddle his hips, and...

I dunked under the water again. I knew how good it felt to straddle Tenn, to have his hands on me. Would I really want to restrain him? Another shiver. Yes, I think I would...

One last time, I dove beneath the cool water, holding my breath until my lungs burned, staying under until I had my head straight.

Tenn was not the point. I wasn't here for Tenn. I was here for Thatcher. Only Thatcher. It was a little scary how often I had to remind myself why I was here. Thatcher. Not Tenn.

I popped back up above the water, my eyes on the boys splashing in the shallowest corner of the pool. If I kept my eyes on the boys, I could try to pretend Tenn wasn't there.

I did my best, but as I tried to ignore him, I had the fleeting thought that maybe when this was over, when Thatcher was safe, maybe I could have Tenn. Just long enough to satisfy us both. Just a taste.

That was a problem for later. I had bigger problems than wanting to jump Tennessee Sawyer.

Still nothing from Thatcher as far as I knew. Tenn wouldn't give me my phone but he'd shown me the locked screen a few times. No missed calls. No texts. It was possible Thatcher had called and Hawk had intercepted him and erased the call history. The screen appeared to be locked, but Hawk looked like a man who had skills. The truth was I had no idea what he could do.

Regardless of the reason, not hearing from Thatcher was making me a little crazy. When I finally caught up to him, I was going to kill him. Even when I was distracted by Tenn, the cataloging project, or August, Thatcher was a buzz in the back of my head.

Was he safe? Where the hell was he and how long was it going to take him to get to Sawyers Bend? I knew I wouldn't be able to relax until I saw with my own eyes that he was okay.

Every second I had free, I spent searching for the ugly little bust of Vitellius. I knew my devotion to the art-cataloging project had to look weird. It wasn't like I was getting paid. As far as they knew, I was doing this for free to fill the time until the police chief caught Vanessa's killer.

That story might have worked if Tenn hadn't busted me for breaking into his cottage. We all knew there was more going on, and I had a feeling the cataloging project was their way of giving me enough rope to hang myself. I wasn't so naive that I thought I was truly wandering the house alone, handling all of their art.

They had to be watching me in some way, either through cameras in the house or through the camera in the tablet. I wasn't bothered. When I did appraisals, my workspace was under surveillance. Ditto for the collections I worked with at the college. They'd have to be stupid or nuts to let a virtual stranger have free rein of their house. From what I'd seen, the Sawyers were neither.

It didn't matter if they were watching. I was there to

search, and they'd given me the perfect excuse. I was running with it. Too bad my hours of work hadn't resulted in much. After the pool, I spent the rest of Sunday working my way through the guest rooms on the second level of the Manor. I'd found mostly empty rooms, some mediocre art, and no Emperor Vitellius.

Dinner that night was a blur. Savannah seated us at the end of the table out of the fray, and I spent most of my time making sure August was behaving himself. Nicky ate in the kitchen, as usual, but August had been deemed a guest and his presence at the table was required.

We got some curious glances, but no one paid us much attention. I had Tenn's little sister Sterling to thank for that. Apparently, she'd brought her new boyfriend to family dinner. Forrest wasn't just Sterling's new boyfriend, he was also the new CFO of the Inn at Sawyers Bend. He seemed to be well-liked, but I could tell Tenn, Royal, and Griffen weren't happy about this development.

Once dinner was over, I got August set up with a movie and slipped out of Tenn's suite with the tablet. Quietly, I left the family wing and crossed to the guest wing and the room I'd been working in earlier.

I'd just started in there earlier when Tenn came to find me for dinner. It had been long enough to discover a second closet door at the back of the main closet. I was hoping I'd find Vitellius stashed inside. I just needed a few minutes alone to find out.

Chapter Eighteen

TENN

Scarlett took off the second dinner was over. She'd been skittish with me ever since the pool. I hadn't laid a finger on her. Hadn't even flirted. I wasn't much of a flirt, to be honest. That was Royal's thing. Usually, I didn't have the patience for it.

Scarlett was different. I loved poking at Scarlett, teasing her, and seeing the heat rise in her green eyes, watching as her breath sped up and she tried to pretend she didn't want me.

My cock wanted me to push, to keep teasing, keep poking at her until she lost control and I could take what I wanted. My cock was going to have to wait. I was going to fuck her eventually, and it wasn't going to be because I pushed her into it. I barely knew Scarlett, but my gut read on her felt solid, like I'd known her all my life. Pushing would only trigger her battle instincts. If I pursued her the way I wanted to, she'd dig in her heels.

Instead, I'd seduce. I'd tempt. I'd be patient. I didn't have much of a choice with August in my suite and the house full of family. Everything—our circumstances, my instincts—told me slow was the way. That kiss told me Scarlett wanted me enough to make the choice herself.

She was going to come to me.

That didn't mean I wouldn't give her a preview of everything I had to offer.

After checking to make sure August was good with his movie, I followed what I guessed was Scarlett's path to the guest wing. Most of the second floor was deserted, the rest of the family still lingering over drinks or watching TV. As I'd expected, I found her in the room she'd been cataloging just before dinner.

A few minutes later and I might have thought I'd missed her. She hadn't bothered to turn on the lights in the room, the sun still high enough in the sky to fill the space with light. I stepped inside, swinging the door mostly shut behind me. Glancing around, I saw oil paintings on three of the walls, a mahogany bed frame with a bare mattress, and a bedside table. No lamp. No wonder she hadn't turned on any lights in here. There weren't any.

Just as I was thinking I had the wrong room, a thump from the closet gave her away. I followed in time to see her disappear into a dark hole at the back. A light flicked on, a bright glare in the dark, illuminating nothing. What was she looking for? A passing survey showed nothing much in the main part of the closet. A few empty hangers. An abandoned shoebox, the lid askew, gold tissue crumpled inside.

I stepped through the dark hole. Not a hole, a door, though a short, narrow one. Ducking my head, I blinked, giving my eyes time to adjust. Here in the dark, the light from Scarlett's tablet wasn't as blinding. Shelves lined the long room, a few cardboard boxes here and there. Scarlett stood over one, trying to angle the tablet so she could see the screen and aim the light.

"Want some help?" I offered, pitching my voice low in the silence of the closet.

Scarlett screeched, spinning to face me, the tablet held up like a weapon, the flashlight stabbing my eyes. She deflated as quickly as she'd snapped to attention, her shoulders sagging as she let out a laughing breath.

"Oh, my god, Tenn, I think I had a heart attack. Were you trying to sneak up on me?"

"A little," I admitted, "but not to scare you. Sorry." I looked around the hidden closet, scanning the low ceiling. "No light in here?"

"Not that I could see."

"I've got you." I pulled my phone from my pocket and tapped until the flashlight came on. "Good?"

Scarlett smiled. "Perfect."

Under the light from my phone, she unfolded the flaps of the first box, revealing neatly folded rectangles of fabric. Taking one out, she spread the snowy white linen over the open box. A napkin. Scarlett's face fell as she carefully dug through the rest of the box, finding only more white linen. She folded the top closed with a slump to her shoulders and moved on.

The next box was no more exciting. An ancient plug-in alarm clock. Equally ancient toothbrushes, still in their wrappers. A half-empty jar of face cream. The detritus left from guests long gone? We'd never know, and it didn't really matter.

Scarlett pushed the box away from the other and moved to the next. More junk. Another held what I guessed was the tablecloth to go with the napkins. Scarlett put that one beside the first.

With each new box, her eyebrows raised in anticipation. With each discovery of more useless junk, her shoulders rounded further. Was she disappointed by the lack of art? Or was it more? My gut insisted it was the second option. I knew it wasn't just me. Griffen and Hawk had seen the same thing. Scarlett was looking for something. And whatever it was, she hadn't found it here.

The last box examined and set aside, Scarlett handed me the tablet and picked up the boxes of table linens. "Savannah might want these," she said in way of an explanation, leading us out of the closets and back into the bedroom.

Rays of the setting sun flooded the room with golden light, drawing Scarlett to the windows facing the woods. She barely noticed me taking the boxes from her arms and setting them by the door.

"The trees go on forever, don't they?" she murmured. "It's so beautiful here."

I stood beside her, taking in the view. I'd lived here for most of my life and, unlike the house, I never got used to the views. Scarlett was right. Perched as we were on the mountain at the edge of the national forest, the trees really did look like they went on forever. Rolling waves of green rose to sharp peaks, stretching as far as we could see.

"I could look at this every day and never get tired of it," she said.

"I know," I agreed, leaning into her until her shoulder pressed my arm. "When I was a kid, I'd disappear out there for hours. I wish I had more time to hike these days. Quinn has it better than the rest of us." At Scarlett's questioning look, I explained. "She runs a gear shop and guide business. She gets paid to spend her days out there."

"Pretty sweet gig," Scarlett agreed. "Do you wish you'd done something like that? Instead of choosing the Inn?"

"No," I answered immediately. I didn't have to think

about it. "I always wanted to run the Inn. When I was younger, I tried to hide it from Prentice. From my father—"

Scarlett drew her gaze from the trees and raised her eyebrows at me. "You called him Prentice?"

I laughed. "In my head. Not to his face. To his face, it was mostly, 'Sir.'"

"Why did you hide it? Didn't he want to raise all of you to run the family businesses?"

"He did, but only on his terms. I think he thought that if he gave us what we wanted, we'd be soft. Or not work hard enough. Or maybe he was just an asshole. When I look back, it's hard to find any logic in his decisions. But whatever his reasoning, it was a guarantee that if he found out you cared about something, he'd find a way to take it from you."

"I'll go with asshole, then," Scarlett said, her green eyes glowing in the golden sunset, warm and filled with sympathy.

"Yeah. That's where I ended up too. When my brother Ford was in college, Prentice gave him this project tracking investments. It sounded boring to me, but Ford had been dying to learn more about that side of the business. He took one look at those spreadsheets and fell in love. A week later, Griffen came home from college for the summer, and Prentice took the project from Ford and gave it to Griffen. No explanation. He just took it. He did that all the time. And he always gave the thing you loved to someone else. He loved setting us against each other."

Scarlett turned to face me, her eyebrows drawn together. "That's twisted. I can't imagine pitting my— How do you all not hate each other?"

"We're not as close as we could be," I said, thinking of Griffen and Ford, once closer than brothers, and now... I didn't know what they were now but calling them family seemed like a stretch.

"It didn't always work," I went on, wanting Scarlett to understand, though I didn't know why. "Sterling found a kitten once. She loved that scraggly thing. Prentice said she was too young for a pet and gave it to Parker. Parker loved the kitten, too, but she snuck it into Sterling's room every chance she got. The kitten loved Sterling more. Then, one day, the kitten was gone. We never found out what he did with it."

"He got rid of their kitten?" Scarlett's voice pitched up in outrage. "He really was an asshole."

"Yeah." I laughed under my breath. "You should see the list of suspects West had for Prentice's murder."

"Long?" Scarlett asked, raising one eyebrow, her lips quirked in a smile.

"Very." I grinned back, at that moment in perfect accord with Scarlett Hall. Without another thought, I raised one hand, drove my fingers into her thick, silky hair, and pulled her face to mine.

I'd been thinking about kissing Scarlett since that morning. There was no way that kiss had been as perfect in reality as it was in my memory. I'd been half asleep. I'd embellished. Sure, it had been good, but it couldn't have been the best kiss of my life.

I'd been right. That first kiss had not been the best kiss of my life.

This one was.

I half-expected her to pull away, but Scarlett leaned into me, tipping her lips up, parting them in welcome. So sweet. Her tongue stroked mine, her hands rising to grip my shoulders, holding on as she tilted her head to the side, drawing me deeper.

My arm went around her waist, pulling her hips to mine, edging her back until her legs met the bare mattress behind her. It didn't take much to hitch my knee on the bed and draw her with me. Her back hit the mattress and she groaned low in her throat, her eyes flashing wide with understanding.

My mouth stayed locked to hers even as I moved, settling between her legs, our bodies a perfect fit. Everything about her was a perfect fit. That thought might have been alarming if I'd been sharp enough to consider it.

I didn't want to think. I didn't want Scarlett thinking. I only wanted to feel. Wanted her hand tight on the back of my neck, holding me close as her soft tongue stroked mine. The full weight of her breast in my hand, the pebble of her nipple tight against the lace of her bra. One fingernail scraped the peak and she arched her back, another low moan vibrating in her throat, her legs moving restlessly beneath me.

I thought about stripping her shirt over her head and finally seeing her...

Not yet. I hadn't locked the door. I was drowning in the feel of her, the taste of her, but I was alert enough to remember that I hadn't locked the door. Okay. Next time. For now, kissing was enough. More than enough. I was beginning to think I could kiss this woman all day.

I couldn't remember the last time I'd kissed a woman like this. Not as a prelude to more, to sex. Kissing for the sake of kissing had disappeared from my life sometime after high school. My cock was hard as hell, ready for the slick heat of her pussy. If kissing her was this good, fucking her would be life-changing.

Was that why I was happy I had an excuse to keep our clothes on? Did some deep, subconscious part of me recognize that fucking Scarlett would be so much more than sex? Or was it because just kissing her was so much more than sex had ever been?

The warm silk of her skin under my mouth, her breath in my ear, hard and fast and just as desperate as mine. The quick thumps of her heart under my fingertips. Those sounds in her throat, low moans and tight gasps—if she sounded like this just from my mouth and my hand, how hot would she be once I was inside her?

I wasn't going to take off her shirt. Not with the door half-open, disguised as we were by the shadows cast in the fading sun. This wasn't high school, and I wouldn't run the risk of anyone catching us. Especially August.

It should have been a warning sign that even the thought of her kid didn't sidetrack me.

Pulling my mouth from hers, I slid up her shirt, baring one perfect breast. Only a few freckles here, ginger spots against the cream of her soft skin. I followed the trail, kissing one high on the inner curve of her breast. Another on the fullest curve, another just beside her hard, pink nipple. She swallowed a gasp at the nip of my teeth, couldn't silence her moan when I sucked hard, drawing her deep.

It should have been enough. It wasn't. I rolled, making enough room to slide my hands down her side, fingertips nudging her shorts—

Scarlett's body froze, one hand flying up to cover my mouth. In the dim light, I just caught her lips moving. *Quiet.*

Quiet? What did she hear? I caught it a second later. The shuffle of a footstep in the dark hallway outside the half-open door. The low thump of wood on wood. A door closing? Other than us, who was sneaking around the guest wing in the dark?

Chapter Nineteen

SCARLETT

I don't know how I heard him in the hallway. I was lost in Tenn, in the feel of him touching me, surrounding me. That man could kiss. All my resolve went out the window when his mouth met mine. I could kiss him forever.

And the worst thing was I felt like I had been kissing him forever. There wasn't any of that first-time awkwardness—not knowing how he liked to be touched or worrying that I wasn't doing it for him. All it took was his body, his mouth, and I was right there with him.

It was perfect. So perfect I shouldn't have heard the sound from the hall, but I did.

Furtive footsteps. A door creaking open. Closing. It took almost a minute for my brain to make sense of the subtle sounds. I was a lot more focused on Tenn, the rumble in his chest as he kissed me, the liquid slide of our lips, our tongues, the rustle of fabric as his hand slipped under my shirt.

It almost killed me to stop. I would have sworn it physically hurt to break our kiss and push him away. A totally different kind of tension swept through me as logic reasserted itself in my brain. No one should be out there. The guest wing was deserted. It was dark.

I pressed my palm over Tenn's mouth, registering the softness of his lips before I silently whispered, "Quiet."

He stilled. Tenn wasn't just the world's greatest kisser, he was also smart. Shifting gears along with me, he slowly pulled down my shirt—sending a stab of regret right to my heart—and shifted his attention to the sounds in the dark hall beyond the door.

Moving carefully, I rolled off the side of the bed, landing on the balls of my feet, my sneakers silent on the polished wood floor. Tenn followed, just as soundless, and we peeked through the half-open door, his head so close to mine his bristled jaw brushed my cheek.

A tall shadow left one room and slipped deeper into the hall, further from the main staircase, and disappeared into the room opposite ours. I recognized the blue dress shirt covering those broad shoulders.

Forrest. The CFO of the Inn.

And Sterling's new boyfriend.

There was no good reason Forrest should be sneaking around in the guest wing.

He could have gotten lost. It was possible, but I doubted it. Heartstone Manor is a ridiculously big house, but it's easy to navigate. At the top of the stairs from the main level, you could go either left or right. I was pretty sure Forrest already knew that the family wing—and Sterling's bedroom—were to the left.

While some of the light fixtures in the hallway of the family wing didn't work and the wallpaper had seen better days, the family wing was in far better shape than the guest wing. Even if Forrest had wandered down the wrong hall at the top of the stairs, he would have immediately known he wasn't in the right place.

In the guest wing hallway, half of the wallpaper had been stripped. Instead of sconces, there were holes with wires dangling out. Most of the bedrooms were missing furniture. There might be a bed frame but no mattress or dressers and an armchair but no bed.

My point is, I've used the whole *'I must have gotten turned around! How did I end up here?'* excuse for being somewhere I wasn't supposed to be. But the room Tenn and I were in was at the far end of the hall. I could see Forrest making a wrong turn and getting halfway down, but this was no wrong turn. How many rooms had he already searched before we realized he was there?

How long before he opened our door and caught us unaware? My gut turned to ice at the thought. We still had Vanessa's killer on the loose. I couldn't remember anyone mentioning Forrest as a suspect. Hadn't he been out of town when she was shot? Was he simply another Bryce, searching for something to steal?

Tenn's chest pressed to my back, warm and solid. Safe. I should have been freaking out at our close call, at the presence of someone else searching Heartstone—I should have been freaked out at a lot of things. Instead, Tenn's arm around my waist, his mouth at my temple, the sheer heat and size of him made me feel safe.

Was it pheromones? It had to be. Pheromones, or hormones, or maybe I was going a little crazy.

I didn't need anyone to make me feel safe. I took care of myself, took care of my family. I hadn't needed a man for that in years, and when I'd had one, I'd still done it all on my own. So why did Tenn's arms around me feel so exactly right? Like I was finally where I was supposed to be?

I blinked away that thought. Now was not the time to get all googly-eyed over a hot guy who can kiss. Remember what happened the last time I got stupid over a hot guy? Except this was not that. For one, Tenn was a much better kisser. And, more importantly, he wasn't that other guy. He was Tenn, and—

The door across the hall swung open and the tall shadow emerged, gliding silently back down the hall toward the main stairs and out of the guest wing. As far as I could tell, his hands were empty. Had he found what he was looking for? Something about his smooth yet impatient stride made me think he hadn't.

"What the hell is he up to?" Tenn breathed by my ear. We watched in silence as Forrest disappeared from view.

"He looked like he had a plan," I said, stepping back into the dark guest room and turning to face Tenn. Sometime while we'd been plastered to each other on the bed, the sun had finished setting. I could barely see Tenn in the deep shadows of the room. It didn't matter. Whatever drew us together was just as alive in the dark. Maybe more so. "Has he been in the house before?" I asked.

Tenn thought for a moment. "I don't think so. I'll have to ask Hawk. He would know. It's possible Sterling's snuck him in before tonight."

"There's no way he got lost."

"No," Tenn agreed, stepping closer. Close enough to touch, though he kept his hands to himself. "He wasn't lost. He's looking for something. Popular activity lately," he commented with a raise of one eyebrow.

I wasn't taking the bait, but Tenn had a point. First Bryce, then me, and now Forrest. Were we all looking for the same thing? The idea seemed preposterous. And somehow, vaguely possible.

"Still not going to talk to me, Scarlett?" Tenn asked, his voice low. Patient.

I didn't say a word.

I wanted to. That was the crazy thing.

I wanted to tell him everything. and even crazier than that, it wasn't because I wanted to beg for his help—even though I needed it. I wanted to tell him everything because somewhere deep inside I hated the idea of lying to Tenn. Hated it.

If I couldn't tell him the truth, he could never know who I was, couldn't know me. Know my heart.

Why did it matter? Nothing would come of it. Tenn was gorgeous, and kind, the best kisser on the planet. And none of that explained my need for him to see me. To know me. To want *me*.

I kept my mouth shut and stared back at him. I wasn't going to give him some bullshit lie or pretend I didn't understand his question.

Before common sense could silence me, I whispered, "I can't, Tenn."

I couldn't see every nuance of his expression in the dark, but I saw his shoulder drop. I felt his disappointment.

If this were only about me, I'd tell him everything.

If this were only about me, I'd be rushing headlong into heartbreak and disaster just for another of his kisses.

I didn't have that luxury. Not anymore. What I wanted didn't come first, no matter how much I wished it could.

I was going to have to figure out a way to put this thing

with Tenn aside and focus. Find the bust of Vitellius. Find Thatcher. That's why I was here.

I was not here to get naked with Tennessee Sawyer. That couldn't happen. And if following my hormones screwed up my life this time, with so much at stake, I'd never be able to live with myself.

Chapter Twenty

TENN

I could get used to this. I woke slowly, content and boneless with relaxation, a warm, soft weight on my chest. Scarlett. Yeah, I could definitely get used to this. In sleep, I'd wrapped an arm around her waist, my hand burrowing under her loose tank to flatten against her spine. Holding her close.

I was a possessive bastard even unconscious. I wanted to keep Scarlett exactly where she was.

After our scene in the guest room, Scarlett fled, using August as an excuse. He'd been curled up on the couch right where we'd left him, watching his movie, content and oblivious. Scarlett tucked him into his temporary bed and, saying she was tired, had disappeared into the bathroom for a shower.

Considering how long she was in there, she should have looked less chilly when she emerged in her tank and boxers. She'd tucked herself into the other side of the bed, practically clutching the edge of the mattress, and pretended to go to sleep.

I pulled up a book on my iPad and settled in, prepared

to be amused at her attempt to sleep so early. It was August's bedtime, not hers. After a flip to her other side then back again, she'd hurtled herself from the bed, grabbed a blanket from the closet, and rolled it into a long tube. Placing the makeshift bolster between us, Scarlett avoided my eyes and tucked herself back under the covers.

I resisted the urge to laugh. Really. It was almost impossible. "Am I that irresistible?"

No answer from Scarlett. Not a verbal one. A single hand rose from the blankets, one elegant finger extended. The middle one.

I choked back a burst of laughter. "Sleep tight."

The hand withdrew and, eventually, Scarlett's breath evened out. I waited until I was sure she was out before I snagged the bolster and tossed it on the floor. Not long after, I joined her in sleep.

I woke with her soft body entwined with mine.

I felt it the second she woke. Face turning to the side, her cheek on my shoulder, her lips brushed my neck. "Did you sleep okay?" I asked, pitching my voice low so I didn't wake August. I could just see him, splayed on his stomach, hair falling over his eyes, and one foot hanging off the couch. Still out cold.

"Mhmm," Scarlett murmured into my skin. Her hand shifted, coming to rest on the shoulder opposite her head, fingers curling in, then relaxing to stroke.

Fingertips swirled, feather-light. Did she realize she was touching me? Just my shoulder, but it was enough to send shivers all the way to my toes. Her sleepy acceptance made me bold. "Do I get a good morning kiss?"

The fingers stopped moving. Everything about her stopped moving. Just when I thought I'd blown it, Scarlett lifted up on her elbow and looked at me across the inches that separated us. Her mouth opened to speak. Before a sound escaped, I said, "He's still asleep."

"Not for long," she breathed just before her mouth closed over mine.

My arms tightened, holding her still as my lips met hers. She was warm, every muscle relaxed, her mouth moving against mine with leisurely appreciation as if we had all the time in the world. It felt like we did. Like we could spend every second of that time just like this. Kissing. Touching.

Don't get me wrong. I wanted to fuck her. More every time we kissed. Wanted to strip off her clothes and see her naked, to taste and touch without any thought to an interruption. I would, I promised myself. It was going to happen. I was only waiting for the right opportunity. And the open door between us and Scarlett's sleeping son meant this was definitely not the right opportunity.

But I had this—Scarlett kissing me, half straddling me, her smooth thigh shifting against my hard cock, my boxers doing little to dull the sparks of pleasure every time she moved. My brain—and my cock—almost exploded when she slid to the side and her hand drifted down, fingers closing around my length, squeezing with a firm grip that had my hips jerking with the need to thrust, to bury myself in her slick heat.

The hungry growl in the back of her throat was almost enough to push me over the edge. Her grip tightened, relaxed, tightened until my hips pumped and her throat rumbled again. Sleepy and greedy. I sucked in a ragged breath, desperate to get my head together. I hadn't been this close to blowing in my shorts since I hit puberty and the slightest breeze had my dick ready to come.

It wasn't her body. Not that alone. Or her passion, as hot as that was. It was everything. It was Scarlett. So guarded, so secretive. She was a fortress barred against me—until we touched. Like turning a lock, everything flipped when I got my hands on her.

I needed more. So did she. We weren't going to get it.

Somehow, I caught the faint thump of little feet on the floor. The even quieter thud of the pillow followed as August made his way from the couch to the bedroom door. I flipped us, rolling to dislodge Scarlett's grip on my cock, though the loss of her hand made me want to cry.

It only took her a second to get what I was up to. By the time August passed through the open door, I was leaning against the headboard, knees cocked up, the blankets hiding any hint of my body's true interest. Scarlett sat beside me, her breathing only a little uneven, a welcoming smile curving her swollen lips.

"You just wake up, Gus?" Her voice was husky, but August didn't notice.

"Uh-huh." He made his way around the bed and climbed in, tucking himself into Scarlett's side, his head on her breast. I tried not to be jealous. "Cartoons?" he asked, angling his neck to meet his mother's eyes.

"Um, sure—" Scarlett looked to me, eyes wide.

I did the only thing that made sense. Grabbing the remote, I flicked on the TV and found the kids' channel August and Nicky had been watching the day before. A show with an Aussie dog came on. "This one good, August?"

His eyes slowly came fully open. Throwing one arm across Scarlett's belly, he relaxed completely before giving me a slow nod. "This is my favorite."

"I figured that," I said, remembering how he'd bounced on the couch when the show had come on before. Setting the remote back on the bedside table, I murmured, "Guess we're watching cartoons."

"Sorry," she said back, looking as if she actually was sorry. Very sorry.

I wasn't sure that I was. Sorry, that is. I mean, in one sense, I was very, very sorry. My cock agreed. And in another sense, I wasn't sorry at all. Sitting up a little, I slung one arm around Scarlett, pulling both of them closer. August tipped his head up a little and smiled at me before looking back at his show. Scarlett made a questioning sound.

"Not the right time, anyway."

With a glance down at the blond head on her chest, Scarlett agreed. "Definitely not."

"Eventually, it's going to be the right time, Scarlett."

Her eyes flashed up to mine, wide and alarmed, anticipation warring with denial. "Tenn—"

I shook my head. "Don't even try that. It's going to happen. Not last night. Not right now. But eventually. It's going to happen."

To her credit, Scarlett pressed her lips in a tight line but didn't try to argue. She knew it as well as I did. It was going to happen. Just not right now. And it was beyond weird how okay I was with that. Having her in my bed, cuddled up on a lazy morning while we watched cartoons was something... I didn't know what it was or why I wanted it. I just knew that I didn't resent August for interrupting us. I liked seeing him there, relaxed and happy, at home where he was. At home with me.

I don't think a single one of my siblings experienced anything like this when we were August's age. I knew I sure as hell hadn't. My mother had been long gone by the time I was eight. Darcy, my stepmother, had been full of love, but early morning cuddles were not something Prentice would allow. I could count on one hand the number of times I'd been in his rooms. His bed? Never. Prentice Sawyer was not a cuddler.

I hadn't put much thought into kids outside of a vague idea that I might like to have a few one day. I'd never envisioned this exact scene or what those kids would look like. Now that I was here, I realized it was this. Being together. Relaxed. Curled up in bed with nowhere to be, watching some cartoons.

Scarlett's hand moved over August's back in an unconscious gesture I'd bet she'd repeated endless times over the years. Her head tipped to the side, resting on my shoulder, the swell of her breast pillowing into me, her hair silk against my arm.

I grabbed my tablet off the bedside table and pulled up a news site. Angling it her way, I hovered a finger over a headline. Scarlett's eyes narrowed. I went to another. The sides of her lips curved up, and I clicked. We read at about the same pace. When we finished the first article, she stopped rubbing August's back long enough to reach out and choose the next. I clicked the one after that. We kept on like that, the sounds of the TV washing over us, reading while August watched the TV until his stomach got the better of him.

Sitting up, hair tousled but eyes bright, he said, "Pancakes?"

I grinned at his hopeful expression. "It's Sunday morning. That usually means something better than pancakes."

Hope turned to doubt. "What's better than pancakes?"

"Belgian waffles. With strawberries and whipped cream."

August threw himself off the side of the bed and went tearing around the rooms, arms waving overhead, shouting, "Waffles! Waffles! Waffles!"

Scarlett shook her head at me. "Now you've got him going. He loves the waffles song. And waffles."

I dipped in for a quick kiss before rolling out of bed and heading for the bathroom. "Be out in a sec. Then we'll go get him filled up on waffles."

Chapter Twenty-One

TENN

Waffles consumed, with a minimum of syrup in his hair, August escaped the adults to join Nicky with Savannah, saying only that he and his friend had 'plans.' Neither of us asked what those plans might be. As long as they didn't burn the house down, I didn't want to know.

Scarlett turned to me, her face flat. She was going to try to put distance between us. I felt it coming. I got there first. "I have some work I have to catch up on. Are you good?"

She stared at me, mouth slightly agape, momentarily speechless. I resisted the urge to grin. Did she think I was going to grab her and drag her into the closest room to have my way with her?

When I put it like that, it sounded like a great idea... But Scarlett was clever, and she was used to having the upper hand. I wasn't going to win her over with a power struggle. I'm pretty clever myself, and I'm definitely used to having the upper hand.

There's something I have that Scarlett hadn't factored

in. Patience. She was going to come to me. She just didn't know it yet.

"Uh, yeah, I, um, still have to finish cataloging the guest wing."

"Sounds good. Keep the panic button in your pocket just in case." Before she could flee, I dipped my head and brushed a casual kiss across her parted lips, my tongue stroking hers for the briefest second before I pulled away. "I'll find you later. Maybe we can have another picnic and a swim."

I left without waiting for a response. I took my laptop to Griffen's office where Royal found me an hour later, and we hashed out details on a few outstanding things at the Inn. West still wanted me to work from the Manor for a few more days. So far, no leads on Vanessa's killer. I wanted her killer found, but if this was the same person who'd shot our father, I wasn't holding out much hope.

I didn't let myself check the hacked camera on Scarlett's tablet. If I did, I'd never get any work done. Besides, spying on Scarlett to make sure she wasn't stealing from us felt a lot less creepy than perving over her via a camera she didn't know was turned on. I was determined, not a creeper.

I did check the camera once, just before I closed my laptop for the day. It was almost lunchtime. Sundays we were on our own for lunch, but I thought we could manage a few sandwiches by the pool. Scarlett was exactly where she'd said she'd be: in the guest wing, cataloging a room.

When I got up there, she was photographing a fragile-looking vase, painted with royal blue fruits and leaves. After a quick glance at me and a flash of a relieved smile when she realized I wasn't Bryce, she went back to her task. "This should be on a shelf in the library," she said absently as she typed on the tablet. "Or behind glass. Somewhere it won't get bumped into."

"We'll take it downstairs when you're finished," I agreed. I didn't know what was valuable about the vase, but in this, I trusted her judgment.

Scarlett clicked off the tablet. Throwing a glance around the room, she said, "Are all the rooms on this side connected?"

When we were kids, we'd played hide and seek up here and I knew exactly what she meant. "Not all of them, just this section. It gives us flexibility if a larger family comes to visit. Each room can be a suite unto itself, or the doors can be open between, turning it into more of an apartment."

"Did you used to have a lot of visitors?"

"Prentice didn't like guests much. Aunt Ophelia and Bryce came sometimes. But my grandfather used to tell me stories about house parties that would go on for weeks."

"Sounds like fun," Scarlett said, following me out of the room and down the hall. "Especially if someone else is doing all of the cooking and cleaning."

I couldn't argue that. Having all my siblings back under Heartstone's roof should have felt like a house party. It might have if we'd had different childhoods. Or a different father. If we trusted each other. Hell, just knowing each other better than casual acquaintances would help.

If we could be like Nicky and August, life would be a house party. Despite their age difference, they were already joined at the hip. The second we opened the door to Savannah's call of welcome, they came at us in a rush, babbling a mile a minute.

"One sec," I said to the boys, holding up a finger until they reluctantly stopped talking. Raising my chin at Savannah in greeting I asked, "They eat yet?"

"No, not yet."

"Okay if we take them to the pool for a picnic and some swimming?"

Savannah's eyes brightened. "That would be great. But they have something to ask you first."

At her words, the floodgates opened and both boys started talking again, their words falling over each other as they pointed back into the room. The sofa had been deconstructed and rebuilt into a massive pillow fort. The boys must have scrounged up every spare blanket in Heartstone.

Dutifully, Scarlett and I followed the boys closer for a tour, marveling over the elaborate floorplan including a play area, classroom—because August was helping Nicky with his letters—and the bedroom they'd set up with two neatly folded blankets and the pillows from Nicky's bed. It was a marvel of construction, held up in places by masking tape, a yardstick, and what looked like the back of one of Savannah's chairs.

"Can we, can we, can we?" they chanted, eyes wide with expectation.

Had there been a question in there somewhere? A look at Scarlett told me there had, and she wasn't very happy about it. "I don't, um, I—"

Savannah was biting back a grin, though when she looked at Scarlett there was a hint of sympathy in her eyes. To me, she explained, "The boys are dying to have a sleepover in the fort. They promise they won't stay up all night, right guys?"

Both boys turned innocent eyes to Scarlett. "We swear," August said, slapping a hand over his heart. "Because Miss Savannah said she has to get up early, and if we keep her awake, she'll make sure there aren't any pancakes for breakfast for at least a week."

"A horrible punishment," I murmured, trying not to grin at Scarlett as she debated what to do. The problem wasn't letting August have a sleepover with Nicky. The problem was, August's sleepover meant she'd be alone with me. All night. It took every ounce of my self-control not to laugh out loud in sheer relief.

"It's okay with you?" Scarlett asked Savannah weakly, her eyes begging Savannah to say, '*No*' and let Scarlett off the hook.

With a sympathetic smile, Savannah dashed her hopes. "It's fine with me. But if they don't go to sleep on time, this will be the last sleepover they ever have," she finished ominously. Both boys launched into another round of promises.

"Then I guess it's okay," Scarlett agreed. Narrowing her eyes at the grin I couldn't quite hold back, she reached out a hand to August.

"Why don't we make some sandwiches to take out to the pool?" I looked to Savannah, trying not to grin wider at her amusement. "We'll take the kids for the afternoon to give you a break."

Scarlett tossed her hair over her shoulder with a scowl. "You get the sandwiches, I'll get the boys dressed for the pool." Without another word, she dismissed me. For now.

I could let Scarlett have the last word. I'd be getting mine later. It looked like 'eventually' was finally here.

Chapter Twenty-Two

SCARLETT

I managed to avoid thinking about the night to come while we were entertaining the boys. It was not easy. Especially considering we spent most of the afternoon in the pool and it was nearly impossible to keep my eyes off Tenn's perfect torso, his muscles flexing as he played the boy's favorite game—tossing them in the air to land with a splash. Droplets of water beaded on his tanned skin, funneling into the chiseled grooves of his abs... Oh, shoot me now.

Why was I even pretending not to look at him? He was gorgeous. I wanted to lick every inch—

No. Absolutely not. I'd already decided *no* about a thousand times. Tenn was not on the menu. Had I forgotten about Thatcher? What was wrong with me? I couldn't afford to get distracted. Not now. Not when I hadn't heard from Thatcher in days. Ice prickled my skin as that thought really sunk in.

I hadn't heard from Thatcher since we'd left for Sawyers Bend. Unless he'd called or texted and Hawk was erasing the messages. It was possible, but I couldn't imagine why he'd bother. No one knew who Thatcher was or why I was here. Hell, I barely knew why I was here.

How could I be thinking about sleeping with some guy I'd just met when Thatcher was missing?

Another glance at Tenn and the hot spike of lust gave me part of the answer. It had been a long time. A very long time. And Tenn was close to irresistible.

I was going to have to resist him. The last thing I needed was another distraction. Or a complication. Tenn was all of that and more. So much more.

I could do this. I had the willpower. I'd made it through most of my adult life by gritting my teeth and getting shit done. I could do the same here. Tenn was just a man. Nothing special.

I told myself that through the afternoon. I had a mission. Tenn was just a guy. I didn't need anything from him. I could resist temptation. He wasn't that great anyway.

I repeated those words until I almost believed them. Almost.

I let Tenn deliver August and Nicky to Savannah for their kids' dinner and sleepover. If I had done it, I probably would have snatched August back and used him as a shield. Not that I needed a shield. It wasn't like Tenn was going to attack me. It wasn't Tenn I was afraid of. At least I had dinner as a buffer before I had to face being alone with Tenn.

Apparently, Sunday dinner was a big deal at Heartstone Manor. Everyone was there except Parker. Despite my hasty packing job, I was not the most underdressed. That award went to Tenn's younger brother, Finn, who showed up in board shorts and a faded t-shirt. In my yellow sundress, I was definitely the most casual of the female contingent, though no one made me feel weird about it.

I sat beside Tenn, avoiding his gaze, letting the conversation wash over me, trying desperately not to think about what would happen after dinner. If this was my house, I could think of a thousand chores to delay bedtime. At Heartstone, I didn't have my own space to retreat to. I didn't have anything.

Every time I glanced at Tenn the side of his mouth was quirked up in a half-grin that was almost as appealing as his full smile. Bastard. He'd been grinning like that ever since I'd agreed to let August stay with Nicky overnight. I'm sure he thought we were going to get naked the second dinner was over.

Well, wouldn't he be in for a surprise? I wasn't that easy.

"Scarlett?"

I looked up, eyes searching the table. I'd been off in space and had no clue who'd said my name.

"How's the cataloging going?" Hope asked, lips curved in a polite smile, a hint of amusement in her eyes. Did everyone know about August and the sleepover? Was I imagining her knowing look?

I'm just being paranoid, I assured myself. "It's going. I finished most of the guest wing before lunch. I haven't decided where to start next."

"Parker asked me to tell you that you can work in her room whenever you want. She'll be gone for at least three or four days."

"Oh, thanks, that works." I hadn't even thought about cataloging rooms that were occupied. I wasn't used to the idea of valuable art being scattered throughout a house as if it were nothing more than an interior design choice.

The vase I'd found in the guest room earlier was Ming dynasty, I thought from the Yongle period. I'd seen one at the auction house a few years before that had gone for a hundred and fifty thousand. And this one was in better shape. It wouldn't stay that way carelessly stashed on a rickety end table in an unused guest room. I'd moved it to a high shelf in the library where no one could bump into it and send it crashing to the floor. I wondered what treasures I'd find in Parker's rooms.

"Where did Parker go?" Finn asked, slouched in his chair, seeming disinterested in his own question.

"Hopefully to talk Tyler into coming back," Bryce said with a smirk. He took a long sip of wine. "He was the only one of you I could stand, so of course, you had to drive him off."

"Bryce!" At the far end of the table, an older woman shot Bryce a surprised look, her darkly drawn eyebrows high, mouth tight.

Bryce ignored her. The woman shook her head and looked around the table. "I'll apologize for my son. I've tried to teach him manners, but none of them stuck." She gave a weak smile and, following her son's example, sipped deeply at her wine. She must be Aunt Ophelia. I hadn't met her personally yet, but if she was Bryce's mother, I could wait. Forever.

Sterling rolled her eyes at both of them. "I hope she's up there serving him with papers. He's a total asshole. Not a surprise you like him so much," she said to Bryce. "I'm just shocked she didn't get rid of him before now. Parker deserves better."

"Here, here," said the brunette beside Sterling. They clicked glasses and grinned matching smiles at each other.

It's funny how genetics works. Sterling could have been Bryce's sibling with her golden blond hair and startling blue eyes. Both of them looked like they'd tumbled off a screen into real life. Quinn, the brunette beside Sterling, couldn't have been more different. She was pretty; that, they had in common, but she was dark to Sterling's light. Taller, rangy, with sharp cheekbones that were austerely elegant rather than beautiful. But when they smiled, they almost looked like twins.

I glanced to Tenn to see what he thought about Parker's... husband? I assumed Tyler was her husband after Sterling had mentioned serving him with papers. Tenn's ever-present grin was gone, replaced with a look of disgust.

"You don't like him either?" I murmured.

"Sterling is right. Parker deserves better. Much better. I hope she *is* serving him with papers."

We all looked to Griffen and Hope at the head of the table, but they gave nothing away. Hope changed the subject to the new cottages at the Inn, and I went back to listening with one ear while I stressed about the empty couch in Tenn's rooms. When Sterling mentioned putting on a movie in the family gathering room, I leaped at the opportunity, ignoring Tenn's sly smile at my obvious attempt to evade him.

I thought about trying to find an armchair to watch the movie, but there wasn't one. While I was standing at the door, trying to figure out where to sit, Tenn took my elbow and guided me to a loveseat. Not good. The whole idea was to avoid being alone with Tenn and I ended up curled into his side, basically in the dark. *Great job, Scarlett.*

Relaxing was impossible. I was braced for a move, ready to fend him off. I had to be vigilant. It didn't take much before my hormones took control of my brain and convinced me that anything to do with Tenn Sawyer was a very good idea.

He barely had to look at me and I felt myself softening,

leaning into him, tilting my head up, ready to be kissed. To be touched. We were already too close on the loveseat, the room dark enough to hide all manner of questionable behavior.

If Tenn slid a hand up my leg or even around my shoulders, I was toast. I shivered at the thought, then tried to hide it. In the dark, I caught the movement of his jaw beside me. The bastard was grinning again. He was torturing me on purpose. I knew it.

I ground my teeth and stared at the screen, completely oblivious to everything except the solid heat of the man beside me. I swear, I heard his every breath, his every heartbeat. I was completely in tune with him, and he didn't seem to care. Maybe he'd just been messing with me. Maybe he was so confident I'd sleep with him he wasn't worried about it. Maybe he—

Ugh. I was making myself crazy. I had to get away from Tenn. Quietly, so I didn't bother anyone else, I murmured, "I'm tired. I'm going to sleep."

Note I said *sleep*, not *bed*. I wasn't saying the word *bed* to Tenn. I didn't even want to think the word *bed*. Not waiting for a response from him, I slipped out of the room. Another cold shower? They didn't seem to be dulling the heat.

Maybe I should just—

No.

Sleeping with Tenn was a terrible idea.

I got ready for bed, choosing my baggiest, most ancient t-shirt and a pair of yoga pants that did not do good things for my ass. See, not trying to sleep with Tenn. A mumu would have been sexier than my sleepwear. Eyeing the king-size bed, I thought about my bolster from the night before. It had ended up on the floor. I assumed after Tenn threw it there.

Grabbing the cushions from the back of the couch, I lined them up in the center of the bed. They were wider than my bolster, leaving a narrow strip on either side for us to sleep. The cushions made a very clear point. I was not interested in sex. Not at all.

Some small part of me looked at that wall of couch cushions and knew I was being crazy. Completely irrational.

I didn't care. I just had to get through this one night and everything would be fine. I'd find Vitellius and Thatcher and get the hell out of this house without doing anything monumentally stupid. Like having sex with Tennessee Sawyer.

By the time Tenn came to the room, I should have been asleep. I tried. I did breathing exercises, counted sheep, tried to remember state capitals... anything I could think of to relax enough to fall asleep. None of it worked. By the time Tenn climbed into his side of the bed, I was wound tight and sleep was a distant dream. I waited, ready to turn him down.

I heard a low chuckle and thump... thump... thump... as one by one, the pillows between us took flight, landing on the floor. If he said one word—

He didn't.

Once the pillows were out of the way, Tenn rolled over, giving me his back, and went to sleep.

He. Went. To. Sleep.

My head was spinning. He was sleeping? We finally had privacy. It was *eventually*.

And he went to sleep?

I wanted to hit him with my pillow. Forget that, I wanted to punch him. I wanted—

Oh, yeah, that was his plan. I'd get pissed, and as soon as I touched him, he'd have me. Not going to happen. I was smarter than that. I lay where I was and waited. After a while, when I thought I'd scream from the tension, a light snore drifted across the bed.

Wait, was he really sleeping?

Not messing with me, or getting ready to reach across the space between us, but actually fast asleep?

Frustration burned in my chest with such a fierce heat that tears pooled in my eyes. Was it just me playing this game? Was it all in my head? How could he be sleeping?

Never mind that he was doing exactly what I'd told myself I wanted. He'd made no demands. Didn't even issue an invitation. I gave very clear signals that I wasn't interested in sex, and he was reading them. How could I possibly be mad about that?

Because I just was.

I knew why. I wanted Tenn to make the choice. To take the decision out of my hands. If he started it, I could blame my hormones and let myself off the hook.

Too scared to trust myself, I'd run from him, going so far as to build a wall between our sides of the bed. And now I was mad at him for respecting my boundaries.

I was a jerk. Tenn was the good guy here. And I was still mad at him.

Grinding my teeth together, I rolled over, facing the windows, and stared out at the stars. I didn't bother trying to fall asleep. It was never going to happen. I was too mad. Too frustrated. And too afraid that by denying both Tenn and myself, I might be making a huge mistake.

Chapter Twenty-Three

SCARLETT

I drifted awake to the sensation of heat on my lower back. A hand. Heat beneath me. Blinking my eyes open, dark green cotton filled my view. Tenn's t-shirt. I was on top of him. Again.

If I hadn't been so worried about waking him, I might have screamed. What was wrong with me? Why couldn't I just stay away from this man? What was so special about him? It had been ages since I'd had an interest in sex. Why Tenn? Why now, at the exact time I couldn't risk getting distracted?

I let out a sigh, turning my head to rest my cheek on his shoulder. So much was crowded in my head I couldn't think straight.

Why exactly was it such a bad idea to have sex with Tenn?

I couldn't remember. Something about keeping my head clear so I could find the bust of Vitellius and Thatcher.

Not a very convincing argument considering how distracted I was by *not* having sex with Tenn. If I slept with him, I'd be more alert, not less, right?

Hard to argue with that point. Not sleeping with Tenn was doing nothing for my brain, that was for sure.

So why? Why did I keep telling Tenn, 'No?' Why did I keep telling myself, 'No?' Didn't I deserve something just for me? It felt like years, thirteen of them to be exact, since I'd done something just for me.

I wanted him. Wanted Tenn. Wanted him in a way I'd never, ever wanted a man. Not even my ex. My want for Tenn was nothing I'd ever experienced.

Letting out another sigh, I knew that was the answer to my question. I was in deep with him after only a few days. All these years of caution, and this one man snuck through my barriers without even trying.

This thing between us couldn't go anywhere. For so many reasons. I had a life a thousand miles away, for one. And I came with baggage. A lot of it, a significant chunk currently sleeping in a pillow fort two stories below. Tenn and I didn't have a future.

I was fending him off because I was afraid for my heart, not my body. My body was pretty clear on what it wanted. Tenn. Full stop. My heart was at a loss. I already wanted more than just his body. I wanted his smile. I wanted to make him laugh. I wanted to curl up in bed and read with him again. I wanted a lot of things that weren't going to happen.

So what?

The thought caught in my head.

So what?

So what if we weren't going to have a fairy tale romance?

Did that mean I should slink off and deny myself at least part of what I wanted?

If I can't have the fairy tale, I won't have anything at all?

Every cell in my body tossed out that idea.

My heart could be a fool, but my body was done with self-denial. What had I thought the other day? *Just a taste.* Even if I couldn't keep Tenn, I could have just a taste, couldn't I? We were both adults. We both wanted it. Why not? Wouldn't a little bit of Tenn be better than none at all?

Finally, in all my confusion, a breath of sanity. I just wanted a taste. It didn't have to be a big deal.

Craning my neck, I stared at the column of Tenn's throat. So close. It took the smallest effort to close the distance and press my mouth to his warm skin. To lick. He tasted so good.

The hand on my lower back moved, sliding into my yoga pants to cup my ass. He squeezed, and liquid heat shot straight between my legs. Shifting up on one elbow, I found his lips with mine.

No going back now.

Our mouths fit as if he'd been made for me, his lips soft, my tongue stroking his. I let out a moan of relief, of need, and the kiss exploded. We were done waiting. Tenn wasn't holding back. Neither was I.

I wasn't sure if it was a battle or a race. He took my mouth with a ferocity I returned, sinking my fingers into his hair, holding him right where I wanted him, tilting my head to kiss him deeper, harder. We broke apart to pant for breath, staring at each other for a silent moment before I sat up, reached down, and grabbed the hem of my t-shirt.

Without a word, I stripped it off and tossed it from the bed. Tenn's eyes flared, his breath frozen for a heartbeat. He reached for me, going for my mouth again when I thought he'd be done with kissing now that my clothes were coming off.

I scrabbled at his chest, trying to find the bottom of his

shirt. I wanted to feel his skin on mine, his chest hair brushing my hard nipples. I found it, yanking up. He broke our kiss long enough to tear the shirt over his head.

My entire body shuddered in pleasure at the scalding heat of him against my bare breasts. Nothing had ever felt this good. Skin. I needed more skin. Fumbling, drugged with lust, I rolled to my back, pushing my yoga pants off, kicking my feet to get free. The second I was naked, I turned back to Tenn to find him just as bare. He was beautiful. Not just his cock, thick and hard, begging for my touch. It was all of him. The hungry glint in his eyes. The set of his jaw. Determination and violent lust. And he waited. For me.

I reached, and he was in my arms, between my legs, the thick head of his cock at my pussy, moving against my wet heat. I was ready. I think I'd been ready before I woke, my body desperate for this. For him filling me.

I tipped my head back, staring blindly at the ceiling, speechless at the impossibly bright, sharp sparks of pleasure, so intense they burned. I couldn't stop moving. Rocking my hips up, taking him deeper, sliding under the wave of sensation at him filling me to the hilt.

So much of him and he fit me so perfectly. And then he started to move. One hand cupped my breast, his mouth found my neck, teeth biting as he slammed his cock into me. Hard. Fast. I met him at each thrust, legs wrapping his hips, a keening cry breaking from my lips. I came. And came. It went on forever, my body still pulsing around him after he'd collapsed half on top of me, panting for breath.

At least Tenn could breathe. My lungs had frozen mid-orgasm. Tenn rolled to his back, taking me with him, one arm holding me to his side. I settled in, my forehead pressed to his neck, fingers trailing down his chest.

For endless minutes, we clung to each other, panting, hearts pounding, brains completely scrambled.

I'd barely caught my breath when the wet heat on the inside of my thigh got my attention. On the same wavelength, Tenn said, "We didn't use anything. I meant to. I—I had a plan—"

"To drive me insane?" I demanded, rising up on my elbows to stare down into his eyes.

He grinned up at me, his smile incandescent even in the dark room. Shifting to one elbow, I raised a hand to trace a finger over the bottom curve of his lip. Dipping my head, I nipped at that curve, wanting a bite of his amusement.

"Not insane, exactly," he said when I pulled back. "Just crazy enough to jump me."

"Mission accomplished," I grumbled, not meaning it at all, and settled back onto his chest. "I'm on the pill. And I haven't slept with anyone since my last physical."

"Neither have I."

I lifted up again to get a look at his face. He was totally serious. "Really? When was your last physical?" I figured he'd say a few weeks ago.

"In October."

October? That was eight months ago. "That's a long time."

"When was your last physical?"

I didn't want to answer that question on the grounds that the answer made me look lame. "Three years," I admitted, ready to see a laugh in his eyes. Instead, the deep blue softened and he lifted a finger to bop my nose.

"You're supposed to go every year, you know?"

"I know. And I mean to. I just get busy and figure I'll go later."

"Three years?" he asked, sliding one hand down my back to cup my ass.

I laughed. "Couldn't you tell?" I'd been desperate to feel him inside me. After that orgasm, all I wanted was more.

"Looks like you have a lot to make up for." Tenn rolled off the bed before he reached for me, pulling me to my feet. "We'd better get to work."

Work, it turned out, meant a steamy shower. I'd spent plenty of time in Tenn's oversized, white-tiled shower. Mostly standing under a frigid spray, trying to ice out my growing lust for him.

This was much better. Soft, warm steam filled the shower. Tenn's hands, slippery with soap, explored every inch of me. The sweet, citrus scent of the soap was everywhere, his fingers touching, sliding until I rubbed my soapy body against his and conducted my own exploration.

I'd been dying to get my hands on his body since... since the day we met and I got a good look at his legs in his running shorts. Had it really only been a few days? My body swore I'd known him a lifetime. He felt like he'd been made for me.

Tenn pulled me down to the deep bench opposite the showerhead, drawing me onto his lap, his stiffening cock pinned between us. Dipping me back over his arm, his lips found one hard nipple and I gasped at the spike of pleasure that went straight to my clit. We hadn't gotten to this part before, too hungry for each other to slow down.

Tenn made up for lost time, sucking and biting, kneading my breast in his strong hand before switching to the other. I wanted him inside me again. Squirming against his length, fully hard and ready for me, I lifted my hips and reached down to guide him into me. I took him in slowly, savoring the stretch.

I barely needed to move. His mouth on my nipple had my head spinning in bliss. His cock filling me, the base right at my clit, was all I needed. I rocked, grinding on him, leaning back into his arm to offer him more of my breasts—I was coming again, my cries echoing off the walls.

Tenn didn't stop. One hand clamped onto my ass, he held me as I rode him through my orgasm, my body chasing every last pulse until I collapsed forward, draped over his chest, my face in his neck. His lips grazed my temple as he rose, hauling me up with him. The movement of his cock inside me sent another wave of pleasure through my over-stimulated nervous system.

Too much and not quite enough. Until he pressed my back to the tile wall and started to fuck. There was no other word for it. That kiss on my temple as he stood was tender. Sweet.

This was primal. I was pinned between wall and man, his cock driving into my pussy, sending me from languid afterglow straight back to the peak. I sank my fingers into his shoulders and went over, everything but pleasure scattering from my mind.

We napped for a while, still wet from the shower, tangled in the bed, sated and exhausted. I woke to Tenn's hands stroking my back, my body splayed across his. "You know, I've never liked sleeping with women."

"Could've fooled me," I mumbled into his shoulder.

Fingers curved around my hip, squeezing tight. "You know what I mean. Even when I'm dating someone, I sleep in my own bed. Alone."

Maybe I should have moved, but I was too comfortable, and he wasn't exactly shoving me off. I gave in to the temptation to tease. "Want me to go sleep on the couch?"

His lips brushed the top of my head. "Try it and I'll find those handcuffs."

"Not sure that's a threat." I didn't have to look up. I could feel his grin.

"I'll keep that in mind." He stroked a hand down my bare back, his cheek against my hair. "I like you exactly where you are. Anytime you want to use me as your mattress, feel free."

I liked me exactly where I was, too. I didn't know why. I needed my space when I slept. I hated feeling crowded in bed. Usually. Apparently, not when it was Tenn since every time I fell asleep, I wrapped myself around him.

I didn't want to think about that. I didn't want to think about anything. Instead of thinking, I kissed him.

That time, I stayed on top, riding him slowly, pinning his hands with mine, changing position to offer him my mouth, my breasts, anything he wanted until we both came, Tenn straining up, hips thrusting until I could barely hold on.

I fell asleep still lying on top of Tenn, temporarily satiated and thoroughly exhausted.

We slept too late. Both of us.

I snapped alert to the sound of the door, and a familiar voice calling, "Mom, I gotta show you—"

A female voice cutting him off. Savannah. "August, I told you she'd be down later—"

"But Mom's always up by now."

I don't know how I got out of bed and into the bathroom so fast. I was the roadrunner, leaving a puff of smoke and a memory in Tenn's bed. I probably should have felt bad about leaving Tenn to fend for himself. I didn't. I was too shocked by the idea of August catching me naked in bed with a man.

Nothing like this had ever happened before. What would I say? What was appropriate to explain to an eight-year-old? And what exactly was I going to explain? Sometimes even moms need to get some? It was true. At this point, I had to admit that. But not the truth I wanted to explain to my almost-third grader.

Ugh. I stood in the shower for a minute, then pulled on Tenn's robe—because, of course, I didn't grab clothes in my mad flight to the bathroom—and tried to do something so the mess on my head didn't scream *sex hair*. I settled for a ponytail and came out to find August bouncing on the end of the bed, telling Tenn—who'd managed to find a pair of cutoff sweats and my abandoned t-shirt—all about his sleepover with Nicky.

I couldn't meet Tenn's eyes. I tried. I'd done all sorts of things with him that should have erased any hint of shyness, but that didn't seem to matter. In the light of morning, post-orgasms, I couldn't seem to handle my son and my new lover at the same time.

It wasn't them; it was me. August hadn't noticed anything different, continuing to talk about their pillow fort and how it had fallen down while they were sleeping as I pulled on shorts beneath the robe and turned my back to yank on a bra and shirt. Spinning around, I avoided Tenn's eyes while stammering something about coffee and taking August outside for some fresh air.

Then, I fled, feeling exactly like the coward I was.

Chapter Twenty-Four

TENN

S he could run, but she couldn't hide. After a quick stop in my room, I crossed to the other side of the second floor and went hunting for Scarlett. It wouldn't take long. She only had one room left in the guest wing before she started in Parker's suite.

I should have known Scarlett would get weird as soon as reality hit her. I might have been able to ease her through it if August hadn't shown up. Or maybe not. I'd been thrown myself. So thrown I'd let her escape, put on my running gear, and hit the trails behind the house. I needed to get to work, but more than that, I'd needed to get my head straight.

Some people like meditation. I run. Something about it —the rhythmic pounding of my feet, the air in my lungs— sets my mind free to think. Or not think. I started out mostly concentrating on my footing and the trail. I do a lot of trail-running, but the trails I usually hit were by the Inn and somewhat flatter and smoother than the narrow, uneven, root-filled trails behind Heartstone.

Once I got into the rhythm of picking my knees up

higher and watching my footing, my thoughts turned to the problem of Scarlett Hall. It was fair to say the night with Scarlett had blown my mind.

I'd wanted to fuck her. Of course, I had. She was hot, and smart, and sleeping in my bed. How could I not think about fucking her?

Had I been thinking about more than that?

In retrospect, I must have been. I'd never dated a woman with children. Had consciously avoided it. Too much commitment. Too much responsibility. Too many people in the relationship. I wanted kids someday, but I'd never felt prepared to put someone else's needs above mine the way you had to as a parent. Especially not for someone else's kids.

All of that sounded flat and empty in the face of August and Scarlett. August wasn't some anchor around my neck. He was a person. He was funny, and sharp, and pretty cool for a little kid. And I was living with them at my own demand. I let out a gust of laughter as I pounded up the trail, thighs burning and my brain finally coming in line with my subconscious.

I never would have slept with Scarlett, especially when she and August were living with me, if I hadn't been planning on keeping her.

Keeping her? As in permanently?

It was too soon for that. Way too soon. We barely knew each other. She was lying to me about something. Something big. She didn't trust me. I wasn't sure I could trust her. She didn't exactly live nearby.

I had a pile of good, solid reasons why wanting something more with Scarlett was a bad idea. And that was before I threw August into the mix. If this went bad, the fallout wouldn't just affect the adults.

All of that was perfectly reasonable. Sensible.

I didn't care.

I could take things slowly.

Really?

I'd moved Scarlett and August in after knowing her less than an hour and had sex with her only a few days later. Okay, I could *start* taking things slowly. I wasn't going to ask her to marry me, but I was done pretending this was just about sex.

Fucking Scarlett had been spectacular. I couldn't wait to do it again. A lot. As often as possible. If it had just been that, I would have been fine. Nothing wrong with some no-strings sex between two consenting adults.

The problem was, I also wanted to watch cartoons with August, Scarlett curled into me while we read the news and she rubbed his back. I wanted more picnics. More splashing in the pool. I wanted to take them hiking and show them the mountains. To bring them to my favorite barbeque place.

I wanted to show them my life. I wanted them to want to be a part of it.

I wanted Scarlett to tell me what put those lines of strain around her mouth and why she kept demanding to see her phone. What was she looking for? Who did she need to talk to? Why couldn't she trust me?

In the back of my head, I could hear someone, maybe Griffen, telling me I was rushing things. It sounded like the kind of thing an older brother might say. He'd probably insist that I couldn't possibly know I wanted something serious with a woman I'd met less than a week ago. Relationships are built over time. You can't just know another person is the right one.

And if Griffen did tell me I was being crazy? Did it matter? I didn't care about any of that. My heart, my soul, whatever it was inside me that operated outside of logic—that part said that when it was the right person, I absolutely could know in a few days. And Scarlett was the right person. She was why everything was different. Scarlett was why this wasn't just about fucking.

I was going to have to be smart.

First, she was up to something, and I had to know what it was before this went too much further. I needed her to trust me. And second, she didn't have a rosy outlook on relationships. What had she said that first day? That if she wanted someone else to take care of, she'd get a dog? Yeah, it was fair to say she wasn't angling for a wedding ring.

It was going to take some work to convince her to give me a shot.

When I pushed away everything else, that was what I wanted: a shot at winning Scarlett.

I finished my run, showered, and got to work. I couldn't keep my finger on the pulse of the Inn the way I liked from home, but Royal and Forrest had things in hand for now. I'd give West another week to track down Vanessa's killer and then I was going back to work. For now, I cleared my inbox, got up to date on a few projects, and made my plans for Scarlett.

I found her exactly where I expected: in the last guest room, finishing cataloging the artwork there. A master bedroom with an ensuite bath that connected to a set of rooms continuing down the hall, the room had a glass case of figurines that had been keeping Scarlett busy. It also had a locking door and a wide, velvet chaise lounge that was more daybed than sofa.

Her cheeks were pink when she turned to face me. Matching pink lips parted as if to speak, then pressed together. The color in her cheeks deepened. Yeah, she was hot, and smart, and amazing in bed. And sometimes, she was just fucking adorable. Did she notice me turning the lock on the door after I closed it behind me? I think she did.

"Are you going to run again?" I asked, closing the distance between us. "Because I think I told you what would happen if you did." Her cheeks flushed dark red as she remembered. Green eyes flashed to my empty hands. I took the tablet from her, tilting it away as I deactivated the hacked camera. I set it on a side table.

"I... uh... August had never... I mean..." Scarlett let out a huff of air and tipped her face up to the ceiling. Drawing in a breath, she finally met my eyes. "I'm sorry I was such a dork this morning. Last night was amazing and I wasn't thinking about August walking in. I freaked. I haven't dated much since I divorced my ex and I've never brought a man around. I didn't know what to do."

"Never?" I hooked a strand of red hair around my finger and tucked it behind her ear.

She shook her head. "Never. And all of a sudden, there's you and he's seeing me sleep in your bed. And we're here, almost a thousand miles from home, living in a castle. Everything's upside down. And last night was... amazing. You were..." Her lids lowered in sensual memory as she swayed toward me a fraction of an inch.

I raised my hand to pull her closer and Scarlett snapped back, spinning on one heel to put some distance between us. "I just—" She tugged at her hair. "I don't know what I'm doing right now, and being in bed with you and August coming in... It was like two parallel universes collided and I couldn't deal."

"Do you regret it?" It was going to kill me if she said yes.

She shot me a look that was half-glare and half-desperate appeal. "I should regret it. My eight-year-old

185

almost caught me naked in bed with a strange man. I'm a terrible mother."

"So, you do regret it?" I took a step closer, wanting to pull her into my arms.

Another desperate glare. "No! I think you're turning me into a crazy woman, but I don't regret it. I feel like I should, but I can't. And I'm sorry I'm being weird. But I'm not sorry because you should have known what you were getting into. Which is nuts because you barely know me."

Another step closer. Scarlett was caught up in her rant and didn't notice.

"I do know you. And I knew this was going to be complicated. For a lot of reasons."

She stopped, studying me. "Do you regret it?" she asked softly.

"Not for a second. I regret not locking the door so you could have time to get yourself together before August came in. That's it. Last night was..." I closed the distance between us and slid my arm around her waist, pulling her against me. "Last night was the best night of my life. And the worst. Ever since the kids mentioned that pillow fort, I was desperate to get you alone in my bed. Not touching you was the hardest thing I've ever done."

Her eyes flew wide. "I thought you went to sleep!"

"Are you kidding? I finally had you in my bed, alone. It took everything I had to fake it."

She was cute when she scowled. "I almost killed you when I heard you snore."

"I thought that was a nice touch."

The annoyance melted off her face, replaced by confusion. "Why? I mean, why didn't you just—" She shrugged a shoulder as if the question wasn't important.

Leaning in, I traced a finger over her cheekbone,

guiding her face up to mine. "Because it had to be you. We're in my house. In my town. I forced you to come here. To sleep in my bed. If we were going to go there, it had to be you who made the choice."

"That's very evolved of you."

"Mmmm," I said in agreement, taking her mouth in a kiss. She was about to see how very un-evolved I could be.

Kissing Scarlett is a full-body experience. Every time my lips touch hers, I drown in her taste, her scent, her touch. I almost dropped the cuffs when I pulled them from my pocket. Somehow, I managed to maneuver us to the chaise lounge.

Scarlett didn't resist when I pulled her down beside me, the deep, lush velvet chaise almost as wide as a bed. Stretching out beside her, pinning her against the back, I coaxed her hands over her head. It took every ounce of concentration I had to keep kissing her as I opened the cuffs and slid one around her wrist. Carefully, I fed the other end through a decorative wooden loop on the arm of the chaise and secured it to her other wrist. Handcuffs fastened, I broke the kiss and sat up, looking down on Scarlett in satisfaction.

She blinked up at me, dazed. I couldn't blame her. I was dazed myself. The woman could fucking kiss. Tilting her head back, she looked up at her hands cuffed to the chaise and back at me. One dark red eyebrow raised.

Slipping my hands under her shirt, I inched it up, my eyes on hers, taking in every nuance of her expression. "I told you what would happen if you ran."

"And I told you that wasn't much of a threat." She sank her teeth into her lower lip, eyes heavy, languid with desire. Pushing her shirt over her breasts, I unsnapped her bra and tugged it out of the way, baring her full curves, her nipples tight and darkly pink. Drawing in a slow breath, I skimmed my hands down her sides and around to the front, flicking open the button on her shorts and pulling them down her long legs, taking her underwear along with them.

I don't remember taking off my own clothes or lying down beside her. I was too focused on Scarlett. I ran my hand down her arm, from her cuffed wrist to her shoulder. "This okay?"

She nodded, raising her mouth to mine. I brushed a kiss across her lips, easing back when she would have deepened the kiss.

"In a minute," I murmured against her ear. Sitting up enough to meet her eyes, I threaded my fingers through her hair, brushing it back from her face. "First, we need to get something straight."

"What?" she asked, a little breathless. The sound went straight to my cock.

"This isn't just sex. I know things are complicated and I know this is crazy, but this is more than sex."

Her eyes closed in a slow blink, and when they opened, they were wet, drenched in sadness. "It can't be. You know it can't."

"I don't, and neither do you." I ran the side of my nose along her jaw, nuzzling her before I kissed the shell of her ear. "I don't know what's going to happen. I don't know why you're here. And I'm getting that neither do you."

"Tenn, I—"

I dropped a finger over her lips. "All I do know is that this isn't just fucking. I can't come inside you and then walk away like it was nothing. I don't want to. I want you."

"I want you, too."

"Just to fuck? Is that all you want?"

"I—" Scarlett stopped, her eyes on mine, and the confusion I saw there stabbed straight to my heart.

All my confidence was bullshit. Maybe I was way off base. Maybe she just wanted to get laid. I fought the urge to brace myself, to shut down.

I waited, searching her face, hoping she wasn't about to destroy me.

Chapter Twenty-Five

SCARLETT

Just to fuck? Is that all you want?

It would have been easier if I could have said, *'Yes. Sure, all I want is some great sex, no strings.'* I could have said that, but I would have been lying. I wanted the sex, absolutely. And the strings? Why did I want strings? I didn't want a relationship, especially an impossibly complicated one. I didn't need another responsibility—

But that was all bullshit. Complete and total crap. I wanted all sorts of strings tying me to Tenn. Because I wanted him. Not just his cock or the phenomenal orgasms he kept giving me. I wanted him. And I wasn't going to lie to either of us.

"I—" I lost my courage and swallowed hard. "I can't make you any promises, Tenn. Not now. I don't know if I ever can. But I wish I could. I want to."

Tenn dipped his head to run his lips along my jaw. "Good enough. I can be patient."

Yes, he could, and he set about showing me exactly how patient he could be. He kissed me, his mouth gentle, lips softly persuasive, one hand teasing my breasts until I chased his mouth with my own, desperate for more.

He refused to give it to me. Moving so gradually it felt like a dream, he abandoned my mouth, leaving a trail of kisses across my breasts and down my torso, his lips moving from one spot to another. "I love your freckles," he murmured. "I think we should spend all day naked so I can kiss every single one."

I was all for that. He reached my hips and crossed just beneath my belly button. I was drenched with heat, my body ready for him. I tilted my hips, moaning for his touch. He sat up, smoothing his hands up my legs, lifting one and hooking it over the low back of the chaise, baring me to him.

In the afternoon sun, every inch of me was exposed. I have no idea why I wasn't embarrassed, but I wasn't. This was Tenn. And me. When it came to our bodies, I had nothing to hide. He traced a finger around my opening, slowing as he passed over my clit. I squirmed. "Tenn, please. Don't make me wait."

He didn't answer except to shake his head, his eyes fixed on my pussy. I bumped his hand with my hips, impatient. Demanding. Another shake of his head and his deep blue eyes met mine, filled with desire and an amused conviction. "Nope. I'm in charge now and you're not going to rush me. We've had it fast and hard. Now I want you slow."

"I like fast and hard," I insisted, my body on fire.

"Me too," he agreed, his eyes leaving mine to study my pussy. I squirmed again. What was he waiting for? "But I also like slow. I want to be thorough. For instance—" One finger traced the darkened line that ran from my belly button to my mound. "How many times do you think I can make you come before I can't stand it anymore and have to fuck you?"

I shook my head, speechless. I had no idea, but I wanted to find out. He dipped his head, licking my clit, and I bowed, legs splaying wider, rocking my clit up into his mouth. Yes. Yes, this was it. The best. This was everything. The first orgasm hit before he even got a finger inside me. He let me come down, stretching out beside me, petting my breasts and whispering in my ear.

"I love the way you look when you come. Your eyes get so wide, and then they squeeze shut. It's so hot. Beautiful. I don't care if I just came, I want you all over again."

Just as I got my breath back, he was there again, filling me with his fingers, licking, sucking, one hand curved around my hip, fingers digging in as he ate my pussy with skill and ferocity. I twisted, rolled my hips, anything I could do to encourage him to lose control and just fuck me, but he refused, making me come again with his mouth before sliding back up to stroke me down and tease me with his soft words and butterfly kisses.

I'd started out wanting another hard and fast fuck. I didn't want to think about more. To think about my feelings. My heart. I wanted hands and mouth and his cock inside me. I tried, using what little freedom I had to try to drive Tenn as wild as I was. It worked, but not the way I'd planned. His grip on my hips got tighter, his mouth on my body hungrier, more demanding.

He didn't break. Didn't fuck me fast and hard like I thought I wanted. He made me come again and again, surrounding me with touch, soft words, so intimate and revealing. He held nothing back, seducing my heart along with my body until I stopped fighting his tenderness and let him have what he wanted.

Everything.

In exchange for so much sweetness, Tenn could have everything.

I was limp after the third orgasm. Or maybe it was the fourth. I lost count. I just know that when he finally pressed his cock inside me, I gave him a blissful smile and wrapped my legs around his hips, wanting Tenn to find the same pleasure he'd given me.

My legs were wobbly when we finally got up, my lips curved in a goofy smile, my brain spinning.

"I have to get back to work," Tenn whispered in my ear, helping me pull my shirt down and straighten my bra.

"K. Me, too."

One more kiss and he was gone, leaving me still wobbling and trying to remember what I had to get back to. Oh, yeah, the figurine case. And then Parker's room, and after that, on to the library. I sank down onto the plush velvet of the chaise and stared at my knees.

I'd never had sex like that. Not even close.

That's because it wasn't sex. That's what they mean by making love. He made love to me.

I shied away from that thought even as I felt its truth. Sex was great, but Tenn had made love to me. Worshipped me with his body, with his words, with everything he had. How was I supposed to resist a man like that?

I wasn't. A man like Tenn was a gift. Someone to be cherished, not resisted.

The thought left me sick at heart. I wasn't in the position to cherish any man. Sex, making love, fucking—it didn't matter what I called it, it was too much. Too much distraction, too much complication, too much whatever. I shook my head, trying to dislodge the arguments I'd been having with myself since the second I set eyes on Tennessee Sawyer.

I had a task at Heartstone Manor and falling for Tenn Sawyer was not it. I tried to remind myself of that, but my worries weren't enough to dim my sexed-out glow. I got started on the rest of the display cabinet, the post-orgasm hum in my body gradually distracting me from my worries. That and the hope that I might find the Vitellius once I finished with the display cabinet.

I was done with the guest wing in another half hour and moved on to Parker's room. Everything there was neat, only a stray hairpin to reveal that someone lived there. Her room wasn't what I'd expected. Based on the little I'd seen of her, I guess I thought it would be conventionally pretty.

Instead, she'd decorated her rooms in a deep navy with accents of cream and aged gold. She'd furnished it with antiques, the pieces substantial but not bulky. Here and there, she had touches of something... different. A delicate glass sculpture of a fairy I instantly coveted. A woven silk scarf in a riot of color draped over the back of an armchair.

She had a few beautiful pieces of art, some valuable and some not as much. None were the Vitellius. Of course not. I could see from her rooms that Parker had an elegant, ageless style with hints of whimsy. She has far too much class and appreciation for beauty to display the squat little bust of Vitellius.

I'd have to arrange to catalog the other family rooms one by one. Moving on, I started on the main level of the house. Here, most of the art was concentrated in the library, Griffen's office, and the family gathering room. I'll admit, I got a little distracted in the library. There was so much there: the books themselves, the pieces I'd spotted on my first tour, and everything I discovered once I wasn't distracted by Tenn.

I didn't see Tenn for the rest of the day. He must have been shut up somewhere with his laptop, working remotely on Inn business. I didn't miss him. Really. I wanted to be left alone to work. It was more efficient. And the faster I could work, the more likely I'd find the bust of Vitellius.

Bryce didn't confront me again, not directly, but he was around. By the end of the day, I felt like every time I looked up he was lurking outside the doorway or waiting in the hall to watch me as I walked by.

He made my skin crawl. It wasn't just him calling me a *tasty little snack* or the predatory way he'd approached me, a combination of intimidation and intent that left no doubt what he would do if he thought he could get away with it. That was bad enough. But there was something else in his eyes when he watched me. A calculation that wasn't sexual. I didn't want his hands on me, not in a million years, but somehow, him watching me like I was a puzzle to be solved was more unnerving than the thought that he might corner me while I was alone.

Thanks to Tenn and Hawk I had that panic button always in my pocket, just a touch away. That would have to be enough.

We ate in Tenn's suite again, joined by Nicky and August, who watched cartoons while eating at the coffee table as they had a few days before. Tenn and I shared another intimate meal at the small table he'd rolled in, almost able to pretend the boys weren't there.

Pushing away my reservations and worries, I let myself relax and enjoy being with Tenn like he was just a guy and we were on a date. Like we were learning each other, enjoying each other, with nothing more to worry about than whether he'd kiss me at the end.

He did kiss me, but that was it, and Tenn didn't seem to mind. He was lying in bed after I got August tucked in, the sheets pulled to his waist, his gorgeous chest on display and the remote in his hand. "Movie?"

"Sure." I got ready for bed and slid in beside him, loving the easy way I curled into him, my head on his chest, his arm around me, his fingertips curving around to graze my breast. A flash of heat went through me. Reluctantly, I glanced through the open door to the couch. "We can't. Not with August—"

Tenn's hand stilled and a soft kiss pressed to the top of my head. "I know. I have plans to find you in a dark corner tomorrow, lock the door, and have my way with you."

I giggled. Actually giggled. "Oh, you do, do you?"

I fell asleep right there, happier than I had any right to be, pretending the man in my arms was mine and all was right with my world.

I couldn't have been more wrong. My peace would only last as long as the night, shattering after the sunrise with a chime from my phone.

Chapter Twenty-Six

SCARLETT

Augustust crawled into bed with us again, the shaking of the mattress waking me gradually. A finger poked me in the shoulder. "Mom. Cartoons?"

I blinked awake to August's familiar eyes, focused on his goal. Cartoons. Never mind that his mother was snuggled up to our host in his bed. August didn't seem to register that there was anything odd about that. I wasn't sure if that said something about his resiliency or his love of cartoons. Maybe both.

While I was still trying to figure that out, squinting against the morning sun, Tenn passed the remote to August, who had no trouble navigating to his preferred channel and, with a contented sigh, leaned into me and lost himself in the dramas of his favorite Australian dog.

I stayed where I was, my head on Tenn's shoulder, his arm around me.

"You sleep well?" he asked in a low tone August missed.

"Mmm-hmm. You?" I traced circles on his chest with my fingertip.

"Mmm-hmm."

That was all we said. It worked for me. I didn't want to talk, I wanted to stay exactly where I was. I didn't want to get up. I didn't want to go anywhere. I wanted to pretend that this was my life now, and I'd always feel as good as I did right there, cuddled up to Tenn, lazing in bed.

My sense of well-being lasted until the next commercial break.

Beneath the loud jingle for an upcoming kids' show, a familiar tone hit my ears. A text alert. On my phone. I popped upright, dislodging August, and twisted to search the room. Where was my phone?

Tenn, catching my distress, opened his bedside table and pulled out the phone, the text alert still showing on the screen.

I'm good. Call soon. <U

I didn't recognize the number, but the message was definitely from Thatcher. That last part was a little joke between us. His own shorthand for *love you more* without the heart because Thatcher said he wasn't a hearts and flowers kind of guy.

I grabbed at the phone, unlocking the screen and dialing the unknown number. It rang once before a mechanical voice alerted me that the mobile user hadn't set up his voice mailbox. I tried again, calling twice more to the same result.

With a grunt of frustration, I tossed the phone on the bed. *He's okay. He said he was, and he wouldn't have texted if he weren't okay.* I tried to reassure myself, but I wasn't buying it. It was a text, not a phone call. Video chat would have been even better. And I had no guarantee Thatcher had even sent it. I didn't think anyone else knew our in-joke, but this whole situation was proving that I didn't know as much as I thought I did.

I sat there, the sounds of August's show ringing in my

ears, and the reality of my situation smacked me in the face. I was lying in bed with a man I barely knew, I was no closer to finding the bust of Vitellius than I had been when I got here, and worse, I'd managed to embroil myself in a murder investigation. I wasn't completely sure why Thatcher had sent me here or how much danger we were in—even before Vanessa's murder—and I'd brought my eight-year-old along for the ride.

There was no other way to look at it. I was a terrible mother, an idiot, and a fool. Here I was, snuggling with Tenn Sawyer, who I barely knew but had slept with too many times, spinning dreams of staying here forever when clearly all of that was impossible. I wanted to pack August up and flee for home. Except I couldn't because there was Thatcher.

"Who was the text from, Scarlett?"

Tenn's quiet question interrupted my spiraling thoughts. Deliberately, he picked up the phone and put it back in his bedside drawer. I couldn't let him do that. Thatcher had said he'd call me later. I needed that phone.

"Give me my phone, Tenn." I tried to hide the worry in my voice. To sound strong. Tenn only stared at me in the same way Bryce did. As if I were a puzzle to be solved.

Finally, he said, "I don't think so. Not until you tell me who that text was from."

Why did he need to know? He couldn't demand I trust him. That wasn't how trust worked.

"Give me back my phone, Tenn." I met his eyes with a steady gaze. "You don't have the right to keep it from me. It's mine."

"This is my house. I have the right to do anything I want."

His words sent a chill through me. Just yesterday, the

handcuffs he'd taken from the police chief had been a sensual promise well-fulfilled. Now, they were a threat. He had my phone. We were trapped here. And I'd let my hormones blind me to our reality. We were prisoners and I'd been sleeping with the enemy.

"Is that really what you think?" I asked, my voice dull.

A hint of discomfort crossed Tenn's face before he repeated his request. "Tell me who the text was from."

And if I did? What if that put Thatcher at risk? I'd made so many stupid mistakes since this whole situation began. I couldn't afford to make any more. "What if I tell you? Will you promise to give me back my phone?"

I wasn't sure it was the right thing to do, but I could compromise if it meant getting my phone back. I couldn't bear the idea that Thatcher would call and I'd miss him. Tenn made the decision easy.

"No phone. Not unless you're prepared to tell me everything. Who sent that text. What you're doing here. Everything." His jaw was set, eyes hard. Nothing about Tenn suggested he was willing to bend. I could meet him halfway but not if he wasn't going to do the same. Not when I had so much at risk.

"I can't," I whispered miserably.

I watched in stunned silence as Tenn got out of bed, grabbing my phone from the drawer. "I guess that's the end of that, then." He went into the bathroom and locked the door, shutting me out.

I didn't know what to do other than sit in bed with August and watch cartoons, hoping Tenn would be in a better mood when he came out of the bathroom. No such luck. He emerged, freshly showered and dressed, my phone sticking out of the front pocket of his jeans, his eyes hard and dark. "I need to get to work." Tenn left without another word.

In a daze, I took my own shower and got dressed, enticing August away from cartoons and into regular clothes with a promise of breakfast and Nicky. Savannah must have noticed something off when I brought Nicky down to their rooms behind the kitchen.

"Hey, you okay?" Her grey eyes were concerned. Kind. I wished I could trust her.

"Fine, just tired. And I had an argument with Tenn," I found myself admitting.

She rolled her eyes. "Not a surprise. He's got a hard head, and he's bossy."

I opened my mouth to stick up for him and remembered that I was furious with him. Savannah was right, he was bossy. And hardheaded. And dictatorial. And— I stopped that train of thought before I opened my mouth and it turned into a full-blown rant.

Savannah flashed me a smile. "Don't worry, he'll get over himself."

"Maybe," I offered, not at all sure that he would. Or that he should. Yes, he should give me my phone. But I also kind of understood why he refused. He had a right to know what I was doing in his house. It wasn't his fault I couldn't tell him.

He should just trust me.

Why, when I refused to trust him?

We were at a stalemate, and I was not at all confident either of us would be able to get over it. I dodged Savannah's comment and changed the subject. "Are you sure you're fine with watching August? I know you have a lot to do and—"

"Not a problem," Savannah reassured me. "My mother

will be here in an hour, and August is wonderful with Nicky. Really, it's fine."

"Okay," I agreed weakly, and without another excuse, took my tablet and made my way to the library to begin another day of searching for the little bust of Vitellius.

The day crawled by. I second-guessed every choice I'd made since Thatcher took off. I should have called the police. I shouldn't have driven to Sawyers Bend or tried to meet a Sawyer so I could search their house. I should have—

I didn't know. The more I ran over it in my head, I didn't have any idea how to move forward except to keep searching for the bust of Vitellius while I waited to hear from Thatcher. Also, I should never have sex with Tenn Sawyer again. Definitely not.

My resolve lasted until shortly after lunch, a meal I skipped in case Tenn was there. Or Bryce. Or anyone. I didn't want people. I wanted to be alone to stress and sulk and generally vacillate between misery and worry.

Tenn scared the hell out of me when he came into the mostly empty gallery by the library, standing in the doorway, watching me much as Bryce had earlier in the day. I tried to ignore him as I had Bryce. It didn't work. After a moment's contemplation, Tenn strode into the room, taking my elbow in his hand, and half-led, half-dragged me to a tiny room off the hall.

Shutting us in the tiny room, he flicked a switch, illuminating the wood-paneled walls and built-in counter with an upholstered chair in front of it. On the counter was an ancient rotary dial phone, the cord frayed and dangling off the side of the table.

"What is this?" I asked, avoiding Tenn's eyes.

"A telephone room. From back in the days when the

house only had one phone. You could come in here to talk privately. No one uses it anymore."

"Oh." I risked a glance at Tenn's face. His expression remained hard, his jaw set, just as it had been that morning.

"Are you ready?" he asked.

I shook my head, not getting it. Ready for what? Not— Hadn't I decided I wasn't— "Ready?" I parroted, stalling.

"To talk to me. Are you ready?"

I had to shake my head, a sorry, stubborn *no*.

I didn't know enough to tell Tenn the truth. What if he was the one who had the Vitellius? I'd searched his rooms, but this was a massive house, filled with cabinets and closets and a million places to hide something that small. A sinking feeling weighted my chest at that thought. The thief could be anyone, and the Vitellius could be anywhere. I was on my own.

"I can't," I forced out. Tenn's jaw flexed, but he gave nothing else away.

He lifted one hand and the light flicked off, blanketing us in darkness. Tenn's hands closed over my shoulders. "That's okay." He dipped his head to rub his cheek against mine, the light scratch of his stubble, the heat of his scent, clouding my head. "We don't have to talk if you don't want to. I can think of other things to do with your mouth."

So could I. I could think of a lot of things I wanted to do with my mouth while closed up in a dark room with Tenn.

Hadn't I just told myself this was a bad idea?

So many things I should have done but didn't. I didn't turn on the light. Or push him away. I didn't leave. I lifted my face to his, accepting his kiss. Kissing him back. I let him unbutton my shorts and pushed them to the floor myself. And when he lifted me to sit on the counter, I spread my legs in welcome.

It was the hard and fast fucking I'd wanted so badly the day before. It didn't take much to push me over the edge, my fingers gripping his arms, heels tight to his ass, holding him close as he followed me into orgasm with a harsh cry.

I almost believed we could work past this stalemate when he whispered, "The only time you're not lying is when I fuck you."

He pulled out, fixed his pants, and left. The brief moment of hope crumbled into dust. I'd wanted hard and fast, had gotten it, and now sat alone, inner thighs sticky and cold, feeling used and stupid.

When Bryce bumped into me after my trip upstairs to clean up and change, I didn't have the heart to bother being afraid of him. I sliced a scathing look his way, said, "I have work," and brushed by him.

By the end of the day, I wanted to curl into a ball and cry. I dodged dinner with the Sawyers in favor of eating with the kids in Savannah's rooms. Not realizing what I was doing, I lingered over putting August to sleep on the couch, delayed getting ready for bed, and finally gave up. Tenn wasn't coming.

I woke in the night to find myself wrapped around him, face tucked into his neck. Mortified, I rolled away until he pulled me back.

"Go to sleep, Scarlett."

I didn't think I could, but I did, the solid thump of his heart lulling me back to sleep.

When I woke, he was gone.

So was my phone. Again.

Chapter Twenty-Seven

SCARLETT

B y Wednesday morning, I was about to pop from the tension. Tenn hadn't spoken to me since his brief words while we slept. As far as I knew, he was holed up in Griffen's office on a conference call with Royal, going over Inn business. August was happily playing with Nicky and Miss Martha, and I was finally finished cataloging the art in the Heartstone Manor library.

I hadn't even touched the books, though, in my opinion, a lot of the older texts were just as much art as the paintings and sculptures scattered through the room. But books were not my area of expertise, so I passed them by and moved down the hall to an expansive space Savannah had referred to as the family gathering room. I hadn't really paid attention to it the night we watched a movie, too obsessed with Tenn to care about decor.

With an oversized fireplace, comfortable couches and armchairs, tables set up for cards or games, and a huge flat-screen TV, the family gathering room was basically an enormous and very elegant rec room. Despite its size, I imagined it would be cozy in the winter with a fire going. No fire at the end of June, but the tall windows let in the bright summer sun, leaving the room cheery and welcoming.

There wasn't much in here to catalog. The card tables and armchairs looked well-used, but the flat screen and couches had definitely been added recently. There were a few small sculptures in nooks here and there. Sadly, none of them were Emperor Vitellius. I photographed what I found and made notes, ready to move the search somewhere new.

I was almost finished when my head snapped up at the thud of the heavy door closing, my heart jolting at the metallic snick that followed. Not just closed, but locked. He'd better be ready to apologize, especially if he thought I was having sex with him. Which I was not going to do ever again.

Clutching the tablet to my chest, I spun on my heel. My heart fell. I hadn't realized how much I was hoping to see Tenn, to fight and make up and maybe settle this thing between us. For him to beg my forgiveness and promise to give me some time to work out my problems.

The last thing I wanted was Bryce striding toward me, determination in blue eyes the exact shade of the summer sky. If he weren't such an asshole he would have been very hot. The sneer twisting his full lips drained away all that hot and left him looking like a petulant toddler.

I slipped one hand into my pocket, my finger on the panic button just in case. I thought I could handle Bryce, but I wasn't taking any chances. Straightening my spine and lifting my chin, I looked down my nose. "Can I help you?"

He folded his arms across his chest, raking me with a look that attempted to strip off my clothes. "You can drop the act," he said. "I know what you're up to. The way I see it, you have two choices. Either you cut me in or keep working alone and I get you thrown out of the house."

All I had for Bryce was a blank stare. Cut him in? My nerves were already cranked to the breaking point. I didn't have anything left to play games with this jerk.

"I honestly don't know what you're talking about," I said. "What exactly is it that you think you know?"

Bryce's smug expression sent a chill of fear down my spine. "I know that you broke into a cottage at the Inn. And I know you're here searching for something. I'm betting your plan is to rob us blind. The truth is, I don't care. I hate every single person in this house except for my mother."

"The cottage thing is pretty much common knowledge at this point," I argued.

"But the rest isn't. I know you're looking for something, and I've overheard enough to know that you're the best person in this house to tell me what I can sell for a nice load of cash. Fucking Prentice left us with nothing."

"I thought he left you and your mother with room and board? That's far from nothing." I shouldn't be poking at the asshole, but I couldn't seem to help myself.

Bryce's sneer deepened, twisting his face, his eyes dark with anger. "Room and board is bullshit. Prentice had billions. He couldn't slide some of that our way? I'm going to get mine one way or another. Either you help me, or I get you thrown out of this house."

He stepped closer, almost in arm's reach. I hadn't realized how much taller than me he was. My thumb grazed the curve of the panic button. I didn't want to press it. Not yet. Not unless I really had to.

Instead of hitting the button, I tried reason. "You can't have me kicked out. Tenn and Griffen want me here. The police chief told me to stay here. What makes you think they'll listen to you?"

The sneer dropped from Bryce's face, his mouth transforming into a wide, satisfied smile that lit his blue eyes with malice. "They will when I tell them about the goodies you have stashed in your duffel bag."

It took a minute for me to understand. I didn't have anything stashed in my duffel bag other than a toiletries case and my dwindling collection of clean clothes. Then, the light came on. There wasn't anything I'd put in my duffel bag. Shit.

"You snuck into Tenn's room and put things in my bag, didn't you? You're a real bastard."

Bryce just grinned wider. "Not a bastard. My parents were married, though you'd hardly know that given how fast my father took off. And you can think of what's in your duffel as insurance. Or incentive. Yours to keep as long as you help me find more."

I opened my mouth to tell him to go to hell. I didn't want whatever he'd stolen and there was no way I'd help him steal more. A heartbeat later, common sense caught up to my temper. Tenn hated Bryce. That meant there was a good chance he'd believe me over his cousin. But Tenn had already caught me committing one crime. It wouldn't be a stretch to believe I'd commit another.

Bryce was right. I only had two choices. He was also wrong because my choices weren't what he thought they were. Getting thrown out of Heartstone Manor couldn't happen. Not until I found Vitellius and Thatcher. Which left me with this: come clean to Tenn or throw my lot in with Bryce.

I didn't have to think for very long. My heart racing so fast I struggled for breath, I forced out, "What do you want me to do?"

"For starters, I want a good faith offer. Think of it as a

down payment on my silence. If you were going to smuggle something out of here, what would you take?"

"Hawk isn't going to let you walk out of this house with the family's art."

"No, Hawk isn't going to let *you* walk out of this house with their art. You don't have to worry about me. I have my ways, and when it's time for you to leave, I'll help you if you help me."

"Fine." I swallowed hard. "There's a small oil painting on an easel, guest wing, right side of the hall, third bedroom down. On the dresser by the window. It needs to be cleaned, but it's fairly valuable."

"Show me in your file." Bryce nodded at the tablet clutched in my hand.

I pulled up the painting in question, a beautiful example of impressionism by an artist who was well-known but not particularly famous. Bryce scanned my entry in the catalog.

"There's no price here," he complained.

"I'm not an appraiser except in very specific circumstances. I didn't put prices down since they wouldn't be useful for insurance or anything legal and Griffen wasn't interested in resale. I'd say if you could get that to someone who knows what it is, you'd walk away with at least seven to ten thousand. More if it's been professionally cleaned, but that's not cheap."

Bryce read the entry in the database again, mulling over my feeble offering. The truth was, there weren't many high-value items lying around the house. I didn't have much better to offer. I didn't even consider telling him about the Roman aryballos or Ming vase in the library. They were a part of history.

Finally, Bryce nodded his agreement at my screen.

"Find me more like this and I'll keep my mouth shut. Got me?"

Gripping the tablet with both hands to keep them from shaking, I asked, "And what if Hawk searches my things? They'll kick me out and you won't have anything."

"That sounds like your problem. And don't even think about moving what I stashed in your bag. I'll be checking. If it's gone, I'll just add more. I own you now."

Bryce closed the scant distance between us, looming over me. I shoved one hand in my pocket to finger the panic button. I couldn't use it. Not now. Not unless I was desperate. Bryce wasn't the first horny asshole I'd had to fend off. I could deal with him. I had to.

Narrowing my eyes, I glared up at him. "Don't even think about it. I'd rather be arrested than let you lay a finger on me."

The sneer was back, Bryce's confidence grating. "What makes you think you get to say no? Have you ever been to jail? Are you sure you're ready to find out what it's like? And what about your kid? What happens to him when you get arrested?"

I was shaking, and Bryce could see it. The tremble in my shoulders, the way my teeth gritted so they wouldn't chatter. My heart raced so fast I was light-headed. Could he have me thrown in jail? Could he hurt August?

My gut said no. My gut said Tenn wouldn't let that happen.

Why not? Who was I to Tenn, really? He wasn't even speaking to me.

And if he thought I was a thief? If he thought I was lying to him even more than he already knew I was?

The only time you're not lying is when I fuck you.

I swallowed again, forcing back my terror at Bryce's

vision of my future. Not even to stay out of jail would I let him touch me. He was just another in a long list of entitled men who thought they had a right to my body because they wanted it. Well, fuck them and fuck him.

Sucking in a tight breath, hating the way my voice shook, I said, "I'll help you steal, but if fucking you is part of the deal, you might as well call Tenn and Griffen in here right now because it's not going to happen. Ever. Got me?"

"You're awfully confident for a woman backed into a corner."

I shook my head, my throat almost too tight to force out words. "We all have lines we won't cross. That's mine. If you want my help, deal with it. Otherwise, you can wait for the next art history professor to move into Heartstone Manor."

The muscles in Bryce's jaw flexed, his lips pressed together in an unhappy line. "We'll see. I'll take this for now. Find me something else by the end of the day. Remember," his gaze stripped me from head to toe, "if you want to stay out of jail, you'd better keep me happy."

I stood frozen as Bryce strode from the room, listening to his footsteps echo down the hall, my mind racing. I'd been wrong. I didn't have two choices. I only had one. I just had to hope it wouldn't come back to bite me on the ass.

Chapter Twenty-Eight

TENN

"Is Forrest up to speed on the changes to the cottages?" Griffen asked Royal, who'd joined us in Griffen's office via the screen on the desk. I had to force my attention back to the meeting. We'd already discussed Forrest sneaking around the house. Royal was keeping an eye on him at the Inn, and so far, he hadn't done anything suspicious. We'd decided to take a watch-and-wait approach.

Scarlett was working down the hall in the family gathering room, and I was trying to pretend it wasn't killing me that she was so close. I was the one who'd shut her out. When she'd refused to tell me about the text, my temper had flared, driven by ugly, sour jealousy.

Who was texting her? I didn't know what it meant, but the *<U more* part felt like a secret language. Was this her boyfriend? Husband?

How could she be getting secret texts from some guy and also sleeping with me?

I'd been okay with her secrets until I thought I had

competition. By the time I realized I was being a jealous ass, I'd already driven a wedge between us.

I should apologize.

But... should I?

We both knew she was lying to me. She was here in town, in my home, under false pretenses. She said she wasn't here to hurt my family, but how could I know that? Soon enough, either West was going to find out who'd shot Vanessa, or he was going to tell us to go about our lives because he didn't have a suspect. No suspect and no hope of one meant that Scarlett wasn't in danger. She'd leave, and this would all be over.

That should have been a relief. It wasn't. It left me feeling hollow. I didn't want her to go. All the other stuff aside, I didn't want her to go, and I had no idea what to do about that.

Royal's voice cut into my thoughts, dragging me back to the meeting. "He's good," Royal said, still talking about Forrest. "It took longer than expected since his trip out of town delayed our meeting, but, at this point, I've shifted most of the oversight to him."

"Great. Anything else you need to go over with Tenn?" Griffen looked up at me. "I can give you my desk if you need it."

"I don't think so—" A tinny jingle sounded from my back pocket. What the fuck? My attention sharpened as I realized it was Scarlett's phone. A phone that hadn't rung since I'd taken it from her. Forgetting all about Royal and Griffen, I pulled the phone from my pocket and looked at it. The same number that had sent the text the day before.

Swiping my thumb across the screen, I held the phone to my ear. "Yes?"

"Who is this?" A suspicious voice. Male, and much younger than I'd expected.

"Who are you?" I countered.

A long heavy pause. I could hear breathing on the other end, the sounds of traffic in the background. "I'm Thatcher Hall."

"Thatcher Hall, I'm Tennessee Sawyer."

"Sawyer," he breathed, the word tinged with surprise and a hint of wonder. Weird. Then, he sucked in a breath and demanded, "Why do you have my mom's phone? Is she okay?"

"She's fine," I said immediately. I'd thought about playing him for a second, but this was a kid worried about his mom. I wanted to know what Scarlett was up to, but I wasn't a total asshole. "Do you want to talk to her? I can bring her the phone."

I looked up to Griffen and pointed at the phone. He nodded back, telling me he could hear Thatcher's side of the conversation. I thought about putting him on speaker so Royal could listen in, but I didn't want the kid to realize he had an audience and get spooked.

"No, uh, that's okay. I have to go. But, uh, you're sure she's okay? Is she... is August..."

"August is here. I promise, they're both fine. Your mom will be upset she missed you. Hang on and I'll get her."

I turned and headed for the door. Scarlett was just down the hall. I could be wrong, but my gut said that Thatcher was the reason Scarlett had been demanding to see her phone.

"No, wait! Are you in Sawyers Bend?"

I stopped. "We are. Where are you?"

Thatcher ignored my question. "Awesome. I have to go. I'm not supposed to have this phone. Just tell my mom that

I'm fine and I'll be there in a few days. I'll call her—" A male voice shouted something. The kid, impatient, yelled back, "I'm coming, one sec—"

The line went dead before I reached the door. I tapped the number to return the call, but it went straight to an announcement telling me I couldn't leave a voicemail. Someone had turned off the phone. Thatcher? Or the person who wouldn't let him have his phone? And why was Scarlett's kid off with someone who wouldn't let him talk to his mother? Had he been kidnapped? But then why hadn't Scarlett called the police? What the fuck was going on?

As if my questions had conjured her from thin air, Scarlett appeared in the doorway, her hand raised to knock on the frame. "Can I come in? We need to talk."

Damn right we did. I shoved the phone in my pocket and gestured to the couch. Glancing back at the desk, I saw Royal still on the screen, watching his view of the office intently. "Is this a private conversation? Just so you know, Royal's on a video call."

Scarlett didn't sit on the couch, but she did turn and give Royal a wave. Her eyes landed on Griffen and she flashed a weak smile. "No, it's better if you're all here. Um—" She scrubbed her palms over her face and I realized how pale she was, her hands trembling as she tucked her hair behind one ear.

"What happened? Is it Bryce? Did he—"

Scarlett cut me off with a shake of her head. "No. I mean, yes, it's Bryce, but—" Snapping shut her mouth, she spun to retrace her steps, closing the door carefully. Turning back, she took two steps into the office and stopped, gripping her hands in front of her.

Eyes on me, she started to talk. "Bryce confronted me in the family room, said he wanted me to help him find items

218

in the house that he could sell. He stashed some things he'd already taken in my duffel bag, and he said if I refused to help him, he'd tell you to search my stuff to prove I was stealing from you."

Scarlett paused to draw in a breath and cross her arms over her chest. "I know he's your family and I'm a stranger you met after I broke into one of your cottages. I know you have no reason to believe me, but I swear, I didn't steal anything."

I stared at her, keeping my face impassive. "What else did he want?"

Scarlet rolled her eyes to the ceiling, a little of her spirit coming back. "The same thing all spoiled dickheads want, but I told him that was where I drew the line. He didn't appreciate it when I said I'd rather go to jail than sleep with him, but a woman has to have standards."

Royal's bark of laughter sounded through the computer speakers, drawing a faint smile to Scarlett's lips.

"What's in your duffel bag?" I asked.

"Other than my clothes and toiletries? I have no idea. I came straight here after Bryce left. But he said he salted it with things he's stolen from the house. He said he had a way of getting things past security. And he said if I put those things back, he'd just do it again."

Griffen typed something into his phone and looked up at Scarlett. "Hawk's on the way." Griffen's phone beeped. He glanced down at the screen. "He said two minutes." Griffen narrowed his eyes on Scarlet, seeming to absorb everything he needed to know in a glance. "Sit down before your knees give out on you, Scarlett." He waited until she crossed the room to one of the couches. "What did he threaten you with? Specifically."

Scarlett sank slowly to the edge of one couch, her shoulders drooping as some of the tension drained out of her. Griffen typed something else into his phone as Scarlett answered. "Specifically, he said that if I didn't help him steal from you, he'd have me thrown out of the house. When I said I wouldn't sleep with him, he threatened me with jail."

"Motherfucker," I muttered. My head snapping up, I threw a look at both my brothers.

Before I could get out a word, Griffen staked his claim. "Dibs. You hit him last time. It's my turn."

"I get a shot after Griffen," Royal added. "Maybe if we catch him trying to fence something, we'll have enough to throw him out of the house."

"We can only hope," Griffen said. He sent me a look, his eyes meeting mine then dropping to the phone in my pocket. One dark eyebrow raised. It was like he was reading my mind.

I withdrew the phone from my pocket and held it up so the screen was facing Scarlett. "Who is Thatcher?"

Scarlett shot to her feet, her neck craning as she frantically searched the room. "Is he here?" Abruptly, she realized why I'd held out the phone and snatched it from my fingers. Tapping the screen, she pulled up the call history.

I'd had some vague plan about using Thatcher's call to pry Scarlett's secrets from her. Staring into her stricken eyes, I couldn't do it. Scarlett wasn't even trying to hide her fear, and the sight of it was a knife in my chest.

"He said he's fine," I assured her. "I told him who I was and where we were. He said he was on his way here and that he was okay. I tried to get him to wait until I could put you on, but he said he wasn't supposed to have the phone and he hung up. When I called back, it went straight to voicemail."

Scarlett plopped down on the couch so fast I thought

her legs went out on her. Bracing her elbows on her knees, she leaned over and rested her face in her hands, a jagged exhale shaking her body. Was she crying? Shit.

She whispered to herself, her voice floating up through the curtain of her hair, her face still buried in her palms. "—never trust my gut, but it's always right—can't make it worse."

Pulling herself together, Scarlet sat up, finger-combing her hair back from her face and wiping away the moisture beneath her eyes. After taking a deep, steadying breath, she looked at the three of us, Griffen and I in front of her and Royal still on the screen.

"Thatcher is my thirteen-year-old son, and we're in some trouble."

I didn't wait to see what Griffen and Royal thought about that. If Scarlett was ready to talk, I wanted to know everything. Crossing the room, I sat beside her, taking her trembling hands in mine. "Do you need some help?"

Scarlett's eyes went wide with hope tinged by fear. "I'm afraid to ask, but yes. I could definitely use some help."

Apparently, that was all Griffen needed. Turning, he rotated the screen on the desk so it faced the seating area, essentially bringing Royal as close to the conversation as he could get. Taking a seat on the couch opposite Scarlett and me, Griffen said, "Hawk will be here in a minute. Hope is on her way down, and Savannah is bringing tea and something to eat. You look like you're about to pass out, Scarlett."

Scarlett's eyes fixed on her fingers twined with mine as she shook her head. "I'm sorry I didn't tell you before now." She looked up at me, her eyes wet and tired. "It's a lot to have at stake, you know? I want to trust you. I do trust you, but it's my baby on the line."

I pulled my hand from hers. I needed more than

holding her hand. So did she. Wrapping my arm around her, I drew her close, resting my chin on the top of her head. "We're going to figure this out. I promise."

Across from us, Griffen shook his head at me. He knew the same thing we all did. I couldn't make that promise. Not without knowing what the hell was going on. I didn't care. I was going to help Scarlett. Thatcher was going to be okay. I wouldn't accept another option, and neither would Scarlett.

Her voice small, she said, "It's just... he's never been away from me this long. And he's smart. He's so freaking smart, but he's thirteen. He's nowhere near as smart as he thinks he is."

She was killing me. I pressed my lips to her temple. I didn't have any more words of empty reassurance. Until we knew more, I wouldn't make any promises. I was optimistic. Not stupid.

It felt like it took an hour for everyone to assemble in Griffen's office. Hawk showed up first, lifting his chin at us and nodding at Scarlet before sitting on the other side of the couch from Griffen and pulling out his phone. He didn't acknowledge anyone except to send another nod in Hope's direction when she sat beside Griffen.

Savannah rolled in the tea cart and left without a word. When everyone had a drink, a snack, or both, we all turned to Scarlett.

Chapter Twenty-Nine

SCARLETT

I leaned into Tenn's arm, working up the courage to bare my secrets. I should have been terrified. I *was* terrified. I hadn't known these people long enough to trust them. That's what I kept telling myself.

You don't know the Sawyers. They have no reason to believe you. No reason to help you.

That was all true. Logical. What if I told them and they turned on me? It was a risk, no question. A huge risk.

Lately, I'd been thinking a lot about risk and listening to my gut. Most of my ill-fated marriage had been a war between my gut telling me to grab the kids and get the hell out and my common sense convincing me to stay. My common sense was lacking the sense part.

Since the day we met, I'd wanted to trust Tenn. I reached for him in my sleep. I looked to him when I laughed. Something about Tenn drew me, something I couldn't define, didn't even recognize, but it was there. Every day, I thought it would fade, and every day, it only got stronger. It was so much more than sex. I already knew I couldn't walk away.

Then there was Thatcher. I needed help. I had to take a chance on the Sawyers.

Taking a sip of tea, I put my thoughts in order. "Five months ago, your father sent a carved crystal bust of Roman Emperor Vitellius to an auction house I work with. Normally, I wouldn't be called in to appraise a piece like that. They have someone more qualified in-house, but she was called out of town on an emergency. They used another qualified appraiser, but they asked me to take an unofficial look while I was there appraising a glass vase. The bust of Vitellius went up for sale a week ago. It was stolen from inventory before the owner could pick it up."

Griffen leaned forward. "What was it worth?"

"It was appraised for $7,500 and went for a little less than that. It was the only item stolen. Everything else was untouched."

"Weird," Tenn murmured under his breath.

"Very," I agreed.

"So, what does this have to do with your son?" Hope asked, her hand on the slight curve of her belly as she sipped her tea.

"It's not so much my son that's the problem. It's my ex-husband. Elliot had a part-time job at the auction house doing maintenance, and apparently, he leveraged that to figure out how to bypass their security. He took the statue as a job for some very scary guys."

Hawk's head popped up. "How scary? Names?"

"Leary," I answered.

"Boston Learys?" Hawk's eyes narrowed on me. I didn't like that he seemed to know who they were. I wasn't ready for the Learys to have a national reputation for badness. Not when they were after my kid.

I nodded. "Yes. Boston Learys. Do you know them?"

"Know of them." His eyes went to Tenn, then Griffen. He gave a short shake of his head that I took as a very bad sign.

"So, Elliot has the bust?" Hope asked.

"I wish," I said, rolling my eyes. "If Elliot had it, he would have given it to the Learys already. He's a dumbass, but he's way too scared of the Learys to double-cross them. And if he was stupid enough to still be holding on to the bust, I would have solved this whole problem and called the police."

"You'd call the police on your ex-husband?" Griffen asked, one dark eyebrow raised.

His speculative look startled a laugh out of me. "Absolutely. He had the boys overnight when he took that damn bust! He couldn't wait one night to commit a felony?" I shook my head. "If I'd had any idea what was going on, I would have had his ass in a cell."

"But Elliot doesn't have the bust anymore, does he?" Tenn was already a step ahead.

"No. Someone broke into his place—while my boys were there—and stole it. Then, Elliot shows up at my house in the middle of the night, trying to drop off the boys so he can run from the Learys until he finds the bust. I managed to get my hands on August, but Thatcher refused to leave his dad. Thatcher said Elliott was going to get in more trouble if he didn't watch out for him. Elliott got tired of arguing, took Thatcher, and they disappeared."

I slumped back into Tenn's arm, relief washing through me. Not total relief. I wouldn't be there until I had my kid back so I could ground him for eternity. But just telling the truth dropped a weight from my heart. I hadn't truly realized how much I hated lying to Tenn.

I met his eyes, to find them soft. "You must be scared shitless," he whispered.

"Pretty much," I whispered back.

"Why would the Learys be after a low-value item like the statue?" Hawk asked.

"I don't know." I shrugged, the gesture not coming close to illustrating my frustration at being unable to answer that one question. "I've been racking my brain to figure out why anyone would go to so much trouble over that specific piece. And the thing is, Elliott only took that one piece. To give you an idea, the top-selling item in that auction went for over half a million dollars and the bulk of the catalog was worth more than the bust of Vitellius. Elliott literally walked past hundreds of thousands of dollars in art to take an ugly little bust that isn't worth that much, either historically or monetarily. Which means the Learys were very clear that they didn't want him getting sticky fingers while he was in there. They must have scared him because Elliot has crappy impulse control."

"Exactly the kind of person who'd add a few things to the take while he was inside," Griffen commented.

I nodded. "So, the fact that he went to all the trouble of getting in there and just took the bust of Vitellius means something. The security was pretty good. Not the best on the market because they like to pinch pennies, but still, not easy to bypass. Which means Elliott went to considerable time and effort to get in and then only took that one thing."

"And that sculpture originally belonged to our father?" Royal asked from the computer screen. "Do you have a picture?"

I flipped through my phone and pulled up the picture I'd downloaded from the website after Elliott and Thatcher had taken off. I'd studied that picture for hours, trying to figure out what was so special about the piece. Was it possible the Sawyers would know?

"Send that to me," Griffen said.

I found him in the list of contacts that popped up on my phone screen and dropped him the picture. A few seconds later, he had it up on the monitor, split-screen with Royal.

We all stared at the bust of Emperor Vitellius with its rock crystal carving, dull in contrast to the bright brass medallions on the white marble base. Royal interrupted the silence. "Do we know how long Dad had that thing?"

Griffen shook his head. "Harvey might be able to dig up the records." He turned to me. "Any chance you'd know if that was the first item our father sent to that auction house?"

"I'm sorry. I usually only do glasswork appraisals for them, and those don't come up that often. I don't have anything to do with the sales and client side. I wouldn't even have known the bust belonged to your father except that I reviewed the other appraiser's report after I finished my examination, and that report included the chain of custody."

"Is that why you came here?" Hope asked.

"No. Not directly." I took another deep breath to steady myself, trying to untangle the threads of the story in my head. Too many people were involved and there was too much I didn't know. "Elliott said something to Thatcher about the thief heading to Sawyers Bend. I think—I don't know, but I think—that Elliot knows who took the statue. And whoever it is, they were headed here."

"Here to Sawyers Bend?" Hawk asked.

"No," I corrected, "here to Heartstone Manor."

Everyone sat back, not expecting that bit of information.

"But you don't know who? Or why they'd be coming

here?" Tenn's eyes searched my face for an answer. I wished I had more to give him than a shake of my head.

"All I really know is that Elliot stole the statue for the Learys, then someone stole the statue from Elliot, and that person is bringing it to Sawyers Bend. And something Elliott said made Thatcher think they weren't just coming to the town, they were coming here, to Heartstone Manor. I have no idea who took it or why they'd want the sculpture. But if Elliot doesn't get it back to the Learys, they're going to kill him. Which would be his problem except he has my son."

Hawk set his phone down on the coffee table and pinned me with intent, dark eyes. "What's our goal here, Scarlett? Get the statue? Find the thief? Help your ex with the Learys? Find Thatcher?"

"Thatcher," I said without a moment of hesitation. "I don't care about the rest of it. I'm done cleaning up after Elliott's messes. He's my kids' dad, and they love him, so I don't want anything bad to happen to him, but this is his problem. He didn't have to steal, he chose to, and then he dragged our son into the line of fire. All I want is Thatcher."

Tenn shared a glance with Griffen. Griffen nodded. "I'll call Cooper, get him moving on this."

I wasn't sure who Cooper was, but I knew what Griffen's job used to be. "I want your help," I said, hating myself for being honest if it meant they'd withdraw their offer, "but I can't afford to call anyone in on this."

"Don't worry about it," Griffen said. "I've had their forensic accountant looking for the missing art and where the money went if it was sold, but it's worse than looking for a needle in a haystack. Finding your son is the priority, but if this leads to uncovering more of what our father was doing with the art collection, I think we can make a case that the Manor trust should cover the cost of the investigation."

My shoulders slumped with relief. Tenn had said Griffen used to work with the best private security company in the country. If anyone could find Thatcher, it would be them. Hawk held out a hand to Tenn, who leaned forward to give him my cell. Using my face to unlock the screen, Hawk pulled up Thatcher's call and started texting on his own phone. Muttering as he worked, he said, "Sending this over to Coop now so he can get moving on tracing the phone."

"They turned it off," I said.

The side of Hawk's mouth lifted in what I think was a smile. "Doesn't matter." Done typing, he lifted his head and shifted on the couch to face Griffen. "They need to go in soft when we find them if we want to recover the ex and the statue along with the kid."

"You think the ex is working with another buyer?" Griffen asked. That thought hadn't even occurred to me. Griffen focused his attention my way. "I know you said he wouldn't double-cross the Learys, but how sure are you about that?"

I wished I had a different answer. "Not sure enough. Elliott isn't stupid so much as greedy and lazy. And he has a gift for electronics. If it weren't for the laziness problem, he could have done something with his life. I want to think he's too smart to double-cross the Learys, but if he was really that smart, he wouldn't have taken the job in the first place. The last time I talked to Thatcher, about twenty-four hours after the statue went missing, Thatcher said he was sure the statue was on its way here."

"And when was that?" Hawk asked.

"Right before I loaded August in the car and headed down here." Thinking back, I added, "Last Thursday night." Less than a week. It felt like a lifetime.

"Who wasn't home Wednesday night?" Hope asked, looking to Hawk. "Were we all accounted for?"

Holding up a finger, he tapped at his phone, eyes glued to the screen. A very long minute later, he looked up and surveyed the room. "Bryce. The only person missing last Wednesday was Bryce. He left just after 10 AM and didn't come back until mid-afternoon on Thursday."

"Well, shit," Griffen said, mostly to himself. "What does he know about that bust that we don't?"

"I've searched his room," Hawk interjected. "I go through it every few days. If he has anything, the bust or other items he's taken from the house, he's not hiding them there."

"Bryce is a problem for later. Right now, we need to focus on finding Thatcher," Tenn said with a comforting squeeze around my shoulders.

Hawk nodded in agreement and looked back at me. "How well do you know your ex-husband?" Hawk asked. "Is he armed? Is Thatcher?"

The thought of my thirteen-year-old son armed with a weapon sent a chill down my spine. "I don't think Thatcher has ever seen a gun except on TV. And Elliott hates them. I can't be sure of anything right now, but I doubt they're armed."

Another long look was shared between Hawk and Griffen. Whatever they were thinking, they appeared to have reached a decision. Hawk went back to typing on his phone, and Griffen looked at Tenn and me. "As soon as Coop gets us a ping on that phone, you two take off to get Thatcher."

"Aren't you guys forgetting something?" Royal's voice boomed through the computer speakers. We all looked up. I'd forgotten he was there. "There's still a week left in the quarter and Tenn already used up most of his days."

I had no idea what that meant, but Tenn's muttered, "Fuck," told me it was a problem. A big one.

Chapter Thirty

Fuck. I'd completely forgotten about the will and the rules. Based on the surprised expressions around me, so had everyone else. Except for Royal. I was glad one of us was thinking.

Scarlett nudged her shoulder into mine. "What's wrong?"

I let out a breath, counting in my head as I explained. "Our father's will requires us to live at Heartstone Manor for five years before our trusts are released to us. We get fourteen days a quarter for travel. Any more and we break the terms of the will."

"How many days were you away this quarter?" Scarlett asked, the hope in her eyes dimming.

"Twelve, I think," I admitted.

"I should have taken that last trip for you and kept it even," Royal said, regret heavy in his voice. I'd insisted he stay home since he had things going on with Daisy and Griffen, and I'd had nothing tying me down but business.

Meeting his eyes through the camera, I shrugged a

shoulder. "We didn't know, and it doesn't matter at this point."

"If you waited a few days, you'd hit the end of the quarter and have another fourteen days," Hawk added absently.

Scarlett's face tightened at the idea of waiting. I'd felt her tension cranking higher with each day that passed. Now that I understood why I knew waiting was out of the question. This was killing her, and Thatcher was a kid who had no business in the crosshairs of people dangerous enough to get Hawk's attention.

"Could you send the Sinclairs after Thatcher?" Hope offered. "Wouldn't that be safer?"

Hawk was already shaking his head. "Coop is tracing the phone, but he's headed out on a job, has to pass the phone off to the in-house team. They're short-staffed right now. Something about an extra bodyguard job that popped up with a regular client who has a stalker and two recoveries." At my questioning look, he clarified, "Kidnappings."

Scarlett's face went pale, but she gave Hawk a nod of understanding. "What happens if Tenn is gone for more than two days?"

I started to answer, but Griffen cut me off. "He loses his inheritance and access to family property, including this house and the Inn."

Scarlett let out a long exhale, her breath blowing her hair back from her face. "So, he doesn't just lose the money, he loses his home and his job, too?" Griffen nodded at her. Scarlett turned to me, her face resolute. "No. You can't risk it. I can go. If August can stay here so I don't have to worry about him—"

"No." I cut her off before she could say more. "You aren't doing this alone. As soon as we have an idea where they are, we'll leave." There was no way in hell Scarlett was going after Thatcher on her own. Not with the Learys in the mix. "We can find him and bring him back in two days."

"And if you can't?" Griffen asked quietly. "I can't change the will. I can't even try without risking everything going to Bryce. Until those five years are up, nothing is really mine anyway. I can't help you if you don't get back in time."

"I know," I said, and there wasn't a doubt in my mind. "I'll have to make sure I'm back here by Friday night." I glanced at Griffen. "Can you talk to Harvey and find out how the fourteen days works? Do I have a full forty-eight hours?"

"I'm on it," Griffen agreed.

Scarlett gripped my hands in hers, tugging them to get my full attention. "I won't let you do this, Tenn. This isn't your problem. You can't risk everything to help me."

"I can. I'm not letting you do this on your own. We'll find him and make it back in time."

"But what if something happens? What if the car breaks down, or we're in an accident, or—"

I pressed my hand over her mouth, stopping her panicked words. "We can do this. We'll wait until we have a solid lead, and then we'll go, grab Thatcher, and be back here before the deadline."

Scarlett ripped my hand from her mouth and looked wildly around the room, her eyes settling on Royal. "Tell him this is insane. Tell him he has to stay here."

Royal just shook his head, a wry smile on his face. "I could try, but it won't do any good."

Scarlett dismissed him and turned to Griffen. "Help me. Anything could happen. It's too big a risk. He barely knows me."

I was curious to see what Griffen would say. He'd

warned me Scarlett could be trouble. Now, her problems had a very real chance of stealing everything I ever thought I wanted. Everything my father had used to manipulate me. Griffen looked at me for a long moment before shifting his glance to Scarlett.

"Here's the thing," he said as if he'd been reading my mind, "our father set the will up like this to control us. He loved the idea of us dancing to his tune even after he was gone. I can't change the will. I can't take away the risk. But I won't try to control my family. Tenn is his own man, and he knows what he wants. If he thinks you're worth taking the chance, then I think he should go for it." Griffen returned his eyes to me. "Just make sure you get your ass back here by Friday at midnight."

Hawk interrupted before I could speak. "Coop has a ping on the phone. The call came out of a cell tower in Winchester, Kentucky. Looks like they really are headed our way. If you waited—"

"No," I cut in. "Not with Thatcher in the mix. If his father was reckless enough to take the kid with him, we can't trust that he'll look out for him if things get sticky." I looked to Scarlett for confirmation.

"I wish I could say you're wrong. Elliott loves his boys, but Elliott's kind of love doesn't hold up under pressure. If they run into trouble, he'll try to look out for Thatcher, but if it comes down to protecting his son or saving his own ass —" She squeezed her eyes shut as untold images of disaster flashed through her mind. Shaking the terrifying thoughts away, she finished, "He'd swear he'd save Thatcher, but he wouldn't. He'd mean to, but he doesn't have the spine to follow through."

"Then let's go pack. The sooner we get moving, the sooner we can bring Thatcher home." I stood, pulling Scarlett up with me. To Hawk, I said, "Can Sinclair Security keep an eye on that phone? Update us if they get another hit?"

"They're on it," Hawk said. "Coop is punting it to Lucas' team. Most of his hackers are out in the field right now, but one of his best is recovering from an injury—"

At Griffen's look of concern, he said, "Floyd, broken ankle, nothing serious." Then, back to me, "Floyd's on Thatcher and Elliott full time until you bring the kid home. He'll find them. He's already got a line on Elliott's burner phone. Trust me, if you're on the run, you don't want Floyd tracking you. Man's a bloodhound. I'll get him your info so he can send you updates."

"I wonder," Hope said absently, her eyes on the teacup in her hand, "if the missing art has anything to do with your father's murder. We keep thinking it's personal, but as we work our way through everything he left behind, the only really odd things are his murder and the missing art."

"Missing art and missing cash," Griffen added. "If he sold it, we still don't know what happened to the money."

"We can figure that part out later," I said, impatient to leave now that we knew where we were going. It was still early enough in the day that we could get to Kentucky by late afternoon if we left right away.

"I know," Hope said, "but if they're related, this might be even more dangerous than you think. Be careful."

I love my sister-in-law, but the last thing I needed was more reasons for Scarlett to insist I stay home. Scarlett looked up at me, panic bright in her green eyes. I put a finger over her lips before she could speak.

"Nope. I'm still coming." Her eyes narrowed. "And every minute you spend arguing is another minute between us and Thatcher."

That got Scarlett moving. She turned and bolted for the door. I followed until Griffen stopped me.

"Take my SUV. Keys are on the board by the garage door. I'll get our stuff out while you're packing."

I shook my head. "I can't. What if you need to go somewhere? That thing is a tank. You—"

"I'll play chauffeur while you're gone," Hawk interrupted without looking up from his phone. "No one's getting assassinated on my watch. Now, get the hell out of here before you lose the day."

"Thanks," I said to Griffen as I headed for the door. "See you all in two days."

Hawk followed me out of the room, jogging ahead of me up the stairs. He beat me to my suite and strode through the open door. "Did you touch the bag?" he demanded as Scarlett came out of the bathroom with a cosmetic case in her hands.

"No, not yet." She set the case on the bed next to a small pile of clothes. "I need to use it, though. Can you—?"

While I grabbed enough clothes and the rest for a few days along with my 9mm and a taser I never used but kept charged anyway, Hawk went through Scarlett's bag, carefully extracting a necklace, a small porcelain figurine, and a rolled-up watercolor. Scarlett winced at the half-assed way the watercolor had been stored.

"Asshole," she breathed as she took the bag from Hawk. We shoved our things inside and finished packing. "Does Savannah know we're leaving? Does she mind keeping August? We can't take him—"

"She knows," Hawk answered. "The boys are down there getting ready for lunch. You have just enough time for a quick goodbye. Try to chill out so you don't scare the hell out of him."

Hawk left with Bryce's stolen art in his hands. Scarlett turned and headed back to the bathroom, splashing cold water on her face and pulling her hair into a neat ponytail. "Better?"

Her eyes were still strained, but August wouldn't be able to tell she'd been on the verge of a nervous breakdown. "Gorgeous," I said honestly. "Now, let's get out of here."

I was behind the wheel of Griffen's massive SUV less than ten minutes later, the GPS set for Winchester, Kentucky.

"Why are we in Griffen's car?" Scarlett asked, twisting in the seat to take in the oversize vehicle. As these things went, it was pretty luxurious, but it wasn't as nice as Griffen could afford. Not at first glance.

"This thing is a tank. Almost literally. It's the same model they use at Sinclair Security. A rocket launcher could probably take us out, but anything less and we can run right over it."

"Really? Like bulletproof glass?" Scarlett rapped her knuckles on the normal-looking window.

"Bulletproof everything. Puncture-proof tires. And I hope it doesn't come to that, but I'm a better-than-average shot." At Scarlett's raised eyebrows, I said, "Family hobby. Probably the only thing any of us ever enjoyed doing with our father."

"Do I want to know why Griffen has a tank for a car?"

"That's a long story." I turned onto the main road, starting the clock on my absence from Heartstone Manor. Scarlett's ankle monitor gave a long beep as we crossed the property line.

"I half expected it to shock me." She stretched out her leg, studying the black band around her ankle. "I kind of forgot it was there. I'm not crazy about looking like I'm under house arrest, but it's kind of comforting knowing Hawk can track us considering."

I knew what she meant. I didn't love the idea of being tracked either, normally, but we didn't know what we'd be walking into when we found Thatcher. It wouldn't hurt to have eyes on us from a distance.

"So, tell me the long story about Griffen's tank." Scarlett pulled her leg back and relaxed into the leather seat.

"I'll tell you the whole story after I make one more phone call." This one wasn't going to go well. Tapping my phone screen with my thumb, I pulled up West's number.

He answered on the second ring. "What now?" he growled.

I almost felt bad for what I was about to do. I gave it to him fast. "Scarlett and I are headed out of town to get her son from her ex. They have a situation. It's complicated, but it doesn't have anything to do with Vanessa. We'll be back by Friday night."

"How the hell do you know it doesn't have anything to do with Vanessa? When did you become a cop?"

"Never. Hawk knows everything we do, you can ask him for details. We'll be back by Friday night. If anything comes up, you can call."

"And if the killer decides you're an easy target now that you're out there without security?"

Beside me, Scarlett sat up straight, turning horror-filled eyes my way. With everything that had happened, she'd temporarily forgotten the reason she was at Heartstone Manor in the first place. I hadn't, but some things were worth the risk. Thatcher's life was one of them.

Chapter Thirty-One

TENN

I shook my head at Scarlett. Vanessa's killer was not our biggest problem right now.

"West, whoever it is would have to find us first. And they don't want me dead, they want me punished. Otherwise, they would have shot me while I was alone in the gardens. Or any number of times I've been alone in the open. Only a handful of people know where we're going, and half of them work for Sinclair Security."

West grunted into the phone but didn't say anything except, "Get your ass back here asap, got me?"

"That's the plan. Call Hawk for more if you need it."

"Yeah, later. Stay safe."

The second I hung up, Scarlett said, "Are you sure about this? I forgot about Vanessa. How could I have forgotten about Vanessa?"

"Because you're scared for your kid and you didn't even know Vanessa. Give yourself a break."

Scarlett stared out the window, watching the trees flash by. "I keep replaying it in my head. Thatcher leaving with Elliott. I keep thinking—if I'd been closer, I could have grabbed him, made him stay. But—" She sighed. "He's thirteen, but he could easily pass for sixteen or seventeen. He's been like that since elementary school, always at least a head taller than everyone else. And he's strong. I couldn't have dragged him back in the house even if I'd tried. He was determined, was positive Elliott would get hurt if he didn't stay to watch out for him."

I reached across to take her hand, squeezing her fingers gently in mine. "We'll find Thatcher. If Hawk says this Floyd guy is a bloodhound, I believe him."

Her fingers squeezed mine back. "I'll feel better when I can put my arms around him." She let out another gust of breath. "I am going to kill Elliott if the Learys don't get to him first."

"Do you share custody?" I wanted to know everything about her ex, but I wasn't sure how to get her talking. Starting with the kids seemed like a good idea.

Scarlett laughed, but the sound was bitter. "No. Not even close. He gets them for the occasional sleepover when he feels like playing Dad. It doesn't happen as often as it should, so I try to make it easy for the boys' sake. They love the asshole no matter how many times he lets them down."

"They'll figure it out eventually." I spoke from experience.

I'd been them once, hanging on to love for a dad who didn't really give a shit about me. I'd wanted him to love me so badly for so long. And then, one day, I didn't want it anymore because I knew my dad's love wasn't worth the cost. If I hadn't figured it out before then, I'd known the day I watched Griffen walk down the long drive of Heartstone, his backpack slung over his shoulder, cast out by his father for trying to do the right thing.

Scarlett sighed again. "I wish Elliott would get it

together so they don't have to figure it out." She glanced over at me. "He's never done anything like this before, you know. Committed a crime—at least that I know of." She stared at the trees for a moment, sifting through her thoughts. "Damn. This isn't the first time, is it?"

I looked over to meet her eyes before looking back to the road. "I doubt it. I don't think you get to know people like the Learys, have them put you to work if you haven't committed a few crimes to get in their orbit."

Scarlett swore under her breath. Shifting in her seat so she faced me, she said, "He's never put the boys in danger as far as I know. Though now, I'm realizing that there's probably a lot that was going on that I didn't know about. But what I'm saying is that I had no clue. Until this happened, I would have said the worst thing he did with the boys was load them up with junk food or show them an R-rated movie. Or bailed on their sleepover night because something came up. Not great stuff, and it bothered me, but none of it was bad enough to cut him off from the kids. Nothing like this."

"Is he the reason you said you don't need another person to take care of?" Her response to the idea of marriage had stuck with me. She laughed again, and this time her laugh was unexpectedly less bitter.

"Oh, yeah. Elliott's not the worst person in the world, but he's a miserable husband as well as a crap father. I never should have married him. He and our parents snowed me. I was young and stupid and I fell for it."

Now I had to know the details. I'd already guessed she'd been young. Twenty, if my math was right. And now she was an art history professor. "What happened?"

"I met Elliott my sophomore year of college. He was a

grad student and he was—" Scarlett looked a little sheepish. "He was really hot."

I rolled my eyes. That was the last thing I'd expected Scarlett to say. She hadn't seemed the least bit affected by looks. Bryce had only earned disdain, and she appeared to be immune to my own better-than-average appearance.

Scarlett's cheeks flushed. "It kills me to admit it, but my studious, focused, nineteen-year-old self was blown away by Elliott Hall. He's so handsome, he's kind of unreal. And he's lazy, but he's even more vain, so he might skip out on work, or chores, or, you know, parenting, but he always has time for the gym. I was a smart girl, but he's the most beautiful human being I've ever seen in real life and I was blinded by him. I mean, what was a guy like that doing with me?"

My ego twinged at her description of her ex. It could have been more than a twinge, but there was no affection in her voice when she spoke of her ex, only amusement at her own idiocy.

"Have you looked in a mirror?" I asked, throwing her a glance. "You're not exactly plain."

"I'm no supermodel, either. Anyway, between his looks and the sex—" Now she flushed a deep red. "I wasn't paying attention to the important stuff. Like how he was skating through his grad program because he was too lazy to handle the higher-level work. The way he couldn't hold down a job. The fact that his mother came by every day to clean and cook for him. I missed everything that mattered. And then the condom broke, and I was pregnant and a junior in college."

"Scary," I commented.

"Terrifying," she agreed. "I wasn't sure what to do, and before I could really think about it, his parents and my parents were pushing marriage. They'd help us buy a little house, and help watch the baby so I could stay in school... If I'd been thinking clearly, I could have taken them up on their offer of help without agreeing to marry Elliott. But he was all for it, too. They found a cute bungalow, and Elliott showed up with a ring, and before I knew it, I was moving out of the dorms and we had a sweet little backyard wedding."

"What about school?"

"Thatcher was born in July, before the start of my senior year. Elliott missed the whole thing. He went on a 'last fun time with the guys' camping trip a week before my due date and left his phone at home."

"What a jackass." I couldn't help it. I had this picture in my head of a barely adult Scarlett going through the pain of labor, her husband nowhere to be seen.

"Totally a jackass. Our moms were there, and they were great, but he was supposed to be my partner. He didn't even apologize, just breezed in the front door—after we'd been discharged from the hospital—and made cute noises over the baby. Everyone wanted me to let it go, and I was too tired to argue."

"I'm surprised you didn't kill him," I said with a sideways glance at Scarlett. This time her laugh was genuine amusement.

"You know, in retrospect, I am, too." She laughed again. "I don't really remember much of my senior year. I had to keep my grades up to keep my scholarship because the last thing I needed was student loans I hadn't planned for. My parents lived an hour away, but Elliott's parents were in the same town. His mom saved my ass that year. I think, if things had been different, she would have encouraged me to be a stay-at-home mom like she was, but it was already clear that Elliott wasn't going to be much good at holding down a job. She knew I had to get through school. She practically lived with us that first year."

"You didn't mind?" I didn't think most young brides would love spending that much time with their mother-in-law.

"No way. I would have drowned without her. She made sure I was getting my work done for school, that I had a ride to class, and she loved Thatch so much, I never worried that he wasn't being cared for. I was so exhausted all the time, it's a blur. Connie cleaned and made dinner, and honestly, I have no idea how she did it all or why Bill, Elliott's dad, didn't mind. When they retired to Florida last year, we all cried. We've been to visit, and they've come back to see us. We video call all the time. Elliott barely even talks to them. They deserve better."

"And your parents?" I wanted to punch her ex, but I was glad his parents had stepped up. At least she wasn't completely alone.

"They were both still working when the kids were babies, and they lived over an hour away in Boston, but they helped as much as they could, especially with the bills and the mortgage. They'd set aside money for a wedding, for someday when I was ready. Instead, they took the cash and put a down payment on our bungalow. The first two years they paid most of the mortgage, though I know it made things really tight on their end. Without our parents, I don't think I would have made it. I definitely wouldn't have graduated from college or been accepted to grad school."

"You went to grad school where you teach now?" It was a guess since she talked about the house like they were still living there.

"That wasn't the plan, but you know how plans go. Forget about Italy or applying to a more prestigious graduate program. At that point, I didn't care. I was head over heels for Thatcher, even if I was starting to have major doubts about Elliott. The college only has a few departments that offer graduate degrees, but their arts program is robust. It's the reason I went there for undergrad. They also offered me an on-campus job that came with childcare, so it was a no-brainer. I worked my way through my graduate degree, basically bringing Thatcher to school with me, while Elliott bounced from job to job and eventually gave up on finishing his own degree."

"Why did you stay with him for so long?" The guy sounded like dead weight, and Scarlett wasn't a woman who took crap from anyone. I know she said he was good-looking, but still...

She let out a huff of breath that pushed her hair from her face. "I don't know. Mostly, those first few years, I was just exhausted and trying to keep my head above water, even with all the help from our families. Then, I finished grad school, got a job as an assistant professor. Thatcher was about to start preschool, and I started thinking about my options. I would have left Elliott then, I think, but I got run down in the winter and caught a sinus infection. The antibiotics messed with my birth control, and we ended up with August."

She glanced over and caught the look of pity on my face. With a sweet smile, she shook her head.

"I know you're thinking I'm nuts and this all sounds like a train wreck, but both my boys were worth every second and more. I'll never regret staying with Elliott long enough to have August. If I'd left earlier, I wouldn't have my little guy, and he's the best."

"He's pretty awesome," I agreed. I wasn't lying. He was a cool little kid, and the bond between the two of them was clear to anyone who spent time with them. If there'd been a way to have the kid without his jackass of a dad, though... that would have been a lot better for Scarlett.

"Elliott missed August's birth because he was playing poker and turned off his phone. *On my actual due date.* That was almost my breaking point. Then Elliott was so happy about the baby, and he offered to stay home with August so I could go back to work, so I decided to give it one more shot. I came home early one day to find Elliott gaming with a headset on while August cried because his diaper was soaked and Thatcher was puking from stealing sips of his dad's rum and Coke. He was five. That was it. I was done."

"He let a five-year-old drink his rum and coke? Poor kid."

"The worst part is, he never even noticed. Just made a drink—at nine in the morning—slapped his headset on and didn't give another thought to the kids. I was afraid Elliott's parents would be angry when I left him. By then, I was as close to them as my own mom and dad—but when I told them what happened, it was the last straw for them, too. They helped me find a lawyer and I kicked Elliott out. They even strong-armed him into signing the papers without trying for part of the house or my car, which was all we owned between us."

"That's good, at least. He could have gone for custody or support since you were the one working."

Scarlett laughed, this one tinged with the bitterness I'd expected earlier. "He threatened to. I'll never know what Connie and Bill said to him, but he dropped all his threats and let us go. In return, I've never kept him from the kids. Never said a bad word about him." She scrunched her nose. "You might have to hold me back when we find them. It's possible I'm going to undo all that maturity and kill him in front of Thatcher."

"What if I kill him for you?" I glanced her way with a raised eyebrow. She thought I was kidding. I wasn't. I was dying to beat the crap out of the guy for so many reasons.

"Not a great idea. Pretty sure they'd hold you for more than two days for that. No sense in losing everything just for the fun of murdering Elliott." She let out a sigh. "Though it would solve a lot of problems." Another sigh. "And it would break Thatcher's heart."

"Not August's?" I asked.

"Maybe August's a little. He doesn't really remember living with his dad. And in the last few years, Elliott has been around less than he was when we first divorced. Lots of broken dates with the kids. A million excuses. August is a practical kid. He's got a good read on his dad. Thatcher still hopes Elliott is going to step up."

"Poor kid." It didn't sound like Elliott Hall was the 'stepping-up' kind of guy.

"Yeah." She stared out the window at the passing scenery. "So, tell me about Griffen coming home after fifteen years. How long has he been married to Hope?"

Sensing that she was ready to change the subject, I launched into the story of the prodigal son's return, starting with murder and ending in true love. Scarlett settled back in the cushy seat, reaching across the center console to rest her hand on my arm, her fingers stroking absentmindedly over my skin, sending shivers of contented pleasure down my spine.

When the story was done, we fell into a companionable silence, watching the miles race by as we moved steadily north to Kentucky. Floyd texted twice, both times letting us know Thatcher's phone hadn't moved from a tight radius around a motel east of town.

We found the motel without any trouble, rolling by slowly, checking it out. The place was run down, with rusted gutters and faded paint, the parking lot crumbling into the weeds. Scarlett sucked in a breath as she spotted something.

"The idiot is driving his own car." Under her breath, she muttered, "At least that makes it easier."

"We've got him now. Just have to grab Thatcher and we can head home."

I should have kept my mouth shut. I already knew nothing is ever that simple.

We weren't the only ones who'd managed to track down Elliott Hall.

And getting Thatcher clear of his father's trouble was going to be a lot trickier than we'd planned.

Chapter Thirty-Two
SCARLETT

Tenn pulled the SUV around the side of the motel, parking next to a dumpster. Smart. The SUV blended in just fine on the freeway, but it would stick out among the aging vehicles in the motel parking lot. On the far side of the dumpster, no one pulling into the motel would see it but we could get to it quickly. He reached into the back seat to grab something. I couldn't quite see what it was and was too wound up to ask.

Thatcher could be only a few feet away. "What if he isn't here?" I whispered as we made our way around to the front of the motel. I passed the first room slowly, trying to glance through the curtains without being obvious about it. A shabby motel room, bed unmade. No personal belongings in sight. Inconclusive.

"We'll find him," Tenn promised, his eyes scanning the parking lot. Thatcher had to be somewhere nearby. Either in his room or within a two-block radius if the mysterious Floyd was as good as Hawk said he was. My heart beat faster just knowing we were close. The next room had its curtains wide open. The third's were completely closed, giving us no way to see inside.

At the fourth, I stopped to tie my shoe, leaning down and peering through the bottom half of the gap between the curtains. A green backpack sewn with gaming patches caught my eye. I knew that backpack. Switching to my other sneaker, I tilted my head to peer deeper into the room, my heart racing so fast it thundered in my ears. He was so close I could almost feel him in my arms.

"This is it," I murmured. For a second, I thought I caught movement. The shift of a shadow, maybe. Something. I waited but didn't see anything else. Standing, I knocked.

Nothing.

I knocked again.

Still nothing. Crap. My stomach turned a little, the letdown painful after the sudden surge of hope.

"Try this." Tenn pulled my little zippered case of lock-picking tools from his back pocket.

"I can't pick this lock," I protested. True, the doors had old-fashioned keyed locks, but surely, they were beyond my skill level. I wasn't a master criminal and there's a big difference between a lockbox lock and the deadbolt on a motel room door.

Tenn wasn't convinced. "You picked the lock on the cottage and it's a lot newer than this one."

"Yeah, but I had almost unlimited time. And it took me a while." I glanced around, taking in the passing cars, the storefronts across the street, the motel office. "If we stand here for too long, someone is going to notice."

Tenn pushed the kit at me again. "Might as well try. If someone comes by, we'll hide the picks, say we lost our key or something."

"Tenn—"

He shoved the kit into my hand. "You can do this, Scarlett."

I took the kit with a shaking hand, tugging at the zipper. Tenn moved to stand behind me at an angle to the rest of the motel rooms, mostly blocking me from sight. He slouched into the door frame, his face a study in boredom. Under his breath, he said, "Relax, Scarlett. You've got this. And if you don't, we'll figure out something else."

His calm assurance steadied my nerves enough for me to focus on my task. I took another look at the lock, then at my set of picks. Grabbing the two I thought would do the trick, I crouched in front of the ancient lock and went to work.

Picking locks is mostly a function of sound and touch. I could do it without hearing the lock, but it was harder. For me, a lot harder. Between the cars on the road and the noise of construction from down the street, I couldn't hear the lock at all. Going by feel is a lot harder on a lock I'd never opened before. Most of my skills had been developed by picking the same few locks at home, not by trying a variety of locks. Like I said, not a master criminal.

I followed Tenn's suggestion and took a long, slow breath. His hand fell on my shoulder, anchoring me, a silent reminder that we were going to figure this out together. That I wasn't alone. It was enough to chase off my nerves, and I focused on the lock.

I slid the lower pick in to hold on to any pins I managed to move, and went to work, feeling my way through the lock. This one should have been easier than the newer, higher quality lock on the cottage at the Inn, but what this lock lacked in security, it made up for with stubborn age.

Twice I thought I had it and met complete resistance

when I tried to turn the bolt. Each time, I closed my eyes, took a deep breath, and tried again. Above me, Tenn kept an eye out, occasionally murmuring, "You're okay. No one is watching. Take your time."

I have no idea how I could have done it without him. Despite his calm encouragement, I was painfully aware of every second slipping by. Even in this run-down part of town, at a motel no one seemed to care about, someone was going to notice me trying to pick the lock to one of the rooms. If I didn't get it soon, it wasn't going to happen.

On my fourth try, I almost had it, the lock turning so far I was sure it would open. It did not. I let out a gusty sigh. "One more time," I muttered.

"You're almost there." Tenn squeezed my shoulder.

I was. By now, I had a feel for the lock. The first two pins slid up easily. I had their number after four tries. The third was trickier. It pushed back at my pick, refusing to slide up until I jiggled it just right. The feel of it clicking into place had my heart racing all over again.

This was it. I was almost there.

Careful not to lose the progress I'd made, I went for the last pin, wiggling and pressing with the curved tip of the pick, raking at the pin gently but firmly. "Come on, baby, I know you're sticky, but slide up, just a little." I thought I had it and tried to turn the lock, almost losing my hold on the pins I'd already moved when the lock jammed.

I squeezed my eyes shut for a second, searching for calm. Shaking hands and a racing heart were not helping. Slowly, I turned the lock back to its original position and went for the last pin one more time. I tried to force it up. No dice. I tried raking again, sliding the pick back and forth and hoping it pushed the pin into place. Raking looks sloppy, but it works on a surprising number of locks. Not this one.

A car door slammed to my right and I jolted against Tenn's legs, my nerves strung too tight, every new sound starting a terrifying avalanche of *what-ifs* in my brain. What if it was the police, catching me in the act of breaking and entering? The motel manager? Another guest? What if—?

I gave it one last effort, jamming the pick up and in with such force I felt it bend. A click vibrated down its length, registering in a burst of relief and triumph. This time, the lock turned easily, the door popping free under the pressure of my hand.

I shot to my feet, pushing it open, not registering Tenn's hasty, "Scarlett, wait—"

I should have listened. The second the door swung open, a hand shot out to close over my wrist, dragging me into the room so fast I stumbled. Before I could hit the ground, an arm looped around my neck, hauling me to my feet, holding me still as a gun pressed to my temple.

Chapter Thirty-Three

SCARLETT

I stumbled, terrified I was going to fall and end up getting shot in the head. The arm around my neck pinned me to a wide chest. Not Elliott or Thatcher. Too broad. Too tall. The arm around my neck tightened, the cold barrel of a gun pressing to my temple.

Tenn stood across the room from me, his face stone, eyes giving away nothing.

"Who the fuck ah you?" demanded a voice to my right in a pronounced Boston accent. My stomach sank. I was a complete idiot. I'd wanted to see Thatcher so badly I hadn't stopped to think about who else might be in the room.

Boston accent plus a gun to my head had to equal the Learys. Fuck.

Tenn was as calm and cool as a mountain lake. Hands loose at his sides, he kept his eyes on the man with the gun to my head. "That's Thatcher's mother you have there. We're here for him. Whatever you've got going on with Elliott doesn't have anything to do with us."

"That fuck'n idgit. Who goes on the run with a kid?" said the one to my right.

"Elliott is an idiot," I said carefully, the arm around my neck cutting into my air. "I don't care what you do with him, we're just here for Thatcher."

I hadn't missed that Tenn didn't identify himself. Right now, the Sawyer name was more of a liability than a help. The last thing we needed was for these guys to decide that taking Tenn hostage would lead to a big payout.

"Can't give 'im to you," the first guy said. I couldn't turn my neck to see any of them, but I could tell by their voices who was speaking. Close enough, at least. I wasn't sure it mattered. All that mattered was Thatcher. A few minutes ago, all I wanted was to see his face. Now, I hoped he was long gone. Unlikely, with his backpack on the bed and Elliott's car in the parking lot.

"What do you need with the kid?" Tenn asked as if this whole thing was an inconvenience. I wouldn't have guessed he'd be such a good actor. I wished I could pull off his cool, but all I could do was try not to pass out from terror.

"Leverage," was the answer. Not good.

"Elliott isn't enough?" Tenn asked, sounding more curious than truly interested.

"He needs motivation."

"What if we—" My voice disappeared at the crank of the arm on my neck. Blinking at the sudden lack of air, everything got a little hazy as the room exploded in sound and motion.

The door swung inward, familiar voices talking in hushed whispers. Like lightening, Tenn lunged, his hand closing over Thatcher's shoulder, hauling Thatch behind him and sending him to the ground with a hard shove. The moment he let go of Thatcher, he caught Elliott with an arm around the neck, his free hand coming up to press a gun to Elliott's temple.

Standoff.

Tenn had moved so fast, I wouldn't have believed it if I hadn't seen it. Maybe he'd spotted their approach through the open curtains. He must have been ready for them, but he'd given no sign. He'd shoved Thatcher out of the line of fire and grabbed Elliott in a heartbeat. With his arm around Elliott's neck, Tenn held Elliott captive in a mirror of my own position.

In a lazy drawl, he said, "Wanna trade?"

My jaw would have dropped if it hadn't been jammed shut by the goon's arm. How could he sound so in control? So relaxed? My insides were ice, my heart and mind screaming in terror. I was barely holding it together and Tenn sounded like he was talking about the last Danish at breakfast.

That was when it hit me. In that exact moment, breathless with fear, I knew I loved Tennessee Sawyer. I knew it because I was afraid, but I was not alone. As long as Tenn was with me, I'd never be alone. I can't tell you how I understood that with such certainty.

Watching him press his gun to Elliott's head, my son almost hidden from view on the floor behind him, I knew.

This man was not going to bail on me, or take advantage, or treat my kids like they weren't important. This man was worth loving, and I wasn't foolish enough to do anything but love him the way he deserved. Just as soon as we got out of here.

If Tenn thought he had the upper hand, the Learys soon disabused him of that notion. They also sounded like this whole situation was an inconvenience. I knew Tenn was putting on a show. I did not think the Learys were doing the same.

I thought they might be perfectly fine with murder if we

made them work too hard to take Elliott. After all, if they'd wanted leverage, they now had both Elliott's son and his ex-wife. Only Tenn was in their way.

One gun was pressed to my head, one to Elliott's, and two more trained on Tenn. My only comfort was that Elliott provided Tenn a full-body shield. Unless the shooter had excellent aim, if one of them shot at Tenn, he'd probably hit Elliott. I couldn't find it in me to care about Elliott. Not when his crappy decisions had landed us in this situation in the first place.

"Look," Tenn said, "we don't care about whatever you want with Elliott. Trade him for Scarlett, we'll take Thatcher, and the three of us will walk away. No interference. We'll disappear."

"I'm keepin' the kid or his ma," the first guy said. "Elliott needs some help stayin' focused."

"Can't let you do that," Tenn said, voice easy, eyes hard.

I started to shake. I couldn't help it. I wanted to hold it together, but Tenn couldn't talk his way out of this. I met Tenn's eyes, trying to communicate without words.

Take Thatcher and go. Leave me.

It's not that I wanted him to abandon me to these guys. I couldn't get my head around what that might mean. I hadn't gotten that far. But he had to get Thatcher out of here. Death aside, the only outcome more horrifying than the Learys taking me was them taking Thatcher. I agreed with Tenn on that point. We were not going to let them take my son.

I don't know if Tenn read my desperate signals. He gave a subtle shake of his head, his eyes flicking to mine. *Please,* I begged silently. How did I get him to leave me?

I couldn't. In my gut, I knew Tenn wasn't going to take

Thatcher and leave me to the Learys no matter how much I begged.

Shocking the hell out of me, Elliott twisted against Tenn's arm until he met my eyes. "Sorry, Scarlett," he gasped out, his crystal blue eyes twisted with remorse. A little late now. I couldn't find it in my heart to come anywhere close to forgiving him. Maybe in about a million years, assuming we got out of this without anyone getting shot. Or worse.

"Let's do what the guy says." Elliott jerked his chin up a fraction, indicating Tenn. "He can take my wife and kid and—"

"She's not your fucking wife." Tenn squeezed his arm tighter around Elliott's neck.

Elliott got his point before I did. "Yeah, yeah, she's not even my wife. We've been divorced for years. She's got nothing to do with this."

"Fine, we let her go and keep the kid." Such a reasonable tone for the inconceivable.

Leave my kid? Not a chance.

I grunted against the arm at my throat.

"See what the little woman has to say," said one of the other Learys. The arm around my neck loosened enough for me to talk if I held completely still.

"Keep me. Let Tenn and Thatcher go."

"Mom, no! You can't—"

"Thatcher, shut up," Elliott and I said in unison. The only thing we'd agreed on in years. Then Elliott had to go and ruin it.

"No way, Scarlett." To the Learys, he entreated, "You don't know her. She's a fucking pain in the ass. Nag, nag, bitch, moan. She'll drive you nuts. And the kid is a pain in the ass, too. Hungry all the time. Misses his games. More bitching and moaning. You don't need anyone else. Just me. I can—"

"You got it?" The first man asked casually.

Elliott stilled. "Not yet, but I know where it might be. I'm going to get it back. I swear on my life—"

"You already swore on your life, ya idgit. Now, I need one of these two so you can swear on theirs."

At the other end of the room, I caught a sound.

A shuffle.

Then a shout, the sound erupting into the room until it was cut off with an abrupt gurgle.

A heavy thud sounded and the arm around my neck loosened just enough for me to turn my head.

One of the Learys was flat on his back, limbs splayed and shaking, wires leading up to a gun-like thing in the hand of a man dressed all in black. He was a wide, tall slab of solid muscle with hard, dark eyes and brutally short brown hair.

I later learned he'd hit the Leary with a taser. He held it in one hand and a handgun in the other, trained on the closest Leary. His partner slid into the room like a ghost, two more weapons drawn, aimed at the other two Learys.

"Let the woman go," the new arrival ordered in a voice as cold and impenetrable as steel. He was almost identical to his partner except slightly smaller, with lighter hair.

The arm around my neck loosened as the new guys closed the distance between us. The second the arm had enough slack, I twisted and ducked, moving straight for Tenn.

The one with the taser kept his eyes on the Learys. "Out. All three of you. Now."

I didn't even consider arguing. Tenn shoved Elliott at the Learys and the two new guys. He reached down to haul

Thatcher to his feet, and we took off out the door. Grabbing Thatcher's hand in mine, I tugged him down the walkway toward the corner of the building and our SUV.

Despite the danger only steps away, I held Thatcher's hand, his strong fingers gripping mine. My baby. A tight band around my chest began to ease.

Tenn sprinted at Thatcher's side, trying to cover our rear and check ahead. An impossible job, especially with how fast we were running. Skidding around the corner past the dumpster, we came to a sudden halt at the sight of a stranger dressed exactly like the two other guys, leaning against the driver's side of our SUV.

Chapter Thirty-Four

SCARLETT

The driver's door was open behind the stranger, the engine running. How? I didn't have time to ask.

"Tenn, Scarlett, and Thatcher?" None of us responded. He tried again. "Cooper Sinclair sent us. Hawk and Griffen said you could use a little help. Assuming you're Tennessee, Scarlett, and Thatcher."

"We are," Tenn confirmed.

"Then get in the car. We have to get on the road ASAP." When Tenn made a move to the driver's door, the stranger slid in ahead of him. "I'm driving. Get in."

Thatcher and I climbed in the back, Tenn in the front passenger seat. With a terse, "Buckle up," the stranger threw the SUV into reverse, and we skidded out from behind the dumpster and rocketed across the parking lot. I lurched forward, then slammed back into the seat, catching sight of Elliott as he dashed to his car and dove into the driver's seat.

I didn't see if he got away or what happened to anyone else, our vehicle already swinging out onto the main road. No one spoke until the driver merged onto the highway, reversing the trip Tenn and I had taken to the motel.

Eyes everywhere—on the rearview, side mirrors, the road ahead—the stranger broke the tense silence. "Kane Black. I used to work with Griffen and Hawk at Sinclair Security. Griffen called in a favor."

"I thought he said you guys were all tied up," Tenn said.

Kane took his eyes from the road to send Tenn a worryingly sympathetic glance. "We are. It was just good luck our job had a hitch and we were on standby only a few hours away. I'm going to drive you as far as Knoxville, then meet back up with the rest of the team and we'll head to Memphis."

"Did Griffen know the Learys would be there? Is that why he called in the favor?" I asked, reaching out to take Thatcher's hand. He squeezed back so tightly my fingers ached. It was the best ache in the world. I glanced at him to see wide eyes in a pale face. *You okay?* I mouthed. All I got was a stiff nod. My eyes filled with tears of relief.

"No," Kane said, answering my question. "More good luck for you. Looks like you were due for some. The whole Leary crew is trouble. Griffen called because—" He paused and cleared his throat. "He said to tell you that you were wrong about the dates. You don't have forty-eight hours. You have a little over six."

"Shit."

That about summed it up. If everything went perfectly, the trip back to Heartstone Manor should take around five hours. If everything went perfectly. That meant no bad weather. No traffic. No flat tires or other emergencies. The margin was way too tight for comfort.

Kane's phone rang and he put it to his ear. "Status," he barked. I heard a voice but couldn't distinguish anything. After a minute, he hung up. "Learys are temporarily out of commission. Hall got away."

Thatcher slumped in relief. "My dad's okay?" he croaked, his voice rough as if he hadn't spoken in years.

Kane met Thatcher's eyes in the rearview mirror. "He got away. That's a good start. Whatever he has going on with the Learys, it's not over, but I can promise you this: he's a lot safer on his own. Now that the Learys know about you and your mom, the best place you can be is with Tenn and his family."

"You're sure he's safer on his own?" My heart broke at Thatcher's desperation. He wanted to help his dad, but he was terrified. Rightfully. Elliott had almost gotten us all killed. I wasn't going to imagine what would have happened to me or Thatcher if they'd been able to use us as leverage. Every image that popped into my head was too terrifying to dwell on.

"I'm sure," Kane said. "He can play this differently if they can't get to anyone they can use against him."

"Okay," Thatcher whispered, sinking back into his seat, finally turning his head to me. His fingers still gripped mine with painful force. I didn't care. "Sorry, Mom."

A tear rolled down my cheek. "You're grounded for the rest of your life. And the next life. All your lives. You're grounded forever."

"Okay," he said, the ghost of a smile playing on his lips.

"I'm not kidding," I said, ignoring the tears that spilled down my cheeks. I had my baby back. We were on the way home to August. Tenn was safe, despite his crazy moves in that motel room.

If we could just get to Heartstone in the next—I checked the clock on the dashboard—five hours and forty-five minutes, everything would be perfect.

And if we didn't, Tenn might hate me for the rest of his life.

He might, but at that moment, he looked completely relaxed. Glancing at me, then to Thatcher, he smiled, slow and sweet. "We got him," he said, his smile curving wider.

"Tenn—" I had too many words. I wasn't going to tell him I loved him with an audience. Especially not when one of them was my thirteen-year-old son who'd never met Tenn before. And I couldn't say I was sorry about the risk to his inheritance. Not yet. Not when we had a good chance of making it in time.

Tenn shook his head at me, telling me without words that I didn't need to say anything. But I did need to. Just not right then. It could wait. Twisting to face the seat behind him, he met Thatcher's curious gaze. "You've been making your mom crazy, you know."

Thatcher's face flooded with color. I waited for him to get pissed, but Tenn winked and Thatcher gave him a wobbly grin. "I usually do."

"No, you don't, not like this," I protested in a watery voice, my emotions ping-ponging all over the place. "When you leave your socks everywhere or when you forget your homework at school. Not by taking off with your dad when he screwed up a job for a bunch of criminals."

Thatcher dropped his head, scratching at a spot on his jeans with his free hand. "I didn't know, Mom. I thought it was one of his dumb friends. Like he owed them poker money or something and they broke in and took it. He was so freaked, I was worried he'd do something stupid. And then—" He sucked in a breath and let it out in a rush, giving me a hopeless look I hated. "I didn't know."

I leaned over and wrapped my arms around him, the seatbelt cutting into my side as I stretched across the wide seat. "I know, buddy. I know. I didn't think it was that serious either. Not until it was too late."

We held on to each other for a while, my face buried in his hair, his tucked under my chin. Hot tears hit my neck and I rubbed his back, knowing his young man's pride would not want the two men in the front to see him cry. "We're okay, baby. Everything is okay now."

"Dad?" he pleaded, looking for a reassurance I couldn't give him.

I'd always straddled the line between not bad-mouthing Elliott to his sons and not lying to make him look better. I didn't lie to my boys. If something wasn't their business, I told them so, but I didn't lie. I wasn't going to start now.

"Your dad made some bad choices, honey. Some really bad choices. I don't know if he knew how bad and decided to take the risk or if he got in over his head. He's involved with dangerous people, and I don't think we can help him with that except by staying out of the way."

"What if he needs us?" Thatcher pressed. Breaking my hold, he reached up to touch Kane's shoulder. "Can't you guys help him? Get him away from the Learys? Make them leave him alone?"

Kane shook his head, sending Thatcher a sympathetic glance. "Can't do it, kid. We don't aid and abet criminals. We have a lot of connections with law enforcement because we keep it clean and play by the rules." Considering, he added, "Mostly. We bend the rules here and there, but not enough to jeopardize those relationships. And we never work with organized crime. The boss has a real thing about that."

"But—" Thatcher protested.

Kane cut him off. "When we leave you in Knoxville, we're headed to Memphis. You know what we're doing there?"

Thatcher shook his head.

"We're helping a family recover their daughter, a three-year-old who was grabbed while they were on vacation. The father's a big exec, deep pockets, and apparently, the people who took her were watching the family for a while. We'd recommended heavier security more than once, but they didn't want to feel trapped. The kidnappers distracted them at an amusement park and snatched the girl."

"Is she okay?" Thatcher asked, a worry line between his eyebrows.

"So far. We're going to get her back as fast as we can. And I can't sideline or delay that mission to help your dad no matter how much you love him and want him to be safe. You understand?"

This time, Thatcher didn't try to hide his tears. He let them fall as he nodded. "Yeah," he said, his voice rough. "I understand. The little girl is more important."

Kane nodded. "She is. And after her, there'll be another. And another after that. All innocent people hurt by bad guys."

Resigned, Thatcher finished his thought. "And you can't spend time helping a kinda bad guy when you could be helping the good guys."

"Yep."

Kane fell silent. Thatcher's mouth worked as he chewed his lip and thought about that. The idea of his dad as one of the bad guys was impossible to refute and so painful to take in.

"Hey, Thatch," Tenn said, turning in his seat to meet Thatcher's eyes. "Remember this—your Dad made some bad choices, but in the end, he was looking out for you. All that stuff he said about you being a pain in the ass, you know he was trying to get you somewhere safe, right?"

Thatcher gave a weak smile. "Well, I am kind of a pain in the ass sometimes."

Tenn raised his eyebrows. "You mean eating all the time and jonesing for your gaming console? That's just being a teenager. He doesn't care about that stuff. He loves you. He wanted you safe. He made some bad decisions, but that doesn't make him a bad guy or mean he doesn't love you, you know? Sometimes, we get in over our heads and there aren't any good choices. But when it came down to it, he tried to get you and your mom somewhere safe."

"Yeah," Thatcher said, turning this over in his mind.

I sat up and reached out to squeeze Tenn's shoulder in thanks. He caught my hand, turning it in his, and kissed my palm. My heart squeezed with love and my eyes flicked to the clock. The road was clear and we were flying, well above the speed limit, but the clock continued to roll ahead, time draining away.

I had a terrible feeling we'd already used all of our good luck.

Grabbing a jacket I'd thrown in the car just in case, I bundled it into a pillow on my lap. Patting it, I said to Thatcher, "Why don't you put your head down and take a nap. We won't get to Knoxville for a few hours."

I wasn't sure he'd take me up on the suggestion. Thatcher could be stubborn as hell. I couldn't complain since he got it from me. All the stress of the last week showed in the instant he said, "Yeah, okay," tugged at his seatbelt to loosen it, and slumped to the side, putting his head on the makeshift pillow.

The position was awkward, his legs too long to stretch out. He jammed his feet under Tenn's seat, settled in, and closed his eyes. I ran my fingers lightly through his hair, noting the film of grease. Typical of both Thatch and his dad to forget about basic stuff like showering. I guess life on the run doesn't lend itself to good grooming. We'd worry about that later.

First, we had to get back to Heartstone Manor before time ran out. I loved Tenn too much to be the reason he lost his legacy.

Chapter Thirty-Five

SCARLETT

Thatcher fell asleep within minutes. I kept watch on the clock and the road. Tenn did the same. So far, so good. Kane drove with clean precision and a sixth sense for lurking police cars. Every time he slowed to just above the speed limit, we invariably passed an officer in hiding, his radar gun at the ready.

Knoxville grew ever closer. I tried not to stress. We had Thatcher. We were going to make it home on time. The Learys were focused on Elliott. They wouldn't come after us in Sawyers Bend. Then why was I so uneasy? Was it that we might not get back to Heartstone Manor in time?

I stared out the window, watching the trees fly by, and tried to examine my roiling emotions. I was mostly stressing because of the deadline, I realized. And beneath that worry was a tangled ball of smaller worries.

All this time, I'd been focused on finding Thatcher and getting him free of Elliott's problems. Well, I had him. What now? Did I keep looking for the bust of Vitellius? If I didn't need to search for the bust anymore, I didn't need to stay at Heartstone.

Though, that part might be up to the police chief. As far as I knew, West didn't have any suspects for Vanessa's murder. More importantly, he didn't have much evidence. If he didn't have any leads, then anything I remembered wouldn't make me a threat to the killer. And if that was the case, I was free to go.

At the twist in my stomach, I realized I'd hit on what was really bothering me, beyond the immediate problem of Tenn's deadline. What was going to happen now? Did I want to go? Did Tenn want me to stay? And what if he did? I had the boys, and our house, and my job. I had to consider what August and Thatcher would want. I couldn't just walk away from my job. Could I?

I'd thought about it more than a few times over the last two years. Ever since the first month my side hustle brought in more than my salary. It didn't happen every month, but it happened more often than not, and the months it fell short, it wasn't by much. At first, I paid off my car, then started paying extra on the mortgage and putting more in the boys' college funds. I was starting to make good headway on those. If I went full-time making jewelry and small sculptures for my online shop, I'd be able to sell more but probably not enough to equal what I was making both teaching and running the shop.

It was a big risk. As those words ran through my head, I hated the sound of them. Everything was a risk. Going to Sawyers Bend. Trusting Tenn. Coming after Thatcher. Was I going to be afraid of risks forever?

Yes, big changes were a risk.

And yes, I had two boys to look after.

I didn't have the right to be reckless, but did that mean I couldn't take a chance?

I didn't know. I knew I was in love with Tenn. No doubt

there. I didn't know what to do about it, or if it could go anywhere, or if he even wanted it to. I was three years older than him with a pain-in-the-ass ex-husband and two great kids. Maybe Tenn didn't want a ready-made family. Maybe he was good with what we had—a fling or whatever this was —and he'd be ready to send us on our way in a week or two.

Or maybe, I thought with a blast of horror, he'd be ready when we got back to the Manor.

No. It was possible, but I didn't believe that. I didn't know if Tenn loved me. We'd barely met, after all. But I was sure he felt something for me. He was the one who'd insisted it wasn't just sex, right? My thoughts drifted as the miles sped by. I watched the clock, wishing we could speed up while the clock slowed down.

I may have dozed off, my head leaning against the cool window, one hand on Thatcher's side, feeling his ribs move with every breath. I must have because I blinked my eyes and we were nearing the outskirts of Knoxville. I looked around, spotting a black SUV identical to ours right behind us.

"Are those guys with you?" I asked.

"That's the rest of the team. We'll pull into a gas station in a minute, you guys can fill up, get some food, and head home."

"I can't thank you enough for everything," I said. "Things were not looking good when you showed up."

Kane smiled as he hit his blinker and slowed for the exit. "No thanks needed. Griffen saved my ass a few times. Glad to help out his family."

At the sound of voices, Thatcher stirred, sitting up and blinking out the window. "Hungry," was all he said. Typical.

"We'll grab some food when we stop," I said, repositioning in my seat now that he wasn't sleeping on me anymore.

We pulled into a gas station attached to a drive-through and parked in a spot off to the side next to the other SUV. One of the guys from the motel room hopped out, Thatcher's backpack in hand. Kane got out, and the rest of us followed.

"I think this is yours," the guy said, holding the bag out to Thatcher.

"My backpack!" Thatcher grabbed the bag. "Thanks! And thanks for, you know, getting us out of there."

"Happy to help."

Kane handed the keys to our SUV to Tenn. "You have three and a half hours to get back. Should be smooth sailing if you make this a quick stop and get back on the road."

"That's the plan." Tenn held out a hand to Kane and they exchanged a firm shake. "Thank you. You guys really saved the day. Good luck in Memphis."

More handshakes, some back slaps, and they were gone. Tenn turned to Thatcher and me. "Hit the bathroom, get gas and food, and then get back on the road?"

"Why don't you tell me what you want to eat, and Thatch and I will get the food while you fill us up? We can save a little time."

Tenn didn't say anything, just reached out and squeezed my arm once before giving me a quick nod. I found myself leaning into him, feeling his need to hold me and mine to hold him back. But not now. Not in front of Thatcher until I could tell him about Tenn and what he was to me. Which would be sometime after I figured that out for myself.

No time to think about it. Together, we headed to the gas station bathrooms, getting in and out as fast as we could.

Thatcher and I met in the brightly lit, tiled hall that led to the fast-food restaurant attached to the gas station. Tenn called out his order as he moved past us to the front door and out to the pumps.

Standing in line, I bounced on my toes, willing the line to move faster. Just when I was about to ditch the idea of food in favor of a few bags of chips, the party ahead of us was gone and it was our turn. I ordered as quickly as I could, shoving my credit card at the cashier.

"What's with the rush? Does Tenn have a curfew?" Thatcher asked, laughing.

"Kind of." Sending a look around the crowded restaurant, I said, "I'll explain later."

Grabbing our bags, I nudged the drinks at Thatcher. "Go easy on yours, okay? We're not stopping for another bathroom break."

"Seriously?"

"Seriously," I confirmed.

When we reached the car, Thatcher said, "You can sit in the front, Mom. Then I can stretch out back here."

I guess he was done with hugs. He'd have to put up with one more. Handing the food and drinks to Tenn, I hauled Thatcher into my arms and gave him the hug I'd been saving up for almost a week. He stood passive in my embrace for a few seconds before his arms came around me in a tight hug. "I'm okay, Mom."

"I know." Planting a smacking kiss on his cheek, I set him free. "Don't forget what I said about the drink. We're not stopping again."

I buckled in and Tenn pulled back onto the highway. "We have until 10:48, according to Griffen," he said, a determined set to his chin.

Thatcher leaned forward, his hand on the back of my

seat. "Why do you have to get back home so fast? What's such a big deal that those guys left their mission to help you?"

Tenn sent me a questioning look. I shrugged. "I think he should know what you risked to help him."

Tenn nodded and appeared to think for a minute. "You know who I am?" he asked Thatcher. "Who my family is?"

"Yeah, kind of. You're a Sawyer. Your dad owns, like, a whole town and a bunch of land and stuff. Your family is really rich but sorta secretive. Like, you're not all over the internet, driving expensive cars and stuff."

"Basically. Did you know my dad died a few months ago?"

Thatcher's face dropped and he shook his head. "No. Was he old?"

"Not really. He was murdered."

Both Thatcher and Tenn looked at me, Thatcher in shock and Tenn wondering if he should have kept that part quiet. Ignoring Thatch for the moment, I asked Tenn something I needed to know even if I didn't want to ask in front of Thatcher.

"Are we staying when we get back? Or is it time to, you know, call it a day?" I tried to ignore the spike of nerves while I waited for his answer. I would not burst into tears if he told me we should call it a day. I would not.

Tenn's dark blue eyes were deadly serious on mine. "You're absolutely staying."

I didn't try to hide my smile. "Then I think he might as well know the truth. He'll find out anyway. Better to hear it from you."

"Okay." Tenn looked up to meet Thatcher's eyes in the rearview mirror. "My dad was murdered in his office at the

Manor. We have no idea who did it, but my brother was set up to take the blame. He's in jail right now. There's some other stuff going on too, but you want to know about the deadline."

I didn't miss how he glossed over Vanessa's murder. I wasn't going to bring it up. Prentice's murder was enough for now. Thatcher could hear about Vanessa another time.

"When my father died, he left a will. Instead of splitting his estate between his kids, he divided the cash into trusts and put our oldest brother, Griffen, in charge of the trusts for the next five years."

"The Griffen who used to work with Kane and those guys?" Thatcher asked, leaning forward as far as his seatbelt would let him.

"The same one. Our father put Griffen in charge of the family company and left him the house, but he didn't leave him any money. He gets access to our trusts and any profits from Sawyer Enterprises. The rest of us don't get anything for the next five years. If we want what's in those trusts, we have to live in the family home, Heartstone Manor, for those five years."

"That doesn't seem that hard. I looked you up and there aren't any pictures of your house online except what someone took from a drone, but it looks huge. Like a castle or something."

"It's a lot like a castle, yeah. And you're right, living there isn't hard. Except there are conditions. One of them is that I can only leave for fourteen days every quarter. If I'm away for more than that, I lose my inheritance."

"Like whatever's in the trusts? How much is it?"

"Thatcher! You can't ask that! It's rude!" My cheeks were on fire with embarrassment. He knew better than to ask someone how much money they had. Tenn put his hand on my leg, squeezing.

"It's okay, Scarlett." Looking up to the rearview again, he said, "The truth is, I don't know the exact number. According to the terms of the will, Griffen isn't supposed to tell us. In the video he left, Prentice told Griffen to take it all. I think he didn't want us to know how much there was. He liked to play games."

"Sounds like it. He wasn't a nice guy?"

Tenn was quiet for a long moment. "No, Thatcher, he was not a nice guy. And he wasn't a good father, either."

"No wonder you guys can't figure out who killed him. Must be a long list."

Tenn laughed. "It's a very long list," he agreed.

Thatcher digested all of this before he put it together. "You were already gone for the fourteen days this quarter, weren't you? And if we don't get back by eleven, you lose your inheritance? That's crazy."

"Not just that," I added. "If we don't get back by eleven, he doesn't only lose the money, he's banned from all the family property, including the house and the inn where Tenn works. He'll lose everything."

Thatcher stared at us, at a loss. "Why? Why would you take the risk? Your house? Your job? And it has to be a lot of money, even if you don't know how much. That's crazy."

Tenn shook his head, a bemused smile on his lips. Letting go of my leg, he reached over and took my hand, resting it on the center console, his fingers wrapped around mine, his thumb absently stroking my skin.

He sent that bemused smile my way before he answered. "First of all, we miscounted, and I thought I had forty-eight hours left, which is slightly less crazy, though I take your point. And second, I don't know exactly how much money we're talking about, but Griffen implied it was a hefty amount and he's not a liar."

"And third?" Thatcher pressed.

"Third, you were missing with some very scary guys after you. I don't care what was at risk for me, there was no way I was letting your mom go after you on her own."

"Couldn't you have waited until the quarter was over?"

"Did you forget what happened in that motel room? How do you think that would have gone down if we hadn't been there? Your dad would have done his best, but he wouldn't have been able to keep you safe. Not when they planned to use you for leverage."

"What did that mean?" Thatcher asked, and I was so grateful he hadn't had to find out.

Tenn's expression darkened. "I'll explain that later."

"So, all we have to do is get to your house by eleven? How much of the drive is left?"

I checked the clock. "Two hours and fifteen minutes. We should have an hour to spare."

Should, but didn't.

Thatcher stretched out in the back seat and dozed off again. I sat beside Tenn, holding his hand and watching the road, willing us to move faster. We left the rolling hills and gentle mountains behind, passing into a narrow stretch of highway that curved tightly through the mountains. According to the map, it was only a few miles until we'd leave the highway for the road to Sawyers Bend.

As we emerged from a long tunnel, the sun setting over the mountains, Tenn slammed on the brakes.

A line of cars stretched in front of us, red lights a snake winding around the curve ahead. Frantic, I scrambled for my phone, pulling up the navigation app. Our section of the highway was a thick red line. Tapping it, I saw the one thing I hadn't considered.

Rockslide.

And just like that, our hour to spare began to slip away.

Chapter Thirty-Six

SCARLETT

T hatcher slept on, unaware of the precarious change in our circumstances. I was sick with worry, but Tenn appeared unbothered.

"I should have thought about this," Tenn said, his voice far too even and calm. "We had a ton of rain last week. It destabilizes the tree roots, and when the trees come down, the mountain comes with them. We haven't had a rockslide in a while, but it happens."

"How long does it usually take to clear?" I asked, my voice taking on a frantic edge. I may have sounded a little unhinged.

Tenn shrugged. "Depends. Looks like there's a crew working right now. And the cars ahead are moving. We should be good."

I peered into the growing dark, the taillights ahead growing fuzzy as it got darker. When the sun hit the ridge-line of the mountain, it went down fast, the sky shading from sunset pink to deep purple in minutes. As hard as I looked, I couldn't see the cars ahead moving. Then one inched forward. And the next. And so on down the line until we inched forward, too.

"Doesn't anyone you know have a helicopter or something?" I muttered.

Tenn laughed. "Don't think so. Griffen might know someone, but not around here."

"There must be something we can do," I insisted, looking around at the road ahead and the slowly moving traffic, hoping for a miracle.

Tenn shrugged again. "We still have some time."

I checked the clock. Only forty-six minutes and we were a good thirty minutes away without the rockslide. We could sit here for an hour, or—

I shut down that thought and tried to follow Tenn's lead and relax. Either we'd get home on time, or we wouldn't.

Nope, not doing the trick. "Why aren't you upset?" I demanded, not caring that my near shriek woke up Thatcher.

Tenn braked behind the hatchback in front of us, coming to another stop. Lifting one hand, he cupped my chin. "Because it doesn't matter, Scarlett."

"Not matter? It's your inheritance! Your home! Your birthright! You love the Inn."

With a slow graze of his thumb along my jaw, Tenn let go of my chin, turning his eyes back to the road. Our pace was agonizingly slow as we inched forward another few feet before stopping again. "I do love the Inn," he said. "And Heartstone Manor. I even love living with my family again, which is something I never thought I'd say. But, Scarlett, the money and the house and the job are just things. They don't really matter."

"Not matter?" I shrieked again. From the back seat,

Thatcher glanced between us before his eyes fixed on the taillights ahead of us.

"What's going on?" he asked Tenn in a low voice, probably deciding that I was too unhinged to bother talking to. He wasn't wrong. I did not have a hold on calm. I was freaking out, and I still didn't get why I was the only one.

"Rockslide," Tenn answered.

Thatcher's eyes flew wide and his face fell. "Oh man, that's bad. I'm sorry—"

"I'm not." Tenn cut him off. Braking again, he turned in his seat to meet Thatcher's eyes. "I'm not sorry, and I don't want you to be either. Whatever happens, I won't regret leaving to come get you. You're more important. Your mom is more important. The rest is just stuff."

"It's not just stuff," I insisted.

Tenn looked over at me. "So, if I lose the house and the money, have to get a job somewhere else, you'd be upset? You wanted to live at Heartstone? Want me to buy you a big diamond?"

"No! I don't care about all of that. You know I don't. But I care about you. I want you to have what you deserve. What's yours. And more than that—" I swallowed hard, afraid to admit the truth. "I don't want you to hate me for being the reason you lost everything."

"Scarlett—" Tenn's voice was warm with affection. Maybe something more than affection. "You could never be the reason I lost anything. You're the reason I have everything."

"Tenn—"

"No," he went on as if I hadn't interrupted, "I need you to understand. The money, the house, the Inn—none of that is mine. Not really. I want to keep running the Inn because I love that place and I love the job. But in the end, it's just a job. There are other jobs. There is no other you. There is no other Thatcher. It wasn't even a question for me. If something had happened to Thatcher, it would have destroyed you."

I reached up to wipe away a tear. He was right. I couldn't fathom how I could have handled something happening to one of my babies. A fresh wave of anger at Elliott washed over me. How could he have put Thatcher anywhere near the Learys? I should have grabbed one of the guns and shot him.

"But what if we don't make it? I don't want to be the reason you lose it all."

"You aren't getting it, Scarlett. My inheritance is just another way for my dad to yank my chain. He could have left the Inn to Royal and me. We've been running it for almost a decade. He didn't, he left it to Griffen just to remind us that none of it was ours. Same with the trusts. That money isn't mine. It may never be. Griffen could decide to buy a small country and clean us all out."

"Griffen isn't going to steal from you." I didn't know Griffen well enough to be sure, but I didn't need to. I was sure anyway.

"Probably not. But it doesn't matter. My father did it this way to remind us we don't have anything without him. But he was wrong. Because there's you and your boys. You matter. Thatcher and August matter. I'll tell you what I couldn't live with: choosing the money over going after Thatcher. Especially given what happened today."

I didn't have a response. He was right. And still, the idea of him losing his inheritance left me with an empty hole in my chest. I wanted to bring goodness to his life, to make him happy. Not be the reason he lost it all.

We inched forward, almost at the curve in the road. I

caught the edge of a road work sign, the kind that points out a coming merge. Okay, this made sense. It was so slow because we were merging into one lane. Maybe things would pick up when we passed the sign. I could only hope.

"I don't get it, though," Thatcher said from behind us, sounding years younger, his voice tight and small. "You don't even know me."

"Want to hear a story? It's not a great one. Sad and kind of scary," Tenn said, flicking his eyes to the rearview to catch Thatcher's attention.

"Sure, I guess," Thatch said, uncertain and worried.

"When I was just out of college, my younger brother Finn was kidnapped. He was on spring break in Mexico to celebrate turning twenty-one, and some bad dudes figured out who he was, slipped something in his drink, and took him."

Finn? I remembered him at dinner the other night in his board shorts and faded shirt, looking like he didn't have a care in the world.

"What happened?" Thatcher asked, his voice rough.

"The kidnappers sent a ransom demand to my father. Prentice Sawyer did not like being told what to do. Even to save one of his sons. He told the kidnappers to do whatever they wanted with Finn."

"What?" I couldn't imagine it. "But he called the FBI, right? Or people like Sinclair Security? It sounds like that's what they do."

Tenn shook his head, inching us another ten feet closer to the merge. Up ahead, I thought I saw cars picking up speed, the bright glare of road work lights and smoke from flares. The clock kept rolling forward. Thirty-two minutes. Not enough time. I felt sick.

"My father could have called someone, but he didn't. If

he paid one set of kidnappers, others would come for us. That was his excuse. The kidnappers didn't believe him, so they tortured Finn, recorded it, and played it back for my father, thinking it would change his mind."

"Did it?" Thatcher whispered.

"No. They kept at it for a few days, a new recording every day. We didn't find out all of this until later, or we would have tried to help. My father kept it a secret. He wasn't giving any kidnappers a red cent, he said."

"Your father was a real piece of work," I said in the understatement of the century.

"And then some," Tenn agreed.

"Did your brother die?" Thatcher asked quietly as if he was afraid of the answer.

"No. Eventually, the kidnappers realized they weren't going to get a payoff, and Finn thinks they planned to kill him. But they got drunk while they were arguing about what to do and he managed to get away. He was out in the desert, and by the time he found help, he was in bad shape. Dehydrated, injured from the torture, and really, really pissed off at Prentice. He dropped off the map for a while. We all thought he was dead. That was when my father told us about the kidnapping."

"Did he regret it?" I asked. We rounded the turn and the traffic started to move. Not at normal highway speeds, but faster than a crawl. It wasn't going to be enough. Unless this SUV had wings, we weren't going to make it.

Tenn gave a wry laugh. "Prentice? Not a chance. He was angry, but not remorseful. I'll never forget how furious he was that Finn had gotten kidnapped in the first place, and after it was over, so annoyed at the idea that Finn was dead. Not grief-stricken or remorseful. Annoyed. Like the whole thing was a big inconvenience. Later, we found out that Finn recuperated at a friend's place, and when he was well enough, he left to wander around the country. He never came home. Not until Prentice died. But I'll never forget the pictures."

"What pictures?"

"They faxed pictures of Finn. I never heard the recordings of the calls, but I saw those pictures. Finn was... I'm pretty sure he spent some time in the hospital. It was bad." Tenn swallowed and blinked hard.

Meeting Thatcher's eyes in the rearview, he said, "I wasn't letting that happen to you or your mom. No fucking way. Maybe if Sinclair Security had a team free and they could have gone in and gotten you out. Maybe then I would have stayed at Heartstone with your mom and waited. Those guys are pros, and we would have only been in the way. But they didn't have a full team to spare, and it was too dangerous to leave you with your dad. As it is, we got very lucky their job in Memphis was delayed."

"I didn't know," Thatch whispered. "I didn't know about the Learys or that they would—" He looked away.

"Hey," Tenn said, getting his attention. "Your heart was in the right place, Thatcher. But maybe avoid scary dudes with guns from now on."

"Yeah, I think I can do that." Thatcher looked at the clock. "We're not going to make it, are we?"

Tenn hit the gas as the traffic sped up even more. "There's always a chance."

I didn't see how there could be. We had less than twenty minutes to make a thirty-minute drive. At least thirty minutes. We passed an exit. And another. Tenn pulled out his phone, dialing and putting it on speaker so he could keep both hands on the wheel.

"Cutting it a little close, aren't you?" demanded a voice I thought I recognized as West. My heart leaped in hope.

"I'm about to hit the exit off 40. Any chance you're around? I've got—"

"I'm sitting here waiting for you, you jackass. Hawk has a tracker on the SUV. Watching you has been torture."

"There's a rockslide, man."

"Yeah, I know. Pull into the emergency lane and hit the gas. I'll have the lights on. We're going to get you home. And if I get fired, you owe me."

"I owe you anyway. See you in two."

Tenn hung up and focused on the road. West had told him to pull onto the emergency lane, but there wasn't much of one. Driving with fearless determination, Tenn used every inch of space, our outside wheels dipping off the pavement, tilting the heavy SUV toward the trees a few times. I grabbed the handle above my door and held on tight. We shot free of the traffic a few seconds later, staying in the emergency lane and passing all the other cars on the exit. Horns blared until a cruiser pulled in front of us, lights flashing.

Then we really took off. I remember it taking at least twenty minutes to make my way from the highway to the town of Sawyers Bend. Not the way West drove. His lights going crazy, sirens blaring, he raced down the country roads, the top-heavy vehicles leaning with every turn, the wheels coming off the ground often enough to have me squeezing my eyes closed.

From behind me, I heard Thatcher's awed, "Wicked."

Ugh. Kids. Everyone around me was insane. On the other hand, if this mad ride would get us to Heartstone Manor in the next—I risked a glance at the clock—seven minutes, I'd deal with my fear of rolling off the side of the mountain.

West took a road I didn't know about, bypassing town and looping around to meet up with the road that wound up the mountain to Heartstone Manor. Five minutes. Four. Three. Two. I clenched my teeth together, trying to hold my stomach in place. Between the crazy ride and my nerves, I seriously thought I was going to puke. Because that was all we needed. Me puking all over the car.

That thought distracted me for a second or two. Finally, the gates came into sight. West must have called ahead. They were open, and we flew through, tight on West's bumper all the way down the long drive to the courtyard in front of the Manor. Skidding to a halt, I checked the clock. 10:50. My heart sank. Surely two minutes wasn't that big of a deal, right?

We spilled out of the SUV to find most of the family gathered on the front steps, surrounding an apple-cheeked man in a suit, peering at an open pocket watch, his brows drawn together, mouth set in a tight line.

He looked up from the watch and met Tenn's gaze. "Tenn. I'm sorry. I'm going to have to escort you off the property—"

"Wait—" Griffen, his phone at his ear, sliced up a hand to stop the man from talking. "Glenn in the booth has Tenn crossing onto Heartstone land at 10:48 exactly. He doesn't have to be in the house itself, he just has to be on the property, correct?"

The man slid the watch into his pocket. Reaching for the phone, he took it from Griffen. "You got him at 10:48? And you can support that in court?" He paused to listen. "Hmm. Uh-hmm. Fine." Handing Griffen back his phone, he said, "Glenn confirmed that the security system recorded the SUV reentering the property at 10:47 and 37 seconds. The system record is admissible in court and Glenn will sign an affidavit confirming the arrival time." As the rest of us relaxed, the man turned to Tenn. "Don't cut it so close again."

"I won't," Tenn promised.

One arm around Thatcher, I threw the other around Tenn, burying my face in his chest and sobbing with relief. Thatcher stiffened in surprise when Tenn pulled us both close, rocking side to side just a little. "Fuck, that was close," he murmured into my hair.

"Too close," Thatcher mumbled, not squirming to get away from Tenn's hold.

"Mom! Thatch! Tenn!" August barreled down the front steps, followed by Savannah.

"Sorry," she called out. "I couldn't get him to go to bed until you got home."

August reached us and slammed into Tenn's legs. Tenn let go of Thatcher and me long enough to haul August into his arms and we were hugging again, me still sobbing and the three guys laughing, a little at me and my tears but mostly in sheer relief.

We were home. Thatcher was safe. And Tenn still had his inheritance.

Now, we just had to figure out what came next. In light of everything we'd been through, that part didn't seem too hard. In my giddy relief, I forgot exactly how complicated life could be, and how impossible it might be to move forward with so much of the past holding us back.

Chapter Thirty-Seven

TENN

All of them had waited up for us. Even Finn and my youngest brother Brax were there, wearing the same relieved smiles as everyone else. Once I let go of Scarlett and the boys, I got backslaps from my brothers and tight hugs from my sisters as well as Hope and Daisy, all of them warning me not to take any crazy chances again. I wasn't planning on it.

The only people missing were Bryce and Ophelia. I didn't ask where they were. This was a celebration, and I'd prefer to pretend they didn't exist. I'd find out what Hawk and Griffen might have discovered about Bryce later.

Just as I was turning to find Scarlett and get us settled for the night, Savannah took my arm, leading me into the house.

"I knew you'd make it back," she said, glancing back to catch Scarlett's eye. At the look, Scarlett gathered her boys and joined us. "I did a little reorganizing while you were gone. Called Billy Bob in for some muscle. I think you'll like this."

Confused, we followed her up the main stairs and to the

right, into the guest wing. The hallway was lit by a floor lamp Savannah had relocated since we'd last been there. Beside Scarlett, Thatcher was looking everywhere at once, his eyes wide with wonder. "This place is huge," he whispered to August.

"It's even bigger than you think," August said with glee. "Nicky and I will show you around tomorrow. Heartstone is the ultimate for hide and seek."

I'd played the same game with my siblings when we were August and Nicky's age. August was right, Heartstone *was* the ultimate for hide and seek. I could give the kids some tips. Warmth spread in my chest at the idea of a whole new generation of kids making Heartstone a home with their laughter when Savannah drew to a halt in front of a door. One room down from the one with my favorite velvet chaise, this room had been empty of furniture the last time I'd seen it.

I barely recognized it after Savannah led us inside. Now, it was set up as a sitting room with a television, two couches, and a desk in one corner. None of the furniture matched, and all of it was well worn, but the room had been transformed from an abandoned space into a functional place to hang out. At the far end, the door was open, a light on in the room beyond.

"Go check that out," Savannah said to the boys, lifting a hand to point to the open door. August and Thatcher made a beeline for it, August shouting, "Awesome!" as he crossed the threshold. We followed at a slower pace to find the formerly empty room decorated with mismatched twin beds, cheerfully made with red plaid comforters and matching pillows, a table with a lamp between them. A door at the other end was open into a white-tiled bathroom.

Leaving the boys to bounce on the beds, Savannah

turned to lead us across the sitting room to the open door on the other side. The chaise was no longer the main piece of furniture in the room. Savannah had found an antique, queen-size four-poster somewhere, probably the attics, along with matching bedside tables and a tall wardrobe she'd placed beside the small closet. Nothing in this wing had been updated, and the closets, while expansive for the standards of a century ago, were tiny to a modern eye. Scarlett didn't seem to care.

"This is amazing! For us?" She turned wide eyes to Savannah. "How did you manage this?"

Savannah laughed. "With the help of some of the day staff and Billy Bob—two brothers who work around Heartstone when we need them. They don't say much, but they work fast."

"I can see that," Scarlett murmured, turning a slow circle then crossing the room to push open another door and finding a second bathroom, also tiled in white.

Savannah followed, explaining, "The plumbing works in both bathrooms, but only about half of the outlets have power. I brought up some extension cords in case you need them."

"We'll make it work," Scarlett assured her.

"Let me know if you need anything at all," Savannah said, heading for the door. Scarlett caught her in a tight hug.

"Thank you for making us feel so at home."

Savannah grinned as she stepped out of the hug. "It's all self-interest. If you're at home, maybe you'll stay. Nicky loves having you here, and so do I."

I caught Savannah before she left. "Thank you."

She surprised me with a quick hug. "It took my mind off watching the clock. You scared the hell out of us."

"Sorry about that."

Patting my shoulder, she said, "No, you're not. You shouldn't be. You did the right thing."

Something occurred to me, and I followed Savannah out into the hall, glancing across to an open door. "I can't stay with Scarlett, but I don't like them alone in this wing with all the trouble Bryce—"

"I have you covered." Savannah strode across the hall and pushed open the door opposite Scarlett's. This room was still mostly empty, but the double bed had fresh sheets and there was a lamp on the dresser. "No bathroom, but it's the closest to the stairs and to Scarlett. If you leave the door cracked, you'll know if anyone comes this way."

"You're the best, Savannah."

She flashed me a very satisfied smile. "I know. Now, go help your woman put those kids to bed before they realize how overtired they are and go bonkers on her."

Shouts of outrage echoed across the hall. Savannah's eyebrows shot up. We both recognized the sounds of a sibling war in the making. "Too late." Patting my arm, she strode away, her laughter floating in her wake.

Getting both boys to calm down enough to go to bed was a new experience. August was wound up tight, over-stimulated by the drama of our last-minute arrival, the late bedtime, and the company of the brother he'd missed so much. We finally got them in bed, Scarlett rubbing August's back while I leaned in the door frame, watching as the younger boy chattered non-stop to his brother, who answered mostly in grunts until August's voice abruptly shut off. He was out.

Scarlett got up and moved to perch on the side of Thatcher's bed, combing her fingers through his hair, murmuring soft words I couldn't hear. I left to go back to my own room and grab a few supplies. Some clothes, a bottle of water, phone charger, toothbrush, and a bottle of whiskey with two tumblers. If ever we deserved a drink, it was now.

Scarlett sank onto the velvet chaise in her new room, curling into me as she took her tumbler of whiskey. "My head is still spinning. Was it really this morning that Bryce threatened to have me arrested? I feel like I've lived two lifetimes since then."

"Me, too." I paused, balanced on a precipice, not sure if I should dive over the edge. Fuck it. Luck was with me so far today. Might as well ride the wave. "Want me to spin your head a little more?"

Scarlett's eyebrows pulled together in disappointment. "We can't. Not with the boys—"

I nudged her shoulder, completely unable to stop the knowing grin that spread across my face. "Not that. Not tonight. Thatcher is holding it together, but today was intense. I know you want to leave the door open in case he needs you."

Scarlett's green eyes studied mine. "How do you know that?"

I leaned in to kiss her, a slow meeting of lips, the taste of whiskey on her tongue. "Because I pay attention."

"You certainly do," she said, her soft lips grazing mine. Pulling back slowly, she sipped her whisky. "Then what? What could you possibly say that would make my head spin even more than it already is?"

I stepped off the cliff. "I want you to stay."

Her eyes widened, mouth curving. "I don't have to be back until—"

"No, Scarlett. I want you to stay. Not 'until.' I want you to stay."

Her mouth dropped open. Staring at me, dumbfounded,

Scarlett didn't say a word. With a sudden move, she drained her glass. I took it, setting it on the floor beside the chaise. I'd known I was going to shock her. I'd shocked myself the first time the idea had hit me.

What if they stayed? What if she was mine? If *they* were mine? The idea was crazy. The list of reasons why not was a mile long.

"You barely know me," she breathed. Clearly, I'd succeeded in making her head spin.

"I know everything I need to know."

"I have the boys—"

"Did you think I missed that? They're great kids."

Scarlett let out a gust of a laugh. "Thatcher—"

"—fucked up. Everyone does. And Elliott was no small part of that. Thatcher's thirteen and he wanted to help his dad."

Scarlett sat back, studying me again. "Where's the rest of that whiskey?"

Obliging, I got the bottle and poured a healthy splash in both of our glasses.

Finally, she asked, "Should I ground him?"

I wasn't sure if this was a test or Scarlett working it out and asking for input. Either way, my answer was the same. "Nope."

"Why not?"

"Because the fallout from today is going to be punishment enough."

Scarlett took a long sip of her whiskey. "Elliott is such an asshole. Thatcher loves him so much, and Elliott..." She drifted off, anguish for her son in her eyes.

"Once this sinks in," I said, "what his dad did, how bad that could have been... He'll still love his father, but he'll never see him the same way. That's a lot for him to handle. He doesn't need to be grounded on top of it."

I didn't know how to be a parent, but I knew what it was to be that kid who lost hope for his father. I knew what it was to realize the father you loved was never going to love you back the same way. Was always going to let you down.

"That's the way I was leaning, too." She tipped her head to rest on my shoulder. "Of all the lessons he has to learn, I hate that this was one of them."

"Me, too." I waited, the quiet darkness cocooning us, the golden light from the lamp giving the room a warm glow. Was she going to ignore what I'd said?

Her voice, when it came, was the softest vibration of sound. If I hadn't been holding my breath, I would have missed it.

"I want to stay with you." A quick intake of air, as if she was surprised the words had escaped. Then again, louder. "I want to stay with you, Tenn. I really do. But it's—" She stopped, searching for the right word.

"Complicated?" I supplied.

"So insanely complicated. There's the boys, and my job, and the house..."

Counseling myself to be patient, I pushed just a little. "Which of those is the biggest complication?"

"The boys," she answered instantly. "I know a lot of people would say I can't let children dictate my life, but they're my boys. We're a team." She turned to face me, entreaty on her face.

"I want you to stay, Scarlett. Not for the summer. I want you to stay forever. You and the boys. If they don't want to be here—" I stopped, not sure what to say. "We'll figure it out."

"They need time," she said, worry creasing a line between her brows.

I kissed the worry line, wishing I could wave a wand and erase everything keeping me from her. I wanted this bedroom to be ours. I wanted those boys to be mine with a visceral need I'd never expected. I wanted it all right now, and I couldn't have it. Not yet. Maybe never.

I wasn't admitting the possibility of defeat. Only delay. They needed time. That was one thing I had in abundance.

"I know. Let them settle in. Relax. Enjoy summer in the mountains. We still have a Roman emperor to find."

The worry line disappeared as Scarlett's brows shot up again. "How could I have forgotten about Vitellius? He has to be here somewhere, right? If Bryce is the one who stole the bust from Elliott—he could have stashed it somewhere else, but Heartstone Manor makes the most sense."

"We'll check in with Hawk and Griffen tomorrow, but that's my guess. And if the Vitellius is here, Elliott will show up eventually."

Scarlett took a quick sip of whiskey, surprised to find the tumbler empty again. "This isn't over, is it?"

"No, it's not."

It wouldn't be over until we found that bust and got it back to the rightful owner. Until that happened, we were all in danger, no matter how much we wanted to pretend saving Thatcher was the end of it.

Thanks to Elliott, it would never be over as long as the bust of Vitellius was still out there.

Chapter Thirty-Eight

SCARLETT

I cracked the door to my room, peering into the dimly lit hallway. The boys were out cold, exhausted after another day of playing with Nicky in the morning and swimming in the afternoon. While August never stopped moving, Thatcher liked to escape to the family gathering room to make use of the gaming console Tenn had shown him or chill in our sitting room with a book. Between the pool, the hours spent gaming or reading, and near-constant raids on the pantry, my oldest child seemed to be okay.

He was and he wasn't. I knew my boy, and he was mostly his usual self. Mostly. He had the cook and Savannah wrapped around his little finger with his shy smile and patience with the younger kids. But there was a heaviness to his eyes, a deep quiet surrounding him that I wasn't used to. I knew I couldn't fix it for him, and I tried not to hover. Parenting had been so much easier when all their hurts could be fixed with a band-aid and a kiss. This was nothing so simple.

I tried to get him to talk to me, an effort that had only

resulted in one of his trademark grunts and an eye roll. "Mom, I'm chill. Stop worrying."

Like that was going to work. I'm a mom. I worry. But I tried to give him space.

Savannah, her mother, and I worked out a deal. They covered the boys in the morning while I continued my cataloging project and, openly now, searched for the ugly little bust of Emperor Vitellius. In the afternoons, I took the kids off her hands, usually with a picnic and a swim.

Tenn played hooky from work in the afternoon most days. To his irritation, everyone agreed he couldn't leave Heartstone Manor for any reason until the last day of the month, even for work. While the will only counted time away from the house if it included an overnight, no one wanted to take any chances.

Tenn gave in with a shrug. Most of a week slipped by that way—work in the morning, play in the afternoon, and me creeping across the hall when the boys were asleep for another kind of play at night.

Across the way, Tenn's door was open, darkness beyond. I didn't need the light. Leaving my own door open, I snuck from my room to his, my body warming as I thought about Tenn. He lay in bed, the sheet at his waist, his chest bared to my eyes.

Yum.

I didn't delay, untying the belt to my robe and dropping it to the floor.

"Efficient," Tenn murmured, flipping back the sheet to welcome me to bed.

I came to him eagerly, fitting my body to his, pulling his lips to mine. I couldn't believe I'd held out so long before getting this man naked. Everything about him was a perfect match for me.

He rolled me to my back, settling between my thighs, kissing me everywhere. My jaw, my collarbone, one hand closing around my breast, his mouth sucking at one hard nipple, then the other.

I was ready, soft and slick with need for him when I raised my knees, pulling him up, urging him inside.

"You're always rushing me," he pretended to complain, his eyes burning as he filled me.

"I can't help it." I rocked up into him, taking more, needing to feel him come, to hear his harsh breaths and thundering heart. "It feels too good to slow down. We can always do it again."

I felt his laugh deep inside, all the way to my core. Nuzzling at my neck as he fucked me in that deliberate pace that always made me crazy, he agreed, "True. And again. And again. Or maybe I should cuff you to the bed and take my time."

At the memory, I shivered. Tenn groaned, moving faster, promising, "Later. I'll cuff you to the bed later. Now, I'm going to make you come so hard you see stars."

It didn't take long. It never did with Tenn.

Since the day we'd met, his body and mine had called to each other. Nothing felt so right as Tenn touching me, loving me. We'd never said the words, but I knew. I'd spent so many years with my walls up, doubting men—at the end with Elliott, and then the few guys I'd dated after the divorce. I started with suspicion and never got far enough to let anyone in.

I don't know if I'd ever really let Elliott in. I'd thought I had. Thought what I'd felt for him had been love, at least in the beginning, even if it had faded later. Now that there was Tenn, I knew I'd never loved Elliott. I'd been blinded by his looks and his easy charm, too young to tell infatuation from love. I'd thought it had been his beauty and the sex, but I was wrong about that, too.

Tenn was a million times more handsome than Elliott. And when it came to sex, there was no comparison. Elliott gave me orgasms. Sometimes. Tenn was... everything. Sex with Tenn was so much more than orgasms. It was connection, the feel of his body, his touch, his kisses, and soft words. I was whole with Tenn, and until him, I'd never known something had been missing.

Turning in his arms, I rose up enough to see his face. "I talked to my department head."

Tenn sat up, taking me with him, pulling the blankets around us. I cuddled in, nervous and not nervous at all. I could talk to Tenn about anything, but this was big. He waited for me to go on.

"Back in the spring, when we discussed my course load and me taking the summer off, I mentioned the idea of a sabbatical. We don't have a funded sabbatical program, but a few professors I've known have done self-funded sabbaticals."

"And?" Tenn prompted when I fell silent.

"And when I brought it up, he said he'd approve a sabbatical, but I had to let him know soon so he'd have time to organize my replacement. I also called a friend who knows everything going on around campus and she has a line on a few people looking for sublets for the year. A visiting professor in the Mathematics Department and one in her department. It's a small town and decent housing can be tough to find. Most of the rentals are for students and they're not in great shape."

"But?" Tenn reached out to tuck a strand of hair behind my ear, then changed his mind and pulled it to the front where it fell over the swell of my breast. His fingertip stroked over my skin, sending shivers down my spine, and still, he waited. So much patience. I wished I had the same.

"I don't want there to be a *but*," I admitted. "I want to say yes. Yes to staying here. Yes to everything."

"But you can't," Tenn said, no trace of anger or frustration in his voice, his eyes.

Perversely, his patience annoyed me, the surge of irritation pushing me past my reservations into spitting out the truth. "I love you, okay? I don't know how it happened so fast or how I can be so sure, but I love you. I'm in love with you."

I didn't mean to sound so aggravated when I finally told him, but every word shot out like a bullet. I crossed my arms over my chest, off-balance after my rushed confession. I wasn't sure I'd been ready, but the words were out now. Too late to take them back.

Tenn just smiled, a slow spread of his lips, a heat in his eyes that told me what I already knew. "I'm in love with you, too."

Something about hearing it chased off all my fears. I'd known he must love me. No one could touch me the way he did without love in there somewhere. I'd known before our mad race to get Thatcher. I definitely knew after.

I hadn't thought I needed the words. I'd been wrong. Struck silent, I sat there, staring at him.

"I love you, Scarlett. I love August. And once I get to know Thatcher better, I'm sure I'll be a goner for him, too."

"That's the *but*," I whispered, my throat dry at the easy way he'd said he loved my sons.

"Have they said they want to go home?" Tenn asked, hesitation in his eyes for the first time.

"No." I shook my head. "I think August would be crushed if I told him we were leaving. He thinks this place is heaven. But Thatcher isn't saying anything, and I haven't had the guts to talk to him about it. He's so—" I couldn't find the right way to describe what was off about my oldest son. "Contained," I finished, for lack of a better word. "He's locked up inside and he won't talk to me. I'm worried about pushing something this big on him when he's already reeling."

Tenn leveled concerned eyes on my face as he leaned in to kiss me. When he pulled back, he stroked a hand down my shoulder, ending with my hand in his, our fingers tangled together. "I don't want to do this long-distance, especially since I can't travel—"

"No, definitely not."

He smiled at my instant refusal. He could tell me a thousand times that his inheritance didn't matter, and I was never going to listen. It wasn't about the money or the house. It was about giving, not taking. I was determined that if we did this, I was not going to take away from his life. Bringing two kids with me was a lot. Being the reason he risked his birthright? Not happening.

Giving me a gentle bop on the nose, he finished, "I don't want to do this long-distance, but I will if that's the only way. Like I told you before, we can figure this out. What's your deadline? When did your department head say he had to know?"

"July 10th."

"We have almost two weeks. We can let Thatcher settle in a little more and see how things go. I think you're right not to push. Not yet."

"Okay." I settled in beside Tenn, my head on his shoulder, his arm around me. I was exactly where I wanted to be. Well, almost. I would have preferred to stay like that all night.

It was way too soon to share a bedroom with him in front of my kids. It was one thing when we were camped out in Tenn's suite. Those days had a dreamy, haphazard quality that made our crazy arrangement make sense. Now that both boys were here and we'd needed our own rooms, suddenly, sleeping in the same bed with Tenn felt wrong.

August wasn't clueless, but he was focused on the priorities of an eight-year-old. The five years between him and Thatcher could have been a lifetime. Thatcher wasn't an adult, but he was close enough. And since I was the actual adult, I had to make the right choices. I was pretty sure those did not include moving my brand-new lover into my bed in front of my boys.

"We're both nuts, you know that right?"

Tenn nuzzled the top of my head. "You might be. I'm completely sane."

"We've basically just met." I still couldn't get my head around it. How could I be so sure about him? Yet I was. I had a million doubts, but none of them were about Tenn.

"Doesn't matter," Tenn said, his lips moving against my temple. "I love you. I think I fell for you that first night when I woke up with you on top of me."

I snorted a laugh. "That was your cock talking."

"A little, maybe." Tenn trailed a finger down my back, tracing across the swell of my hip. "Mostly, it was that I didn't want to push you off. I wanted you to stay exactly where you were even though I knew I wasn't getting laid. It only got worse from there."

A giggle snuck out. "You didn't have to wait long. I couldn't keep my hands off you. I should have known it was love. All these years of not being interested and all I wanted was to strip you naked."

Tenn rolled and I was on my back, legs spread, staring up at a devilish grin. "I'm naked now."

"Yes, you are." Reaching down between us, I wrapped my fingers around his hard cock, tilting my hips to lead him inside me. "I like you naked."

Those were the last words I managed before Tenn pinned my hands above my head and started to move. Nothing was resolved. Not really. We knew we were in love like a million idiots before us. It was the rest we had to work out. And we would. Eventually. Later. After I had my fill of naked Tenn.

A last thought drifted through my head before my mind blanked out.

If I waited until after I had my fill of Tenn, I'd never get another thing done.

I'd never have my fill of this man, but I was going to spend the rest of my life trying.

Chapter Thirty-Nine

TENN

My phone in my hand, I went in search of the elusive Thatcher Hall. I had a project and questions only he could answer. I hoped. I hadn't found him with Miss Martha and the younger kids. He wasn't with Scarlett or in their sitting room reading. For an active kid who loved gaming, I'd been surprised at how often I found him buried in a book.

If he wasn't with his brother, his mom, or reading, there was only one place he could be. We might not have been BFFs, but I was getting to know the kid. I found him in the gathering room, his eyes fixed on the screen where he methodically tracked and shot alien after alien, smirking as they exploded into purple goo.

Dropping onto the couch beside him, I waited. After a second, he shot me a sidelong look. Fuck, the kid was the spitting image of his father, only a spray of freckles across his nose reminding me of Scarlett. He was just thirteen, but the promise of the man within showed clearly.

Just like Elliott, his thick hair was so dark it was almost black, falling across his forehead in a perfect swoop as if he'd spent hours in front of the mirror to get it just right. Elliott might have, but I doubted Thatcher had done more than drag a brush through it, and that at his mother's insistence.

Instead of Scarlett's green eyes, Thatcher's were an arresting arctic blue, his cheekbones, nose, and jaw sculpted like a work of art. It killed to admit it, but I could see why a teenage Scarlett had fallen head over heels for this kind of beauty. Everything I'd heard and seen about Elliott led me to think he was an idiot. In contrast, Thatcher's eyes held a wary intelligence I had to respect.

"What's up?" he said, his eyes fixed on the screen.

"I wanted to ask you about something. I can wait." I wasn't a gamer like Thatcher, but Royal and I like to unwind with Madden or FIFA. I knew all about waiting until it was a good time to take a break. Thatcher grunted his assent and went back to his mission, clearing the level with a precision that told me this wasn't his first go-round.

I split my time between watching him and watching the screen. He was good, but I'd expect that of any gamer his age. I was a little surprised at his planning and tactics. He didn't rush through, blasting with the highest-powered weapon he could get his hands on. He switched seamlessly between weapons and methods of attack, the sides of his mouth curving up as he demolished the final boss.

Tossing the controller to the cushion beside him, he said, "You play this one?"

"No, FIFA's my game."

A wide grin split Thatcher's face, his mother coming into focus in that smile. "I kill at FIFA. I'll destroy you."

"Probably," I agreed. "Do you have a sec?"

Thatcher leaned back, the smile dropping off his face, guard up. "Sure, I guess."

The nerves swirling in my gut knocked me off-kilter as I pulled up my tablet. I hadn't spent any time with Thatcher on my own. I understood his reserve, even approved, but it was terrifying. If this kid decided he hated me, all my plans would go up in smoke. He was too smart to bribe or manipulate, not that I'd do either anyway.

He either liked me or he didn't, and I couldn't remember the last time that choice had me so rattled.

"So," I began, trying to sound more confident than I was, "I want to get your mom a surprise. She didn't bring her lampwork supplies down here, and I've seen her sketching. She wants to get back to it, and I thought I'd get her some basic stuff to get started. Do you know anything about her tools? Can you tell me which torch she'd like?"

Thatcher's eyes were wary as he leaned over to take the tablet from me, tapping and swiping until he'd looked at the various pages I had open. Pointing to a torch with over a thousand five-star reviews, he said, "She's been looking at that one. She wants to upgrade, but the one she has is okay so she hasn't wanted to spend the money." He flipped to a different tab and pointed to a basic lampwork kit. "That's enough to get her started. And she'll need a good worktable. Something sturdy that won't catch fire."

I took the tablet when he handed it back. "Does she usually set things on fire?"

I could see Thatcher weighing his answer, deciding if he was going to fuck with me. "Nah. But sometimes, the torch or her tools are hot and they scorch the table." He straightened, turning on the couch to face me, arms crossed over his chest. Like this, he looked a lot older than thirteen. It wasn't just his size—Scarlett was right, he could have easily passed for sixteen, even a young eighteen. It was the gravity in his icy blue eyes, the challenge. He was still a kid, but he was no child.

"Why are you buying this stuff for my mom? She has everything she needs at home. Are we going to stay here?" An edge of panic tinged his voice at the end.

I didn't know what to say, so I went with the truth. "I want you to, but nothing has been decided."

"What about what I want?" Thatcher demanded, his chin thrust forward, teeth clamping together the second the words were out.

I sat back, trying to look relaxed when I was anything but. "That's why nothing has been decided. You guys are a team. Your mom isn't going to make any decisions without you and your brother."

"She hasn't said anything," Thatcher muttered, his arms falling to the sides, his eyes on a scuff at the end of his sneaker. He rubbed at it with the heel of his other shoe. "She just hugs me and tells me we'll talk about it later."

"She's worried about you."

"I'm fine."

I paused, not sure what to say next. "I'm not trying to make you feel bad, but while you and your dad were missing, she was terrified." Thatcher's face fell, misery and guilt weighing his features, shading his bright eyes. I tapped his foot with mine to get his attention. "I meant it. I'm not trying to make you feel bad. I get why you did it."

A grunt. More scrubbing at the scuff on his sneaker.

"Look, I loved my dad, too."

"You said he was an asshole."

"He was. I still loved him for a long time. Especially when I was around your age. If I'd thought he was in big trouble, that I could help—" I shrugged, saying honestly, "I'm not sure what I would have done."

A raised eyebrow and a sullen look. "My dad's not an asshole like yours."

Something we could agree on. My smile was thin but real. "Yeah, I got that. My father was his own breed of asshole. Your dad—he's made some really bad decisions. He almost got you and your mom killed. I don't want to think about what would have happened if we hadn't come after you, if Sinclair Security hadn't saved all our asses. We're going to have to deal with the fact that he's mixed up with some really dangerous people. That doesn't mean you stop loving him. He's still your dad."

"Is my mom mad at me?" he asked, his voice sounding far too young for his body.

"No," I said immediately. "Your mom loves you more than anything in this world aside from August. She was scared. And if you do anything like that again, she may kill you herself. But right now, she's not mad, she's just grateful you're okay and that you're with her."

"So, why isn't she asking me what I think about all this?" That chin jutting forward in defiance reminded me so much of Scarlett, I felt an instant connection to Thatcher. I had to remind myself that just because I was head over heels for his mother, that didn't make us friends.

Scarlett aside, I liked him. He was honest and smart, and despite fighting with his brother half the time, he was a good kid. Polite. Kind. Usually pretty thoughtful. That part stuck with me. This was not a selfish kid. He shared with his brother, had way more patience with August and Nicky than I would have had at his age. He had to love his dad a lot to have put his mom through so much.

I tried to think of the right answer. I was totally at sea here. "I, uh, I think she's trying to give you space."

Another grunt, this one amused. "She's hugging me like every five seconds."

"She was really scared," I said quietly. "And I think she's worried about you. She knows how much you love your dad and she's afraid he's going to get into more trouble and you're going to get hurt."

"She never says anything bad about him," Thatcher said, his eyes still fixed on his shoes. "Sometimes her mouth gets weird when he makes her mad, but she never says anything mean about him."

"Does he say stuff like that about her?" Maybe I shouldn't pry, but I was dying to get inside Thatcher's head, to figure out what he was thinking.

"Nah. He makes jokes about her being a hard-ass and not letting us have junk food and stuff, but he never... I think he sometimes wishes they were back together."

"Only sometimes?"

A flash of that grin that reminded me of Scarlett. "Yeah. He's right, she doesn't put up with a lot of crap." He raised an eyebrow at me, a pure teenage smirk on his face. "Dad wouldn't make it five minutes in our house. He'd leave his shoes on the floor or forget to throw his laundry in the hamper and she'd kick his butt." The smirk melted away. "She wouldn't take him back anyway."

"Do you wish she would?" I asked quietly, not sure he'd answer.

After an endless minute he spent rubbing the heel of his sneaker on the carpet, he said, "No. My dad is fun when he's around, but my mom works really hard. August and I try to do our stuff, like take out the trash and help with the dishes, but she's tired a lot. My dad wouldn't make her happy."

There was nothing I could say to that. I was glad he didn't have fantasies of his parents getting back together.

One hurdle we didn't have to worry about. Thatcher slanted me an incisive look, and I had the distinct feeling he was mentally dissecting me.

"She needs someone who can make her happy."

"I agree," I said carefully.

His arms crossed over his chest again and he was back in full interrogation mode. "So, what makes you think that could be you? She only met you, what, like a week ago?"

"Ten days," I corrected before I could think better of it.

His grunt was more of a scoff. "Like that's any better."

Thatcher wasn't wrong. It was crazy. We'd just met. We should have been in second-date territory, not exchanging vows of love and talking about moving in together. If anyone else said they were in love after barely more than a week, I'd be all over them with warnings to slow it down, to give it time.

And the kid was right to worry about his mom. He loved her. I wondered if he felt like he'd left his dad in the middle of a dangerous mess only to find his mom in the same. Different kind of danger, but still...

With nothing else to work with, I stuck with honesty. "I know it's fast. Your mom knows it's fast. We also know we love each other. Sometimes, it happens like that. And your mom is an amazing woman. She's smart and funny, and I don't just love her, I love being with her. I don't want you guys to leave. I want you to stay and we can see how this goes. But it's up to you and August and your mom. If you decide not to stay..." I shrugged a shoulder. "We'll work it out."

"What does that mean?" Thatcher demanded, eyebrows pulled together, making a worry line identical to his mother's.

I shrugged again. "I don't know. I guess we'll see when

we get there. I know I love your mom and she loves me. I know I like you and your brother and I want you guys in my life. I also know this is a complicated situation, and it's happening fast, and there's a lot to consider. It's also hard for me to travel because of the will and my job."

"Your dad was a real jerk," Thatcher said.

"Believe me, I'm aware. If you guys go back home, it's more complicated, but it doesn't change how I feel about your mom or you and your brother. I can't give you a concrete answer. All I can say is that we'll work together to figure it out."

Thatcher nodded, not meeting my eyes. I couldn't get a read on him. We sat there in silence for a while. "You going to order that stuff?" he asked, lifting his chin in the direction of my tablet.

"Do you think I should?"

"Yeah, she'll like the torch. And—" His phone beeped with a text. Pulling it up, his eyes went dark. He read the text, then read it again, his eyes scanning the words until he must have had them memorized. Silent, he turned the phone to me.

Headed to SB. Got a line on the statue. See you soon.

My gut sank. Elliott. I met Thatcher's worried eyes. Carefully, I said, "You met Hawk?" He nodded. "Did your mom tell you how we found you?"

"He tracked my phone," Thatcher said slowly. He put the pieces together and clicked his screen closed. "Hawk saw this?"

"I'm sure he did."

"Is he going to hurt my dad?" I barely knew the kid and already I hated hearing his voice go small. If Elliott Hall had been here, I would have knocked him out cold.

"Not unless your dad tries to hurt someone in this house."

"Do you think those Leary guys are going to follow my dad? Here?"

I shook my head. "I have no idea. Hawk probably has a better guess than me. Do you want to go find him? Show him your phone?"

Thatcher sat there holding his breath, staring at the dark screen of his phone. Finally, he stood, the movement slow and awkward as if he was tired all the way to the bone. Shoving his phone in his pocket, he said, "Yeah, I think maybe we should."

I squeezed his shoulder, my chest going tight when he leaned into me for just a second. He didn't hate me. That was a start. "Everything's going to be okay, Thatcher."

I knew better than to make promises about things I couldn't control. I did it anyway. He'd been through enough. I wasn't going to let his dad make things worse. Not if I could stop him.

Chapter Forty

TENN

"You're not helping." I'm sure Scarlett meant to sound firm, but her breathless words only drew me back for another kiss.

"Did I promise to help?"

"I thought it was implied when you sat down and started going through that storage bin."

I couldn't help giving her a raised eyebrow and a matching smug smile. "You thought wrong. I'm here to distract you with kisses."

Her eyes sparkled in the golden light flooding through the small attic window. "Well, okay then. As long as the kisses keep coming."

The lid of the storage bin in my hands, I leaned in to press my mouth to hers one more time. Despite my teasing, I'd come up to the attics with the intention of helping. I'd tried to concentrate on work, but I hadn't seen Scarlett alone in daylight for a few days, and I missed her.

I loved our stolen nights in my room across the hall. I wasn't pushing for more. Not now. Not yet. But I wanted this, too. Just being with her, helping her or her helping me. When I was with Scarlett, something deep inside me relaxed, at ease and at the same time more alive than I'd ever been. I was at home and on an adventure at once. All I wanted was more.

I'd hold off the kissing for a few more minutes. Maybe one. We did have a job to do. Tossing the lid to the floor, I dug into the plastic storage bin at my feet. A small smile curving her mouth, Scarlett did the same with the bin in front of her.

She'd finished the main areas of the house and had started on the attics. Plural. Each wing of the house had its own attic, and all three were a rabbit warren of small rooms, most of them packed with stuff. Furniture and boxes. So many boxes. Everything from ancient crates and antique steamer trunks to faded cardboard and more modern plastic storage bins. It looked like none of my ancestors had ever thrown away a single thing.

Scarlett ducked her head to the side, landing a quick kiss on my jaw. "Did I say thank you for the torch and glass? And the space by the kitchens?"

"Several times." Her thanks had involved the handcuffs, my bed, and hours of delicious sexual torture. "If that's the way you say thank you, I'll have to think of more things to buy you."

She poked me in the side. "That wasn't my thank you. That was just for you. I owed you one."

"In that case, I'll have to think of more ways to get you in my debt."

She hummed in the back of her throat, a sound of pure satisfaction spiked with a thread of anticipation. "Anytime, cowboy."

I resisted the urge to tumble her to the floor and have

my way with her. It felt like we were alone, but I had no idea if these doors locked. Later. I'd get my hands on her later. I went back to sifting through the bin in front of me. Nothing interesting yet. We'd stumbled onto a random assortment of my father's papers, stored up here who knew how long ago. So far, my bin held everything from a roofing estimate to dental bills.

"How was your hike this morning?" she murmured, opening a manila envelope and scanning the contents.

"Good. Quiet." At breakfast, I'd said something about hitting the trails before work and Thatcher had asked if he could come. Shocked, I'd immediately shifted my plans from a run to a hike. If Thatcher was asking to spend time with me, I wasn't going to say no.

Scarlett let out a short chuckle. "Sounds about right. I swear, since he hit puberty, his vocabulary has devolved into mostly grunts and annoyed sighs. We used to have great conversations. We still do, sometimes, but he's made silence into an art form."

"It was okay. I'm good with a quiet hike. He said he liked it, so that was something. He wants to do it again. And he thought it was cool I can fly fish and asked me to show him how." I swallowed. "I want him to like it here."

This thing with Scarlett was so new, I was still adjusting to the idea of exposing my vulnerabilities, still surprised by how many I had when it came to Scarlett and her boys.

"I want him to like it here, too." She leaned her head against my shoulder for a moment, her love filling that dark hollow of worry inside me. Scarlett fit me like a puzzle piece. I hoped she'd stay with fierce desperation. I couldn't imagine the hole she and the boys would leave if they went back up north.

"I'm glad he had a good time. I liked showing him the

trails." It had been too long since I slowed down and really paid attention to my home. Too long since I'd seen it with new eyes.

With Thatcher beside me, everything was new. The mist clinging to the treetops, the way the branches seemed to brush the sky above moss-covered rocks and roots in every shade of green and grey and brown. Thatcher had stopped, stunned, when we'd surprised a family of wild turkeys, his eyes wide at the sight of the small, plump poults guarded by the hen and tom who gobbled at us until we backed away.

"We could grab one for dinner," Thatcher had joked.

"We could, but check out their feet. Those claws are no joke."

Thatcher had stepped behind me, crouching down to take a closer look without scaring the birds. "They're so big."

"Sometimes they wander down to the house and hang out on the lawn."

Thatcher turned to look up at me, the fascination on his face reminding me how young he really was. "So, you have wild animals hanging out around the house? No one shoots them or anything?"

"Turkey season is only a few weeks, and they don't bother anyone. It's the bears you have to watch out for. When I was a kid and the fountain in the gardens worked, sometimes a mama bear would bring her cubs for a swim."

"For real? Are there still bears now?" His eyes were wide with a hint of worry.

"Oh, yeah, but they aren't much trouble. They have plenty of room to spread out here. As long as you never get between a mama and her cubs, you'll be fine."

At the memory of the disbelieving look on Thatcher's face, I grinned. "It was cool showing him around." I hoped he took me up on the offer to do it again or take him fishing. It had been way too long since I'd taken my fly rod out to the river.

"Did he say anything about Elliott?" Scarlett asked.

"Not to me. Did he say anything to you?"

She shook her head. "Only that he was worried about the Learys following his dad. I wish we had the stupid bust of Vitellius so we could put an end to the whole thing." She shook her head again, this time in disgust. "Fucking Elliott."

I had nothing to say to that. I'd only spent a few minutes with the guy, but I had the feeling he didn't grasp the danger he'd brought to his family. Or maybe he did, and he didn't care. Either way, they were mine now, and I wasn't going to let him hurt them. That didn't mean we didn't have another set of problems on my side of the family equation.

"Hawk still doesn't have anything solid on Bryce. Plenty of suspicions and circumstantial evidence, but not enough for West to bring charges on anything. And if Bryce is the one who took Vitellius, Hawk hasn't found it."

"And neither have we," Scarlett finished, lifting her head to look around the crowded attic. "He could have stashed it anywhere."

I wrapped an arm around her, pulling her into my side and kissing her temple. "We'll get through this. I'm not going to let anything happen to you or the boys."

Scarlett turned her head to kiss my jaw. "Or you, right? I haven't forgotten all those guns pointed at you. That's not happening again, either."

"Agreed. Not the high point of my summer. I'm good with no more guns pointed at any of us for the rest of forever."

"Maybe we can—" Scarlett stopped, arrested by the

papers in her hand. Her alert green eyes scanned the lines of text. Hurriedly, she swapped the page she was reading for the one beneath, then the one beneath that. With a quick intake of breath, she shoved the stack at me. "Is this what I think it is?"

It took me a minute to absorb what I was seeing. Hot damn, this wasn't the Vitellius, but it might be part of what we were looking for, buried in a stack of grocery bills and outdated legal documents.

"It looks like this is a contract to put an oil painting up for auction." I shuffled to another piece of paper, this one thin, the writing uniformly grey as if it were a part of a duplicate pad. "And this looks like a receipt for a cashier's check with the same account number as the contract with the auction house."

I set the two papers aside and looked through the rest, quickly matching a second contract with a different auction house and a handwritten receipt for another cashier's check. We dug through the rest of the pile, matching five more works of art with five more receipts.

When we were done, Scarlett gave a low whistle through her teeth. "This adds up to almost half a million dollars. Didn't Griffen say he had a forensic accountant looking for the money?"

"Wherever this cash went, it wasn't into any of the accounts she was able to find. No way she would have missed this much money. Griffen said she's the best."

"Do you think he stashed the money somewhere?" Scarlett gazed around the attic with renewed interest.

"Maybe," I said slowly, digging beneath an old newspaper to pull out a manila envelope, the flap tucked inside to keep the contents in place. Pulling it open, three handwritten notes slid out.

My heart stopped in my chest. I knew that handwriting.

I shot to my feet, heart pounding in my ears, my own voice tinny and far away. "Grab those papers. We need to bring this to Griffen."

"What is it? What did you find?" Scarlett kept pace behind me as I jogged down the narrow staircase from the attic to the second level.

Scarlett had been working in the attic above the family wing. The stairs let out beside the linen closet, the stairwell door designed to blend in with the wall itself. When it was fully closed, it was almost invisible. I'd shut it behind me when I went up to see how Scarlett was doing.

Despite my haste, the sound of angry voices on the other side had me stopping short at the closed door. Turning the handle slowly, I opened it an inch instead of rushing through. Scarlett wiggled in beside me, the soft press of her breasts momentarily drawing my attention from the scene in the hall.

"What is it?" Her mouth was at my ear, her words barely audible. In answer, I opened the door another inch. "Ohh," she breathed, watching along with me, the receipts and contracts momentarily forgotten.

In the hallway, Sterling argued with Forrest. I couldn't make out any distinct words—they could have been arguing about a game of cricket for all I knew—but whatever they were fighting about, they were pissed. Sterling's cheeks were flushed, her finger pointed, jabbing him in the chest.

Where another man might have backed away, Forrest leaned in, ignoring the poke of her long fingernail, looming over her to say something in a low, furious tone. I started to shove the door open, every brotherly instinct telling me to get this overbearing asshole away from my sister.

Sterling had been taking care of herself for a long time. Far too long. It had taken Griffen's return for me to see how alone my youngest sister was. How much she needed her family. I wasn't the best big brother, but I wasn't going to let this guy push her around.

Scarlett's hand closed over my arm, pulling me back. She shook her head, unbothered by my glare. "Give her a minute. I think—" She smiled in satisfaction. "Yeah, see?"

Turning back, I scowled as Forrest slid a hand around the back of Sterling's neck, pulling her up and slamming his mouth down on hers. She melted into him, her arms going around his neck, kissing him back with a hunger I did not need to see.

Pivoting back to Scarlett, I growled, "You should have let me stop them."

Giving my arm a light slap, she peeked around me, eyes wide. "They look good together."

"Shut it. I do not need that image in my head." I really did not. "She's my baby sister."

"Well, she's not my sister, and he's not my brother, and all I can say is... they're hot. If they're not going to get a room, I'm sticking around for the show."

Letting out a groan they would have heard in the hall if they hadn't been drowning in a fog of lust, I pulled the door shut, closing us off in the dark of the stairwell. Pinning

Scarlett against the wall, I dipped my head to nip at her earlobe. "You need a show, Scarlett? Not getting what you need?"

As a distraction, it worked perfectly. Scarlett twined her arms around my neck, tipping her head back, offering herself to me. "I'm so deprived. I haven't gotten you naked in almost twelve hours. I don't know how you expect me to—"

She let out a shriek as I cupped her ass and lifted her against the wall, settling myself between her legs and kissing her until we both stopped thinking about anything but each other.

She wasn't the only one who needed a diversion. With Scarlett in my arms, I couldn't have cared less about whatever my sister and Forrest were up to. Scarlett filled my senses. The warm scent of her skin, the little sounds she made as I kissed her, satisfied and eager, the clasp of her legs around my hips, her fingers digging into my neck.

I didn't get my senses back until the crackle of paper hit my ears, sharp and out of place among the soft sounds of our breath and bodies.

The contracts.

Damn.

Slowly, I set Scarlett on her feet, looking down to make sure we weren't standing on top of everything we'd dropped.

"We have to get this to Griffen," I said, bending down to pick up the papers and slide them into the manila envelope.

Scarlett brushed her hair back, blinking at me in the dim stairwell. "I almost forgot why we were coming downstairs." She turned the handle to the door, peeking out a narrow crack. "Coast's clear. Let's go before I drag you into an empty room to have my way with you."

"As soon as we talk to Griffen, I'm finding a room with

at least five locks and I'm handcuffing myself to you again. After we're naked."

"I like your plan." She pressed a quick kiss to my neck and led me down to the front hall, her hand in mine, tugging me along.

I didn't bother to knock on Griffen's office door, flinging it open and pulling Scarlett in behind me. "Griffen, we found— Oh, fuck, sorry—"

I spun around, blocking Scarlett's view of Hope straddling Griffen's lap, his mouth on her neck, hand inside her shirt and half her buttons undone. "Sorry," I said to the ceiling. "We have something to show you, but we'll come back."

Griffen cleared his throat. "Later would be good. Or never—"

It sounded like Hope covered his mouth with her hand. "It's fine, we're fine, just one sec. Don't go."

"No, go," Griffen added. "It's not fine."

"Griffen—" Hope sounded torn between regret and amusement. Over a rustle of fabric, she said, "You can turn around, I'm decent."

"I'm not," Griffen muttered.

I turned to find him seated behind his desk, Hope beside him, her fingers still fumbling on her buttons, cheeks sweetly pink.

"Sorry," Scarlett said, taking the manila envelope from my hand and shoving it at Griffen. "We should have knocked, but we found this and wanted to show you right away."

"What is it?" Griffen asked immediately, taking the envelope and pulling out the contents.

"Auction contracts for five pieces and receipts for almost half a million dollars." I paused. "And something else you need to see."

Griffen spread the first few papers out across his desk. "Tell me what I'm looking at."

Scarlett leaned over and lined up the contracts with their matching receipts. Griffen didn't need further explanation. "That's a lot of missing cash. And what's the 'something else?'"

I shook out the three letters I'd found and set them on Griffen's desk in front of him. Reading over his shoulder, I waited for Griffen's response.

It was Hope who spoke first. "That's Vanessa's handwriting. I recognize it from the notes she'd send Ford." At Griffen's curious look, she explained, "They'd get mixed up in the business correspondence and sometimes I'd open them by mistake. Or because I was nosy," she added, rolling her eyes in sheepish amusement at herself.

Before marrying Griffen, Hope had been her Uncle Edgar's assistant. Edgar, Prentice, and our brother, Ford, had worked closely together, much of the Sawyer business intertwined with Edgar's. Hope knew more about the details of both Ford and our father's life than anyone except her uncle.

The letters in front of us were neither addressed nor signed. One was on a heavy-weight notecard. The other two appeared to have been hastily scribbled on lined notepaper. On all three, the handwriting was unmistakably Vanessa's, a distinctively odd combination of sweeping curves and hard angles. I'd have recognized it anywhere. None of the letters were dated, but they followed a clear progression. The first was short.

I know who the new Mrs. Sawyer will be, and I know why you're marrying her.

500k or I tell him everything.

"So there really was a new Mrs. Sawyer," Hope

breathed. "He'd hinted, but no one ever met her. Uncle Edgar and I joked that he found a woman on one of those dating apps."

"Maybe no one ever met her because she was married." I pointed at the last words. "'500k or I tell him everything.' Who else could the *him* be?"

"A father?" Hope offered.

Griffen shook his head. "This isn't Victorian England. I'd bet it was a husband. Unless she was underage..." He shook his head again, this time a scowl of disgust twisting his face.

"Ugh. I hope she was married," Hope said, moving the second letter to the top of the pile.

Cutting it a little close, aren't you? You don't have long before you're out of time. Get me the rest of the money or I tell him all your plans. Once he knows the truth, he'll never let her go.

"I'm voting the *he* is her husband." I racked my brain for any woman I'd ever heard my father mention. I came up with nothing. "We can ask the girls, but I have no clue who he might have been involved with, and Royal wouldn't either. We didn't deal with Prentice much in the last few years. Sterling's the only one who was living here. She might have seen or heard something."

"I'll ask Uncle Edgar again," Hope murmured, pulling up the last letter.

If he finds out what you did to him, what you stole from him, he'll destroy you. Once he knows the truth, there won't be anywhere you can run that he won't find you. 300k more and I'll keep my mouth shut. Pay me and you'll never see me again.

"Is this what I think it is?" Scarlett asked, head tilted to the side as she studied the small sheet of notepaper.

332

"If you think this could be the motive for our father's murder, then I think you might be right," Griffen said, sitting back his chair. "I'd almost convinced myself it was about business."

"This looks pretty personal," Scarlett said, "but I'm not sure I'm putting the pieces together. How would Vanessa know about your father's love life when no one else did?"

"No clue," I answered. "But that's nothing new. We don't know much about what was going on. There's no date on these, but I'm guessing this was around the time he started doing all the renovations in the family wing. About three years ago." I looked to Hope.

"That's the only time period when we had any hint there might be a new Mrs. Sawyer," she agreed. "And he hadn't bothered with updating the house until whoever she was came along. I always assumed the two were connected."

"What does this mean?" Scarlett pointed to the words *out of time*.

"No idea." I shook my head in disgust. "We don't even know all three of these notes are about the same thing. The first two reference a woman, but the third doesn't. It could be about something else."

"Could be," Scarlett mused, "but I doubt it. How connected was Vanessa to Prentice? What are the odds she stumbled onto not one but two separate reasons to black-mail him?"

I hoped Scarlett was right. All we needed was another complication. I shoved the notes into a rough pile. "This doesn't help at all. We have more questions and no real answers."

"I disagree," Griffen said calmly, gathering the loose papers into a stack with the notes and sliding them into the manila envelope. "We know Vanessa was blackmailing our father. We know that when she claimed to know who killed him, she might have been telling the truth. And we know whoever killed them both was a lot smarter than they thought he was."

"It could be a *she*," Hope added. We all stared at her. "The killer," Hope explained. "It could be a *she*. We don't know what happened to the mysterious future Mrs. Sawyer. Maybe Prentice pissed her off and she killed him, then killed Vanessa for threatening to expose her."

Thinking it over, I played back my last conversation with Vanessa. "She said, '*When he finds out I told you, my life won't be worth anything.*'" Everyone shifted their gazes from Hope to me. "Vanessa. That morning in the garden, right before she was shot. She said, '*When he finds out I told you, my life won't be worth anything.*' She was trying to talk me into paying her for the name of Dad's killer. I wish—"

"Don't." Scarlett slid her arm around my waist, her eyes heavy with concern as they met mine. "If you'd talked to her longer or gone to get her the money, you might have been killed, too. We have no idea if the killer had a plan to set you up for her death or if you just had bad timing. If it was the second, he might have shot you, too."

"If he thought you were a witness, he undoubtedly would have killed you," Griffen added, and I was reminded that while he was doing a stellar job running Sawyer Enterprises, he wasn't a businessman by trade. Before our father died and stuck him with all of this, he'd been with the best private security company in the country. This wasn't Griffen's first run-in with a killer.

"Hey, Griffen— Oh, sorry—" Sterling hovered in the open door, her eyes searching for Griffen.

Smoothly, he slid the manila envelope into a drawer, his

eyes warming as he leaned back in his chair. "It's okay, Sterling, what's up?"

"I just wanted to let you know I won't be home for dinner."

Griffen slanted her a big brother look, his eyes narrowed on her face. I wondered if he caught her swollen lips or the hint of beard burn on her cheeks. "Hot date?"

Sterling narrowed her eyes back at him before her face broke into a sunny smile, lighting her blue eyes until she was so beautiful it made my heart hurt. "None of your beeswax, but yes, I do." Sticking out her tongue, she turned to flounce out of the room, reminding me painfully of the little girl she'd been.

"Wait a sec, we want to ask you a question about Dad."

Sterling deflated, the spring gone from her step as she pivoted to face us. "What about Dad?" she asked, her voice weighted with caution. Anything to do with our father had Sterling gathering her armor, barricading herself deep inside where she was safe.

"Do you remember if he was seeing anyone a few years ago? Around the time he started fixing up the family wing? Or after?"

Sterling shook her head slowly, eyes focused on the ceiling as if she were flipping through her memories. "I don't..." She shrugged, eyes dark, her light dimmed. "I was drinking a lot back then and he was..." She stopped, gathering her thoughts. "He was gone a lot. Not always overnight, but he missed dinner pretty often. I remember that because I'd skip dinner if he was around and eat in the kitchen after the staff went home, but if he was gone, they'd serve me his meal in the dining room." She shrugged a shoulder. "I was drinking too much then, but I was eating pretty well."

I hated knowing that. Why hadn't it ever occurred to me that Sterling was hiding in the kitchen to eat alone when Prentice was home? Why hadn't we checked in on her? Back then, it had felt like it was every Sawyer for himself. Avoiding Prentice and Heartstone Manor had been my modus operandi. I hadn't spared much thought for my youngest sister, assuming she and Prentice must get along alright or she would have left too.

"Why did you stay?" I wished I'd kept my mouth shut when Sterling looked away.

Hope answered for her. "Sometimes, being alone is scarier than being with someone who makes you miserable." Sterling's lips quirked into a half-smile that didn't reach her eyes.

"You moved out, though," Sterling said, referencing Hope's great act of rebellion against her Uncle Edgar.

Hope smiled, shaking her head in denial. "I did, but not until I was older than you are now. It took me ages to work up the nerve, and while Uncle Edgar can be an ass, he was never a match for your father."

Finally, Sterling's face cracked into a genuine smile, though it didn't quite reach her eyes. "That's true. Even at his worst, Edgar is nowhere close to dear old Dad." Straightening her shoulders, she studied Griffen. "Why'd you ask about Dad? Did something happen?"

Griffen shook his head. "Nothing happened, we were just trying to work out what he might have been up to."

Sterling snorted and turned for the door. "Good luck with that. He was up to a lot, and none of it was good. Now, I'm going to follow in his footsteps and get up to some trouble myself." She winked and shut the door behind her.

Griffen stared at the closed door for a long moment

before letting out a breath. "I don't like her with Powell. She's going to get her heart broken."

I sank into the chair opposite his desk. "Agreed. He's working out well as CFO for the Inn, and he seems like a good guy, but—"

"Any chance you two are just being overprotective?" Hope asked. "She's a grown woman and he seems to care about her."

"There's a few things you don't know—" Leaning forward, I told Griffen and Hope about the fight in the hall and reminded them about catching Forrest searching the guest wing.

"Other than that, he seems above board," Griffen said. "But I'm with you. I don't like it."

"Too bad it isn't any of your business who Sterling goes out with," Scarlett said, one eyebrow raised and a hand on her hip. "And if you badger her about Forrest, she'll probably drag him off to Vegas and marry him just to show you who's in charge."

Griffen laughed. "You're right. They're in the honeymoon phase. There's no arguing good sense with all those hormones flooding her brain."

Scarlett leaned in to whisper to Hope, "You should have seen them in the hall. I thought they were going to set the wallpaper on fire."

"Ooh, tell me more—"

Griffen pulled Hope into his lap. "Why don't we stop talking about my baby sister kissing some guy, get rid of these two, and go back to what we were doing before they barged in?"

I got to my feet and took Scarlett's hand, tugging her toward the door. "I believe we had plans involving a door with locks?" I loved the way her cheeks went pink at being teased in front of Griffen and Hope.

Scarlett on my mind, I forgot all about Forrest Powell. In retrospect, I wish I hadn't.

In the end, I'm not sure it would have made a difference.

All around us, unseen forces were moving toward each other on a collision course. One we wouldn't see coming until it was far too late to stop the explosion.

Chapter Forty-Two

oom! My ears rang from the concussion, the sparkling crackle of the fireworks popping against my senses, my eyes dazzled by the splash of color where the stars should be. Fourth of July fireworks lit the night sky above the Inn and we had a front-row seat. Tenn and Royal had gone all out, transforming Tenn's office into a party room complete with a picnic and champagne.

The penthouse had the best view, but the Inn at Sawyers Bend was sold out for the holiday, the grounds below packed with guests and locals who'd bought the Fireworks Package; An elegant picnic dinner and reserved lounge chair, complete with pre-toasted s'mores.

We'd gone a little crazy with our own picnic, and I'd had a few too many glasses of champagne. Enough that my smile stretched my cheeks and the fireworks set off matching sparkles in my giddy brain. August and Thatcher had plowed their way through most of our picnic basket as well as the Fourth-of-July-themed cookies and other treats the staff had sent up. I made a half-hearted attempt to grab yet another cookie out of August's hand only for him to evade me and jam the cookie in his mouth, crumbs flying everywhere.

"Housekeeping is going to cry when they see what we did to your office," I murmured to Tenn.

He tightened his arm around me, dropping his mouth to graze the side of my neck. "They'll survive. It's not that bad."

A hitching gurgle sounded in the corner of the room. One cookie too many for poor August. "Thatcher!" I cried out, seeing my oldest was closer to August than we were. He jolted into action, grabbing Tenn's trashcan and shoving it at August.

Too late. Damn. So much for our picnic and fireworks. August raised his head, his face and t-shirt splattered with vomit, matching the mess he'd left on his sneakers and Tenn's carpet. Pulling away from Tenn, I crossed the room to my little guy.

"Come on, babe, let's get you to the bathroom." Over my shoulder, I said to Tenn, "Had enough of the Hall family throwing up on you?"

"Hey, August didn't puke on me, just my carpet." He winked at August, whose head hung as he rubbed his roiling tummy. "Want a ginger ale, buddy?"

August nodded, swallowing hard. "Mom, I think I'm not done—"

"I know kiddo." I ushered him into the bathroom just in time for him to lose the rest of his dinner in the toilet. At least he missed the floor.

Tenn stuck his head through the door. "He okay?"

My heart squeezed when August lifted a shaky thumbs-up, turning his head to look at Tenn. "Sometimes, when I eat too much junk, I puke."

"Me too, August." To me, Tenn added, "If you want to

throw him in the shower, I'll get something from the shop for him to wear. And a ginger ale."

"Thanks, Tenn."

"I've got you guys." He was gone, and August's next heave had me rubbing his back and murmuring meaningless words of comfort.

I should have been watching him more closely. This hadn't happened in a while, but I knew better than to let August have free run of junk food. A quick glance told me Thatcher wasn't having any such problem. He stood in front of the big window, riveted by the fireworks, shoving yet another sandwich into his mouth. I couldn't believe how much food the kid could pack away.

When August was sure he was finished throwing up, he let me strip him of his puke-covered clothes and push him into the shower. Thank God for Tenn and Royal's early morning runs, necessitating a private shower in their office bathroom. With all the guest rooms—and their showers—occupied, we would not have enjoyed driving home with August smelling of puke. Yuck.

Tenn was back a few minutes later, handing me a bag with an adult size t-shirt. "We didn't have anything his size. If he feels weird about it, we can go out the staff exit and he won't see anyone."

"I don't care," August announced cheerily. True to form, now that his stomach was empty of all the crap he'd eaten, he was back to normal. "I'm hungry, Mom."

"No way, little man." I pulled the t-shirt over his head and handed him the open ginger ale Tenn brought. The t-shirt covered him to his knees, engulfing his small form. I shoved his soiled clothes and sneakers into the bag from the Inn's shop, grimacing as August sucked down half the ginger ale in one long sip. "You can have some toast when we get back to the house if you're still feeling okay."

Tenn already had our stuff together when we left the bathroom. "I thought we should get him home."

"Yeah, good idea." I looked to Thatcher, who was still engrossed in the fireworks. "Maybe Thatch can stay?"

Thatcher turned, leaving the window to join us. "It's almost over anyway. We can go."

"You sure?" Tenn asked, scooping up August to carry him since his shoes were in the bag with the rest of his clothes.

"You could get a ride back with us," Royal called out. "And I think Sterling, Quinn, and Avery are around here somewhere."

"Nah, I'm cool. I'll go home with Mom and Tenn." Thatcher followed us down the back stairs to the employee parking lot, laughing as August's begging for more treats was drowned out by the finale of the fireworks show.

The explosions of sound didn't stop until we were walking around the side of the building to the employee parking lot. The second he could be heard, August started up again.

"But Mom, Thatcher ate all the s'mores. All of them! And I didn't even get one because they just got to the room before I got sick. It's not fair! You know I'm not going to throw up again. My tummy's all empty and it's not bubbly anymore because of the ginger ale and— Hey, what's he doing?"

Bryce stood beside Tenn's SUV, holding out a black key fob and clicking the button. The lights on the car flashed, the locks popping open.

"What the f—" Tenn glanced at Thatcher and August. "What are you doing with my keys?"

Handing me August, he strode to Bryce and grabbed for the keys. Bryce didn't fight, letting Tenn yank the keys out of his hand while he leaned into the SUV. What was he doing?

Tenn reached for his collar to drag him back, but Bryce twisted, leaning further into the back seat. It looked like he was pulling at the floor. Tenn's SUV had captain's chairs in the second row, and the floor was equipped with hidden storage to maximize packing space.

He must have stashed it in one of those hidden storage wells because I absolutely would have noticed riding to the Inn with the freaking bust of Emperor Vitellius sitting beside me.

Bryce held the bust of Vitellius against his chest, a triumphant smirk on his handsome face. "I told you I had a way to get this stuff off the grounds. Hawk and his goons always search my car, but they never search Tenn's, and you don't keep track of your extra keys."

Tenn reached for the bust, clearly intending to rip it from Bryce's hands.

Before he could grab it, a familiar voice called, "Wait, don't!" We spun around to see Elliott melt out of the darkness. "Don't take it from him, I need it."

He strolled across the parking lot to our little group by the SUV as casually as if he were joining us for dinner. Bryce zeroed in on Elliott. Whatever else we could say about Bryce, it appeared he was no idiot. Looking between Elliott and Thatcher, understanding spread across his face and he began to laugh, his gaze landing on me.

"I thought you were just here to steal whatever you could find, but you were after this ugly piece of shit the whole time. Did you know," he asked Tenn, "or was she just taking you for a ride? That's a sweet deal, trading pussy for—"

Bryce didn't finish his sentence. Tenn swung, his fist connecting with Bryce's cheek, his other hand coming around to pluck Vitellius from Bryce's hands as he crumpled to the pavement. "Still can't take a punch, you asshole." Looking up, Tenn caught sight of the kids. "Sorry."

"He is an asshole," Thatcher said with a shrug. I didn't admonish him for his language, too shocked by Elliott's sudden appearance.

"Elliott?" Puzzle pieces shifted into place in my mind. "Bryce was the one who stole the bust from you? Did you know it was him?"

"I knew it was one of them." Elliott tossed his hair off his forehead in a move that would have had nineteen-year-old me swooning. Now, it just looked contrived. Maybe I'd still be susceptible if I hadn't seen him practice it in the mirror a thousand times. Hair toss followed by a devastating smile. So predictable.

"How?" I pressed, trying to make the pieces fit together in my mind.

"They told you, didn't they?" Bryce demanded of Elliott. Bryce lurched to his feet, swaying a little, and shot Elliott a look of utter scorn. Elliott tried to look innocent, and Bryce moved his glare to Tenn and me. "I hired the Learys to steal the bust for me. They double-crossed me and decided to keep it for themselves."

"Only because you told them how much it was really worth," Elliott accused, shaking his head. "Fucking moron."

"I'm the moron? I was watching the auction house the whole time, saw you break in, followed you home, and you never spotted me. I let you do all the hard work. Like taking candy from a baby." Bryce's sneer was getting to Elliott.

Before this whole thing devolved into an infantile pissing contest, I cut in. "If Bryce stole it from you," I asked Elliott, "is he going to give it back? Is that why you're here?" I looked between my ex-husband and Tenn's cousin.

"Fucking waste of time. I spent weeks trying to crack it. Good fucking luck, man. Prentice's story is bullshit. It's just an ugly statue. Give me my cash and it's yours."

Elliott put on his most charming smile and aimed it straight at me. "I'd love to, but there's a slight hitch in my offer."

Oh yeah, I knew what was coming. I'd lived this enough times while we were married. "Let me guess," I butted in, "You promised to pay Bryce for the bust, but you don't actually have any cash."

"I'm a little short right now. I won't get paid until I have the bust, and I can't get the bust without the cash."

"What was your plan, Elliott?" I demanded, too exasperated to tone it down for the kids. "Just roll into town and hit me up for—" I speared Bryce with a furious glare. "How much?"

"Fifty thousand dollars," Bryce supplied, eyes narrowed at Elliott.

"What?" Thatcher's outrage knocked me back a step. "You wanted Mom to give you fifty thousand dollars? We don't have fifty thousand dollars! Where was she—" The answer to his question came clear before he finished asking. Throwing a glance at Tenn, he refocused on his father. "You were going to ask her to hit Tenn up for it, weren't you?"

Elliott shrugged and tried his charming smile on his son. "He wouldn't even notice that much, and he's so nuts over your mom, he'd—"

Thatcher wasn't having it. "Shut up! Just shut up!"

Shouts exploded in the air. "Turn and face the car.

Hands where I can see them!" I spun around to see West and Hawk bearing down on us, guns drawn, two deputies behind them.

West was on Bryce a second later, dragging his raised hands down and behind his back, cuffing him with expert ease before shoving Bryce at the deputy. "We have you breaking into Tenn's vehicle and admitting to using it to smuggle art off the property."

"You can't arrest me!" Bryce protested. "Tenn was driving the car. It was his—"

"You can tell your story at the station. The deputy's going to bring you in, and we'll have a nice long chat about all that missing art and what you did with it."

"He owes me!" Bryce protested, trying to twist away from the deputy.

"Owes you for what, exactly?" West asked slowly. "For the transfer of stolen property? Can you produce a receipt showing you're the rightful owner of that ugly little statue?"

"No," a new voice interrupted. "That would be me."

Forrest Powell stepped into view, a folded packet of papers in his hand. Handing them to West, he waited while West looked them over. West shoved the papers into his pocket with a nod and stepped to Tenn to take the bust of Vitellius. I expected him to hand it to Forrest, but he shook his head.

"If you're the rightful owner of this piece, you can have it after I verify your paperwork. Stop by my office Monday morning and we'll work it out."

Forrest gave a resigned nod. "Another day or two doesn't matter, but make sure that thing is locked up. This idiot's bosses are still after it," he added, nodding at Elliott.

"Why?" I asked, champagne and adrenaline loosening

my tongue. "Why that piece? It's not worth anything close to fifty thousand dollars."

Forrest paused, scanning the small group. His eyes landed on Bryce, still held by the deputy. "He knows."

Bryce's handsome face twisted. "Prentice was full of shit. He said it was a puzzle, and the person who could solve it would be rich beyond his wildest dreams. Fairy tale bullshit. Prentice never solved it. He would have told me."

"Because you were so close?" Tenn asked, one eyebrow raised, his expression one of withering scorn. "You found out Prentice put it up for auction and figured you'd help yourself? Are you the reason the Learys knew about it?"

Bryce didn't respond, his brain in control of his mouth for once. Tenn gave Forrest a considering look. "And you know how to solve the puzzle?"

Forrest shook his head in a negative I didn't quite believe. "There is no puzzle. The bust of Vitellius was my father's. Prentice took it from him, and I want it back. I knew it was here in Sawyers Bend, but I didn't know your father had sent it to the auction house or I could have saved myself a lot of trouble—"

A scuff of shoes on the pavement had us turning to see Sterling staring at Forrest, her mouth open and her beautiful blue eyes shattered. "Is that why you came here? Why you wanted to spend the night at Heartstone? So you could look for that thing?"

"Sterling—" Forrest took a step towards her, flinching when she stepped away.

"Answer me!" Sterling demanded.

"I—" Forrest stalled and it was clear that he couldn't make himself lie and couldn't bring himself to tell her the truth, knowing it would sever what was between them.

Sterling's head dropped, her eyes swimming in tears. "I

should have known. I should have known it wasn't about me."

"Sterling—" Forrest started toward her and found himself blocked by both West and Tenn. "Let me explain."

"I don't want to hear it," Sterling said, her voice flat, eyes broken. "Just stay away from me." She turned to go, looking around the parking lot with unseeing eyes. With a nod at West, Tenn intercepted Sterling, pulling her into a tight hug as he led her back toward the Inn.

West looked at the deputy who still held a cuffed Bryce. "Take him in. I'll be right behind you."

The deputy pushed Bryce in the direction of his patrol car, ignoring Bryce's threats to call his mother.

West speared Elliott with a hard look. "I don't have anything on you. Let's keep it that way. I'd suggest you don't spend the night in Sawyers Bend. Got me?"

Another dazzling smile. "Of course, officer. I'll just get my family and we'll be on our way."

West didn't bother to hide his laugh. "Good luck with that. Make sure I don't see you again." To Forrest, he said, "First thing Monday, in my office."

"I'll be there," Forrest promised, his dark eyes troubled, mouth tight.

Tenn strode back into the parking lot. "Stay away from Sterling," he ordered.

"Am I fired?" Forrest asked warily.

"Are you kidding me?" Tenn stared at Forrest as if his CFO was an alien who'd suddenly stripped off his human suit.

"Let me explain. Please. I did this all wrong, but once I'd started, I didn't know how to fix it."

Tenn stared at Forrest for a long time. "You know, I liked

you. Didn't like you with my sister, but aside from that, I liked you. Thought you were a good guy."

"I am a good guy. I just— I knew your father. I knew you, even though you don't remember. But I didn't know if all of you grew up like him. I couldn't trust you." He rolled his shoulders, straightening with resolve. "I wish I could go back and do this over, but I can't. At least let me tell you everything before you toss me out."

Tenn appeared to consider. "I'll make you a deal. You stay away from Sterling tonight. Come to the house tomorrow and say your piece then."

"I can't walk away from her." Forrest protested, his voice breaking under the effort to force out the words.

"You just admitted you used her for access to Heartstone Manor. If you know her at all, you know that kind of bullshit was the last thing she needed. She's with her family now. We'll look after her. If she's still willing to see you after tomorrow, that's up to her."

Forrest's shoulders dropped and he nodded. "If that's the best deal I can get, I'll take it. For now."

He strode off into the night, the darkness closing around him, leaving Tenn, me, and the boys alone with Elliott.

Chapter Forty-Three

SCARLETT

"Well, that didn't go the way I'd planned," Elliott said with a practiced smile, this one just a little sheepish. He had, '*Aww shucks, I didn't mean it,*' painted all over his face.

I shifted August on my hip, my arms aching from his weight, ready to put him in the car and go home. Elliott stepped forward as if to take August, but Tenn was already there, plucking August from my hold and settling him easily in his arms.

August wrapped an arm around Tenn's neck and whispered something that sounded suspiciously like '*s'mores.*' Tenn chuckled. "Maybe tomorrow, buddy," he said in a low voice, his eyes on Elliott.

Elliott pretended he didn't mind seeing his son in Tenn's arms. "I could use a ride home," he said, his eyes on Thatcher, maybe sensing that Thatch was the easiest target. After all, Thatcher had stuck by his side through so much already. What was a little more?

Thatcher's face hurt my heart. He stared at his father, his shoulders set, jaw tight. "You want a ride home?" Before

Elliott could repeat his request, Thatcher pressed on. "What are you going to do about the Learys?"

Elliott tried on another charming smile, this one meant to be reassuring. I knew all of his smiles and I didn't buy a single one. Not anymore.

Neither did Thatcher.

He crossed his arms over his chest and waited. In the distance, car doors slammed over in the guest parking lot, the festivities winding down.

"It'll be fine," Elliott reassured. "I'll explain everything and tell them I'll make it up to them."

"So, you're still going to work for them? Even after what happened?" Thatcher waited, his voice raised in disbelief.

"Hey, everything worked out okay, didn't it?" Elliott appeased.

"Only because Tenn's brother sent freaking commandos in to save us. If they hadn't shown up, Tenn would have been shot and they would have taken me and Mom." Thatcher paused, giving Elliott a chance to defend himself. Elliott stared at his oldest child, stymied by Thatcher's anger.

"They were going to torture us!" Thatcher shouted, his patience gone.

"I'm sure it wouldn't have come to that, Thatcher," Elliott said in an annoyingly superior tone as if Thatcher hadn't been there, hadn't heard exactly how the Learys planned to use him.

"Bullshit," Thatcher shot back. "I talked to Hawk about the Learys."

Tenn and I shared a look. Neither of us knew Thatcher had been talking to Hawk about his father's situation. He couldn't have picked a better source considering Hawk knew more about the Learys than anyone else in Sawyers Bend.

"I don't know who this Hawk is, but—"

Thatcher cut him off. "He's the Sawyers' security expert and he used to work with the best security team in the country. He knows who the Learys are and he told me how dangerous they are. He told me what they would have done with me or Mom if they'd taken us."

"Thatcher, I've been working with these guys for a while. Their bark is worse than their bite."

Thatcher shook his head. "If you think that, you're stupid. Now I know some of the things they've done. You can't protect us. As long as you work for them, we'll be in danger."

"I'm not going to let anything happen to you, Thatcher. We can talk about this at home later. We've imposed on the Sawyers long enough."

I was gearing up to tell Elliott to go fuck himself—without the profanity—when Thatcher took a step back, coming in line with me and Tenn. "We aren't coming home. We're staying here."

Every single one of us stared at Thatcher. I'd been planning to talk to him about staying, trying to give him as much time as I could before my deadline.

"Thatcher," I breathed, "are you sure?"

"Yeah, I'm sure. I like it here." A swift glance at Tenn still holding August. His eyes came back to me, anguish and fury swirling in their depths. "And it isn't safe at home. Not anymore."

I slipped my arm around him, pulling him in until his face pressed against my shoulder. "Honey..." I squeezed him tight, my heart breaking along with his. I knew Elliott was a complete asshole, but I hadn't wanted Thatcher or August to know. I'd always hoped Elliott would get it together before they were old enough to really understand. But he hadn't, and now he'd forced Thatcher into a choice a child should never have to make.

"It's okay, Mom," Thatcher said, low enough that only I could hear. "I want to stay. And I don't want to go home and worry something is going to happen."

"Okay, love bug. If you're okay with it, we'll stay." Usually, he scowled at me when I called him *love bug*, but this time, he just stood there, swiping at his eyes with the back of his hand. I could have killed Elliott for putting Thatcher through this.

"Elliott," I said, getting his attention. "Thatcher's right. We're not coming back except to pack up the house."

"You're staying here?" It was as if he was only now seeing August in Tenn's arms, the way Thatcher stood between us. We were a united front and Elliott had no part of it.

Reality finally penetrated.

"You can't stay here! You don't even know these people!"

"I'm in love with Tenn. He loves me and he wants us to stay. That's all I need to know."

Elliott sneered. "Right, sure. Find a guy with a nice fat wallet and your morals go right out the window, don't they?"

I was done with Elliott's temper tantrums. "Elliott, you don't know anything about me, and you don't know anything about Tenn. The size of his wallet isn't even on the list of reasons I love him. The fact that he risked everything to help me find Thatcher when you put our son in danger is definitely at the top."

"Whatever." Elliott dismissed Tenn. "Look at him! He's got everything. What did he risk? An afternoon of driving? And for that, he gets my family?"

"Dad." Thatcher's voice was weary in a way I never wanted to hear again, his disappointment soul deep. "Just shut up. You don't know anything about Tenn, and we haven't been your family in a long time."

For the first time, Elliott's carefully constructed facade crumpled, his eyes seeking something from Thatcher that Thatcher didn't have to give. "But if you stay here, I'll never see you."

A small voice piped up. "You didn't see us that much when we lived in the same place. And Grandma and Grandpa will be closer to us here." August looked up at Tenn. "Right? Florida is closer to North Carolina than Massachusetts."

"That's right, buddy," Tenn said in a low, tight voice. "Florida is closer to North Carolina than Massachusetts."

"See?" August pinned Elliott with an innocently solemn look, unaware he was driving nails into his father's heart with every word. "We can see Grandma and Grandpa more, and we didn't really see you that much before anyway, so you won't miss us. And we have friends here now." He bit his lip at the sad look on Elliott's face. "You shouldn't have taken Thatcher with you when the bad guys were after you. Mom was really scared. And you lied to Thatch. We're not supposed to lie."

"You want to stay too, August?" I asked, needing to hear him say it.

He gave me a look that clearly said, *Duh.* "I thought we already decided."

"Not for sure," I said slowly. "I wouldn't decide anything like that without talking to you and Thatcher about it."

Shocking the hell out of me, Thatcher said, "We talked about it already, August and me. We want to stay here."

Elliott was speechless. I hadn't seen him without words

since I told him I wanted a divorce. After a long silence, he pulled himself together. Typical Elliott—his first thought was for himself. His son had just told him he was going to live a thousand miles away and all Elliott had was, "How am I supposed to get home?"

I couldn't help it. I rolled my eyes, staring at the night sky. "I cannot fathom how this is my problem."

"Why don't you give me your car?" Elliott wheedled. "I bet this guy has a car you can use—"

"I just got it paid off, you—" I bit off my words before I could call him a name I couldn't take back in front of his children. Sucking in a breath to clear my head, I said, "I like my car, Elliott. You can't have it. Figure out your own way home."

Beside Thatcher, Tenn shifted. Reading his mind, I muttered, "Don't even think about it. We cave once and it'll never end."

"I don't want him in my town," Tenn muttered back.

He had a point. The idea of Elliott hanging around Sawyers Bend made me a little nauseous. Against my better judgment, I was about to offer to buy Elliott a bus ticket when Hawk stepped into the light.

Ignoring Elliott, he said, "Sterling is in your office with Royal, Daisy, her sisters, and a few bottles of champagne."

"I'm going to kill Forrest Powell," Tenn said under his breath. I knew from Tenn that Sterling had a pretty big problem with drinking until a few months ago. A broken heart was not a great speed bump in her recovery. I kind of wanted to kill Forrest, too. Or at least kick him in the balls really, really hard. Poor Sterling.

"I'll give Hall a ride to the bus station in Asheville. You won't see him again," Hawk promised.

"Thanks, man," Tenn said, turning toward his SUV. "You guys ready to go home?"

"Yeah," Thatcher said, pulling me along with him.

From behind me, Elliott called, "That's it? You're just leaving me with this guy? We aren't going to talk about this?"

I didn't bother to answer. Stopping at the open door to the backseat, I hugged Thatcher tight. "You okay?"

"Love you, Mom," his voice hitched, his arms coming around me so tight I lost my breath.

"Love you too, Thatcher." I rocked him from side to side, the way I had when I'd carried him as a baby. "Love you so much."

He shuddered against me once before getting himself under control. "Can we make s'mores at home? I'm hungry."

Of course, he was. Wiping away the moisture under my eyes, I let out a watery laugh. "It's pretty late, kiddo."

"It's a Saturday," Thatcher countered.

I sighed. "Why don't we get home and see what's stashed in the pantry? I'm sure we can find something to fill your hollow leg."

Shutting his door as he clicked in his seatbelt, I rounded the back of the SUV to get in. Elliott was following Hawk to his vehicle, his shoulders slumped, dejection hanging over him like a cloak of misery. I couldn't bring myself to feel more than a vague sense of pity.

I was done saving Elliott. I'd been done for a long time. Elliott was going to have to save himself.

August, Thatcher, and I had our lives to live, and we were going to do it far from Elliott's bad decisions. We were going to live a new life here, where we were loved.

My hand met Tenn's, my fingers twining with his. He smiled at me, his expression soft, transforming gradually into a grin, his eyes sparkling as he asked, "How do you feel about s'mores before bed? Thatcher looks like he's starving to death and August never got any."

A bit of sweet to balance the sour of saying goodbye to their dad. I was willing to meet Elliott halfway if he wanted to see the boys, but I didn't have much hope he'd bother. Yeah, bedtime and junk food aside, my guys could use a little sweet.

"Sounds good to me," I said to cheers from the back seat. "Let's go home."

Chapter Forty-Four
SCARLETT

B right and early the next morning, Forrest Powell arrived at Heartstone Manor to plead his case. He must have ice-cold blood in his veins. Not a single person in Griffen's crowded office looked happy to see him. Most of them could easily have been planning his murder. Given Griffen and Hawk's background and our relative isolation on the Sawyer Estate, I would have been terrified I was going to end up disappearing in the mountains surrounding the house.

Forrest just sat there, his face neutral, his eyes on Sterling. For her part, Sterling sat on the sofa furthest from Forrest, her sister Parker beside her. They wore identical expressions of composed disinterest as if nothing said in this room could possibly affect them. Expertly applied makeup hid the circles beneath Sterling's arresting blue eyes.

I wasn't betting on Forrest winning her over. No one liked being played for a fool, and I'd seen them together. Sterling had liked him. A lot. If I found out Tenn was just using me? My chest burned with fury at the thought. Yeah, if I were in Sterling's shoes, I could only hope I'd be able to manage icy disregard. More likely, I'd set him on fire with my torch.

And yes, I'm aware I was using Tenn for access to his house when we first met—not so different from Forrest—but Tenn knew I was up to something from the beginning. Sterling had no clue.

Griffen's face was a thundercloud. He sat behind his desk, Hope beside him, her usually kind smile replaced by a solemn mask. Except when her eyes moved to Sterling. Then, they were soft with compassion and worry. When she looked at Forrest, all she showed was anger. She wasn't alone.

Glancing at Griffen, Forrest raised an eyebrow. Griffen scanned the room, maybe checking to make sure everyone was here.

Forrest sat in an armchair slightly in front and to the side of Griffen's desk where we could all see him easily. I was next to Tenn on the sofa, Royal on his other side. Finn and Hawk flanked the cold fireplace, Hawk's alert eyes fixed on Forrest, Finn lounging against the mantel, appearing half asleep though it was mid-morning. West leaned on the door frame, separate from the family but close enough to hear every word.

No one spoke, the silence growing heavier until Griffen finally broke it. "We're all here. Say what you need to say so I can throw you out of my town." I hadn't known Griffen long, but I'd never imagined he could sound so hard.

Forrest sat up straighter until his spine looked like it had been fused to an iron rod. His eyes on Sterling, he started to speak. "Before I tell you who I am and why I came back, I just need to say—" His calm dissolved, anguish suffusing his moss-green eyes. "If I could go back to the beginning, I would have told you who I was. Who I am. Because getting what I came here for isn't worth losing you. Nothing is, and I wish I'd known that in the beginning. But I didn't." He leaned back a fraction, glancing around the room. "I didn't just come here for the job or the bust. I was here for revenge."

Revenge? Revenge for what? I glanced around, wondering if this was inside Sawyer info I wasn't privy to, but everyone else looked just as clueless as I was.

"I know Griffen remembers Alan Buckley." Forrest paused, glancing at Griffen, who drew in a breath, comprehension and confusion warring on his face.

"I don't," Parker said, her voice clear and crisp. "Who was Alan Buckley?"

Griffen sighed, rubbing his palm against his jaw before answering, "Alan Buckley was Dad's partner in the VoIP business."

"The one you fought over?" Tenn asked. "Wasn't that part of the reason Dad threw you out?"

Griffen looked at Forrest. "I want to know who he is before I say anything else."

"You remember Alan Buckley," Forrest prodded. "Do you remember Buck? He only brought me a few times. I was probably too young for you to notice. I mostly hung around with Finn."

Finn's eyes narrowed on Forrest. "You're Buck? Did you change your name?"

"I was always Forrest, but my dad hated that name, so he called me Buck. After he was gone, my mother changed our names and I stopped going by Buck." He focused on Griffen. "Your father threw you out? After?"

Griffen ignored Forrest's question in favor of one of his own. "What do you mean, *after he was gone*?"

Realizing he wasn't going to get an answer from Griffen,

Forrest explained. "He killed himself on Christmas Eve, two weeks after your father stole the company and the bust of Vitellius. Once he realized he wasn't going to get it back, that he'd lost everything, he just gave up."

Griffen looked down at his desk, drawing in a deep breath and letting it out in a shuddering sigh. Hope reached over, stroking her palm down his arm in a gesture of comfort. "You did everything you could to stop him."

"I could have told Alan what he was up to before it was too late."

"Wasn't that Ford's job? Didn't he promise he was going to work things out with Alan?" Hope prompted. I had no clue what she was talking about. Royal reminded me that I wasn't the only one still confused.

"Was that how Ford double-crossed you?" Royal asked. "None of us knew the details, just that something went wrong with a deal and Vanessa left you for Ford."

Griffen sighed again, turning to face Forrest. "You remember my brother, Ford?" Forrest inclined his head in assent. "We'd only been working for my father full time for a few months. The company he started with your father was our first big project. We handled the business side and your dad and his team built the code. It was going to revolutionize VoIP communications."

"It did," Forrest said bitterly. "After your father stole it from mine and sold it to the highest bidder."

"Ford and I found out what Prentice had planned. I was working on legal and financial ways to stop him from taking the company. Ford was supposed to be working with your father to safeguard the company from takeover. It never occurred to me that he was lying the whole time. Back then he was—" Griffen faltered. "We were close."

"Why would Ford have done that?" Parker asked,

wilting a little, her hand reaching for Sterling's. "He was always a little distant, but to help our father steal from a business partner? I never understood his marrying Vanessa. I thought he was just young and she'd seduced him into betraying you, but this? How could he be so cruel?" Looking at Forrest, she asked, "Did Prentice know about your father? About what happened? Did Ford know?"

"You'd have to ask Ford. After my father died, my mom packed us up and we moved to Oregon to be closer to her family. I don't remember hearing anything about the Sawyers after that."

"He regretted it." Sterling's voice cut into the room for the first time, low and a little husky from the tears she'd shed. "Ford was never the same after Griffen left. He pretended to be. I was just a kid, but I remember he was almost manic at his wedding. His smile was so fake it was kind of scary. He was like that for a while, and then he was just sad all the time."

She still couldn't bring herself to look directly at Forrest, but she said, "I know he had so many regrets. Not Prentice. Prentice didn't have a conscience. But Ford isn't like him. If he was here, he'd tell you he was sorry."

Forrest jerked up a shoulder in a shrug. "He's not here, and his apology wouldn't bring back my father." Pain flashed across his face as he turned to Griffen. "You were trying to stop the sale?"

Griffen nodded. "I thought I had it, but Ford was undoing my work behind the scenes. He and Prentice did it all in secrecy. Sold the company out from under your father, disinherited me, and once my fiancée found out, she married Ford instead. Your dad wasn't the only one who lost everything. But I didn't have a family to support."

"What did you do?" Forrest asked, his eyebrow raised.

"I've heard the gossip around town, that you've been gone for years and only came back when Prentice died, but I didn't know when you left or why."

Griffen smiled wryly and shook his head. "I hitchhiked to West's house and he took me to the army recruiter's office. I stayed with him until boot camp, and I never came back. Not until Prentice died, and then only because he set up the will so if I didn't come back I'd bankrupt the entire town."

"You might be the only person who hated Prentice Sawyer as much as I do," Forrest said.

"Maybe," Griffen agreed. "Did you kill him?" he asked casually as if the answer wasn't relevant but he was curious anyway.

Forrest's eyes flared wide and he recoiled until his back hit his chair. "No! I wanted revenge. I wanted the bust of Vitellius back. I didn't want to kill anyone."

"His alibi checked out," Hawk added.

Parker turned her head to pin Hawk with an icy glare. "So, you investigated him enough to know he didn't kill our father, but you couldn't figure out who he really was? I thought you were the best of the best?" Her glare pivoted to include Griffen. Made sense.

While Griffen wasn't head of security, he'd hired Hawk and had worked side by side with him on the family's security plan. I'd also gotten the impression from Tenn that Griffen had been Hawk's boss in some way before they'd both come to Sawyers Bend. Hawk moved to speak, but Griffen cut him off.

"We went back to high school. Everything about Forrest Powell checked out. And before you ask, he didn't hire a hitman either. No suspicious financial activity of any kind."

A tiny smile cracked his face as he looked at Forrest. "That's what we call playing the long game."

Forrest returned his smile with the smallest curve of his lips. "I'd love to say I'm a mastermind who's been planning this since I was thirteen, but I never thought about coming back here until I was in my twenties and my mother mentioned something about the bust of Vitellius. My grandparents were both sick and their medical costs were killing her and my stepfather. I tried to help out, but I had student loans and I was just starting out, so I wasn't making much. She said if only my father hadn't told Prentice Sawyer about the bust, we'd have all the money we'd ever need."

"So, there is a puzzle," I said under my breath. "Prentice wasn't lying to Bryce?"

"He wasn't lying." Forrest stopped, appearing to struggle with his next words.

Looking around the room, he said slowly, "I broke your trust. I came here with a vague plan to find the bust and steal it back, and maybe make you pay for what your father had done. I wasn't expecting all of you to be so different from Prentice. And once I was here, I remembered how much I liked being in Sawyers Bend. How much I liked your family before everything went bad."

He looked right at Sterling, waiting until her eyes rose to meet his, drawn by a force stronger than her broken heart. "Looking back, I can think of a thousand times I should have come clean, but I didn't. I lied to you. I don't know how to fix that except to tell you the truth and hope you don't use it against me."

Sterling looked away without saying a word. Forrest gave a slight nod of acceptance before turning his attention to West. I'd almost forgotten he was there, he'd been so quiet. "You have the bust?"

"Not here. It's locked in my office safe."

"Who has the combination?" Forrest asked.

"Only me."

Forrest nodded again, this time with more conviction before he looked my way. "You were right. The bust isn't worth that much as a work of art, or as a historical artifact. It isn't the bust itself that's valuable..."

He hesitated, and I wondered if he was finally going to tell us the truth.

Chapter Forty-Five

"It isn't the bust that's valuable," he said slowly, "it's the numbers engraved on the base."

I thought back. "I don't remember any numbers on the base."

"They're almost impossible to see without a magnifying glass, and they're not in a place anyone would examine closely."

"Account numbers," Griffen guessed.

"Coded account numbers. My father was brilliant, but he was paranoid. He sold his first company for millions and put almost every penny into investment accounts he kept from everyone, even my mother. He protected them by putting the account numbers and access key in a code. He engraved the code into the bust, saying no one would ever know how to get to the money except him. He always promised my mother the money was there to protect us. Until he told Prentice about the bust, and then, when things went wrong, there was nothing."

It wasn't my business, but I had to ask. "Do you know how to break the code?"

"I guess I'll find out after your police chief verifies that I'm the rightful owner."

"So, you came all the way down here," West said, "just to find out Prentice had sent the bust up north to auction, and then you had to buy back your own property only for Scarlett's ex and then Bryce to steal it out from under you?"

"Basically," Forrest admitted. "I told you, I'm not a criminal mastermind. I am what I said I am. A guy who's made his career in hospitality with a focus on high-end boutique hotels, and for the last few years I've been a damn good CFO." He looked to Tenn and Royal. "I know you're angry and you have a right to be, but at least admit I've been an asset to the Inn."

Royal scowled at Forrest. Grudgingly, he admitted, "You know you have. If it hadn't been for you sneaking off with our sister, we would have been patting ourselves on the back for making such a good hire."

"My personal life doesn't have anything to do with your business," Sterling cut in, looking angry for the first time since I'd walked in the room.

"You're our baby sister," Tenn argued.

Sterling tossed her hair back and raised her chin. "Really? Now you decide to be big brother of the year? Where were you when Dad was still alive and I was alone in this house with him? When I was slowly drinking myself to death? Don't make this about me."

"It wasn't about you," Forrest interrupted. "And then it was. Somewhere along the way, it stopped being about revenge and it was all about you. Sterling, please, give me another chance."

"No," Sterling shot back. "I did a lot of thinking last night. About more than you." Composing herself, she shut out Forrest and turned her attention to Tenn and Royal. "I don't want you to fire Forrest. Not because of me. I know you've both been happier with him to lighten the load, and I'm quitting the Inn anyway."

"Quitting? Why would you quit?" Royal demanded.

"Marcy is back from maternity leave. You don't need both of us, and I need... I don't know what I need except to work on me a little, I think. I appreciate you giving me the job at the Inn. I really do. I needed that. I needed to know I could do something positive, that I was smart and I could make good decisions. I don't want to go back to what I was."

"What do you want, honey?" Griffen asked, gently.

"I don't know. That's the problem. I need to figure it out. I was talking to Quinn last night and she needs someone to run the office at her guide business. I can do that. I want to do it."

She looked down at her fingernails, scraping at the polish while she worked through her thoughts. Miraculously, her overbearing brothers managed to keep their mouths shut while she did it.

Finally, she looked up, her eyes swimming in tears. "Everything is different now." Her voice hitched and she swallowed hard. "I spent so much of my life hiding from Dad or fighting with Dad and not knowing who *I* was. And then you guys came back. And I know we're all still a mess, but for the first time, I feel like I have a family. But with all of us living in this house..." She stared up at the ceiling. "I know this is crazy since Heartstone is practically a castle, but I need some space. Some time to myself. I need space, but I also need to know I'm coming home to all of you." She pushed her hair behind one ear and shrugged. "I know I sound nuts—"

"You don't," Finn said, surprising me. "I know exactly what you mean. Being alone is better when you know you have people to come home to. And sometimes you need to be alone to figure shit out."

"Yeah." Sterling shared a smile with her brother. "That's it exactly. I'm not really alone now. And since I'm not, I need some time by myself to think."

"We can give you space," Tenn said, looking a little baffled at her contradictory needs.

"Not really. I loved working with you guys, but it's busy and crowded and there's a lot of pressure when we have an event. I love that, too, but right now, I need a break. And aside from dealing with the groups that come in, there aren't really any people at Quinn's place."

"You have a job with us whenever you want to come back," Royal said softly.

"Anytime, Sterling," Tenn added. "I know Marcy's going to miss you, and so will we."

The wobbly smile she gave Tenn and Royal made me want to wrap them all up in a hug.

"So, that's it for us?" Forrest interrupted. "You're just done?"

"Yeah, that's it." Sterling's eyes were guarded as she looked at Forrest. "Maybe we just had bad timing. Or maybe you shouldn't have lied to me from the day we met. I don't know, take your pick." She crossed her arms over her chest. "One thing I realized last night after I was done crying my eyes out after half a bottle of champagne is that I'm tired of trying to drink away my problems, and the last thing I need is some guy I can't trust. I spent my whole life trying to please my father or at least get his attention. All I got out of it was shitty self-esteem and a drinking problem. When I decide I'm ready for a man, I need someone I can depend on. That isn't going to be you."

Forrest looked like he wanted to protest but, wisely, he kept his mouth shut, and Sterling plowed on.

"So, yeah, we're done. I don't want to ruin your life. I don't want you to lose your job. You're great at the Inn, and I know my brothers like you. But I have one favor to ask." Knowing he had the final say, Sterling spoke directly to Griffen. "I don't want Forrest in this house. I have to live here." She rethought what she'd said. "No, I *want* to live here. I know half of you guys probably hate it, but I love having everyone here. It was like a fucking mausoleum when it was just Dad and me. But I don't want to have to worry I'm going to bump into him in my home."

"I can make you that promise," Griffen said gravely. He raised his chin at Hawk, who aimed a look at Forrest.

"Security's going to have instructions to keep you off the property. Don't try to sneak in or you won't like the consequences," Hawk said.

Forrest caught West's nod of agreement and kept his mouth shut.

Tenn and Royal looked at each other, sharing some silent communication I couldn't translate. When they were done, Royal said to Forrest, "Be in the office Monday morning. We'll talk. I'm not making any promises, though."

Forrest stood. "I'll take it."

No one else seemed to have anything to say, and he turned for the door. As he passed through, he said to West, "Call me Monday after you verify things with the auction house."

"Count on it," West replied.

After Forrest left, everyone else gradually filtered out of the room. Parker stayed with Sterling, talking to her quietly. Griffen and Hope were having a conversation I couldn't overhear. Finn and Hawk had already slipped out.

Royal glanced at Tenn. "I'm headed to the Inn to check on a few things after the party last night."

"Do you need a hand?"

"No, you're good. You didn't exactly have an uneventful night from what I heard. Take the day off. I'll call you later to talk about the Forrest situation."

"Works for me." Royal left and Tenn stood, reaching for my hand and pulling me to my feet.

"What do you want to do, gorgeous?"

There were about a thousand things I wanted to do. Drag Tenn into the closest room with a lock on the door and strip him naked. Put on my suit and jump in the pool, with or without the kids. Check in on said kids and take their temperature after the upheaval of the night before.

All good options, but I was a little embarrassed to admit that the thing I wanted to do most was get back to my little workroom near the kitchens and finish the piece I'd been working on before we left for the Fourth of July celebrations.

I shoved my hands in my pockets and cocked my head to the side, looking into Tenn's deep blue eyes, wondering how he'd react if I picked my lampwork over him. I shouldn't have worried. I was gnawing on my lower lip, still thinking about what to say, when Tenn answered the question for me.

"You want to finish that little bluebird, don't you?"

I exhaled a relieved breath. "I do. Do you mind? He's been in my head all day. I want to perch him on a little branch and maybe find something cool for a base. Can we go hiking later? I bet I'll find what I need in the woods—"

Tenn laughed, wrapping his arms around my shoulders and pulling me close, kissing the top of my head. "I want to come down and see how far you got on him yesterday. And then I'll go find something to do while you work. Maybe I'll take the kids to the pool. And we can definitely go for a hike later."

We walked hand in hand down the hall to the stairs, me picking up speed as I got closer to my workroom, excited to show Tenn what I'd been working on.

The workroom was a few doors down from the main kitchens, a decent-sized space that had been a storage closet. Unlike the others, this one had been mostly empty. Savannah hadn't had any trouble relocating the linens and extra dishes that had been haphazardly stored on the shelves. They'd brought in a huge wooden table with a thick, scarred top telling of decades of loving use. Most importantly, the room had excellent lighting and plenty of shelves to store my supplies.

I'd had this little bluebird in my head for two weeks. Letting him out of my imagination into the glass was its own kind of ecstasy. Tenn checked out my small creation, running a careful finger over the bluebird's sharp black beak, up into the curve of his blue head. I hadn't worked too much detail into the wings, still deciding how I wanted them to look. Smooth and clear or etched with the shape of his feathers? I'd figure it out eventually.

My heart beat faster as I looked at my new space. Mine to use as I saw fit. Suddenly, I had space and time. Space to work and time to try new things. Time to make all the pieces crowding my head. Projects that were bigger. Riskier.

And more than that, time with my boys. Time with Tenn. Time to make the family I knew we could become. It wasn't going to be easy. Nothing good ever is, but my boys and I had proven we could handle the hard stuff.

Tenn was worth it. My boys and I, we deserved Tenn, and he deserved us.

Tenn picked up the bluebird carefully, turning it in the light. "Scarlett, it's amazing. I can't wait to see it when it's finished. When you have some pieces done you should take them around town. We have a few galleries and shops I bet would love to carry your work."

"I'll have to think about that once I get my stuff together," I said, my brain turning over the idea of living in an area known as an artists' haven. Tourists flocked to this part of North Carolina to visit galleries and artists' workshops. Even in my limited trips around town, I'd seen plenty of places that might want to sell my work. I'd always been so focused on my online shop since our college town up north didn't have the same options. But here I had the opportunity for more. More of everything.

Tenn nudged me to the other side of the big worktable away from the bluebird and my torch. "I'm gonna get out of your hair and let you work. I just want to say this: I love you, Scarlett. And I'm so fucking happy that you love me, too."

"I do. I really, really do." I lifted my hands to cup his face, running my thumbs along his cheeks before my fingers dove into his silky hair and pulled him close.

I could kiss Tenn Sawyer all day. One of these days, I would. I don't know how much time passed with his mouth on mine. I'd given up trying to keep track of anything but him when he was kissing me.

When he pulled back, I was sitting on my work table, legs spread, Tenn between them, his eyes warm with love and lust. "You know, I think that door locks."

I pulled him down for another kiss, whispering against his lips, "Why don't you go find out, and we'll see how sturdy this table really is?"

He did. And we quickly learned it was exactly sturdy enough.

Epilogue

TENN

L ife found a new rhythm faster than I expected. Once Scarlett and her boys decided to stay, it was as if it had never been a question in the first place.

Thatcher and August spent the rest of the summer swimming, hiking, and generally hanging out. For two weeks, they were in a day camp Quinn had started out of her guide business, filling her small van with kids and taking them on adventures in the mountains.

I offered to pick them up every day of the camp, partly because the small cottage housing Quinn's guide business and gear shop was only a few blocks from the Inn. And mostly so I could check in on Sterling. She wore a T-shirt and cargo shorts as comfortably as she did a cocktail dress, her golden hair pulled back in a ponytail, her face free of makeup.

I resisted the urge to talk her into coming back to the Inn, not just because Forrest was still working with us. I missed seeing her every day in the office, but at Quinn's, she seemed happy enough and steady in a way she hadn't been before.

I'd worried she'd start drinking again after she'd dumped Forrest, but no one had seen her with more than a glass of wine with dinner after that first night. She was keeping more to herself, but she'd said that was what she needed, and she was doing it sober, so I tried to give her the space she'd asked for. She'd been right—knowing she was coming home to Heartstone Manor every night made it easier.

When I'd asked her how things were working out, she'd said simply, "I like it here. I haven't hiked this much since I was a kid. Quinn makes it seem like we're living in the middle of the best amusement park in the world. I might come back to the Inn one day, but not yet."

She didn't mention Forrest ever. Neither did I.

Royal and I were getting along with him at work well enough, considering. Despite everything else, he hadn't lied about his capacity for the job. He was excellent at it. Sometimes, I thought he loved The Inn at Sawyers Bend as much as I did.

We avoided talking about anything personal, our budding friendship all but dead. The situation wasn't perfect, but I could live with it for the time being. Especially since having Forrest around meant I could take more time off to spend with Scarlett and the boys.

Toward the end of July, Scarlett, me, Thatcher, and August flew up north to deal with their house. Scarlett had agreed to leave basic kitchen equipment, all the appliances, and most of the furniture so the subletting professor didn't have to start from scratch.

That still left closets, dressers, and everything else. Good thing we have plenty of storage at Heartstone Manor. I worried that the kids or Scarlett might have second thoughts once they were in their old house. They had some quiet moments, especially packing up their rooms, but no one changed their minds.

Elliot, the asshole, didn't bother to come by and see his kids while we were there. Not once. Maybe I should have been glad he wasn't around to mess with the boys' heads, but it just made me want to punch him.

With the help of the movers I'd hired, we got the house packed and loaded on the moving truck in two days. Boarding the plane in Boston, all Thatcher and August could talk about was getting back to Heartstone and the pool. I had to agree—packing a house in the summer heat was not as fun as floating in the pool.

Scarlett disappeared on us for almost two weeks after we got back. She was around in the morning and evening, but now that she had all her supplies from the tiny workshop she'd carved out in her house, she couldn't wait to get settled in her new space. The room by Heartstone's kitchens was several times larger than what she'd had before and she used every inch, getting lost in two or three projects at the same time.

It was a good thing because after she showed her work to some of the local galleries, she couldn't keep them in stock fast enough. By the time fall came around, Scarlett had secured a featured spot in two local galleries and a jewelry store that only featured local artisans.

Once the boys started school, our lives fell into a welcome routine. Savannah's Nicky was finally old enough for kindergarten. Griffen had surprised us all, especially Savannah, by saying that he was paying Nicky's tuition to the school Thatcher and August would attend.

Laurel Country Day, the school William Sawyer had founded and named after his mother, Dorothy Laurel Sawyer, had grown into a formidable institution over the years. Every Sawyer child had attended Laurel Country Day since the doors opened in 1893, just in time for William's son James to attend the inaugural first-grade class.

The only exception was Finn, who'd been expelled in his junior year. Even the Sawyer name and Prentice's generous donations hadn't been able to convince the school to allow Finn back. Setting fire to the principal's office tended to make school administrators cranky.

On their own, the boys might have been more nervous about starting a new school, but going together eased some of their anxiety. I dropped off all three of them in the morning before heading to the Inn. If you'd told me a year ago that driving three kids to school would be one of the highlights of my day, I would have laughed my ass off. Shows what I know.

I handled drop off and Scarlett covered pick-up. After she got August and Thatcher dressed for school, she headed down to her workshop. By three, when it was time to get the boys, she'd put in a full day and was ready to put down her torch.

Everything was going so well those first few months, I wasn't ready when Scarlett's parents announced they were coming for a visit. Only a few days after their call, their RV pulled through the gates. I couldn't relax, even after they spread their arms wide for their grandsons and Scarlett, hugging them tight until August squirmed away. He jumped up and down, excited beyond measure to show them his new home.

After a few days of getting to know each other, Scarlett's father clapped me on the shoulder and said it would be nice to worry a little less about his girl and her boys. I promised him Scarlett's days of handling everything on her own were over.

If I was nervous about meeting Scarlett's parents, the prospect of Elliott's parents visiting sent a ball of ice to my gut. Hawk had quietly informed me that Elliott was only getting in deeper with the Learys. I worried his parents would somehow blame me or Scarlett for Elliott's situation.

They didn't. Whatever illusions they'd had about their son had worn away years ago. Connie and Bill Hall were devoted to Thatcher and August and treated Scarlett like she was their own daughter.

Connie couldn't have been happier about everything— she loved Heartstone, raving over the boys' rooms, how nice my family was, how happy Scarlett and I were together. They stayed ten days, and when they left, Scarlett's former mother-in-law gave me a tight hug and said she looked forward to coming back for the wedding.

I hadn't proposed yet, but Connie was no fool.

I hadn't proposed because I was still waiting on the ring. I realize proposing four months after meeting Scarlett was pretty fast. At least on paper. To me, it felt like an eternity. I'd been ready to marry her after two weeks, but with the kids to consider, it felt better to let everyone settle in before throwing them into another big change.

Anyway, having a ring custom designed took time. Scarlett had been making jewelry, mostly lampwork earrings, for a shop on Main Street that specialized in local artisans. The owner had taken to Scarlett immediately, instantly in love with her work. Every time I'd accompanied her to the shop, I'd noticed Scarlett's eyes straying to a specific display of rings, her gaze lingering over the twists and turns of metal, the intricate settings.

When it was time to find a ring for Scarlet, I knew it had to be something unique. She has the heart of an artist, and she needed a ring as unique and visionary as she was. Unfortunately for me, the designer's schedule was packed with commissions. I managed to persuade her to work me in after talking to Griffen about finding exactly the right stone.

We went through the family jewelry and unearthed a ring that had belonged to Lady Estelle Ophelia Sawyer, the English bride for whom William Sawyer had built Heartstone Manor. The ring itself was heavy and outdated. Nothing any modern bride would want to wear, but the stones had been remarkable. A perfect, emerald-cut ruby with a handful of smaller diamonds whose fire set off the ruby to perfection.

I slid the ring onto Scarlett's finger one night after I'd made love to her as we lay in my bed under the covers, our heads close on the pillow, whispering in the dark, stretching out the time before she went back to her own room.

I wasn't marrying Scarlett so we could share a bed in front of the kids, but that was definitely a perk I was looking forward to. She lay beside me, an orgasm-induced smile curving her lips. I lifted her hand, kissing her palm before sliding the ring into place.

I hadn't expected the tears that filled her eyes, her kiss tinged with salt, her eyes bright with love. "Yes. A thousand times, yes."

"What do you think about a Christmas wedding?" I asked, hoping she wasn't going to suggest a long engagement or a wedding so big it would take a year to plan.

Even knowing she wouldn't want something big and splashy, she surprised me. "Christmas Eve, here at the house, in the library. Just family. My parents and Connie and Bill are already coming for the holiday, so it'll be perfect. And I don't want to wait any longer."

I kissed her, taking her hand in mine, the feel of the ring on her finger filling my heart with fierce joy. I wanted them to be mine. Officially. I wanted to claim Scarlett, claim her boys, in front of both of our families.

We had our first kiss in the library. It felt right that we'd marry there, in front of the big fireplace, our family surrounding us, a mile-high Christmas tree filling the room with festive light.

Thatcher and August walked their mother down the makeshift aisle. Thatcher looked uncomfortable in his tuxedo while August strutted as if he'd been born in a bow tie. Scarlett was incandescent, her champagne silk gown skimming her body to fall in a glowing pool at her feet. She'd left her hair loose and wild, the way I loved it best.

Flanked by her boys, she was the most beautiful woman I'd ever seen, a goddess of love, and she was about to be mine. Holding Scarlett's hands as they escorted her to my side, they each gave her a kiss before taking their positions. August moved beside me, standing as my best man. Thatcher took his place beside his mother as her man of honor.

When it was time, Scarlett said, "I do," her voice solemn, a brilliant smile beaming from her face, her eyes shining with happy tears. I promised to honor and cherish her for the rest of my life, and I knew our adventure together was only beginning.

That night, as I lay my head on the pillow beside my wife, my Scarlett, my love, my heart was full enough to burst. She turned her head to face me, her eyes dancing with amusement.

"As far as Christmas presents go," Scarlett said, "you're going to have a hard time topping this one."

I rolled to face her, pausing to kiss her slow and deep. "I have a whole year to think of something really spectacular."

Framing my face in her hands, Scarlett shook her head. "You're all the spectacular I need. And I was thinking—" She wiggled closer, her lips at my ear, and whispered something about handcuffs and chocolate and champagne. That was all I needed.

I wasn't sure I could top a wedding, but I planned to blow Scarlett's mind every way I could imagine, as often as I could, for the rest of our lives.

TURN THE PAGE FOR A SNEAK PEEK OF
REBEL HEART,
BOOK FOUR OF THE HEARTS OF SAWYERS
BEND

Rebel Heart

CHAPTER ONE
NASH

The day my brother got married was the worst day of my life.

It didn't start out that way.

When it started, I thought it was going to be another typical day with my family. Long stretches of boredom punctuated by flares of irritation. My family was frequently both boring and irritating. I love my mother, so for her, I tolerated the boredom and irritation. My father and I had worked out a policy of ignoring each other in an effort to keep the peace for my mother, who we both loved.

My brother, Tyler, was a different thing altogether. Tyler, I avoided completely. I tried to stick with that tactic when it came to his wedding. I had no interest in watching him marry some society airhead in a spectacle that would easily run into seven figures. I wasn't going to suffer through a tedious weekend I'd never get back when they'd be divorced in a year.

I had my strategy all planned. I'd have a last-minute emergency meeting. In Tokyo. Maybe I'd miss my flight back. My mother put an end to that. I'd learned over the years that firm boundaries are the key to loving Claudia Kingsley. Very firm. As in sky-high and rock-solid. Once Claudia knew she couldn't yank my chain, we'd settled into a comfortable affection that worked for both of us.

Then Tyler proposed to Parker Sawyer, and my mother decided my boundaries could go to hell. She wanted her whole family at the wedding of the century and wouldn't accept anything less. I managed to get out of the engagement party and rehearsal dinner but agreed through gritted teeth to come home long enough to attend the ceremony and reception.

Skipping the engagement party was the biggest mistake of my life.

After, my mother's words rang in my ear. '*You have to meet her, Nash. I really think Parker will be the making of your brother. She's perfection. You're going to love her.*'

For once, my mother was right, 100%. And 100% wrong. Parker Sawyer wouldn't be the making of Tyler. He was a lost cause. He was greedy, jealous, entitled, and excelled at the kind of manipulation that kept everyone around him dancing to his tune. No woman could be the making of Tyler. He'd destroy anyone foolish enough to tie herself to him. That's what Tyler always did with his toys.

My mother was wrong about Parker and Tyler, but she was right about one thing: I was going to love Parker Sawyer.

For the rest of my life, I'll never forgive myself for waiting until the wedding to meet the bride. The first time I set eyes on her, she was heading down the aisle on her father's arm, her slight, fragile form elegantly sheathed in a white satin column of a dress, its spare design highlighting her small stature, her pale hair in a refined knot that accentuated her stunning features.

Everything about her was understated beauty except for her eyes. A golden hazel, they glowed with serenity. And deeper, beneath the shell of perfection, there was a spark, a hint of life that was nothing as serene and orderly as her exterior suggested.

I'll never know how I alone saw it—Parker's secret chaos, the wild spark she hid so well. See it I did, and as she walked down that aisle, I experienced the first moment of genuine regret in my life, a sense of something precious slipping through my fingers, gone before I could make it my own. My heart ached, an unfamiliar sick pulse in my chest, loss spreading through my limbs, saturating my soul.

So much regret in that one moment. I make it a policy not to have regrets. I make decisions, and I move forward. If I fuck up, I try not to do it again. Simple and efficient. I don't waste energy dwelling on things I can't change.

Until Parker.

There's nothing I regret more than turning down my mother's invitation to Tyler's engagement party. I have no doubt that if I'd been at that engagement party, I would have left with Parker.

Unfortunately, at the time, I wasn't speaking to our father and all my mother's pleadings fell on deaf ears. I was done helping them enable Tyler. If I'd known my father wouldn't live more than a few months after the wedding, if I'd known who Parker would be to me, I would have come to the engagement party. I would have taken one look at Parker and changed all of our lives instead of putting us through what came later.

I watched Parker proceed up the aisle in a daze, thunderstruck, something elemental inside me demanding I leap from my seat to steal her for my own. I couldn't compute, couldn't reconcile this primal need to take her with the ultra-civilized wedding happening in front of me.

Vows were spoken, falling on my deaf ears.

The bride and groom left the church in a spray of soft pink flower petals.

I headed straight to the bar.

Two whiskeys and I wasn't any closer to getting my head on straight. Something inside me had shifted, a puzzle piece moving and another sliding into place. I'd seen Parker for only a moment and I knew. She was meant to be mine. And she was my brother's wife. Not just any brother; she was Tyler's wife. Fucking Tyler. Even Parker's formidable shell wasn't enough to protect her from the insidious poison that was Tyler.

She'd chosen him. I tried to remind myself of that through whiskies number three and four. *She had chosen him.* She probably thought she loved him. It wasn't my place to tell her who she should love.

That feeble protest didn't get very far. I'd grown up with Tyler, after all. I knew exactly how charming he could be when it served his purposes. Parker, my Parker, likely had no idea what she'd done in marrying my brother.

I held it together when my mother tracked me down and dragged me to the receiving line to congratulate the happy couple. Tyler wasn't the only Kingsley who could pull off charming. I'd almost convinced myself I'd imagined everything I felt the moment I saw Parker walking down the aisle.

Love at first sight is a child's fairy tale. I knew nothing about this woman, and she was married to Tyler. Not a choice that spoke highly of her character. I'd been momentarily deluded, had been having a weird moment, a flashback to the parties of my childhood, and had fixated on this woman, my brother's bride. I'd made more of her than she was.

Parker Sawyer—no, Parker *Kingsley*—was just a woman. She was my sister-in-law. She was married to my dickhead of a brother. She was no one special.

Then my mother pushed me at the bride and groom. Parker leveled her practiced, cool smile on my face as she slid her hand into mine. The moment we touched, the second her eyes met mine, we both went still, and that spark, the wild flicker of chaos in her depths, flared to life. Reflexively, her fingers tightened on mine, her breath caught in her throat. Wonder suffused her face, her body tilted forward, closing the distance between us—

I don't know what would have happened if my mother hadn't cut in, her voice shrill, manic in her excitement. "Nash, this is Parker! I can't believe you haven't met—"

Her voice faded. Everything faded as the light in Parker's eyes dimmed, filmed over. Her hand slid from mine, her cool shell pulled tight around her. I caught the flash of awareness in her eyes as they flicked over Tyler, my mother, my father, before landing on me. The tiniest burst of anguish, sharp and desperate, and then it was all gone. The light in her eyes, the soft touch of her skin on mine. I made some excuse and headed straight for whiskey number five, my heart pounding in hollow thuds of loss.

I'm not proud of what happened next.

Not proud, but in that whole clusterfuck of a wedding, what happened next is the one thing I don't regret. I'm self-aware enough to know I *should* regret it. It was an asshole move. But I never said I wasn't an asshole. I'm more like my brother than I want to admit. When I see something I want,

I'm ruthless. I was going to walk away from Parker Kingsley. I had to. I'd seen that flare of awareness in her eyes. And I'd seen it dim as she made her choice.

But she hadn't made a choice. Not really. Not until she knew what she was giving up.

Like I said, I'm not proud of what happened next. At least, I can honestly say I didn't plan it.

It was a happy coincidence that I, six whiskies deep, strode down the darkened hallway, determined to get the hell out and away from this fiasco, when who did I see but the bride herself coming toward me. Parker's shoulders were slumped, her eyes fixed on the carpet.

If she'd been looking where she was going, she would have had time.

Time to escape.

Time to see what was coming and run.

Whatever had caught her attention, it had taken it all and she had none left for her surroundings, which made it so incredibly easy to slide my arm around her shoulders and yank her into a dark supply closet.

I didn't say a word. I didn't have any words to say. This sliver of time was all we'd ever have, and I wasn't going to waste a minute of it on words. The dark settled around us, the sounds of the party cut off as I pulled Parker close, bending my head to her small frame.

The back of my fingers brushed her cheeks, warm and smooth. Her lips were fuller, softer than I'd expected, parting as I brushed her mouth with mine. Parker didn't shrink away. She didn't protest. She tilted her head back, wound her arms around my neck, and kissed me.

That kiss was fire, burning me from the inside out. Her eager mouth demanded mine, Parker as desperate as I was to make the most of every second we had. The only seconds

we'd ever have. Parker's kiss was like nothing I'd ever imagined—the low growl in her throat, the desperate way she
nipped at me, her teeth sinking into my lower lip, her
tongue sliding against mine.

I barely had a thought for how her passion would translate to sex. This kiss was so much more than a prelude to
something that could never be. For the first time, a kiss
wasn't about an end goal. Wasn't about the first step to
fucking.

This kiss was all we had. And it was everything.

Everything I'd never imagined I wanted.

Everything I knew I'd never have. Not now. Not ever.
And not because of me. I would have done anything to have
Parker. Burned every bridge, laid waste to the party outside
our dark closet. I have no limits when it comes to Parker,
even then, after one kiss.

No, we'd never have more than this one kiss—because of
Parker. Because of what happened next.

Someone in the hall must have tripped, bumped into
the door, rattling it in its frame. Parker startled, tearing her
mouth from mine, twisting her body away as I fumbled for
the light switch, slapping it on and casting us both in harsh
fluorescent light.

Flags of red stood out on Parker's high cheekbones. Her
breath came hard and fast, her eyes wide and panicked. Her
serene, perfect shell was gone, shredded by our kiss.

"I thought— I thought—" Her voice caught on a choke
and she finished weakly, "I thought you were Tyler."

Disappointment stained the beauty of that kiss, the
promise of everything I felt between us. "No, you didn't." I
wasn't going to let her lie to me. I couldn't do anything about
the lies she told herself.

Parker drew in a harsh breath and let it out, shoulders

slumping in defeat. "No." She shook her head. "No, I didn't. I knew it was you. I wanted—" She caught herself, cutting off whatever she'd been about to say. "I can't. I just married your brother. And I'm not that kind of woman."

"You could be," I pushed. "You could take my hand and walk out of here with me." Something flickered in her eyes, and I pushed harder. "Take a chance, Parker. Take a chance with me and I promise you won't regret it."

I was insane. Definitely. I was insane. The look Parker gave me said she agreed. Still, she squeezed her eyes shut and drew in another breath, her fingers tangled together in a grip that left her knuckles bone white.

My heart stopped beating, my breath frozen in my lungs as I waited, balanced on a precipice, every cell in my body straining for the words I needed. Words that would give me hope. Give us a chance, a future—give us anything. I would have taken anything.

An eternity later, Parker opened her eyes. Wiping beneath her lashes to clear away the hint of tears, she whispered, "I can't. I'm sorry, Nash. I can't."

That was it. Her final answer. Parker wrenched open the door and disappeared back into her wedding reception. That was the last I saw of Parker Sawyer for a very long time.

Parker Sawyer was a bomb. I don't mean a bombshell, though she could fit that bill when she wanted to. No, Parker was a bomb, as in an incendiary device. She fell into my life out of nowhere and exploded, changing everything. My mind, my heart, my life. The goals I thought I had and the dreams I thought I wanted. Nothing was the same after Parker.

And now I'm here again, Parker Sawyer falling like a bomb into my life once more. This time into my bed. In the moonlight, her skin is incandescent, her hair almost silver, her mysterious gold and green eyes closed in sleep. She reminds me of a fairy, of some mythical creature who lives in moonlight, who'll turn to dust at the first touch of dawn.

But Parker isn't a mythical creature. She's a woman. And now that I've touched her, made love to her, she's mine. I know what I suspected all those years ago. This woman was made for me.

The night I fell in love with her, I let her get away. This time, there's no escape. Parker can run—I already know she'll bolt the first chance she gets—but it won't work. I have a plan, and this time, when all is said and done, Parker will finally be mine.

ARE YOU READY FOR NASH & PARKER'S STORY?

Visit IvyLayne.com/RebelHeart
to see what happens next!

Never Miss a New Release:

Join Ivy's Reader's Group

@ ivylayne.com/readers
&
Get two books for free!

Also by Ivy Layne

Don't Miss Out on New Releases, Exclusive Giveaways, and More!!

Join Ivy's Readers Group @ ivylayne.com/readers

THE HEARTS OF SAWYERS BEND

Stolen Heart

Sweet Heart

Scheming Heart

Rebel Heart

THE UNTANGLED SERIES

Unraveled

Undone

Uncovered

THE WINTERS SAGA

The Billionaire's Secret Heart (Novella)

The Billionaire's Secret Love (Novella)

The Billionaire's Pet

The Billionaire's Promise

The Rebel Billionaire

The Billionaire's Secret Kiss (Novella)

About Ivy Layne

Ivy Layne has had her nose stuck in a book since she first learned to decipher the English language. Sometime in her early teens, she stumbled across her first Romance, and the die was cast. Though she pretended to pay attention to her creative writing professors, she dreamed of writing steamy romance instead of literary fiction. These days, she's neck deep in alpha heroes and the smart, sexy women who love them.

Married to her very own alpha hero (who rubs her back after a long day of typing, but also leaves his socks on the floor). Ivy lives in the mountains of North Carolina where she and her other half are having a blast raising two energetic little boys. Aside from her family, Ivy's greatest loves are coffee and chocolate, preferably together.

For More Information:
www.ivylayne.com
books@ivylayne.com
Facebook.com/AuthorIvyLayne
Instagram.com/authorivylayne/

Printed in Great Britain
by Amazon